LOVE AND SURVIVAL | BOOK 2

AFTERMATH

INTO THE UNKNOWN

LENA GIBSON

Black Rose Writing | Texas

©2024 by Lena Gibson
All rights reserved. No part of this book may be reproduced, stored in a retrieval system or transmitted in any form or by any means without the prior written permission of the publishers, except by a reviewer who may quote brief passages in a review to be printed in a newspaper, magazine or journal.

The author grants the final approval for this literary material.

First printing

This is a work of fiction. Names, characters, businesses, places, events, and incidents are either the products of the author's imagination or used in a fictitious manner. Any resemblance to actual persons, living or dead, or actual events is purely coincidental.

ISBN: 978-1-68513-529-4
PUBLISHED BY BLACK ROSE WRITING
www.blackrosewriting.com

Printed in the United States of America
Suggested Retail Price (SRP) $23.95

Aftermath is printed in Chaparral Pro

*As a planet-friendly publisher, Black Rose Writing does its best to eliminate unnecessary waste to reduce paper usage and energy costs, while never compromising the reading experience. As a result, the final word count vs. page count may not meet common expectations.

PRAISE FOR
AFTERMATH

"Compelling, riveting, and ultimately a testimony to the power of belief in something better, *Aftermath* is Gibson's best to date."
–Karen K. Brees, author of
The WWII Adventures of MI6 Agent Katrin Nissen

"Highly-recommended for lovers of dystopian/post-apocalyptic fiction and those who enjoy a sizzling contemporary romance with an edge."
–Troy Hollan, author of *Clucked*

"Life is tenuous. Love isn't. *Aftermath* is Stephen King's *The Stand* on a collision course with HBO's *The Last of Us!*"
–Cam Torrens, award-winning author of the *Tyler Zahn series*

"Lena Gibson is quickly becoming one of my favorite writers, and this book did not disappoint. I was hooked from the very first page."
–Diane Hawley Nagatomo, award-winning author of
The Butterfly Cafe* and *Finding Naomi

"*Aftermath* is a powerful story of survival, perseverance and love as a young couple battles enemies and the elements to find a new life. Gibson delivers an instant classic in the post-apocalyptic genre."."
–Gary Gerlacher, author of the *AJ Docker* series

"Lena Gibson's latest novel is a fast-paced, tension-filled read that will keep you rooting for Robin and Kory all the way to the end. The meticulous plotting, vivid descriptions, and well-drawn characters make *Aftermath: Into the Unknown* a must-read adventure! Don't miss this one!
–Travis Tougaw, author of the
Marcotte/Collins Investigative Thrillers

For Rob, always and forever

AFTERMATH

CHAPTER 1: ROBIN

Robin's youth ended three years ago when the asteroid smashed into the Earth. Everything she'd taken for granted in her previous life was gone. To survive, she had additional responsibilities—such as scavenging for food and taking care of her grandfather. She looked around her sparse surroundings and a sense of unease crept over her as she finished dressing in the cold, windowless room.

The odor of wet concrete overpowered the smell of her meager breakfast, while the shadows where the light from her flickering candle didn't reach seemed ominous. The feeling persisted while she ate. Something nagged at her, something more than the regular struggle for survival.

Maybe it had to do with the numerous flocks of geese flying south yesterday. The changing seasons lent urgency to her daily errands. It might be autumn, but with winter imminent, she had further preparations, so she and her grandfather didn't starve. She glanced over her shoulder to where he still slept. Time to go.

Poking her head through the small crack she'd made opening the door, she scanned the almost dark, empty parking garage on the P3 level under the Towne Square Mall. She dashed out from the secure windowless room she now called home and headed for her shortcut upstairs. Afterward, she'd proceed outside for a gathering excursion in town.

Robin peeked around a cement column on P1. It was lighter here than on the gloomy lower levels, and she stared at the rust-flecked, sky-blue door across the final stretch of gritty pavement. This last open expanse before the stairs was the most nerve-wracking. Only the faint drip, drip of water, and the faint sound of her breathing met her ears. Waiting for the pounding of her heart to subside, she glanced back the way she'd come. If someone saw where she came from, she and Grandpa could lose their secure hideaway—they didn't have the strength to protect it, so she was always careful.

Her pulse normal, Robin dashed the last fifty yards along the cement wall toward the blue metal door—another quick check. Nobody else was around. With the key clutched in her sweaty hand, she inserted it into the lock and eased the door open. The interior was as black as the inside of her eyelids, but she didn't flick on her lighter until she'd closed the heavy steel barrier.

Lighting one of her two half-candles, she climbed the stairs by its amber glow, careful not to clink her backpack against the metal rail. She always listened for out-of-place sounds—people might be anywhere—but there was nothing. Still, best to play it safe.

On the top landing, she opened the door with the same key, closing it with a faint click as she stepped into the windowless hall that connected the mall service areas. With no natural light, there would have been total darkness without the warm glow of candles that lit a path for her quiet feet. There was less chance of discovery here, but the most dangerous part, the mall itself, was ahead.

Last fall, she'd discovered the desiccated corpse of the security guard in the main concourse, still clutching his key ring. That gruesome find had opened up a world of possibilities. The keys allowed Robin and her grandfather access to little-known places in the mall they'd never have found otherwise. It had surprised her how much space was behind the scenes and not intended for the public. The stock rooms had been incredible treasure troves.

The air in the hall was warm and stale, but not a concern as she walked, the smoke from her candle the most pervasive scent. She hadn't been upstairs for a few days, but it appeared undisturbed. One needed keys to access this hall, and as far as they'd been able to determine, they had the only set. Several locked doors branched off in either direction, but there was no point in opening them. She and Grandpa had already cleaned out anything useful.

She turned left, heading for the exit at the other end, ignoring the openings in this section. There had been little of value in the old kitchens and prep rooms on the right, behind the food court. Without electricity or refrigeration, most of the food had spoiled long before they'd arrived. They'd eaten the remaining cans last winter. Some offices upstairs had held surprising treasures, such as stashes of stale candy, a handgun with half a dozen rounds of ammunition, and a bottle of whiskey. Grandpa had savored the amber liquid, a tiny glass at a time, eking the alcohol out over several months.

The two of them had lived in the parkade below the Boise Towne Square Mall for close to a year now.

At the end of the dusty hall, the pale glow emanating from the main concourse shone through the window inset in the last door. Beyond this lay the section of the building where anyone could have wandered around, long ago. This mall had been, like many others, scattered across the country, filled with high-end clothing shops, designer handbags, and jewelry stores that suited a lost lifestyle. Most of the merchandise had little value now. Well, diamonds and gold might be worth something, but she'd need to interact with people to find out, and that was a situation they avoided.

Robin laughed aloud, the sound startling her as it echoed through the confined space. Three years was now long ago—a different life. Not that there were many people left in Boise since the final evacuation order. Or Idaho, it seemed. Once the military had pulled out, it had gotten quiet.

Here in the city, they'd seen half a dozen sets of travelers in pairs and a few family groups at a distance on separate occasions. There'd also been a few additional lone wanderers on the road since leaving the farm. Gangs and convoys were the greater danger. Several had come, but luckily they were just passing through.

She grabbed the plastic milk crate she left stationed by the door, climbed up, and peered through the window. They'd seen no one else in the mall, but twice they'd encountered people close to the Walgreens up the street. She preferred to avoid that part of town if possible, making this shortcut useful. As pickings became slimmer, it was only a matter of time before others risked the upscale mall, even if it contained few shops carrying practical items.

Looters had targeted and gutted the big box stores in the early days of the apocalypse. Opportunists had grabbed the alcohol, junk food, and valuable items first. The next wave had been more practical. People had taken non-perishable food, equipment from sporting goods stores, and everyday medicines—things now in short supply, unless you knew where to hunt.

By the time Robin and her grandfather had left his farm, those stores had been stripped of anything useful. Still, they'd made do by thinking on a smaller scale. She and her grandfather hadn't boarded up the smashed plate glass entrances of the mall. Instead, they'd lowered the security grates and dividers where possible. The barriers wouldn't hold back someone determined to enter, but they made the Towne Square look closed and inhospitable, discouraging the casual intruder.

She watched for several minutes before determining that the coast was clear. No sign of movement and no strange sounds. She jumped down, returned the crate to its storage position, and unlocked the door. Taking a deep breath, she slipped the key into her right pocket and checked she still had the second one she needed—an inside master key, which provided access to the individual stores of the abandoned mall.

She blew out her candle and shoved the door open, relying on natural light filtering in through the dirty overhead glass. The leaf-covered roof over the food court proved it hadn't seen maintenance in a long time. Despite living under and exploring the mall for a year, she and her grandfather tried not to disturb it, allowing dust to settle everywhere. She stuck to the edges by the wall where they'd made a footpath so they didn't leave obvious footprints.

Still in a reflective mood, Robin worked her way toward the far mall exit, considering her life. Not everyone could pinpoint the pivotal moment when they'd transitioned from teen to adult. For some, it might have been losing their virginity to a high school sweetheart, graduating, or leaving for university. Those were typical landmarks that separated childhood from adulthood and responsibilities. None of those things had happened for Robin.

Before the asteroid, this change would have been gradual, but in one fell swoop, civilization had died and obliterated her innocence. She'd been one week from high school graduation and had secured a full scholarship to Yale university. Then the chunks of NR 2025 collided in a series of destructive strikes across North America, changing her life forever—so much for a lifetime of straight A's. In the end, they hadn't mattered. She should be bitter, but there was no point. Everyone had lost everything normal.

After the asteroid, she'd become just another survivor. And she'd like to keep it that way. The initial brutal and lonely months of the apocalypse, back in the spring of 2025, had been the worst. She hadn't owned a vehicle, but a friend fleeing the city had dropped her and her sister Shelby off outside the Portland city limits. A few hours before the first strike, the friend had disappeared, driving north, heading for Canada.

For a while, part of Robin wished she'd gone, too. She discovered later, thanks to the Emergency Broadcast System, that California and the cities along the Pacific coast were almost decimated by volcanic activity. The only home she'd known had been eradicated. The largest chunk of the meteorite had taken out ninety-five percent of the population of southern California, while subsequent environmental problems and flooding plagued the coastline.

She and Shelby had no means of contacting anyone, including their mother, because cell towers were destroyed and most power grids sustained unrepaired damage. On the second day, after the asteroid and thirty hours of silence, Robin had sent a Hail-Mary text with the last two percent of her iPhone battery to her grandfather. He lived inland on his farm—letting him know she was alive. To her relief, he'd replied, giving her a destination and hope.

She and Shelby had hiked east, into the mountains, heading for his place. After twenty-four hours, they'd come across an empty log cabin with a supply of canned goods. They had taken shelter in the coastal mountain range for over a week during the seismic and volcanic activity caused by the asteroid strikes. Their trip had stalled with everything coated in thick chunks of black cinders, and powdery ashfall like snow. It hadn't been safe to venture outside, and traveling had been a bitch.

Then the bikers had come.

Robin's throat constricted. She couldn't cope with those thoughts and returned her focus to the present, pushing aside the past. Today was unusual. She seldom thought about those days, and she tried not to think more than a week or two forward or back. Live in the now. Sometimes it worked. The farm had been good while it lasted and the parkade and mall were better. Or they had been until her most recent worry.

She sighed as she slipped out through the east entrance of the wall, using her key once she'd determined that she was alone. She couldn't be too careful because, despite its unkempt look, the mall was a gold mine. Walgreens, six blocks north, had been gutted. Fred Meyer, several blocks south, was no better. Most survivors hadn't cared about designer clothing and health food supplements, so they had mainly ignored the shops in this mall.

Last fall, she'd scouted around the mall in widening circles until she'd found a smaller, almost undamaged drugstore. Someone had removed the signs in the front, making it blend in with the small real estate offices and stationery store that were its neighbors. Her grandfather had shown her how to pick the lock with bent wire and a wrench to align the inside mechanism. They'd stockpiled antibiotics, various vitamins and supplements, basic first aid supplies, and all the extra soft toothbrushes they could find.

Today she had three missions. Over the last six weeks, as the temperatures dropped, her grandfather's cough became a deep rattle in his chest. His seal-like bark had her concerned, especially knowing colder weather was just around the corner.

She frowned as she walked, unable to shake her uneasy feeling. Twice now, she'd glimpsed blood flecks spotting his handkerchiefs, and her fear was that his condition was serious. He'd started asking her questions, as though testing her survival knowledge. Her chest tightened at the thought. He might not think he had much time left.

If her grandfather died, she'd be alone.

Living in a dank basement didn't help his health, no matter how homey they'd tried to make it, with carpets and bedding. Perhaps they should move upstairs into the mall offices on the third floor. Less secure, but there would be better light and it would be less damp. That, however, was a not-yet problem. For today, she would look through the cough remedies again to see if there was anything she might give him, at least to relieve his pain or help him sleep.

She would end her trip inside the mall on the way home. There was an Eddie Bauer with durable clothing, hiking shoes, and camping equipment. She'd already outfitted herself with the backpack she now wore, as well as her pants, but the chill mornings and leaves turning red and yellow had reminded her it was time to choose a proper winter jacket. The mall supplied a lot of their needs, but she couldn't only live indoors. Last winter, they'd stayed inside to avoid leaving trails in the snow. She would figure something out, so she didn't have to do that again. She needed to feel the wind and sun on her face and to breathe fresh air.

Rounding the corner, into the pharmacy's back alley, a gray cat scurried away, trotting between buildings and disappearing through a gap in the fence. A rat dangled from its maw. Robin hoped she was as successful a provider as the feral cats that roamed the city, most sleek and healthy, even without owners and dishes of kibble. Most of them had become skittish. She'd love to make friends with a cat, but she and her grandfather couldn't afford another mouth to feed.

She utilized bent wire and her multi-tool to unlock the pharmacy door, snuck inside, and relit her candle. The pale glow shouldn't show from the front of the partially boarded-up front of the store, but still she shielded it with her hand. The gritty floor crunched underneath her boots.

She scooped up a few extra items and stowed them in her backpack, including toothpaste, soap, and an assortment of cough syrups. Even if they just soothed his throat, they'd be worth having. She ran her free hand through her short brown hair, trying to decide if she should ask her grandfather to cut it again. Sometimes she yearned for the shiny, long tresses of her past, but maintaining something like that would be a luxury and a waste of water. On a whim, she packed a mini bottle of fruity shampoo. She missed feeling clean.

Turning to leave, Robin froze, listening. An uneasiness settled in her chest as she waited for the unfamiliar sound outside to become clearer. She donned her still-light pack, checked the laces on her sturdy hiking shoes, and crossed the dirty linoleum to the front of the pharmacy. Pausing, she listened by the windows. She hadn't imagined it. A faint rumble, then louder as the vibration increased. Then a roar. Motorcycles. Someone must have found a way to make or store fuel. It was a long shot, but she had to know who the riders were.

She pressed her eye to a crack in the metal blinds and watched as a dozen motorcycles with riders clad in black leathers rode up the street, continuing deeper into the once quiet city. She'd run into their kind before, but didn't recognize anyone. Where was their baggage or trailers if they were passing through? Where were the goods they'd collected? Her blood ran cold. Or had they already set up in the city and were here to stay?

She'd have to maintain her watchfulness. These bikers might be part of a larger group. When the roar had faded to a distant nothing, it was time to go. After checking the street, she slipped out the rear door and locked it.

Halfway back to the mall, still listening for the bikes, she ducked down a residential street into the nearby neighborhood, planning to use this outside opportunity to collect food for the next few days. Robin and her grandfather had taken over several raised vegetable beds that had been left behind and planted a garden behind an empty house with a fenced backyard. They'd grown beans, lettuce, and tomatoes to eat fresh all spring and summer. They had potatoes, squash, and cabbages remaining to harvest through the fall and keep over the winter.

This was the first year since the asteroid that crops had grown properly. Robin had noticed the relief on her grandfather's wrinkled face when their plants had sprouted last spring. In the two previous years on the farm, the sparse vegetables had been puny, stunted things that had tasted bitter. The crop had been better than nothing, but not a lot. Too often the last year on the farm, they had gone hungry. Now that they could grow food, maybe they should return there in the spring and try again.

This summer, the ever-present ash-filled clouds had at last relented, at least sometimes. It was a good thing too. Her stock of vitamins wouldn't last forever. She'd been careful to supplement her diet with calcium and magnesium pills, iron, and vitamins C and D— wanting to keep her teeth intact and her bones healthy. No need to get scurvy or suffer from malnutrition.

Planting and caring for the garden, and spending time outside, sunny or not, had also been beneficial for their mental health. Last winter, they'd stayed inside the mall living on scavenged dry rations and slightly expired canned goods. They had limited their outside time to the lowest level of the parkade, near their bunker. They'd been in closer quarters than she ever would have considered in the old days, when even sharing a room with her younger sister had been torture.

She blinked back tears at the thoughts of Shelby stirred up by the bikers, took a deep breath, and shoved the memories of her sister downward. She focused on the idea of fresh veggies and plunged onward. Maybe she would dig up a handful of new potatoes and check for the last round of new green beans for dinner to augment their usual fare of rice and dried beans. Best not to give in to her worries. Food was more important. Besides, perhaps the bikes had been passing through after all.

•　　•　　•

Robin didn't linger after harvesting the garden. Sliding through the loose board "gate", she checked the street as a nervous reflex before trotting back toward the mall—her pack jiggling with the extra supplies. Despite not seeing anyone, she practiced her silent heel-to-toe steps and maneuvered around the trash and abandoned items. For all her care, she couldn't shake the sensation of being watched, and hoped it was just her imagination triggered by the motorbikes and their riders.

She circled the mall, which still appeared undisturbed. No motorcycles in sight. That didn't mean they hadn't stopped somewhere in town, but it was promising that they weren't here. She slipped inside through a service entrance with her key and popped out of the long hall near the Eddie Bauer.

Trying on jackets was the most fun she'd had shopping in some time, forgetting the chaos of the world for a moment. Despite the pleasure of enjoying something as mundane as finding winter clothes, the itch between her shoulders grew. Twice she whirled, expecting to see someone.

Robin was always alone, and she scoffed at her imagination—it must all be in her head. She avoided the flashier colors, like bright red and neon orange in favor of a purplish-gray fleece and a gray, down-filled winter jacket. After a quick check of her surroundings, she stuffed another pair of travel pants and a pair of jeans in petite size 2 into her pack. Extra thermal socks followed. Hard to believe owning three pairs of pants now made her feel rich.

She hesitated, burdened by her load, then grabbed a large navy-blue jacket from the men's section for her grandfather. Rather than return another day, she should get everything now. Turning the corner after restocking her supply of waterproof matches, she ran into a slim young man dressed in black leather and dirty jeans. She bounced off him and stumbled to the floor.

Tears pricked her eyes in fear, and she struggled to control her panic. Someone had bypassed the security grates after all. It had remained quiet, so they must have entered the mall while she'd been outside. So much for sneaking. How long had he been here? Had he been watching her?

"Don't go." He held out a hand to help her off the floor, but she ignored it. "I was hoping I could talk to you." The man showed no expression while she scrambled at the floor, backing away before standing, now several yards away.

His presence explained the uneasy sensation she'd had since entering the store. She didn't answer and lurched to her feet, preparing to bolt. From out of nowhere, a second man grabbed her from behind. She panicked and flailed, trying to free herself, but only succeeded in having the gigantic man at her back hold her tighter. She peeked over her shoulder as she lunged, trying to get loose. He was almost a foot and a half taller than her five-foot-three frame—practically a giant. Maybe six-foot-six or seven, and he smelled like campfire and pine trees.

"Chill kid. Where'd you come from?" The voice came from the short man, so she refocused her attention on him, instead of on the massive hands clamping her upper arms together behind her back. When she struggled, shooting pains raced into her shoulders. She stopped struggling, and the pain relented. His grip wasn't cruel, just firm.

The guy in front of her was probably only twenty-five. Perhaps younger. He had greasy reddish-brown hair and a hard mouth set in a scowl.

"Well," he said again. "I don't appreciate repeating myself."

She shook her head, having already forgotten his question.

Her confusion must have shown on her face, because he sighed. "Where'd you come from?"

She struggled to keep her voice steady and less feminine. "We live in town."

His eyes narrowed. "Who's we? Are you part of a group?"

"Just me and my grandfather." Robin's whole body trembled. With her words, the grip on her lessened. The truth was probably better. Non-threatening. Inventing a fictional group was more likely to cause suspicion or bring trouble.

"I thought it unlikely a kid like you would be on your own," he said with a slow smile that showed his yellowed canines, reminding her of a shark. "Maybe you can show us around town. Me and Kory are part of a club that arrived in town a couple of days ago."

Kory and I. In her head, she corrected his grammar, something her mother might have done. Still, Robin would have felt better if his shallow smile had reached his eyes. As it was, she remained on guard. She would tell him as much as she had to in order to get loose, then hide.

"I heard motorbikes this afternoon," she said, the words reluctant to leave her throat. Her voice sounded raspy and unused. She'd left this morning while her grandfather still slept, and until now, she hadn't spoken today.

"Did you see us?" said the deeper voice behind her. He must be Kory.

She blinked at the rough tone and glanced back, shaking her head. She didn't recognize them.

"He knows nothing. Too stupid to be of use," said Kory.

He? Good. They believed she was a he. A side-benefit to easy-to-care-for short hair and a slight frame. They thought she was a teenage boy. She relaxed a little while, remaining watchful.

"I'm Dillan, by the way." The redhead flashed another false smile.

Who was he kidding? He looked sharp enough to slice anyone who let down their guard. Which she wouldn't.

"What's your name?" He stepped closer.

"Rob." Close enough to her real name that she'd answer or react if it was spoken.

"Mind if we look in your pack?" He nodded his head to the other man.

Her heart sank. She would rather they didn't know there was a drugstore that still had supplies on the shelves and it was important that they didn't realize that she had a garden with food for the winter. That had to remain secret or they would lose everything.

The man holding her arms released her on one side when he hefted her backpack, bouncing it against her back. She couldn't get a read on him, but he didn't seem as scary as his companion, who pretended to be pleasant.

"Not much in it. Mostly clothes. Not worth looking at." His voice was so deep it was almost a growl.

He was lying. Potatoes and bottles of cough syrup weren't that light.

Dillan shrugged. "Where were you scavenging today?" His hand strayed to a sheath on his hip. A blade.

"Houses," she lied. "I found a couple mealy potatoes in an old garden. Some socks and jeans here." Inside, she was quaking. Dillan's flat black eyes and thin lips looked unconvinced. Would he ask where? Force her to show him?

"Time for you to be on your way." The big man released her other arm.

Despite her surprise, without wasting a second, she stooped to collect the new jackets from where they'd scattered on the floor, and dashed for the mall. Her heart hammered against her ribs. That had been too close.

She left the mall at the closest exit, forcing the locked door open with the emergency crash bar. No way was she going to reveal her keys. To get back downstairs, she traveled the long way around, hoping the bikers were alone and didn't follow. When she stopped to catch her breath, the trail behind was silent.

Chapter 2: Kory

Kory watched the young woman flee; a fistful of jackets clutched to her side. He hadn't corrected Dillan's assumption that the stranger was a boy. It would be safer for everyone that way. Dillan and the others didn't need to fight over another woman. There were already plenty of other issues that caused tension within their group, like food, fuel, and clean water. Essentials.

Kory pushed her from his thoughts and kept his mind on the mission. They were scouting to find a new location to hunker down for the winter, having left Idaho Falls last week. They'd picked that city clean, and they needed somewhere with untapped stores of food. Their leader had banked on the almost total evacuation of the West after the asteroid strike. Most remaining civilians had already moved east, away from the impact zones, so there wasn't a ton of competition. The Wings planned to push further west next spring, to see what had survived in the worst-hit area along the coast.

The upside of the move was that they wouldn't have to contend with many survivors. If the houses were standing, there should be non-perishable food items. Boise just needed to get them through the winter months.

He examined this section of the mall. It had potential. The ceiling seemed to have remained intact, otherwise there would have been mold and invasive plants already. He scowled. It was just a matter of time. He'd been surprised by how much water and root damage many places had sustained in only three years. He refocused on the inspection. If the Wings took over several stores, they could have bedrooms instead of thirty smelly bikers crammed together. Plus, they could park the bikes inside the mall and keep them from being damaged or stolen.

The girl might not have seen their motorbikes outside, since they'd hidden them in bushes a block away, but others might. They couldn't afford to lose their wheels.

Kory cracked his knuckles and turned to Dillan. "You satisfied? The kid's not a threat."

Dillan shrugged; his dark eyes guarded as always. That one gave little away unless you looked for subtle clues. He reserved his genuine smiles for things that caused others pain. The other man wasn't Kory's ideal scouting partner, but with Kory's size, Dillan wouldn't dare pick on him; he preferred weaker prey, like the "kid" who'd just left. If he'd run into her alone, things might have fallen out differently.

Seeing Dillan's speculative gaze still fixed in the direction "Rob" had taken, it might mean the other man was interested, anyway. Prey was prey.

"I think we have what we need," said Kory, aiming to distract his partner.

Dillan turned. "And what is that?"

"We could live in the mall this winter. Rig a stove or two for heat, there's fuel. Park the bikes in the concourse and sleep in stores."

"Can I talk to my uncle about it?" said Dillan, his narrow eyes shifting toward the main section of the mall, as though visualizing Kory's idea.

Kory shrugged. He didn't need credit. Besides, Jake was shrewd, and he'd realize where the idea came from.

The corner of Dillan's mouth curved up, almost a sneer.

Being underestimated might keep Kory alive someday. The Wings could be ruthless in their competitiveness.

Before he left, he checked the back of the outdoor store for better boots than what he wore and claimed a pair, plus an XXL fleece sweater. While some of the stockroom had been picked through, size twelve was uncommon, giving him three choices. He grabbed a lined, waterproof pair to try on and stamped his feet into them. They seemed decent. Bending over to lace them, Kory took a moment to consider his next move. The look in Dillan's eyes had triggered that discomfort he had ignored for too long.

Kory hadn't planned on staying with the Wings for much longer. He would need to decide soon though, because Jake had informed Kory that if he stayed for the winter, he'd need to complete his initiation. He shuddered at the thought. Despite occasional necessity, he preferred non-violence. Once snow settled on the ground, his choice might be made for him and he would do whatever it took to stay.

The last winters had been harsh. They'd spent weeks socked in during blizzards and white-out conditions while several feet of snow accumulated, making roads impassable for months. The cold snaps had also been severe, with temperatures well below zero. As long as he didn't take a bike, the Wings should let him leave—though he didn't plan to ask permission.

Kory wasn't keen to cross the mountains and head back into the coastal zone. That's where he'd lived, on the streets of Seattle. Before that Portland. Unlike most, he'd lived a nomadic life before the asteroid. There'd been rumors that others had gotten out of Portland and Seattle, but he had met no one once he'd left the refugee center in Spokane four months after the impact. Before the Wings, he'd been alone for years. No clean house or loving wife. In that way, he'd been lucky and had less to miss.

He hadn't stayed at the center long. He could look after himself and had felt guilty taking food rations that others needed more. Not that any of them had much, but kids had been going hungry and there wasn't anything he could do to fix it. He left, leaving one less person to feed, but being on his own was risky. Pockets of armed militias and gangs roamed the countryside, and had claimed most of the bigger cities. Still, better alone than beholden forever to the Wings.

Rumors had made their way west of a thriving walled city in South Dakota. A fortress with underground bunkers where hundreds, perhaps thousands, of people had survived. A place like that might be safe and have opportunities. The other option was the Mormons, but he'd never bought into religion and might be unwelcome. He'd looked at the maps and considered trying for the bunker city next year. In his old life, he'd been a bouncer twice and worked a short stint as security. He was strong enough that he would be an asset, even if they only let him in on a trial. As long as the place wasn't just a myth, he could use a home.

•   •   •

The Wings, fifty members strong, had camped in the Walgreens six blocks north of the mall. The space was adequate with sunny fall weather, but it would be a bitch to heat for the winter. High ceilings, little insulation, and wide open. Therefore, their stay would be temporary. In the two days since they'd arrived, the guys had torn down and moved the empty shelving to build sections for each of the three factions: the old guard, the newbies, and the criminal element.

Jake would have to watch the latter group. There might yet be a power struggle for leadership.

Kory hummed as he walked through the former drugstore, ignoring the other bikers, though a few jumped out of his way as he tromped past in his new boots. Some followed him with their eyes, but he didn't stop to socialize. The only sounds were ordinary, the buzz of voices in the background. He missed music and wished for the thousandth time that he could charge his old phone, which lay dormant at the bottom of his pack. He should have tossed it ages ago, but couldn't part with the possibility of listening to familiar songs.

Though he'd collected a few of his favorite albums as CDs when scavenging, he didn't have space to carry more than half a dozen. He'd also been on the lookout for a portable discman or small CD player. That and a stash of decent batteries—many had expired or only had juice for playing something quick. Perhaps if he settled somewhere on his own, he'd find a place with a source of power, maybe solar or even a generator.

He would give his right arm to blast some Foo Fighters or Rush right now. Something old school with instruments and actual music. None of that boy band crap or noisy, distorted rap. Too bad so many people had gotten rid of their CDs in favor of digital files. They were probably kicking themselves, too. With no internet, electricity, or Wi-Fi, streaming music was a thing of the past. He'd come across some kick-ass stereo equipment, abandoned and useless. What a waste.

He turned toward his new digs in the back left corner, bunked down with the former thieves and drug dealers, near the real bikers, where he felt most at home. Many reminded him of the Seattle homeless. He nodded to Jake on the way past where the leader sat at a table with his inner circle. Four gray-haired, tough-looking road warriors were hard at work, hand-rolling smokes. They must have found a substantial stash of tobacco and paper filters. The heavily tattooed older man who led the Wings used them to incentivize his guys—the smokes were both currency and reward.

A part of Kory itched for one, but he'd quit everything back in the refugee center. He didn't want to kick an addiction again or be beholden to someone for a fix, even nicotine. He threw himself down on his sleeping bag, lit the candle he left by his bedside and, groping under his pillow, removed a tattered paperback. This book was almost done. He'd taken to reading science fiction the last few years, even if real life was as weird as some stories.

Flipping to the dollar bill he used as a bookmark, he angled the page into his pool of light. Who'd have thought he'd be a reader? Maybe only Ms. Wilson, his high school English teacher, who'd encouraged him by loaning him books—even stuff from her personal collection. He leaned against the flimsy wall, left his new boots on, crossed them at the ankle, and got comfortable, refusing to dwell on the past.

He lost himself in his book until a shadow fell across his page. He glanced up to see Jake and stopped reading. There weren't many people who'd interrupt him. Kory kept to himself and interacted little with most of the men, but Jake was in charge.

"The mall. That your idea or Dillan's?" Jake didn't sound annoyed, more curious.

Kory shrugged.

"It's a solid one, but my nephew was thin on the details." Jake raised a bushy gray eyebrow.

"His idea to check it out. Mine to set up there. Pick a store or two to make comfortable and keep heated. There's a central, open area to park the bikes out of the weather. Might be possible to rig something for water from the city pipes. Could be gas stoves in the food court."

Jake pursed his weathered lips and tapped them with a grease and tobacco-stained finger as he nodded. "Thought as much. Anyone occupying it already?"

His question seemed innocent, but Dillan may or may not have mentioned the girl. That might go either way.

Kory would play it safe. "Doesn't look lived in. Lots of stuff still lying around. No garbage, beds, or signs of people."

"You see people?" Jake's steely eyes fixed on Kory.

"Some kid. Maybe sixteen. Dillan's going to chase him down if he can." Kory shrugged—like it didn't matter. Even if she was nothing to him, helping someone, anyone decent, had felt good. Still. He couldn't shake the look he'd seen in her startled blue eyes. She'd been familiar with the store and thought she'd been alone. That one was smart. She hadn't reacted to being referred to as a guy, or given anything away about scavenging or her full pack. Dillan wouldn't find her without a lot of effort.

"Let me know if my nephew gets in over his head," said Jake as he turned to go. He held out a bundle with eight or ten smokes. "I know you don't smoke them, but they might come in handy to trade." He winked. "I hear Bill is smoking a new batch of venison jerky."

Kory took them with a nod. "Thanks." He had a case with a stash he would add them to once he was sure nobody was watching. That was the thing about bunking with thieves. At all times, he kept his valuables on him. His pack doubled as a pillow just to keep everything important safe.

After Jake left, Kory leaned back against the wall, thinking of the young woman from the mall. For all the difference in their sizes, she'd been more scared of Dillan than him. That had surprised him. People were often frightened of Kory simply because of his size. He'd been over six feet by the time he was twelve, so he was used to their reactions. Now he was six-foot-seven, and a hard life had kept him tough and lean. Most folk gave him his space.

There'd been strength in her arms, too. Tough and wiry. She would be a hot number in tight leather on the back of his bike. That fantasy crumbled to dust on the spot. If she was half as smart as he suspected, she would have made herself scarce. If they met again, it would be by chance, not design.

•   •   •

Jake presented the mall idea to the Wings at dinner and assigned a group to further investigate. The leader selected Kory for the team, but not Dillan. Kory nodded at Jake, but otherwise kept his head down as he shoveled in the stew Cook had made.

On his way back from the "bathroom" in the bushes in the dark, Dillan stepped in front of him.

"You fucking told Jake the mall was your idea." He kept his voice to a quiet hiss. "Trying to steal my credit. My uncle has expectations. You're an asshole." Silvery orange firelight reflected gleamed from the blade he tried to hide against his leg.

Dillan might think he was sneaky, but Kory could disarm him faster than the man could strike. Kory kept his eyes up and pretended not to notice the threat.

"Jake asked. I didn't lie." Kory tensed his muscles, ready to grab the knife arm if Dillan struck.

"He pay you?" Dillan's eyes narrowed to slits, almost impossible to see in the dark.

"Nope." A gift wasn't payment. No need to tell this weasel anything.

"Then you're stupid. You should have asked him for a half dozen cigarettes. He was rolling today." Dillan's voice held the sneer that the darkness hid.

"I don't smoke." Kory maintained an even tone.

"What about the kid? You mention him?"

"Ya. Said we saw a teenager who ran off."

"God. You can't keep your mouth shut about anything, can you? I should have been on the mall team since it was my discovery."

Kory didn't correct him. "Volunteer to help then." He kept his eyes trained on Dillan, watching for the slightest twitch from the knife.

"Na. I'm going to see if I can find that kid on my own. Steal their stash or bring them in. Just him and a grandfather. Not much fight in that." He slid his knife back into its sheath as he stepped backward. "I'll have more time this way, even if I'm out the finder's fee." He spat near Kory's boots and stalked away, toward the fire.

Kory went to bed that night, still thinking about the young woman. It had been hard to tell her age, but she might be older than his first impression. It was her petite size that made her seem young. He was twenty-five and she might not be much younger. Plus, with the things they'd all seen the last three years, she wasn't a girl, but a woman.

Maybe he should borrow her idea and search old gardens for leftover vegetables, something he hadn't done since the first year. Some plants self-seeded, like potatoes, which he hadn't considered.

Also, he was more likely to run into her scavenging than anything else. The search for food often consumed life.

As he lay in his sleeping bag, the stale darkness pressed inward while he listened to the low murmurs of those playing cards, the rustle of sleeping bags, and the usual nighttime grunts, farts, and coughs that came with a large group of men sharing the same space. Sometimes their indoor camps grew pretty ripe. From the back of the room came the whimper of the women. They had three right now, and they got used hard.

Their crying twisted something inside him, but just like the hungry kids at the center, there was nothing he could do for them. But he'd had enough. He couldn't stay with the Wings for the winter.

Kory decided. He would finish this scouting and prep job for Jake because he owed the man that much for taking him in. The leader had also been patient about an answer regarding initiation. Kory would collect a few covert supplies and split in a week, which should be before snow flew. He'd look for somewhere to hole up solo for the winter, then head for that city in South Dakota come spring. The walled city might need some muscle.

Chapter 3: Robin

"How'd it go today?" Grandpa Clay said, sitting up when Robin returned to their hideaway. He'd probably heard her key in the lock. "You were gone for hours." These days he spent a lot of time sitting on his mattress, which they'd laboriously dragged down from the bedding store so he would be comfortable.

She slipped off her pack and lined up six different cough syrups on the coffee table where they ate, the fronts facing her grandfather. She moved one to correct its position, so they were in height order, from tallest to shortest. That appealed to her sense of rightness.

"Don't think any of those will cure what I've got, Honey." He tugged a handkerchief from his back pocket and blew his nose.

He wasn't fooling her with that move as he dabbed moisture from his azure eyes that matched her own. When she'd arrived on the farm three years ago, her grandfather had been strong and hale. He'd been close to six-two and ran half-marathons. Every widow in his county had asked him out over the last ten years. He'd turned them down, but that hadn't stopped them from coming around. Now, her grandfather was spindle thin, frail, and stooped. He seemed to have aged at least ten years in the last six months. When he coughed, his whole body convulsed. He was dying in front of her and she was at a loss about how to help.

"Not a cure, but something might help you sleep." She was desperate to make a difference.

"I'll sleep when I'm dead." He sounded flippant.

How could he joke about death?

She turned away, a solid lump in her throat. He was all she had left, and she couldn't handle it when he spoke like that. Didn't he understand she was terrified of being alone?

"Robin. Look at me." He struggled to his feet beside her.

She angled her head toward him because she couldn't deny his request. She'd do anything for Grandpa Clay. He'd saved her when everyone else was lost and he understood her better than anyone, except maybe her missing younger sister.

"We have to face facts. I'm not improving. We need to make a plan." He rested his hand on her arm, though he seldom touched her, knowing she often found it uncomfortable. "I have to believe you won't stay here on your own. You need a proper home. Somewhere safe and with other people. With family."

She shook her head, hot tears pricking her eyes. She blinked several times, trying to clear them while the tightness in her chest expanded. He needed to be okay.

"Sweetheart," he said, his voice quieter. "Leave. Go look for your Uncle Luke and Aunt Ella. They're out there. If anyone made it, they did."

"I can't leave you. I won't. We're a team." Her chin wobbled.

His voice was gentle, making his words even harder to take. "We've been a great team, but I don't want you stuck here with a dying old man. My Laura's been gone sixteen years. It's time I joined her. She was my one and only true love."

Robin clenched her jaw. She didn't remember her grandmother and didn't have that connection to missing her, but life without her grandfather was unfathomable. "We have no idea if Uncle Luke is even alive." Her tears poured out, and she was helpless to stop them. Dammit. She wasn't a goddamn baby, just terrible at handling her emotions. Despite being an adult, she cried too much—often when angry or frustrated. Or miserable.

She turned back to the table and removed the four large yellow potatoes from her bag. She thumped them onto the surface, bouncing two boxes of cough syrup off the edge. They dropped onto the carpet samples that covered the concrete floor.

"I brought dinner." Her voice was too loud for their cramped quarters and held an undertone of lurking anger.

"You're not changing the subject this time. Tell me where Luke and Ella went. I need to know you have every detail filed away in that smart brain of yours." His stare was piercing.

His persistence made her uneasy.

"Vita xTerra." She shifted her gaze while trying to catch her breath before she spiraled out of control. "South Dakota. It's a thousand miles away." The bunker city may as well be Europe or the moon. It would be better to stop talking. She clenched her jaw tighter.

"Less than eight hundred," he said with a wracking cough that bent him in half.

She stepped toward him as he wiped his bloody mouth with a cloth, but he held his hand up to stop her. The blood had started last week.

"How am I supposed to get there?" Her voice became heated. "Walk?"

Grandpa Clay remained calm. "If you have to. Or maybe you can scrounge a bicycle and ride to xTerra. Where's the map I gave you?"

She sighed and wiped her stupid tears on her sleeve. "I keep it in my backpack, but I memorized at least half a dozen routes, just in case."

Grandpa passed her a clean handkerchief from the shelf and she blew her nose.

"I'm sorry for crying." Her face burned and her throat thickened.

"Crying is natural," he said. "So's feeling sad, but I need to know you'll try not to be alone forever. I feel in my bones that Luke's family is safe. Like you, they're survivors. You need to join them, and I'm not strong enough to travel with you." Why wouldn't he let her change the subject? They'd been over this months ago, but he held her eyes to make his point.

"Speaking of bikes, there are bikers in town. A sizeable group." Perhaps a more immediate threat would distract him.

Her grandfather coughed again, and she grabbed him a mug of boiled water, already cooled to room temperature. He sipped while she shared what she'd seen and about her encounter with Dillan and Kory.

"Dillan's a creep and Kory's the size of a mountain. My best bet was to run."

Her grandfather's creased face looked worried as his mouth turned down. "You should leave now. Before it snows. I don't want to worry about you running into bikers all over town. It won't be safe to go out."

"I'm not talking about this again tonight. Should I cook dinner or not?" She set her jaw. This conversation was over.

He nodded, indicating a truce, and she boiled the potatoes and they dipped into their stash of salt to sprinkle on them as a treat. Fresh food brought so much to their limited diet.

Later that night, trying to sleep, she stared at the dark concrete above while she tossed back and forth. Her grandfather's familiar soft snores filled the room, but she wasn't comforted. The bunker reeked of damp and sickness, with an undertone of the metallic scent she now associated with blood, and Robin cried herself to sleep.

•   •   •

The next morning, Robin became ghost-like, deciding she would flit into and out of places unseen. If someone spotted her, she'd be gone before they chased her—a figment of their imagination. After a summer outside, she felt fit and could be quick. She cooked oatmeal for breakfast, added a few dried apple slices to the mix, and left some for her grandfather, who was still sleeping. She took her vitamins and ate mechanically while she planned her next few days.

Robin glanced over her shoulder at her grandfather's prone form just before she closed the door as she snuck outside. He looked so tiny, lying there. It was probable that he was going to die this winter. If he made it that long. No matter how sad that would be, she was staying. She would head for xTerra come spring. That should be soon enough. She'd tell him this afternoon when she returned. He'd have to accept that as her final decision.

She left via the parkade rather than through the mall, winding her way up the dark ramps; she listened for unexpected noises, but there was nothing except for the soft echo of her footsteps. This way used to feel risky, but after the encounter with Dillan and Kory, she planned to avoid the mall for a while.

She turned right, avoiding the main mall entrance and the ramp to the outside parking lot before heading out on her route to the garden. She'd brought a couple of extra cloth shopping bags to carry her spoils. The garden could use proper harvesting. With the bikers around town, it wouldn't hurt to collect as much as possible this week. She'd be furious if they cleaned out her garden after all her hard work.

Her grandfather had kept a careful tally of the date since the beginning, even accounting for the extra day this year in February. Though it was unseasonably warm and dry, that was an indicator of climate change more than the season. It *was* October, though she had no way of predicting when the weather would change and become cold and wintery.

The last couple of years had been atypical because of all the ash in the atmosphere, and before that she'd lived on the coast where the climate was more moderate. Based on last year's experience, a regular winter in this area might already be extreme by her standards. Still, she wouldn't gather everything from the garden, but she could make it look less tended and collect a stockpile for their bins. Grandpa Clay couldn't complain about that. Though she had a feeling that he would. Though potatoes were versatile and stored well, they weren't the most portable of foods.

It was early and the chilly air still held the hush of dawn as she slunk from the parkade entrance, skirting the main mall entrance and the exit by the Eddie Bauer. She intended to avoid the mall interior.

Perhaps this afternoon she'd sneak over to the Barnes and Noble a few blocks away to select a few new books. If she was going to lie low, she'd rather have reading material than idle hands or an idle brain. She needed things to occupy her mind. If they had to stay inside for several days at a stretch, at least their water supply was reliable. There was a tap in the bunker from the old city water, which still worked. They boiled the water before drinking and heated it for washing because there was just one temperature. Cold.

Some days, she'd kill for a hot shower but, like many luxuries from her past, they might be gone forever. Their current home had originally been a security break room or panic room. They'd found long-term supplies in the mall and added them to what had been an empty concrete room with a two-burner gas stove, sink, and bathroom. At least the toilet still worked. That had been a bonus.

A faint rumble in the distance broke the early morning silence. Her heart sank. Bikers again. Robin froze on the ring road around the parking area near the last section of the mall. She ducked behind a bank of scraggly bushes at the far end of the parking lot. Palms sweating, she flattened herself against the cracked pavement and peered through the bushes. Half a dozen motorbikes roared up the street in a cloud of exhaust, slowing as they approached. Once she might not have noticed the scent, but in the absence of regular vehicle traffic, it was obvious.

The motorcycles turned, one by one, into the mall parking and rode onto the paved area outside the south entrance. None of the riders wore helmets today. Wherever they were staying probably wasn't far away. She remained hidden, watching to see what they were doing. Though she was over a hundred yards away, she recognized Kory's massive frame, towering above the smaller men. From this distance, she couldn't see any expression on his face.

He got off the lead bike and waited for the others as they lined up their bikes in a row on the sidewalk. One of the smallest riders, one who'd ridden double on the last bike, hopped off and dragged an empty crate over and sat. The others headed toward the entrance.

"We're going to be working in there most of the day, getting it ready to move in. I'll send Jack to spell you off for a while so you can eat." His booming voice carried in the still morning. Kory put a hand on the kid's shoulder as he turned to the mall.

Robin's stomach dropped. They *were* going to live in the mall. It was her nightmare come true. Getting in and out of the parkade would always be risky and exercising in the snow-free mall would be impossible.

Kory pried up the metal grate over one door and held it while the others slipped inside the building, past her line of sight. He turned to the kid on the crate. "Blow the whistle if anyone shows up. We'll come running on the double."

The boy must be guarding their bikes.

She bit her lip and scooted away. Retreating a couple of blocks, she detoured through a different section of town before slinking into the deserted alley near her garden. It was still quiet here, and she couldn't sense anyone watching. Still, she looked all around before proceeding. She moved the loose board, swinging it aside and sliding in before replacing it. Sometimes she used the front gate on the main street, but this was more direct.

Inside the backyard, she and her grandfather had planted their garden in four raised vegetable beds. Two were already empty of food, as she'd finished the beans yesterday and they'd removed the lettuce stalks when they'd gone to seed six weeks earlier. She grabbed her leather gardening gloves and clippers from her backpack. She chopped the unruly dead tomato plants that were now a mottled gray and brown tangled mass. It must have frozen again overnight. Hauling them away to the compost bin at the far side of the empty house, she stuffed them inside and drank from her canteen.

Next, she dug potatoes from the mounds in one of the remaining beds. Most of the potatoes were fist-sized or larger and she washed them off in a barrel beside the house, where they caught rainwater. Her hands ached from the cold water, but she continued until all the potatoes were clean and her hands were bright red.

Some kind of beetle or worm had attacked many of the smaller potatoes in the second bed, making them inedible. What a waste. She piled the intact ones together. The pile was smaller than she'd imagined after the first section. There wouldn't be enough to last the winter unless they dipped into their travel supplies. Gathering more dehydrated food from the mall storeroom had just become an issue. She sighed and scrubbed the few extra potatoes, wishing there'd been more.

Spreading out her meager harvest to dry in the warmth of the mid-morning sun, she shook out her picnic blanket, flopped onto it with her book, and soaked up the sunshine and vitamin D while she had a chance. She read for an hour and a half, turning the potatoes over to dry on all sides. She couldn't store them damp, or they'd spoil.

Too bad there wasn't a way to disguise the cabbages that still grew at the far end of the final gardening bed. She cut two to take back with her. They'd keep a long time in cold storage. She didn't like the way raw cabbage tasted or how it squeaked in her teeth but boiled it was okay—or chopped up in soup, it added flavor. They were also chock full of vitamins.

She gathered up the dry potatoes and her cabbages and headed toward home. As soon as she left the safety of the alley, she was on edge. Her head turned back and forth and her heart pounded though the neighborhood was quiet. Twice she caught the rumble of motorbikes coming from afar and froze until she determined they were elsewhere. She wasn't sure she could stand being around motorcycles so much with all the memories they dredged up.

Passing the mall, the bikes remained, and the same teenage guard sat beside them. Kory and the others had been in the mall for hours. Clearly, they had settled in. Her heart sank. No more easy indoor scavenging. With the bikers around town, gathering food anywhere would be risky.

Once Robin was certain that the rest of the way to the parkade was clear, she backtracked another street over and made her way back to the ramp. She was careful to check all around before descending underground when she determined she was alone.

After arriving home, she unlocked the door and lugged her produce inside, relieved to set down the load. She shook out her arms and looked around. To her surprise, Grandpa wasn't there. He'd eaten the breakfast she'd left and washed the dishes, but he wasn't home. For the last few months, he'd only left the bunker when she'd accompanied him, but she had to trust he knew what he was doing. He'd locked up and could return any time he wanted.

After a long drink, she scanned the room, searching for clues about what he might be doing. She'd left the main key ring behind, but couldn't see it. Surely, he hadn't gone upstairs into the mall knowing the danger.

Still, the quiet room seemed odd without his presence.

Robin loaded the potatoes into the bins and covered them with a blanket to store them in the dark. Time ticked slowly by while she waited for her grandfather's return. What was taking him so long? She hoped he hadn't run into trouble with the bikers. Or his breathing, because walking left him pale and short of breath. She grabbed a handful of mixed nuts and ate them, savoring their saltiness.

Minutes ticked by and still no sign of him. She fought the rising panic. Sitting inside and worrying was pointless. He was probably fine. She would go to the bookstore as planned, and watch for any sign of her grandfather, who must have an errand of his own.

Just before she left, she spotted the main key ring. He hadn't taken it after all. A sense of relief washed over her because he probably hadn't gone upstairs.

While she couldn't keep many books and hated the idea of abandoning them, she'd worked out a new system. She often read half a dozen books at a time, depending on her mood—like her favorite TV character from her old life, Rory Gilmore. At first, she'd missed the routine of going to the library for new books each week, but since they'd arrived in Boise, she'd used the Barnes and Noble for loans. When she finished reading something, she took it back and borrowed something different. Grabbing both books she'd finished this week, she headed out with her almost empty backpack clipped in place. You never knew what you'd find, so it was best to be prepared.

CHAPTER 4: KORY

"Hey, I'm headed upstairs for a bit. See what I can find in the offices," Kory yelled to a pair of the work crew who'd been fixing things in one of the larger kitchens. They seemed optimistic about getting the gas stove working. Each of the men did his own thing, but Jake had chosen everyone for their abilities to turn the mall into a functioning winter hall. It would be a helluva lot more comfortable than whatever he would find on the road. The simple path would be to stay, but his reasons still stood. Comfort wasn't enough to make him change his mind.

The closest man waved while the other shrugged and then said, "Whatever."

Kory could probably disappear for hours before anyone would wonder what had happened. Members of the Wings didn't keep strict tabs on one another. Most of them preferred privacy and many had ulterior motives and hidden agendas—not all as wholesome as stockpiling food. He would take a quick look upstairs, but his real goal lay outside; he just didn't want anyone to know where he went or follow him. Gathering his own supplies, people might see as holding out from the group. Best to hide his efforts and his stash elsewhere.

After a brief but fruitless search in the offices, he headed downstairs and located another blocked exit that was accessible without too much work. Someone had picked through upstairs already. The usual hidden items had been scarce. Usually, in quiet towns like this, he might find a half-empty liquor bottle or some stale hard candies in a desk drawer. Maybe some old-school porn mags. Here, nothing. Even behind the files in the filing cabinets, he came up empty. Not that he was looking for a drink, but he craved those butterscotch candies. Kicking a sugar habit had been almost as tough and more insidious than giving up weed and nicotine.

Having struck out upstairs, he ducked outside and strolled a couple of blocks north, prepared to hide if the roar of motorbikes headed his way. It remained silent, though the wind was picking up, sending fallen leaves racing up the empty street and cutting through his leather jacket. He should go back to that outdoor store and see if they had any winter jackets his size. Sometimes the abandoned world seemed normal. Other times, like now, it jarred against his image of the old world with ATMs and traffic. He could just take whatever he wanted without paying.

He continued up the street, walking up the middle of what had been a four-lane road. The lines had faded, becoming almost invisible after three years without touch-up paint, and weeds clawed at the broken pavement, sending root tendrils into the cracks. It wouldn't be long before the road would crumble into ruin, even here where the summers were hot and arid while the winters were frigid.

Thinking of winter, he shivered and walked faster towards his destination. As he got closer, he noticed the large Barnes and Noble front door had been smashed, though someone had cleaned up most of the scattered glass and nailed crooked boards across the largest of the openings. Perhaps a fellow book lover.

Stepping through the empty frame of the door, finer glass particles crunched underfoot and the mixed aroma of warm paper and dust met him. Open to the elements and without air conditioning, the store reeked of mold, ash, and dust. These books wouldn't last long. In a few years, they'd be moldy and falling apart. He should read them while he could. It was a shame that one day all of this would be ruined—lost to mildew and decay. Maybe he should take an extra.

Though there was no electricity, just like everywhere else, the extensive front windows that were still intact let in enough light that he moved deeper into the store with ease. He navigated using the genre signs at the ends of rows, passing Bestsellers, Romance, and Mystery before he turned into the dimmer section for Science Fiction and Fantasy at the back. As usual. While darker back here, there was adequate light to read most titles on the shelves.

He removed the used paperback from his pack and scanned the books arranged in alphabetical order, finding where his last book belonged on the shelf. Tattered or not, he slid it into place with the other Orson Scott Card books—returning the books gave him a sense of normalcy. He hoped others were still around and enjoying these stories. There should be more to life than just survival. He scanned the shelf for a copy of *Ender in Exile*. He'd been searching for that one for a while. A-ha. This store had a copy. He slipped it from its place, surprised to find it too looked used. It wasn't dog-eared, just faded and creased.

Maybe he wasn't the only one using bookstores as lending libraries. His policy was to take a book, read it, and bring it back before taking another. He needed to travel light and seldom had more than one book at a time, but he liked variety. He'd never been able to pick just one favorite of anything, movie, book, or music. Well, except he favored brunettes.

Thumbing through the pages, he ran his thumb down the rigid crease on the spine. He flipped the cover open and inside, someone had recorded a name and date in purple ink.

"Robin Wilson. Read August 2 to August 7th, 2028."

This past summer. "Rob," he said aloud as a piece clicked into place. The girl yesterday. Robin, not Rob. He'd bet money, or anything else with current value, that they were the same person. He dropped the new-to-him Ender book into his backpack. Instead of leaving, he skimmed the titles, shelf by shelf, row by row, throughout the section, searching for paperbacks that looked as if they'd been read.

Each time he found one, he checked inside for her name and the date. She'd read close to fifty books here by his best estimate, dating from last September to as recently as this fall, not that he was certain of today's date. He'd lost track of the date, long since using the seasons to measure time. A year's worth of reading. On a whim, he checked the fiction sections nearby. He struck out with Mystery but hit solid gold in the Romance section. He chuckled when he found several books that looked well worn. Perhaps they'd had multiple reads. She'd read a helluva lot more than fifty books this year. Perhaps double.

A quick scan of these shelves showed the same bookends for dates. She'd probably been in Boise for about a year and enjoyed Romance, Fantasy, and Sci-fi.

Grabbing one called *The Hating Game*, there was a sequence of half a dozen dates in the front. She must like this one a lot. Out of impulse, without reading the back, he dropped it into his pack on the floor.

"Not what I expected a big guy like you to choose to read," said a raspy voice from somewhere in the shadows to his right. "Aren't you too masculine and tough for romance novels?"

Kory spun around, slipping his knife from its sheath as he sank to a crouch, his eyes searching for the source.

"Put that thing away," said the unfamiliar man's voice. "I've got you in my sights. If I wanted to shoot you, I'd have done it already."

His voice carried a ring of truth. Kory could kick himself. He'd forgotten his surroundings for several minutes, engrossed in his discovery. He should be more careful.

"How long have you been watching?" While his heart thumped hard, Kory peered at the darkness, zeroing in on the speaker's position. Maybe he should rush him before the man got off a shot.

"Long enough to know you've been looking at my granddaughter's reads. I recognize a bunch of them." The man coughed a dry rattling sound at first, then wet. It echoed through the otherwise empty bookstore.

This guy didn't seem like much of a threat. Not sick. Still, Kory's shoulders remained tight and his knife ready.

"Robin." The name felt good on his tongue and suited the slight, but curious, young woman he'd met with birdlike mannerisms. He straightened and put his knife away—a show of faith. He could reach it quick if necessary.

"You met her yesterday, when she picked up the cough syrup." Though remaining in the shadows, the grandfather shuffled closer; he was a spare old man in worn jeans and a navy blue down jacket—a recent score from Eddie Bauer. Once he'd clearly been rangy, but now he was skeletal thin and stooped.

"I did." Kory kept his eyes riveted on the stranger. He couldn't afford to ignore the threat of a gun. He'd made it this far by not trusting anyone.

"Supposedly, you thought she was a boy."

Kory snorted. "Dillan did. I just didn't tell him he was wrong."

"Why would you do that?" The old man cocked his head, reminding Kory of the girl. Was this a test?

"Dillan would have raped her and relished every scream." That came out too casual and sounded creepy as hell. He shook his head. "Not my thing."

The old man studied him and then nodded. Hopefully, he believed him, but trusting strangers wasn't common these days. Probably not. Kory was a stranger and times were tough. The grandfather cleared his throat and coughed. Not just once, but over and over, grabbing the nearest bookshelf for support.

Kory slung his canteen from his shoulder and walked into the shadows between the tall wooden bookshelves. He handed his water to the old man, who took a drink. He met the old man's eyes as he struggled to catch his breath. There was no gun, just an empty holster. When at last he stopped coughing, his breath came out as a wheeze. He slugged more water and wiped his mouth with a blood-spotted handkerchief.

"Cough syrup won't fix that." Kory wasn't trying to be cruel, just stating a fact. Sounded like the old man was operating with half a lung.

"Robin is in serious denial," said her grandfather after several additional sips. He wiped his mouth again and used his sleeve to clean the top of the canteen. He looked at Kory as he returned the container. "Thanks. It's not catching. Lung cancer, I mean."

Kory nodded. Cancer these days would be a terrible death sentence. No chemo or treatment of any kind. Hell, he hadn't seen a doctor or medical professional since the refugee center in the early days. They'd been stretched beyond the limit, working insane hours with limited supplies. At the back of his mind, he tallied another point for xTerra. They probably had doctors.

"Can I ask you a favor?" said the old man. "It's going to sound odd."

Kory shrugged. "First, what's your name?"

The old man nodded, as if in approval of introductions. "I'm Clay Wilson, out of Idaho. Robin's from Portland."

Before Seattle, Kory had grown up in Portland, and the image of the rivers and the bridges flashed through his mind. He missed the wild weather on the Oregon Coast and the windswept beaches littered with haystack rocks. An expected wave of homesickness rocked him. "The two of you were lucky to be together when the asteroid hit."

Clay shook his head. "She hiked a couple of hundred miles on her own through the mountains to get to my place. She hasn't ever said much about her journey, but she's scared to be alone. Something happened out there that separated her from her sister. She doesn't talk about it. The usual bad things that happen to young women when society crumbles, I imagine." His eyes took on a steely look. "The girl's got grit."

Kory shifted. He would never take advantage of someone, but there was a certain lawlessness about the world these days, and he wouldn't be surprised if someone with fewer scruples had hurt her. Her disguise, if that's what it was, made sense. Kory yearned for a purpose, to make a difference. Ninety-five percent of decent people had evacuated, and the rest had hidden. The world sucked.

He didn't mean to ask, but curiosity won out. "What's the favor?"

"I'm leaving." Once more Clay coughed, this time into a new rag he removed from his coat pocket. "Please don't tell Robin you saw me. These days, I need a head start. I came here to leave her a note."

Clay wasn't carrying a pack, which meant he was traveling light. No water. No food.

"You're dying sooner rather than later, then." Kory examined the old man again. Even in the dim light, his eyes had a cloudy aspect, the kind he'd seen only on the ancient and sick, like his childhood retriever, Sunny. He and his dog had been thirteen when, one day, Sunny had hobbled into the forest and never returned.

"I'm leaving town," said Kory. "I'm not staying here for the winter." He wasn't sure why he was volunteering this information. Maybe because Clay was dying and wouldn't be around to double-cross him. "If you were going to ask me to look out for her, that isn't in the cards." It came out more of a growl than intended.

"I keep telling her to leave." Clay shook his head. "Girl's as stubborn as her grandmother was." That was an admirable quality, and they both knew it. More than ever these days. "I was going to leave the note in that book you grabbed. That's her favorite."

Kory unzipped his backpack and groped inside. "You want it back?"

Clay made another negative motion with his head. "I'll just stick my letter on the shelf where the book belongs. Robin will find it. She sneaks over here to read—more than she thinks I realize. She'll be along today, or perhaps tomorrow, unless she gets caught up looking for me."

The note must be a goodbye or an explanation. Clay wouldn't want Robin to worry. Fat chance. She'd probably still be upset. Kory had heard stories about elders doing this long ago. In tough times, the old and infirm chose their time of dying, heading off alone into the elements. Much like his dog. They would die on their own terms, so as not to be a burden to their loved ones. There was something noble about Clay putting his granddaughter first.

Kory had never had anyone put him first as far back as he could remember. None of his parents, including the father he'd never met. Certainly neither of his stepfathers and they'd been better than the series of foster parents. Even though the old man was dying, Kory envied him. He'd made a difference. He hadn't sat around and done nothing.

"Once she knows I'm dead and gone, she's more likely to move on. Her uncle is farther east. I want her to find him." Clay glanced to the east.

"So, I just don't tell her I saw you?" Kory raised an eyebrow. That didn't seem like much of a favor. There was probably more.

"It's true. I hoped you could watch over her for a few days. Maybe check if she gets my letter and leaves town." It became difficult to look away from the old man's piercing gaze.

There it was. Of course. He wanted something more. "What makes you think you can trust me?" Kory's eyes narrowed. It seemed a little too convenient to run into first one of this pair, then the other. Was this some kind of con? Something to throw him off guard?

"Let's just say, I watched you for a while. You like my girl, or you are at least interested in finding another reader who loves the same books. You spent half an hour grinning about finding her name in books, like a goddamn treasure hunt."

Kory clenched a fist. Fuck. He wasn't usually so easy to sneak up on, or get a read on. "I don't have the best track record of looking out for others." Wasn't that the truth? He still couldn't get the cries of the Wings' women out of his head. Damn useless is what he was. He shifted his feet and considered spitting. He settled for cracking his knuckles. "I don't know where to find her. Doubt you're going to share where you two live." He raised an eyebrow, daring the old man to show that level of trust.

Clay didn't bite. "You know she'll come here. Think about it." He stepped closer and slid a sealed blue envelope, marked 'Robin', onto the shelf near Kory's arm.

His hand twitched. What did Clay's letter say?

"Where's this uncle? Far?" said Kory. Why was he even asking? He shouldn't get the old man's hopes up.

"South Dakota," said the old man as he turned away.

Kory's head shot up. "There's supposed to be some walled city out that way." A place like that might have some sort of justice, a place where he could be part of building a decent society.

"You've heard of it," said Clay, with what sounded like satisfaction and a faint smile on his grizzled face. "In the early days, my boy, Luke, and his wife took their baby to Vita xTerra. He does what he sets out to do. They have a bunker inside the wall and are still alive. I can feel it."

"You think your teenage granddaughter is going to walk to South Dakota?" Kory felt the disbelief break his impassive face. "That's almost a thousand miles away."

"She's twenty-one, not a teenager. You sound like her. It's only another eight hundred miles." Clay turned once more. "I'm leaving now. No matter what you say, I'm still hoping you'll be around to check on her for a few days. She's going to be furious with me, and I hope she doesn't do something stupid."

"Why now?" said Kory, still rocked by the knowledge that xTerra was real. This time, he would actually leave and search for it.

"If I wait any longer, she's going to have to deal with my corpse. It's one thing to know I'm dying, another to see it. I'd spare her that. Besides, she needs to leave before the snow flies. Think about it."

Clay left, fading into the shadows. His footfalls were light, but Kory waited to move until after the faint crunching of glass by the entrance signaled the other man's departure.

Looking at the daylight outside as he exited, Kory headed toward the mall. It must be late afternoon. He'd stayed at the bookstore longer than he'd expected, and all he had to show for his time was a couple of books. At this rate, his travel rations would be pretty scant.

He would come back to talk to Robin tomorrow. She knew the town and what would be productive. Working with her would make better use of his scrounging time. They could put together supplies. If she planned to winter here, she must have food, or ways to find it. The weight of her backpack yesterday had been substantial.

Every step, his thoughts circled back to Robin. Maybe he could give her advice or they could travel together after all. She needed safety, and he needed more than being a low-life drifter, existing through intimidation and theft. For the first time in a long time, maybe he could do something. No more being a bystander. This time, he would help.

Kory tromped across the windy town without incident, slipped back into the mall, and joined the others where they'd gathered near the food court. Just in time.

Dillan had arrived with a message from Jake. His dark eyes glinted when Kory walked downstairs empty-handed. That one was too sharp.

"Productive search," said Dillan with a soft sneer.

"What's the word?" Kory leaned against the wall, his arms crossed.

"We're supposed to pick our top three stores as room choices. Jake's coming to inspect the mall tomorrow. He wants to move in before anyone gets too attached and settled in the Walgreens."

Kory's mind shifted to the task, and he nodded. This was easy; he'd chosen first thing this morning. "Follow me."

Chapter 5: Robin

Robin woke with a gasp, covered in a slick sheen of sweat, the grip of unyielding fingers fading from her throat. She took a second to orient herself, taking a shuddering breath. She'd left the mountains behind long ago. She was in Boise, in the security panic room in the far reaches of the parkade under the Towne Square Mall on P3. This was as safe as her life got. As her breathing returned to normal, she sat up, fumbling for the ready candle lantern by her elbow and for her lighter.

Flicking it on, the pale light it cast confirmed her fear. Grandpa's bed remained flat and empty. He'd been missing for three days and nights. She'd searched his usual haunts, other than the mall and the bookstore. Twice, she'd been stymied trying to get to the Barnes and Noble by that Dillan who'd been skulking near the western exit of the parkade. She'd turned back, unwilling to chance a confrontation on her own.

Since searching, she hadn't taken time for herself, not even to collect new books—those were the places she still needed to check. Her grandfather might not want to be found, but she wasn't ready to give up. She also wasn't ready to admit he might be dead. Today, the bookstore was her priority. She needed to try again because she was running out of time.

Her stomach grumbled. She would need to cook and eat actual food today instead of using the travel rations. With the bikers in the mall, she couldn't get more.

She lit her candle and got up, blinking back tears while she ran through her plan for the day. The bikers had been all over near the mall for the last couple of days—the roar of their engines' constant. She'd seen Dillan's fiery hair several times. He seemed to be everywhere. Each time, she'd ducked away and changed directions. Dillan might be out there still. Maybe she should try upstairs first—being extremely careful. She could use the service halls and get a read on the activity before heading into town. If she lost the mall for good, her life would become immeasurably more confined.

Perhaps Grandpa had gone upstairs to inspect the situation with the bikers for himself and gotten pinched. Her lungs constricted. Or he might be lying somewhere, passed out and in pain. Maybe he'd already died. She couldn't shake the fearful thoughts as she got ready and headed out, keys in hand. Her breath plumed white as she walked and the tip of her nose and her cheeks burned from the chill air. The season was on winter's doorstep. The warm fall weather wouldn't linger after the autumn storms hit.

She reached the metal door with the chipped blue paint and headed into the stairwell, locking everything behind her as she went. Checking for her grandfather in the shadows and corners, she was disappointed to reach the door to the main concourse with no sign he'd been here. Taking her crate, she positioned it against the door. She stepped up and peered through the glass, her eyes almost pressed against the window. A startled man with long hair on the other side of the glass met her gaze and let out a shout.

Three other men came running as the first pointed to the door.

She gasped and dropped, her heart racing. They'd filled the concourse with rows of motorcycles. The food court resembled a dining hall next to a motorcycle parking lot. She'd only had a second to look, but they'd seen her. She cursed. How long until the bikers found a way into the service hall? Now they'd be searching for her near the mall. They might even find her home.

Sweat ran down Robin's back as she kicked her crate and backed away. Had someone been close to the door because they'd noticed her dim light? She should have shielded it better with her hand. Blowing out her candle, she held her breath and tried to remain calm. How could she have been so careless? Outside, someone tried the handle, rattling the solid door. It remained closed. For now.

The darkness pressed inward, then someone pounded on the door. Shit. Without her light, the gray square in the door seemed bright. She needed to get far away. She was no longer safe. How hard would they search? The door held. But what if someone used a crowbar? Or found another entrance? The halls weren't completely secure. In her panic, she couldn't remember the last time she'd checked all the locks. She needed to leave. Now.

Keeping her hand on the wall for balance, she retraced her steps toward the stairs, checking each knob she passed. Her sweaty hands shook, but each one remained locked. She didn't breathe until she was inside the pitch-black stairwell, with another barrier between herself and the startled face at the window. She dropped her unlit candle into her pocket, still too nervous to light it again. Plus, a light down here would give away where she'd gone. Let her disappearance remain a mystery. She slid her hand along the chilly metal railing, and worked her way downstairs, listening for sounds of pursuit. Nothing yet. She'd fucked up. She'd known better than to go back to the mall. Now what? Wait and hide.

•　　•　　•

Robin didn't emerge for another two days. Boredom and fear together forced her out of her room. Her grandfather still hadn't returned. As each day passed without him, her hope dwindled. It was time to face facts; he wasn't coming back. The bikers were here to stay, and she was alone. To keep herself from panicking, she made a plan—one more trip to the garden and one more for books. Then she'd hunker down for the duration and hope the bikers left town in the spring.

She pressed her ear to the door. It was quiet outside, so she eased the door open and stuck her head out. No sign of movement. Clear.

Her hands shook as the locked door clicked shut behind her and she slunk along the rough cement walls. At each new level, she stopped and listened. It was slow going because each time she ascended a ramp, she waited until her heartbeat no longer pounded in her ears. As she neared the surface, the cold, blustery wind whistled through the uprights, carrying the odor of damp earth and rotten leaves.

In the days since her last real outing, five days earlier, the leaves had changed color—a riot of brilliant yellow, dull brown, pumpkin orange, and ripe apple red. A smattering of cold mist landed on her face when she stepped onto the cracked street, and leaves scuttled ahead on the rain-spotted pavement. Branches whipped through the air, rattling against each other. High above, another flock of geese winged south, perhaps racing the wind.

Robin kept her eyes peeled, but so far, so good, there didn't seem to be anyone else around. Maybe the stormy weather was a blessing. The further she walked from safety, the more she worried. Were the bikers actively searching for her? She bit her lip, her head on a swivel as she crept through the quiet streets, scurrying through open patches and sticking close to the walls when possible. No sign of her grandfather out here, either. Not that she'd expected anything, she'd just hoped.

At last, she reached the bookstore. The walk had her on edge, but she'd come this far and didn't want to turn back. She checked in all directions and slipped inside, wincing at the crystalline crunch of gritty glass underfoot. Once through the jagged door, she stepped to the edge, avoiding the rest. When she'd cleaned the glass, she'd left some as an alarm for when she was in the store, but that only worked if she was the one already inside.

Her breath was the only sound inside the cavernous store. Usually, she felt safe here, but not today. Creeping along, she checked the Biography section first. The World War Two hardcover her grandfather had finished last week had been returned. Hope surged inside her. He'd been in the store since he'd left their place. Her pulse quickened as she slipped the volume from its shelf. She shook it. She fanned the pages, but there was nothing. Maybe he'd left her a message with her books. Something they'd agreed to do if ever they became separated.

Turning into the Romance section, Robin scanned the shelves. Halfway to the floor, where there should have been three copies of *The Hating Game*, there were only two. Beside them, propped in the empty slot, sat a blue envelope. With shaking hands, she snatched it. She held it up to the light. Her grandfather had written her name on the outside in his spidery handwriting.

She held back tears, tore open the flap, and, trembling all over, she removed a single sheet of paper.

Dearest Robin,

Be mad at me if you want, but my departure is overdue, and you know it. You've been my everything the last few years and without you, I'd have stayed at the farm and given up long ago.

A tear splashed the paper, leaving a damp patch. No crying. Gulping in a deep breath, she returned to the letter.

I'm dying, Honey. I can't hold you back anymore. You need to leave Boise. These bikers make it too dangerous for you to stay on your own. If I'd been braver, I would have gone a month ago.

I hope one day you'll learn to trust people again. Find Luke and Ella and make a new home. They're family and will welcome you with open arms. Eight hundred miles sounds like an impossible distance, but I believe in you. You're stronger than you think.

Love always,

Grandpa xoxo

P.S. You could do worse than to trust the giant biker. He reads.

Robin sniffed, refolded the note, and returned it to the envelope.

"You came back. It took longer than your grandfather expected," said a man's deep voice.

She whirled to run, but he grabbed her arm. His grip didn't hurt, being just enough to prevent her from leaving. Though she recognized Kory's voice, she cursed until he covered her mouth with one of his massive hands, which smelled faintly bitter, like ink.

Though tempted to bite him, she restrained herself. She didn't want to anger someone this huge. Then his words sunk in. He'd spoken to her grandfather. She stopped.

Slowly, Kory removed his meaty hand from her mouth.

"You saw him." She remained conscious of his strength and size while he stood behind her, his other hand wrapped around her forearm.

"Days ago. He wanted a head start. He got it." His voice was calm.

"Let me go," she hissed. Why would her grandfather have spoken to this behemoth?

"Will you stay and listen?" He smelled clean today—less campfire, more soap.

Robin didn't trust her voice, so she nodded. Her every muscle remained tense in case she got a chance to bolt.

His powerful grip released her, and she spun around to face him, her arms crossed. Her gaze continued upward to his face, which was hard as granite.

"What did you do to him?" She didn't really think he would have hurt her grandfather, though she couldn't say why, except maybe the postscript of the note which had been written in different ink. Her grandfather must have added it for a reason.

"Do you remember me?" Kory kept his voice pitched low.

She nodded. Of course she did. "From the mall. What do you know about my grandfather?" She needed to get to the point. She wanted to leave.

"You read the letter. He said goodbye, right?" Kory's face remained difficult to read.

She took a deep breath and inched further away, hoping he wouldn't notice if she kept talking. What was his range if he lunged? Far. Someone his size might be slow, but she couldn't take a chance. "When did you see him?"

"Five days ago." His eyes didn't match his stoney face. They must be what had set him apart that day in the mall. He had kind eyes that were brown and warm.

Robin didn't want his sympathy. Her heart sank. Five days was too long. Grandpa hadn't changed his mind and he wouldn't be back. Maybe he'd just holed up somewhere else across town, but she would never find him. She had no interest in staying here any longer, and she turned to leave.

"He said you would be leaving town," said Kory.

She shook her head, not wanting to have this discussion with a stranger. She might leave in the spring, but that was none of his business, no matter what her grandfather had told him.

"It was you near the food court the other day, wasn't it?" Kory's words stopped her in her tracks. "Dillan is obsessed with finding the intruder."

She turned and cocked her head, trying to decide what to tell him. Saying nothing would be safest, but she couldn't deny this. She stared, hoping he'd say more, but he didn't. At last, she nodded.

"The others think you live in the mall somewhere." He hesitated, but she wouldn't confirm or deny his statement, so he continued. "You look smarter than that, so my guess is you live underneath. Somewhere in the basement or the parkade."

She swallowed, feeling the blood leave her face as the seriousness of his words sunk in. Had he told anyone his suspicion? It might be only a matter of time before the bikers found her refuge. Boise was too dangerous.

She shook her head, but he raised an eyebrow—a skeptical look that reminded her of her mother. A pang of loneliness swept over her. With her grandfather's loss, she was truly alone for the first time in years.

Robin resumed walking toward the exit.

"Your grandfather wanted you to leave town. He suggested I might go with you."

Robin whirled around, startled into meeting Kory's deep brown eyes. "He did not." She pursed her lips, weighing her options. Could she trust him? Fat chance. She narrowed her eyes. "Did he tell you where he wants me to go?"

"To your uncle in South Dakota."

Shocked to the core, she stumbled backward. Grandpa had told the plan to someone he barely knew. Why? "I'm not going until spring," she said, still reeling and surprised into confiding anything, even such a minor detail.

Kory shook his head. "I was hoping we could leave in the next few days. Leave Boise at least. Hole up elsewhere for the winter."

She recrossed her arms. "What about your friends?"

He shrugged. "Not so much friends, as acquaintances I've been with for some time. I don't owe most of them anything."

She needed time to think. "I need to process the letter." It was true. Her grandfather was gone and as good as dead. She swallowed the tears bubbling up.

"Can we meet here tomorrow?" Kory seemed reluctant to let her go. "To talk."

If lying was the only way to escape, she had no problem. "I'll come back in the morning." She had no intention of returning.

He shot her a pointed look and didn't look convinced—the eyebrow lifting once more. Too bad. Robin needed to go somewhere and cry, and she didn't want him anywhere near. She also couldn't face the empty bunker yet. She was about to go lock herself in for months. Today, she'd go to the garden as planned. One last taste of fresh air and freedom.

"I'll be here," he said. "Tomorrow morning."

Robin turned and ran. She hopped through the door frame and took off at a sprint. She went in the opposite direction of her destination for several blocks, then doubled back before heading for the garden. Slowing, when she was out of breath, she checked for followers. She didn't see any sign of Kory or Dillan or anyone else. The weather was definitely a blessing in disguise.

Her route took her past the south of the mall. The bikers seemed to be busy in their new home inside and she hadn't seen many since the first days. They must have rigged a fireplace as smoke rose from the metal pipe on the roof.

The rain picked up, and she shivered, wishing she'd worn a warmer jacket. This one wasn't more than a waterproof shell. She jumped at a crash nearby, but calmed when a cat slunk out from between two buildings. There didn't seem to be anyone nearby. It must have knocked something over.

She picked her way through the quiet neighborhood until she came to the alley behind the row of houses with her garden. She looked right, then left, then swung the loose board and slipped inside. Everything looked the same here—undisturbed.

The wind whipped the almost bare tree branches overhead, and a chill ran through her. The bare garden wasn't much comfort. She looked at the house, picturing the layout from when she and Grandpa had explored last spring. Maybe she'd hang out inside. It would be cold without heat or lights, but at least she'd be out of the wind. There might be a couple of books too, since she'd grabbed nothing new at the store.

Her teeth chattered as she picked the lock with cold, red hands. Entering, she relocked the door and went upstairs to the living room, avoiding passing in front of windows. If someone came here, she wouldn't be cornered, with exits on each floor. She curled up on the couch and let herself cry, great wracking sobs that left her wrung out, but she felt better for the release.

Robin wrapped herself in a blanket and lay there a little longer, trying to decide what to do. She didn't want to stay in the damp cold parkade alone, but South Dakota was unrealistic and so far. It was too late this fall. She would have to stay until spring, then she would travel. Wiping away the tears, she took a deep breath. Time to stop the pity party and get on with it. She got up and went looking for books.

Stuffing half a dozen old-fashioned, lurid-looking romance novels from the bedroom into her bag, she slung it over her shoulder and let herself out the back door—they would be better than nothing. She was a dozen feet into the yard when she realized she'd made a serious mistake.

The rain clouds had dissipated, and the garden was swathed in a patch of golden sunshine, but that wasn't what had caught her attention.

As though enjoying the sun, Dillan stood in the middle of the backyard, staring at the garden, his red hair glinting in the sun. At first, she didn't think that he'd seen her and she backed away, trying not to make any noise.

"Don't bother. You've been in the house for over an hour. Nobody else is anywhere near this neighborhood. I saw you running this way from the mall and followed. I figured you'd come back outside at some point. Is this where you live?" He turned to face her.

Robin didn't answer and stared at him—not daring to look away. She couldn't get back inside and lock the door before he'd follow. She needed to get away from the house. It would be too easy to trap her against the wall. She took a few steps forward, closer to the gap in the fence.

"Stop. We haven't finished our conversation." Dillan's voice took on an edge. "There was something about you I couldn't place the other day." He strolled toward her, stopping about ten feet away with a knife gripped in his right hand.

"What's that?" she said, trying to project a confidence she didn't feel. This situation could go sideways in an instant. He was dangerous, in a nasty, sneaky way, like a viper. She'd seen his type before. Maybe if she played along, she could escape unscathed. She ran through the other places nearby where she might hide short-term. Not a lot of options.

"You're not a boy." The gleam in his cold eyes chilled her insides.

She shook her head. Not denying his statement, but unwilling to discuss this. Robin took another step toward her exit. Dillan lunged. She stumbled, and he caught her. Using her momentum, he slid his knife against her throat. She froze. He applied pressure and her skin parted in a stinging line. A warm trail slid down the side of her neck. She closed her eyes and concentrated on breathing. She had to stay alive. Her skin crawled and she broke out in a sweat. This was going to hurt.

"Let her go," said Kory's deep voice.

How was he here, too? Robin allowed herself a modicum of hope.

"Just in time. Hold her down. We can take turns," said Dillan. "Doubt you've been with a woman in ages." His indifferent tone told her he was serious. She couldn't look at Kory.

"Woman?" scoffed Kory. "I don't fuck kids."

She wasn't a kid, but she wouldn't argue. Anything to get Dillan to release her.

"Close enough to a woman for me," said Dillan.

"Let her go," Kory repeated from closer. His voice had also become deeper, yet quieter, giving it an intense quality.

Dillan yanked her closer, hauling her side tight against his front. He wrapped one arm around her waist while the other held the knife. She shuddered at the close contact. She couldn't see his face, but he clearly hadn't recognized the menace in Kory's voice.

"Fuck off. I'll tell my uncle you've been hiding food for yourself. You've been stashing stuff on your own for almost a week. I'll also say that you've found yourself a tasty piece of ass and wouldn't share. You're just an initiate. You don't tell me what to do."

"I'm not forcing her." Kory's massive body came into view and she begged him with her eyes to intervene. Perhaps he'd followed Dillan and not her. Would he understand? Would he care enough to help?

Dillan shrugged. "Then you can watch." He whispered in Robin's ear. "Take your pack off. Set it down nice and easy. If you don't fight, I won't hurt you more than necessary." His fetid breath made her gag.

With trembling hands, Robin unclipped her pack and let it drop, the icy blade still burning against her skin. Bile rose in her throat as Dillan stroked her cheek with his free hand. "Now slide your pants down and get on all fours."

Without moving her head, she shot a panicked look at Kory. He turned away and her throat seized. The bastard was going to let his friend rape her. Of course. Just because he'd talked to her grandfather didn't mean he'd help her. To him, she was nobody. Dillan pressed harder with the knife, reminding her she was at his mercy. Another trail of blood slid down her neck. Her lips shook as Kory stepped out of her line of sight. Had he left?

"Take them off," insisted Dillan. "I don't want to cut you, but I will if you fight."

Warmth flooded Robin's pants and ran down her leg. This was too familiar. Maybe he felt her terror because he laughed. Her shaking knees wouldn't hold her up much longer. She reached for her belt and unfastened the buckle. Cringing away from the knife, she unzipped her wet pants but made no move to lower them.

"Hurry." Dillan unzipped her jacket, the sound making her knees weak and her legs unsteady. He slid his free hand beneath her shirt, grabbed her breast, and squeezed, pinching her nipple through her sports bra. He released the chokehold on her throat for just a second. With a quick slash, he sliced her shirt open from the neck downward. Goosebumps broke out on her bare flesh. Before she caught her breath, he tightened his grip once more.

The blade returned to her neck. "Now."

Robin flinched. She wouldn't do it, but she had to make him think she was compliant. She reached for her pants, inching them downward as though they were tight across the hips. The knife at her throat drifted away as he leaned down to speed up the job. She struck, elbowing Dillan. His nose crunched, and he crumpled backward, his hands pressed to his face. Blood oozed between his fingers and dripped onto his jacket. She adjusted her pants, grabbed her pack, and scrambled for the hole in the fence.

She didn't make it.

Dillan tackled her, and she hit the ground hard, knocking the wind from her lungs with a sickening thud. Blood still streamed from his nose and his hard face was twisted, but it was the glint in his dark eyes that scared her the most. What was wrong with him? She struggled to rise. He shoved her back to the frozen ground, and sat on her, pinning her in place with both his hands and his shark smile.

He wrapped one hand around her neck, pushed aside the tattered front of her shirt, and sliced through her bra. Her panic shot off the charts and it became hard to breathe.

He stared at her bare breasts. "Nice tits." Smiling, he wrapped his second hand around her neck—like her hazy memory. Like her nightmares.

Robin screamed, wasting her last breath in her terror.

It made no difference. She was alone. There was no help.

With a soft smile, Dillan tightened his grip while she struggled to free herself, and the sound ceased. First, her lungs burned, then the pressure on her throat hurt. Her vision spotted, turning dark at the edges. Her movement grew less, and still he squeezed, the blackness dancing across her vision. Would he stop? Choke her to death?

A scraping sound almost beyond her notice caught her attention.

"You changed your mind," Dillan said, as though from far away.

She couldn't concentrate and the world disappeared into blackness.

•   •   •

Robin came to, bumping against a man's leather-clad back, slung over his shoulder. She couldn't see who carried her, but this high above the ground, she'd bet it was Kory. She moaned and squirmed—being carted like a sack of potatoes was undignified.

He stopped and let her down.

Her knees wouldn't take her weight and she sagged toward the ground. Kory grabbed her by the elbow, holding her up.

Her pack rested over his shoulder next to his and she looked up to find his eyes waiting for her to recognize him. She blinked back tears. Kory wasn't much better than Dillan. He'd left her behind to be raped. Had he come back to deliver her to the biker group? Had Dillan finished? Her pants were on. She couldn't remember, but she didn't hurt as much as she feared. She glanced down, scared to meet Kory's eyes again. Clutched in his other hand was a blood-covered knife.

She flinched and touched the cut on her neck and found it drying and tacky. It wasn't her blood on the knife and his arm. There was too much. She glanced up again, avoiding Kory's eyes in her confusion. What had happened?

"We're leaving town." His intense whisper brought her back to the moment.

"I'm not going anywhere with you." Her voice shook.

"I killed a full member of the Wings. Jake can't overlook that. I can't go back." His eyes had become enormous—winter lakes without a bottom.

"You killed him?" Her unsteady legs sagged again and Kory held her up once more, touching only her arm. Her gut clenched. "I thought you were taking me to the others." Her relief was palpable.

"We're going to your place to get cleaned up. We leave today." He sounded resigned, not angry.

Robin still wasn't going anywhere with him.

Speaking hurt, so she didn't answer, and she avoided his gaze. She blinked. If she started crying again, she might not stop. Her jaw ached with the effort. One breakdown today was enough.

"Look," said Kory. "I'm sorry I left at first. I didn't think I could stand seeing you raped. Turns out, I couldn't leave either. Your grandfather asked me to look out for you and I was doing a shit job. And, Dillan needed to be put down."

Tears flooded her eyes. Not because she was sad for that creep, but a delayed reaction to the attack. She'd been terrified this time she would be killed.

Kory ran one of his gore-splattered hands through his hair, standing it on end. Huge and angry, covered in blood, he was the epitome of a barbarian. "Look, I don't know where else to go. I need to get cleaned up and off the streets. We need to leave. When Dillan isn't back at dinner, it will raise suspicions. The leader of the Wings is his uncle. When neither Dillan nor I have returned by morning, they'll initiate a full-scale search. It might take them a few days, but if we're still here, they'll find you, your hideout, me. There will be no hiding in Boise."

"You could wash up and go back and they'll never suspect a thing." Her voice quavered.

He nodded. "Maybe. I was planning to leave before winter and I'm out of time. If I don't go now, they'll make me a full member, and I don't want that." He watched her while she tried to figure out what to do.

"My hiding place is pretty exceptional." Her voice was raspy. She sucked her lower lip in and nibbled.

He shook his head. "Not good enough. Not for a real organized search. I'm not the only one who has seen you, remember? You got careless."

Until now, Robin had forgotten their conversation this morning about living in or under the mall. The panic room door was solid, but not impenetrable. If someone had patience and the right tools, they could catch her like a rabbit in a trap.

"You'll help me?" She shifted from one foot to the other, all too conscious of her soggy pants and the crimson stain soaking her clothes. Her sliced shirt was sticky and drenched, but she needed a moment. Kory was a brute, but Grampa trusted him. He was a biker, and he just killed someone. But, he'd saved her life.

She took a deep breath. Trusting Kory was a big ask, but perhaps they might call a truce or make an agreement. If the other bikers knew where to look, she didn't stand a chance on her own.

"We won't get far on foot." She had to take a chance.

"We'll take my bike. Ditch it somewhere out of sight when we run out of gas. That should help us get some distance. But we have to go this afternoon."

Still, she hesitated. "We'll never make it to South Dakota before winter."

"Suit yourself." He turned away, his face closed down again and difficult to read. "We can't stay." He clenched a fist but made no move toward her. "I'll leave alone."

"You can wash at my place." She gained nothing by turning him away.

"Can you walk?" He lifted an eyebrow.

Robin nodded and got her bearings. They were a few streets over from the south entrance of the parkade. If she took him there, they would spend less time above ground. Right now, that might be safest. With both of them drenched in blood, they needed to get off the street. Could she trust him? It was a gamble. She didn't move.

"Where do you live?" Kory probably wanted to nudge her into a decision.

She faced the most direct route. "The parking garage." No point in hiding where she couldn't stay.

A faint smile made his lips twitch. "Lead the way."

His reaction made her wish she could kick him.

Chapter 6: Kory

Until today, Kory had never killed a man. He'd steered clear, feeling it was a line he shouldn't cross. The act he'd avoided as his final initiation into the Wings, hadn't been so difficult when it had come to it. Still, he'd taken a life. In the old days, he'd have gone to jail. In this world, there were often no repercussions for violent crime. Not that he intended to do it again. Life was strange. Now he qualified as one of the Wings, but since he'd killed one of their members, leaving had become a matter of his own life or death.

Shit. He watched as Robin stumbled ahead of him, unable to put a finger on why he'd acted now. He looked after himself. She should take care of herself, too. If you couldn't manage it then, you accepted the consequences. That's how the world worked. Always had. He just hadn't had the illusion of family, safety, and society for longer than most. But, damn, it had felt great to take action for once.

The image of his sister flashed through his mind—the haunted look in her hazel eyes after her boyfriend had smacked her for an imaginary infraction. Kory hadn't thought of Alice in years. She'd left home at sixteen after their parents had died, unwilling to try foster care. She'd disappeared. Even run away from her boyfriend. She'd never written, and now, years later, he had no way of knowing if she was even alive.

Robin had nothing to do with Alice. Nothing. He hadn't been able to protect his sister, since he'd been just a kid, so this wasn't the same.

He kept an ear cocked and his eyes peeled for Wings' scavengers or guards, but they were so busy in the mall, they hadn't bothered to set a full perimeter. Robin might be shaken and injured, but she still took precautions not to be seen as she led him to the parkade. She checked as carefully for watchers as he did. She hadn't lost her wits even after Dillan's assault. Despite her youth and size, she was tougher than she looked. Clay had called it grit. Kory understood what the older man had meant.

At the entrance to the underground, they scuttled down the ramp to the first level. With his height, the ceiling hung closer than he was comfortable, but not so close he had to stoop—it just felt like it. He looked around. He couldn't imagine anywhere less hospitable in town than this desolate parkade.

Water pooled in greasy puddles and the wind whistled through the concrete pillars in sharp gusts. Everything was gray, damp, and dripping. Black mildew spots climbed the walls and infused the air with the scent of mold. After a couple of ramps and turns, it became darker and a steady cold emanated not just from the air, but from the surrounding concrete. At least they were out of the chill wind. Overhead, icy drips fell and occasionally landed on him, stinging the exposed skin of his neck and hands.

She led him through a descending maze under the mall and he lost track of what was above them or how far down they'd come, but she never hesitated. At one of the multitudes of service doors, she stopped, fishing out a key from the front pocket of her pants. She unlocked the door and held it open for him. Inside was black as night and he couldn't see beyond the entrance. What if it was a trap? He tossed his chin, letting her know he'd prefer her to go first.

She sighed and produced a candle nub and a silver lighter from her jacket pocket. With a practiced flick, she lit the wick of her candle, closed the lighter, and walked inside without a backward glance.

Kory followed and closed the door.

They'd carpeted the inside in an array of patchwork swatches. At one end, two twin mattresses rested on the floor—the one surrounded by close to a dozen books resembled a nest more than a bed. He'd bet that was where Robin slept. The second mattress had been made without a wrinkle, the blankets pulled tight. Several fluffy pillows sat at one end. Against the back wall stood a narrow stove with a large stainless pot covering both burners, and a sink with a couple of bowls beside it. Did they have running water?

Despite the gloom outside, someone had attempted to make this room hospitable. From outside, it looked the same as the dozen other doors and he never would have guessed there was an actual place to stay here. He'd bet this hidey-hole was one-of-kind and almost as secure as she thought. There was a slim chance it wouldn't be found in a search, but he wasn't about to tell her that. They were better off taking their chances on the road.

While he looked around, Robin lit additional candles, then turned on the gas under the pot on the stovetop. The blue flame caught right away. Water and gas to cook.

She folded her arms as she stared at him. "We have water, but it's all cold." When he didn't answer, she pointed to another door in the back corner. "The bathroom's in there. You wanted to wash." Her voice sounded hoarse. Dillan had done a number on her throat.

A bathroom? Hell, this dismal concrete hole was a five-star hotel in disguise. Kory picked up a candleholder and went where she'd indicated. In the flickering yellow light, he glimpsed his reflection in the mirror and winced. He was a mess. Patches of brownish-red crusted his face and concentrated in the grooves of his fingers and in the creases of his skin. He resembled a horror movie survivor and looked much older than twenty-five. He swallowed. Not just blood, Dillan's lifeblood.

There'd been so much.

Kory's hands shook as he peeled off his shirt and tossed it in the sink, which he filled with cold water. Swirls of darkening pink spread through the water around his soaking garment, and his stomach clenched. Best not to think too hard. He looked around. The bathroom also had a narrow bathtub and a toilet. He turned on the water and rinsed his face, bracing himself for the first chilly splash, using the darker of the two towels to dry his face. It smelled faintly of shaving cream. Must be the grandfather's.

Kory turned the faucet above the tub to run a quick bath, and watched the water cascade into the basin, the sound filling the enclosed bathroom. His knees would be up to his ears when he sat, but it would still be his best wash in ages. He enjoyed being clean, but long ago, he'd adjusted his standards. He couldn't remember his last actual bath. Years. He removed his boots and socks, setting them aside. He prepared to freeze his balls off in the icy water. Before he slipped off his jeans, Robin knocked.

He opened the door, and she stepped in beside him without speaking and leaned over to check the level of the water. In this light, the purpling bruises ringing her throat were already apparent. It must hurt like hell to swallow. The cuts from Dillan's knife didn't look serious, but she'd need to wash and disinfect them.

"Fill it another inch or two. I'll be back with the hot water." She returned to the other room. He didn't know what else she was doing out there. Perhaps packing.

He turned off the tap after another inch of water and held the door wide open, staying out of her way as she returned carrying a steaming pot.

Her arms shook as she poured the hot water into the tub.

Kory reached around her, his hands steadying her tiny ones. Her eyes flicked to his arms and ducked underneath his circling arms to step away. She averted her gaze, and he tried not to show his amusement. He wasn't the only one affected by their proximity.

She was young enough that she wouldn't have been around many men. Just boys, her aged grandfather, and men who'd hurt her. That would mess you up. He'd have to go carefully to get her used to him being around, or she'd be a constant flight risk. He'd forgotten he was only half-dressed and practically a giant compared to her. She wouldn't meet his eyes as she left with the empty pot, closing the door.

He took a deep breath.

From the other room came the sound of more running water as it ran into her pot. She must be heating some for herself, too. He'd have to hurry. They couldn't waste all day and she also needed a bath. Maybe more than he did. Not that you could scour away violence. His brain flashed back to the garden. He'd pulled the blood-soaked, tattered pieces of her shirt closed and zipped her jacket before heaving her over his shoulder. Between splatters, her flesh had been as white as snow, with purple veins trailing underneath. He hadn't meant to notice. Focus Kory.

Before he finished undressing, he opened the door and called, "Get your pack ready to travel. Essentials only. I don't have access to much food, so if you do, please pack it. That's what we'll need most of all." He didn't wait for an answer. He closed the door, stripped, and hopped into the hot water, wedging himself into the limited tub space. His knees jutted over the side, but there was enough depth to get clean. He grabbed the bar of soap and scrubbed the blood from his skin, stopping only when every trace was gone. Then he shampooed and rinsed his crunchy hair.

In the end, killing had been too damn easy.

Kory leaned back and closed his eyes while the scene from the garden played out again. He'd come up behind Dillan and slit his throat, ripping him off the unconscious Robin at the same time. Dillan would have killed her. Taking Dillan from behind had been the coward's way, but from the second Kory had followed, he'd known that was the way events would play out. The crimson flood had stained the ground, soaking into the bare earth.

Dillan had made a horrible gurgling sound, perhaps trying to speak. Then his eyes had rolled back in his pasty face and he'd gone limp. He hadn't lasted long or put up a fight. He must not have expected Kory to be a threat.

Kory would have nightmares about the fountain of red mist.

He took a deep breath and stood; the water sluicing off his steaming body. For once, he felt clean all over. At least outside. He glanced down. Robin would need fresh water. He drained the discolored tub water, grabbed the towel, and dried himself before rummaging in his pack for clean clothes. No one back at the mall would notice that he'd changed. The Wings were a bunch of guys and jeans were jeans.

He wrung out his wet shirt until the water no longer ran red, then he let the sink water drain. Running a fresh sinkful, he shaved with the razor from his pack. He didn't know when he'd have the luxury of running water and a full-size mirror again. It might be awhile. He didn't know what they'd find on the road.

His thoughts turned to the next task. He'd made it sound like getting his bike would be a piece of cake, but it might not be so seamless. Maybe they should leave on foot. He put on his socks and boots while he considered. The bike was worth the risk. They might ride a hundred miles in an hour or two instead of walking the same distance over several days. It would kick start their journey toward South Dakota. Too bad they wouldn't have wheels for longer, not once they ran out of gas. He didn't have a connection to someone who sold or mixed gas. Jake did. Whatever Kory put in the tank before they left town, would be it.

He'd have to think of a reason to take the bike out because the day before yesterday they'd parked them inside, anticipating bad weather. Perhaps a supply run. He snapped his fingers. All those boxes of cough syrup in the other room gave him an idea. He'd say he'd found a drugstore and wanted to bring back a load of medical supplies. That would be worth the gas.

He pulled a clean T-shirt over his head and went to inspect the food situation.

•   •   •

Kory marched into the mall an hour later. He'd attract less attention if he ignored everyone except Jake, like usual. He made his way straight to the leader where he sat playing poker with his regular group, now at the edge of the food court where he'd set up shop. A second table with mainly the more violent thieves sat three tables over, watching. Jake might have trouble with them one of these days.

"You just drained the bikes, but I found a small drugstore across town. No signs out front, so it's pretty stocked. You good if I put in a gallon? I want to load up." It was best to be direct. If he made it sound too spectacular, Jake would either want to see for himself or send someone along to help.

"You need help?" Jake asked, leaning back.

"Na. Just thought I'd do it before dark. Bike will be quicker than several trips on foot."

"Weather's getting nasty out there," Jake said, his attention returning to his cards. "My storm thumb aches like a son-of-a-bitch. Snow by tomorrow." He gave Kory one more considering look. "This might be your last chance for a joyride. Go ahead." He waved his hand in dismissal. "Have fun."

"Thanks." Kory was thankful that while Jake may have guessed it wasn't just about supplies, the astute leader hadn't suspected the actual reason. Kory headed for where he'd slept the last few nights. He took only a second to assess what he could grab, and what he couldn't. It didn't look like anyone was paying attention, but he didn't want his packing to be obvious. He'd left his few unpacked belongings in an out-of-the-way corner for this reason.

Kory shoved his sleeping bag into a stuff sack and jammed it into his pack. He spread his spare blanket over his mattress to make it less obvious he'd taken anything. He left his partial candle and his old boots. Someone would claim them. But, he took his solitaire cards.

He glanced around, noting nothing else worth taking. Everything of value stayed with him all the time. Shouldering his bag, he left the Banana Republic many of the others called their new winter home, feeling a few sets of speculative eyes as he left. Was his departure too conspicuous? His shoulder blades twitched as he strode down the concourse, his boots thumping on the hard floor.

He stopped by the guarded fuel supply near the exit for a small jerry can, where the pungent scent of gas filled the air, making him almost miss gas stations.

"Jake said I can take a bike for the afternoon. Shouldn't be more than a few hours."

Zeke, another of the regular Wings grunted and handed him a three-quarters-full can. "Some guys have all the luck. Jake know you just want a spin before the snow?"

Kory shrugged. "I got permission."

The older man winked. "You're pretty high in his favor right now after scoping out the mall. It's pretty cherry in here. If you see Dillan out there, let him know he's late. Jake wanted to talk to him at lunch."

Kory kept his face expressionless. "Will do." Dillan's disappearance would be noted soon, though Kory doubted they'd search far afield until morning. Still, it was a complication that would limit their lead. He and Robin would have to make the most of it.

Kory emptied the gas into his bike, kicked up the stand, and pushed it outside, going through the east mall exit where the guys had cleared the main entrance. He didn't take the trailer, after all. If everyone thought he was fooling around, why spoil the image? He nodded to the guard and started the bike with a roar and a toothy grin. He'd miss the bike when he left it behind. Maybe he would get another, but without a supply of gas, this one wouldn't be of much use.

Pulling out, he swerved around a couple of fallen branches, turned south onto a major street, and gunned it straight down the middle, adding to the illusion of one last chance to goof off. It wasn't all an act. He loved the rush of air on his face, his hair blowing in the wind, and the power of the bike under his control. He turned west and did another run, enjoying the freedom.

Still, he couldn't afford to waste his limited fuel and soon zigzagged his way toward the drugstore where he and Robin had gone before he'd left to collect his bike. He'd thought it best that he went where he'd told Jake he was headed. Not just in case someone followed, but for when the search started in earnest, they'd know he'd told a partial truth and made it as far as the drugstore. Perhaps they'd wonder what happened next and wouldn't condemn him right away.

Still, this wasn't too far from where they'd find Dillan's body in the backyard. Then they'd understand his reason for a hasty departure.

Kory turned his mind to the next stage of their journey. They'd taken Robin's pack to the drugstore when she showed him where she'd wait. He'd been impressed with her gear. Not only had she outfitted herself with a top-of-the-line winter sleeping bag and a decent backpack, but she also had warm clothes and a hefty supply of lightweight back-packing rations in pouches. She also had a ridiculous number of vitamins in labeled bags and potatoes. Of all the things she'd grown, why something so heavy? At least they were filling and nutritious.

They'd jammed several dozen of them into a daypack that he would carry clipped onto the lower portion of his backpack to distribute their weight. He didn't know everything else she'd packed, but she'd been on the road before. He trusted her to bring what she needed with little excess weight—after all, she'd have to lug it on her own. Other than the potatoes, which they would eat soon to lighten their load, her pack didn't seem burdensome for someone of her size. But it wasn't light either. Good thing she was tough and wiry.

He parked behind the drugstore and dismounted. So far, so good. He slipped in through the back door she'd left closed but unlocked.

"It's me," he said, his voice a loud whisper. "I'm alone." He couldn't see her, but she was in here somewhere. Maybe at the front. He worked his way forward from the back room and into the store, where he grabbed a few useful items from the shelves, stowing them in his bag. He stopped at the dusty counter and tried on sunglasses until he found a pair he liked, and added them to his pack too. "Where are you? I'm alone," he said again. He scanned the nearby racks while he waited for Robin to show herself. He tapped his toe with a sigh.

Kory didn't have long to wait.

"You ready to ride?" He turned at a faint noise. She was quiet on her feet.

"Sorry, I was watching the street. I wanted to be sure it's clear out there."

He gave her a once over, approving of her trim figure in dark colors and close-fitting clothes that wouldn't flap on the bike. Solid call.

"You ridden a bike before?"

She shook her head. Was she quiet because of her throat? Or was it something more?

He would have been surprised if she answered yes. Everything about her screamed "good girl" vibes. He bet she would have been a valedictorian somewhere. Not someone he would have guessed would have made it this far into the apocalypse. Still, brains were strength too; after all, she was still alive.

"One more stop before we leave town."

He'd spotted a bike shop to the east and wanted to add a sissy bar on the back. For even an hour or two, it might make a difference with an inexperienced rider on the back.

Outside, he took her pack and jammed it into the hard pannier on the left. He'd already stowed his in the right.

He gave her a brief run-down as a mini-lesson and hoped it would be enough. "Don't worry about leaning. Your job is to stay on. Hang onto me and don't make sudden movements."

She nodded. Her wide eyes looked serious, and she was worrying at her bottom lip again. He threw his leg over the bike, raised the kickstand, and started the bike, which came to life with a thunderous roar. She clapped her hands to her ears and stepped back. Wide-eyed, she looked terrified. He reminded himself not to be impatient.

"Jump on." He shouted, patting the seat behind him.

She took a deep breath, lowered her hands, and walked stiffly to the bike, wincing at the noise.

"Use the footpeg," he shouted, gesturing to the metal bar behind his boot.

She awkwardly climbed on and plopped onto the seat behind him, almost as far back as she could go and still be on the seat. He reached behind and slid her closer.

"Hold on." He squeezed her calf in what he hoped was reassurance.

Kory pulled out, trying to keep the bike smooth as the only thing she had to hold on to was him. He rode several blocks to the bike shop without incident.

He parked the bike by the curb and jumped off. "Stay here." Not waiting to see if she listened, he smashed the window with his gloved fist, opened the door, and strode inside. With the afternoon sunlight streaming in, he located a screwdriver and a sissy bar that looked like it would fit. Ripping off the packaging, he returned outside and attached it via the back fender struts. His bike didn't look as tough, but it would give Robin stability while they rode.

He dumped the screwdriver into his pannier. Returning inside the store, he grabbed a handful of earplugs packets and a small helmet. It might just be for this ride, but it would help keep her warm. He hesitated and grabbed a large one as well. For something like this, he wanted a helmet for himself too.

He shoved the extra earplugs in his pocket, zipped his jacket, and strode back outside. Without a word, he handed her a pair of earplugs, waited while she put them in, then passed her a helmet. She shoved it on and fumbled at the chin straps to adjust it while he did his own. Her eyes looked enormous.

They were in a hurry, but he tried to control his impatience, reminding himself that she had an "in" at the bunker city in South Dakota. She would be an asset. He ripped off his gloves and helped, fixing her strap so it wasn't so loose. He rested his hand on the top of her helmet, tipping her face upward. "You good?"

At her nod, Kory passed her a pair of riding gloves and demonstrated how to tighten them with the Velcro around the wrists, while fastening his own.

"Hold the sissy bar, or grab onto me when we go fast. I'll lean. You just stay on. Ready?" She nodded again, so he remounted and started the bike. She climbed on behind again. He gave her a few seconds to settle before he left, heading for the highway southeast of town. He ran a few calculations in his head. If his tank was full, he'd be able to get close to a hundred and fifty miles before they'd run out of gas. If they were lucky, they might get over a hundred today. They had three to four hours of daylight, but they'd be on foot before dark.

The interstate would be the place to start. They'd make excellent time. There weren't too many abandoned cars on it anymore because the gangs had cleared most of the derelict vehicles near the city. When he reached the city limits, he took the exit for I-84 East. Revving the engine, he accelerated, feeling the horsepower of the bike surge beneath him. He leaned into the bike, changed gears, and twisted the throttle. He liked to ride fast.

Robin's arms clamped hard around his middle, and he chuckled to himself. Sissy bar or not, holding him would feel a hell of a lot more secure for a beginner. She made an excellent back warmer and was light enough she made no difference to how the powerful bike handled.

Soon after they hit the freeway, the rain descended in a torrent. He slowed at first, but pushed on through the afternoon. They would be wet, but they couldn't afford to stop. They would probably run out of gas before they ran out of light. At least it wasn't snow.

Chapter 7: Robin

The vibration of the bike settled in Robin's chest and even with earplugs, the roar of the bike made it difficult to hear or think of anything else. The vibrational thrum was distracting, even more than Kory's solid presence in front of her. Being on the motorcycle was a lot of sensory information at once. She might have been exhilarated if she wasn't also scared. She hadn't wanted to leave Boise, but with the attack and Dillan's death, it had become necessary.

The idea of the Wings searching and finding her in her hideout was a horrible thought. Groups of strange men were terrifying after what had happened a few years ago.

That pain had nothing to do with her life anymore. Today mattered. Despite his help today, could she count on Kory? He could have abandoned her and gone off alone, but he hadn't. Would he be willing to stick with her until South Dakota? He was just one man—even though he was big and strong. If he tried anything, she'd cut and run. Holding on to him, trusting his skill and his driving, she took a leap of faith. She wiggled a fraction of an inch closer, despite her misgivings. He had a gentleness at odds with his brute strength that made her feel somehow safe.

Kory drove the bike faster than she was comfortable, but he seemed to be a confident and skilled rider. With his size, he blocked her view in front, so she tilted her head to the right to watch the dreary golden-brown landscape roll past. They seemed to make excellent time. The noise of the bike made it difficult to believe they wouldn't be followed right away. This wasn't a stealthy departure.

At first, the rain came in a drizzle, but soon it poured down and created limited visibility. Kory slowed the bike, still riding faster than she liked, but it seemed a more reasonable speed, especially for the slippery road conditions. Each time they slid even a fraction of an inch, she clenched her eyes shut and tightened her grip.

Her rain jacket and motorcycle helmet kept most of the water off her, but her pants were soon soaked through. Maybe jeans hadn't been the best option. She had waterproof pants to wear over her clothes but hadn't worn them, thinking snow pants would be too warm, and it was too late to change. She grit her teeth and held on, grateful for Kory's solid warmth.

After about three-quarters of an hour, Kory exited the highway toward a town called Mountain Home and turned into a parking lot of a smashed-in, empty IGA. He stopped the bike and turned it off. The quiet was a relief. Were they already low on gas?

Robin slid off the bike and flipped up her visor. "Are we out?"

His answer was as growly as usual. "Nope. Just wanted to talk about the route."

"Oh." She hadn't expected the big bossy oaf to want her opinion. It was possible he wouldn't be a horrible travel companion.

"The weather's turning. We'll probably have snow tonight, maybe tomorrow. We might be able to ride another forty-five minutes. An hour if we're lucky. We have two options."

"Stay on the interstate?" That wasn't her first choice.

He nodded. "More small towns, more houses. But there's also been a fair bit of scavenging, as it was the main evacuation route."

She nodded. "Or along Highways 20 and 26 and through Craters of the Moon."

He nodded. "You've done your homework. Fewer houses, fewer towns, but we might find better supplies in quiet areas that haven't been picked clean."

"I vote we get off the interstate." She put confidence into her words, trying not to think about how foolish and misguided traveling with a strange man at the edge of winter seemed.

"That's my thinking too. Let's go." He restarted the bike, its sound once more filling her chest. She was grateful for the earplugs.

Robin jumped back on. This time it was a smoother transition, and they continued through the abandoned town. Some businesses had been boarded up, but most were destroyed and exposed to the elements. They'd been closed for years, and in the fading light, there wasn't much to see. According to the Emergency Broadcast System, in the first years after the asteroid, tens of thousands of people had fled the West, hoping to find shreds of civilization elsewhere. Tens of thousands more had died of starvation and violence, leaving the countryside's population sparse.

For most people, safety was back east or in large groups, squatting in the ruins of former cities. Neither option was appealing.

Robin shivered as they returned to the highway and the rushing air. She clung on and tuned out until Kory slowed the bike. He pointed to a mileage sign: Fairfield, ten miles. He must hope they'd have enough gas to get that far.

Soon after, he drove into a half-overgrown parking lot with rows of metal storage containers amid yellowed bushes and scraggly dead weeds. He drove the bike behind the containers, to the row farthest from the road, where it sputtered and died. He'd timed that well. She hopped off, and he pushed the motorcycle behind the last metal box and parked.

They removed their helmets, and he placed them on the bike seat, against the steel wall of the container where they'd be hidden. He unloaded the hard cases, passing her backpack to her. She hefted it onto her back, clipped the strap around her waist, and adjusted the side straps for better support; the pack had a heavier load than usual. She'd brought a squash for dinner tonight, so it would be lighter tomorrow. He removed a tarp from the hard case and draped it over the bike. He shoved a second folded tarp into his pack.

She looked around as Kory suited up too, adding a navy-blue rain slicker over his jacket and pack. She threw on her rain pants and poncho, hoping her pack wouldn't get wet inside. At least she'd packed her books and clothes in plastic bags and the dehydrated food was in foil pouches. There wasn't much daylight remaining, but they seemed too close to Boise for her comfort. Kory adjusted the bike's tarp again, tucking it in at the bottom. Did he plan to return?

Perhaps noting her interest, he said. "No need to make the bike easy to find. We're on foot from now on. You ready?"

Robin nodded, and they started back toward the road. At first, it wasn't so hard to keep up, though she took two steps to each of Kory's longer strides. It felt good to stretch her legs after the time on the bike and the long days of confinement. Still, as the day wore on and her muscles tired, it got harder.

As the pale sun set behind the thick gray clouds, the light faded and she let out the yawn she'd been fighting. Her pack wasn't overloaded, but its weight was substantial. Still, she tried to keep a steady speed. Her throat ached and her wet clothes made it difficult to feel optimistic about the success of this trip. Quiet and alone with her thoughts because of the exertion of walking, the day came sweeping back.

When she'd wept on the couch in the house with the garden, she'd let her grandfather go—his suffering was over and he'd left to spare her pain. His loss created a gaping hole inside and the ache made her admit what she'd known for days. Grandpa Clay had died. He was gone, forever. Just like everyone else she cared about. Despite Kory's solid frame leading the way, she felt more alone than ever.

●　　　●　　　●

Robin's stomach growled and reminded her of the passing evening. They'd been hiking for hours, passing dinnertime some time ago, and there had been no sign of stopping for a meal. The sky had darkened early with the swirling clouds and it had become difficult to see, though Kory wore a functional headlamp that lit the road ahead, reflecting off puddles and illuminating shadows that marked holes in the crumbly pavement. The road was uneven and patched and she'd stumbled a few times. Its surface had suffered from the lack of road crews who were no longer around to fix up the quiet two-lane highway.

"How far do you think we've come?" It hurt to speak, and her voice didn't sound right.

Kory didn't answer. Maybe he hadn't heard, or she'd missed a shrug in the darkness. Or perhaps he didn't know either.

The air had a still quality as they crested another hill, continuing their climb on the steady slope as Highway 20 headed through the wilderness—a scenic byway in the old days. The roadside markers read, *"From Peaks to Craters."* In the darkness, it was hard to see beyond the long, straight road that disappeared ahead in the gloom. Though the threat remained, pursuit seemed distant; it was like they were alone in the world, cut off by the rainstorm.

When Kory still didn't answer, she kept trudging. What was she doing out here with this silent giant? Perhaps leaving with him had been a colossal mistake.

"At least we have the weather on our side." His comment seemed to come from left field.

"How do you figure?" she snapped.

"It's turning to snow." He stopped walking.

His words startled her from her hungry funk. Robin had paid little attention to anything beyond placing one foot in front of the other, but now that he mentioned it, a faint silvery sheen covered the expanse of road and the grassy shoulders. Kory tipped his light upward to show a thickening flurry of white as the flakes twirled and fell.

"This doesn't seem good to me." Her teeth chattered as she stared at the slushy road.

"Motorcycles don't ride well in the snow. It's too slippery. Jake and the Wings won't risk them."

"People will see our tracks." She shivered. It had only been a minute or two, but her muscles were already getting cold. She'd been warmer when moving.

"Aren't many people out here." He readjusted his light and continued while she hurried to keep abreast.

They remained quiet a little longer as they trudged along, the snow becoming drier and sticking to the cold ground. Soon the snow became deep enough that they left tracks down the middle of the road and the light reflected off the white, making everything seem brighter.

Kory glanced her way and seemed to reach a decision. "Next driveway we see, we should leave the road. Find a place to stop for the night."

She was too tired and hungry to argue or complain. Robin hadn't slept well since her grandfather's disappearance and today had been an emotional roller coaster, with more downs than ups. She welcomed the idea of falling into bed and crying herself to sleep. She hurt inside and out, and holding herself together was taking a toll.

It had been difficult to keep track of the time without the sun or moon for reference, but for some distance, the land had been flat. A wooden fence stretched on either side of the road, just visible at the edge of the glow from Kory's headlamp. Her footing had been solid on the hillside, but now the snow was thicker and the ground slippery in sections. As the temperature plummeted, she stuffed her hands, gloves and all, deep into her pockets, determined to keep up and stay warm.

When a gap in the fence opened on their left, Kory turned, shining his light back and forth, searching for a building. She held her breath, hoping there would be shelter. It wouldn't be a pleasant night to sleep outside. She'd freeze.

It was difficult to be sure in the thick flurry, but there might be a house or structure of some kind not too far back—one with windows that his light reflected from.

"I think there's a place back there. Wanna try it?"

She nodded, not trusting the pain in her throat to speak, especially in the cold.

He said nothing, just resumed walking in a new direction. Again, she trotted to keep up with his long strides. At the end of a short driveway, they arrived at a two-story house tucked amid a grove of bare trees swaying in the wind. An empty carport, half-filled with grey, weathered firewood, sat beside the house—no welcoming lights cast from a lamp or candles to indicate if it might be inhabited. Still, she would approach with caution.

The house remained pitch black and silent as they tromped up the stairs, their feet loud in the quiet night with only the snow hissing softly around them as it fell. Robin peered through a window. Like almost everywhere, it seemed abandoned.

Kory pounded on the door and Robin stepped back, ready to bolt in case they disturbed someone who'd rather be left alone. She shivered at the edge of the porch. Nobody came. He thumped the door two more times before he grabbed the handle. It was unlocked, so he opened the door and they walked inside.

"Don't get your hopes up. We aren't staying here long. Overnight. That's it." He gave her a backward glance.

She clenched her jaw. His condescending tone grated on her nerves. One night was all she expected. She didn't feel safe this close to the bikers that might come after them, snow or no snow. Plus, if South Dakota was the goal, they had another seven hundred miles to go. There was no way they'd make it before winter, but they needed to get farther. She'd have considered hiding out here for the winter if she'd been on her own and if it weren't so close to Boise.

"I'll see if anyone left candles anywhere," he said, closing the door to the outside. Robin shook the snow from her hood and stomped her feet, knocking chunks of wet snow onto the mat covering the wooden floor in the dark hallway. Kory and his light moved down the hall, the floor creaking. Robin's breath froze even inside while she waited.

Cold had seeped into the house, giving it a desolate feel. This, more than anything, convinced her that the house was empty. It was like returning to a house after a long winter vacation where the heat had been turned off for weeks. Cold radiated from the bare walls and the furniture. However, it was dry and out of the falling snow, which was only worsening as the night progressed.

With firewood outside, there should be a fireplace or a wood-burning stove. Maybe they could cook somewhere sheltered. If not inside over flame, maybe on the covered back porch. Kory returned after a short time with two tall candles in holders. Robin fished in her pocket for her lighter and lit their wicks; the flames weaved back and forth, making shadows flicker and dance at the boundary of her sight, pushing at the frigid darkness. They each took a candle and Kory clicked off his headlamp.

"Someone stayed here at some point," he said, "But the air is musty and the furniture is covered in dust. They've been gone awhile. No bodies either. At least not downstairs."

That was good. So many had died of starvation and disease that sometimes the dried-up husks remained where they'd fallen. Others had given up and ended their own lives. Plus, this close to the road, death by violence would also have been a possibility. At least she wouldn't be moving remains for a place to sleep.

Kory led the way down the hall and into the living room where a flat-topped wood stove sat. Perfect for cooking. Doors at either end of the room would keep the heat in, plus the inside was small enough that it might even get warm.

"We can cook some of your potatoes." Kory's deep voice startled her.

"I brought a squash too," she said. "I'll steam it." She missed butter, but there might be salt and pepper in the kitchen if they'd been stored in glass or metal containers. Anything in cardboard would be long gone, either contaminated by mice or moldy. Holding up her candle, she turned to look for a pan and supplies.

"I'll build a fire," said Kory behind her as the stove door clanged open.

"I could go outside for more wood," she said, turning back toward the door.

He put a mammoth hand on her shoulder, surprising her enough that she flinched. "You see about the squash. I'll take care of the wood and the fire."

She nodded, feeling the warmth where his hand rested. She preferred staying inside, as long as he believed she was doing her share.

Already the house felt less frigid, just from their breath and the candles. A fire would make them comfortable, as well as dry their clothes and heat their food. Robin was thankful not to have to return outside into the wind and storm, so she turned and went hunting for the kitchen. Behind her, the door closed and Kory's footsteps crunched across the snow.

•   •   •

Later that night, her stomach full after a dinner of peanuts, steamed squash with salt, pepper, and a scraping of crystallized honey she'd discovered in the kitchen, Robin huddled in her down sleeping bag on the musty couch. She'd been cold for so long that her body was having a hard time warming up. One of the cushions had been inhabited by mice, but they, too, were now gone. There'd been no question of who got to sleep on the floor. Kory didn't fit the couch. There were some advantages to being petite.

Across the room, in front of the living room door, he rigged an alarm built with a length of cord from his pack and several metal utensils from the kitchen. He stretched out a thin inflatable mattress with his sleeping bag close to the stove and placed his pack as a pillow. It never left his side. What did he have that he considered so valuable?

He filled the stove with wood one last time before turning down the damper for the night. She hoped the banked embers continued to burn for hours as they were supposed to set on low. She'd learned how to use wood stoves when she and Grandpa had lived on the farm.

Kory laid back on his bed with a long sigh. Turning onto his side, he faced away from her. Before long, his even breathing told her he'd fallen asleep. No matter how tired her body, it was her brain that wouldn't settle. Robin let her mind wander, something she rarely did, but being back on the road brought the memories flooding back.

It had been a miracle that she'd made it to her grandfather's farm. Weeks earlier, she'd been assaulted, left for dead, and her supplies stolen. She arrived skittish and half-feral in her starvation, having eaten only what she'd been able to steal, traveling on her own. Hiding from everyone. At first, she'd been desperate to go back and search for Shelby, but that would have been suicide.

Her grandfather had hoped to follow Luke and his family later that summer, but the roads had been unsafe. The military had blocked many, first for safety, then the evacuation, but then they'd suddenly left those roads; not long after, less savory types had taken over the patrol. So, she and Grandpa had turned back and waited. The first winter, he'd fed her, and helped her deal with her PTSD. She'd assisted him on the farm and learned a multitude of useful skills, always hoping her mom or Shelby might arrive.

During the second winter, she and her grandfather had slowly starved.

The crops hadn't grown. The garden offerings had been limited for a second year, so they'd subsisted on stale oatmeal, rice, and a bag of dried navy beans with occasional raisins or dried apple slices. Come spring, they'd left again, headed to South Dakota, scavenging on the way. Without supplies, it had been slow-going.

They'd often stayed for a few days or even a week in productive areas, only to be halted in Boise by harsh storms last fall. The mall had provided food enough for a recovery. She was always hungry, but now seemed to need less food to get by. Late summer had been almost plentiful with the garden produce augmenting their diet. It had surprised her to discover she could no longer see each of her ribs as her health improved.

This spring, it had been her grandfather's lung cancer that had kept them from continuing their journey. They'd planted the garden and eaten well, but perhaps she'd put down too many roots. It seemed strange to be on the road without Grandpa Clay. She blinked back tears. At least he'd be pleased she was at last underway.

Kory's deep breathing and gentle snores filled the room and returned her to reality. Even asleep, he took up a lot of space, almost the width of the room. Robin's neck and throat ached. She'd dug into her stash of ibuprofen, hoping it would help with the swelling and the pain. She seldom took painkillers for little things anymore, but the attack today had been brutal.

Flipping over again, she winced at the rustling sound and the creaking springs of the couch. She snuck a peek at Kory, who slept on. Outside, the wind buffeted the house as the gusts increased in tempo and rattled the windows. After living underground for the last year, it felt comforting to be inside listening to the weather. At least they'd found shelter; it had become quite a storm.

Their room was warm enough, but her mind still refused to settle. If she stayed awake much longer, she'd need to get up and disconnect Kory's alarm to get to the bathroom. He'd probably hear, and she was reluctant to wake him. What if he became angry? Not that he seemed volatile, but he was a stranger and, therefore, unpredictable.

Eventually, she must have drifted off, because when next she opened her eyes, light filtered in through the curtains over the windows. She glanced outside. It was morning and still snowing, but the wind had died down. Across the room, Kory sat reading, making the most of the natural light. He'd let her sleep in. Not late, but past dawn. She sat up and stretched, inhaling. Oatmeal bubbled in a pot on the stove. Her stomach growled. She'd recognize the smell anywhere and was hungry enough that it smelled delicious.

"You must have needed the sleep," he said, his eyes meeting hers. "Breakfast. Then we hit the road?"

She nodded and went about getting ready. She slipped out to use the facilities and straighten up before repacking her now dry clothes that she'd left draped near the fire and rolled her sleeping bag. The living room was toasty compared to the rest of the house and she settled cross-legged on the threadbare couch to eat while basking in its warmth.

Kory was still a stranger, but somehow less threatening by daylight. Maybe she should try to get to know him better if they were going to travel together. That could be a long-term goal. She wasn't great with people, but she was willing to make the effort. For now, she ate, packed, and made a quick sweep upstairs. She was always on the lookout for anything useful. One room had a tube-like pillow that smushed up small, so she added it to her backpack. It was lighter than the squash it replaced.

Then they headed out into the snow-covered world.

CHAPTER 8: KORY

Kory rubbed his bleary eyes as they turned left, back on the road. He'd wanted to leave so the still-falling snow would cover their tracks, at least partially. They shouldn't have to worry about the Wings for long. If winter had descended back in Boise, they might not find Dillan's body for a couple of days. Though because it had been left outside, the crows might give its location away. The Wings might guess Dillan and Kory had fought simply because they disappeared at the same time.

His shoulders tightened, and he rotated his neck to loosen the pressure. Jake would be upset with him for leaving and incensed about his nephew's death. The leader hadn't approved of some of Dillan's habits, but they were kin. It could cause dissent within the group, too, deciding what to do about Kory and his disappearance.

He might have slept longer this morning, but for the second half of the night, Robin had snored like a trucker. Before that, she'd whimpered and called out in her sleep, waking him up. Twice. Seemed like she'd slept through her restlessness, though. He never slept well somewhere different or new. The brain's primary job was to keep a person alive, so it didn't fully rest if it perceived a threat. He remembered hearing that somewhere, long ago—probably in a distant high school Science class. True rest often eluded him unless he felt safe. In the past, he'd developed unusual habits, such as sleeping with his eyes open. It hadn't been deliberate, but he'd freaked out at least one set of foster parents that way.

Robin must have been exhausted to sleep so soundly outside her concrete walls.

A ring of livid bruises with darker thumb marks encircled her neck. Nestled among them were two knife cuts, each close to two inches long. Neither looked that deep, and she'd put some kind of shiny ointment on them. Should keep out infection. Good she knew how to look after herself and didn't expect him to do anything. He'd pretended to sleep right away last night, hoping to avoid the expected tears. After all, she'd admitted that her grandfather was dead, almost been killed, and her throat must hurt. He hadn't heard anything, and he was surprised yet again by her strength.

Robin hadn't whined about leaving the warm house to head back into the snow. He wasn't sure what he'd expected, but he liked her quiet determination. Maybe this could work.

It snowed half the day while they walked, lazy clumps of snowflakes falling steadily. For lunch, he shared some homemade venison jerky he'd traded his smokes for a couple of days ago. It was better than going hungry and easy to eat without stopping. It was dry and salty, but at least they had plenty of water. He'd refilled the canteens before cooking the oatmeal this morning. Any water in this godforsaken world should be boiled in case it carried ash, bacteria, or disease. In some places, water might be scarce, but in a pinch, there was a river nearby.

As long as they kept moving, he stayed plenty warm.

In the early afternoon, the snowfall petered out, leaving a muffled and white world with everything blanketed in thick puffs of snow. He wore his new sunglasses to shade his eyes from the blinding glare of the sun's rays reflecting off the white expanse. Robin, too, wore dark glasses and a hat to shade her face as they marched single file. This afternoon, he forged ahead, breaking a trail through the drifts, over a foot in depth, leaving her to walk in his footsteps. He shortened his strides to accommodate her shorter stature. At least because of the temperature, the snow wasn't too wet or heavy. Still, plowing through it was more strenuous than walking on pavement.

The landscape was quiet, with few sounds other than an occasional raven's caw in the distance. A creek dipped down out of the hills, close to the highway at one point, the gurgling water drowning out their squeaky footsteps. They refilled their water, boiling it roadside on a backpack burner while they warmed their hands at the small blaze. They could melt snow, but creek water was often cleaner and didn't boil down as much, requiring less fuel.

Kory sipped still-warm water from his canteen as he walked. Despite the thick covering of snow, the road remained easy to follow. Barbed wire fences lined both sides, with white-capped posts stretching into the distance. The highway seldom branched, and if it did, road signs kept them traveling Highway 20. He kept hiking, putting one size twelve in front of the other, zoning out to make the time pass.

They traveled another hour and a half from the creek. Maybe two. Startled out of his reverie by the silence behind him, he checked over his shoulder where the sun sat low on the horizon. Robin had stopped and now stood a dozen feet behind. She unzipped the front pocket of her pack, removed a paper map, checked something with a sigh, and shoved the map back into its slot.

She was probably checking on their progress along what had been a long, empty stretch of highway. They'd walked close to twenty miles and soon the sun would set. There was no reason to go much farther.

He hadn't seen a house or barn in hours. Nothing since this morning, back near Fairfield. Judging by the road signs, there weren't any settlements within reach before dark. Maybe tomorrow night they'd find something. There were a couple of small towns farther up the highway. Tonight, he would make a tarp tent, hopefully in a sheltered place—if he could find one. He glanced around, searching for somewhere off the road and out of the persistent breeze that sprayed fine snow and ice crystals into the air.

Robin probably wouldn't enjoy sharing a makeshift tent with him. He'd noticed she preferred to keep to her own personal space, but at least sharing would be warm.

His cheeks and nose tingled with the frosty air. With the sun breaking through the clouds, burning them away, tonight looked to be clear and cold. Setting up camp while they still had some daylight would be best.

"How much farther can you go today?" They were his first words since lunch.

"I think we need to stop soon," she said, scanning both sides of the road, perhaps searching for a building. There wasn't one. "I didn't think we'd make it anywhere with shelter tonight and there are no buildings anywhere. I've been watching."

That was more than he'd done.

Off to the left stood a hill with a few trees near the base. He pointed. "There's firewood that way. I can rig a sleeping shelter." He looked down and met her brilliant blue eyes. "I'll share, but it'll be cozy."

Her neck muscles convulsed as she swallowed before nodding, and she followed when he tramped through the snow toward the trees. They worked together to cross the barbed wire fence. She slipped through while he held her pack, then she put it on and hung his on a fence post on her side before holding a strand of wire down with her boot and lifting another as high as possible—stretched as far as the strands would allow—for him to slide between. Crouching as low as he could, he just fit.

Closer to the hill, animal trails criss-crossed the fields. Mostly deer, it looked like from their narrow cloven-hoofed tracks. If he had a rifle and bullets, or somewhere to stay and keep the extra meat, that might be useful. Still, it gave him a goal. If they found a place farther along, maybe he could shoot something to supplement their diet and stay in one place long enough to process it. He'd gone hunting with Jake and the guys last fall and helped butcher the animals they'd killed. His mouth watered at the idea of roasted meat.

Someone his size required a lot of rations. Kory might have a little padding on him now after being with the Wings and having steady food, but a diet of plain potatoes and backpacking pouches would strip it off again, leaving him whipcord thin and ravenous—the way he'd been when Jake had found him. Maybe they'd find a stash along the way to supplement their food. Somewhere not picked clean by travelers. The idea of being weak from hunger again was a constant background worry. He relied on his strength.

The few trees by the hill turned out to be a mixed grove, better than he'd expected. The snow wasn't as deep underneath their sheltering branches.

"Can you clear the snow under those trees?" He pointed to a pair with a decent number of yellow leaves still clinging above and a taller pine with thick branches. "That's where I'll build the shelter and we can make a fire."

With a hatchet, he chopped a few lower pine boughs from another tree to lie on the cleared ground when it was ready. They would need insulation from the frozen ground or it would leach away their heat. He lashed a thick fallen branch in place between the two trees about two feet from the ground, balancing it on existing branches before tying it into place. He draped his large tarp across the branch and tucked the ends underneath, using the excess to close one end. Chopping additional boughs, he turned them into a front screen they could put in place when they entered the shelter to keep the front tarp from blowing in. He unearthed several wedge-shaped black rocks in the snow as he worked and deposited them into a fire ring.

Robin had said nothing as they worked, but several times she glanced at the low structure, a crease deepening between her brows. They'd have to crawl to get in and sleep side by side. While he finished building, she collected bits of dryish wood and branches from beneath the nearby trees, dumping a substantial pile near the outer edge she'd cleared for a fire.

Kory watched with approval as she prepared a fire with dry bark, fine branches, and a handful of pinecones at the center. She built a larger teepee of sticks around it and lit it with a single match. In no time, she had a roaring fire, which she fed pieces of wood until it was in no danger of guttering out. He chose four large potatoes, stabbed them with his knife, and set them inside the margin of the firepit to roast.

The last of the daylight faded to gray and navy as they crouched near the crackling fire. Sparks snapped and glowing bits floated into the air while the hiss of the steaming potatoes filled the air. Damn. They smelled fantastic. He couldn't remember his last baked potato. Suddenly, he wished for sour cream and bacon bits. Even butter would go a long way. He pushed the thoughts away, grateful for hot food, especially something not dry or from a can.

Before it became too dark to see, he shoved his air mattress into the tent and his sleeping bag facing the opening toward the fire. He would slide in foot-first, leaving his boots near the entrance and within easy reach to shove his feet into in case of emergency.

Without him asking, Robin placed hers next to his, the mattresses so close they overlapped.

"What did you do before the asteroid?" she said, returning to the circle of firelight.

He didn't answer at first. He added another chunk of damp wood to the blaze and watched it steam. Meeting her gaze across the flames, he felt compelled to tell the truth. In the past, he'd said things like driving a truck, delivering pizza, and ranch hand. Those jobs sounded better than his real life. However, he was sick of making shit up and keeping track of his lies. He and Robin were together for another seven hundred miles, so he might as well be honest. If she didn't respect his life choices, which had brought them to the same place, that was her damn problem. Not his. Still, he swallowed his pride before he spoke.

"I was homeless. I picked up odd jobs for food, or sometimes for cigarettes or drugs. Sometimes washing dishes, or late-night grunt work on construction sites. Whatever people wanted for cash under the table."

Maybe he shouldn't have mentioned drugs. He hadn't always made the best decisions, but he was done with that. He also didn't want to lie. Not to an ally.

She didn't respond and sat, poking at the fire.

"You?" His tone held an edge. Her lack of reaction had him pissed off. Who was she to judge?

"I was in high school. I was supposed to go to Yale in September. Pre-law." Her words had a mechanical feel like she'd said it often so it wouldn't hurt anymore—like a bruise you pressed to see if it still stung.

He'd been right. The asteroid had derailed a life of privilege. Poor little rich girl couldn't live her dream of being a lawyer.

"Mommy and Daddy must have been so proud." He couldn't keep the envy from his voice. A flash of hurt crossed her face, gone in an instant. As soon as the words left his mouth, he wished he could take them back; he may have gone too far. "Look, I'm an ass. We all lost people and our old life. Some of you just had more to lose." Was she going to cry?

Her jaw flared as she jabbed her stick into the fire, kicking up a spray of sparks. "My mom was a sharp-tongued, single mom, who worked two jobs and didn't take shit from anyone. Most of the time, she was as prickly as a cactus and hard to please. I earned a full scholarship to university, and all she said was, 'Good. At least you can look after yourself.' My dad left when I was three." She looked at him with blazing eyes and took a deep breath. "If they were proud of me, it's not like they're here to ask, is it?" Her gaze became haunted as she sipped her water, perhaps lost in memory.

"I'm sorry," he repeated. He'd shoved his whole boot into his mouth that time. His wasn't the only life that had been rough. Her distrust of men had an extra layer, one worn since childhood. Much like his own. So he wouldn't have to meet her eyes, he got up to fill the cooking pot with fresh snow and to heat wash water.

Robin rotated the potatoes with her sharp stick and the aroma of cooked food intensified. She tilted her head, considering, and punctured one again. They must be almost ready.

"You remind me of someone I knew back in Portland. Before the streets of Seattle." The words tumbled from his mouth.

She looked up, a crease appearing between her eyes. "You're older than I am, but I'm from Portland. What school did you go to?"

"Grant," he said, the word sounding foreign now. Most of the Portland public schools had been named after dead presidents that had ceased to be relevant.

"My mom taught there," she said. Her voice was barely audible. "A million years ago." Her face softened. "And my sister and I went there too."

His skin broke out in goosebumps despite the heat thrown by the fire. What were the chances? His old life crept back into focus. Her name in the books. Robin Wilson. The way a certain tilt of her head seemed familiar. It wasn't his sister she reminded him of, it was his English teacher. Her mother. Plus, he'd seen her before. Long, long ago. Years before the asteroid.

He'd been a senior, and Robin had been a freshman. Just a kid. For all they'd gone to the same high school. A memory flashed before him. She'd come to her mother's classroom after school to drop something off. She'd had long golden-brown hair, loose in shining multi-colored waves. He remembered admiring the glint when it caught the afternoon's sunlight. A wave of unexpected nostalgia swept over him.

He'd stayed after class to do his homework where it was warm. He'd already been expelled from the house by his last alcoholic foster parents, but he'd stayed in Portland through the spring to graduate. Ms. Wilson had brought him food for lunch and dinner every day, encouraging him to stay in school. He'd never thought about it, but as a single mom with two daughters, she'd been especially generous.

"Ms. Wilson was your mom." A grapefruit-sized lump filled his throat, making him unable to speak. She'd definitely had a sharp tongue, but she'd been good to him. She'd tried to convince him to find a job and stick around town. Instead, he'd graduated and fled the city, not wanting to run into anyone he knew, seldom sparing her a thought since.

He'd wanted a fresh start. Not as fresh as an asteroid destroying everything four years later, but that's what he'd gotten.

Robin stared at him, the flush leaving her face as her eyes filled with unshed tears. She hugged her knees tighter to her chest where she sat. Putting her head down, she sobbed, her whole body convulsing.

What had he done? He should have known better than to bring up the old days. From before. He felt bludgeoned by the truth. Robin wasn't a stranger, and he'd never be able to pay back her mother for her kindness. He could do better than just put up with the daughter. He could make sure she arrived in South Dakota. Not for his sake, but for hers.

He scooted closer to Robin, resting his hip next to hers, expecting her to shove him away or tell him to get lost. When she didn't, he stretched an arm and wrapped it around her shoulders, pulling her into a long sideways hug. To his surprise, she let him hold her while she cried.

He smoothed her now short hair and whispered, "I'm sorry you lost her. She was a fine person." Ms. Wilson had framed pictures of two daughters. He didn't ask Robin about her younger sister. A missing sibling was another thing they had in common.

Robin didn't cry for long. She straightened with a sniffle, and he retracted his arm, letting her regain her composure.

"Those potatoes ready? I'm so hungry I could eat them all." He inhaled. They smelled done.

"Well, you only get half," she said, leaning forward to roll two potatoes farther from the glowing embers. She wouldn't meet his eyes anymore.

He grabbed two bowls, two knives, and two forks from his pack and dished up. The potato skins were crusty and blackened in patches, but the aroma was divine. He slit his open to let it cool, the steam rising and dissipating in the night air.

One at a time, they ate the flaky golden insides. He almost burned his mouth at first, but couldn't stop. When he'd finished that, he chopped up the peel and ate that too before stabbing his second and transferring it to his dish. He didn't waste anything edible.

"I figured we could eat two tonight, since we walked all day." She nodded and reached for her second, too. They gobbled their seconds almost as quickly as the first.

With a hot meal in his belly, he washed up and got ready for bed. He brushed his teeth, using the new toothpaste he'd snatched from the drugstore yesterday. It may have expired, but it did the job. Most things like that were still usable. He unlaced his boots and stood on his sleeping bag with stocking feet, arranged his boots inside the tarp entrance, and slid into bed. He didn't need clean clothes yet, and it was too cold to undress. These would be good for a couple of days yet.

Robin disappeared in the darkness for a few minutes and returned to bank the coals of the fire before joining him at the shelter. She slipped off her boots and placed them by her side, and slid into her sleeping bag next to him—her body stiff as a board, facing the other direction.

He rearranged the pine boughs in front of the opening and folded the tarp down partially to cover them, leaving a slim air hole open to the frozen night. Despite the boughs and the lightweight hiking air mattress beneath him, the cold still seeped into his bones, even as he and Robin warmed the interior with their breath. Hopefully, they wouldn't freeze.

"It's probably only seven p.m.," she said, her voice startling him. "If I fall asleep now, I'll be up hours too early."

His tired body and throbbing feet didn't agree, but he didn't want to be woken up at four a.m. either. "You like to read," he said. "Tell me about your favorite books." He might not listen for long, but it would give her something relaxing to think about.

Kory let her talk, her voice washing over him as his eyelids drooped. He should try reading *The Hating Game* next. She made it sound interesting, for a romance. Despite the hoarse quality, her words were expressive and soon fell into a rhythm while he drifted off to sleep.

In the middle of the night, he woke and took stock, trying to figure out why he was awake. He was cool, not freezing; they'd warmed the tent's air. Beside him, Robin thrashed in her sleep and shouted. She'd probably woken him. He rolled closer and spooned her sleeping bag from behind and draped an arm over her to hold her close. She settled, becoming quiet. He fell asleep again, listening to her breathe.

Chapter 9: Robin

When Robin woke, at first, she couldn't move and she panicked, her lungs feeling tight. She wiggled to free her arms from her tight sleeping bag. She wiggled sideways to better see. The morning light entering through the tent's airhole illuminated Kory's bulk beside her, one arm wrapped around her, holding her in place. What the hell?

She flushed hot, though they each had their own sleeping bag. She hadn't planned to sleep with him that way. Not that he wasn't attractive, but she didn't see a reason to get involved with a man whom she'd just met days ago. His strength and the protection might be nice, but she wasn't willing to trade for it. He might be less terrifying than most men. Still, it wouldn't do to let him too close. This situation was temporary—he'd made that clear.

She tried to slide out from beneath his trunk-like arm, but instead, it tightened.

"Warmer in here," he muttered. "Stay a minute. I don't want to get up."

His sleepy tone helped her to relax. "Ya. Five more minutes." She snuggled deeper into her cozy sleeping bag, her arms once more inside as she shrugged to loosen his hold. Outside was cold, and they'd have to walk all day. With luck tonight, maybe they'd find somewhere better to sleep than the rock-solid ground beneath some scrubby trees. A snowbank? Or a house.

Kory yawned, removing his arm. "You had nightmares last night."

It surprised her how much warmth departed with it.

She flipped around to face him and was immediately sorry. He needed a shave—up close, his stubble looked bristly. Her hand itched to stroke it and find out, but she restrained the impulse. His dark eyes were hard to read and at this range, it felt like they saw too much. Last night's revelation that he'd known her mother shouldn't change anything. But it did. She just wasn't sure how.

Time to get moving.

The second day of walking resembled the first, though their footsteps didn't disappear. The frozen snow had become harder, crunching as they waded through the crystalized top crust. If they got more snow, it would be deeper than her boots. Snowshoes would have been helpful. Toward late morning, they came to a steel bridge stretching across the river below. The bridge looked to be intact, somehow undamaged by the earthquakes following the asteroid impact—at least solid enough for foot traffic.

Robin peeked over the guard rail and her stomach dropped. She stepped away from the edge in case she slipped. The water was a long way down.

Across the bridge, Kory dug out more venison jerky for lunch. She hoped he had an ample supply because it was light, filling, and easy to eat. Also, for her, it was something different. It also had a lot of iron, something she couldn't always get. After a steady diet of protein from slightly expired cans of tuna and ham, it was smoky and delicious.

"Thanks," she said as she ripped off another chunk. Her throat still hurt when she spoke, but forty-eight hours and a couple of Tylenol later, the pain was bearable.

"You're welcome." He cleared his throat. "Would you consider cooking something with flavor for dinner tonight? Even if it's just add-water food. I'm already ravenous."

"You probably need more to eat than I do." She eyed his bulky frame, made more immense by wearing a sweater and a down jacket. He was like a living mountain with tree trunks for legs. No matter how careful they were with their supplies, they didn't have enough food to walk to South Dakota. They'd need to find additional sources. "While we're traveling, maybe you should eat extra." The words came out as though forced. She hoped she didn't sound ungracious or stingy.

"I don't want to eat all your food." His stomach growled loud enough to be heard. Just the thought of food must have made it gurgle.

She laughed. "Still, you need more to eat."

He grimaced. "Sorry. I'm used to bigger meals. With the Wings, we ate well."

They resumed walking. Tonight she would find something with tangy tomato sauce. Those were her favorites. She might even lick her bowl if she could get away with it without embarrassing herself.

That evening, when the sun dipped below the horizon, the light faded, making the snow appear blue as they reached the ghost town of Carey. It was remote enough here that little looked disturbed by scavengers or gangs, just abandoned. Maybe there was so little out this way that nobody had bothered with this route in a long time. She could hope.

Glancing around as they walked through town, most businesses, although boarded up, didn't appear broken or gutted. It was also quiet, with just the soft crunch of their footsteps and the gentle breeze. There didn't seem to be anyone around. Finding deserted towns used to bother her. The emptiness reminded her of loss. Now they seemed the best-case scenario—no territorial gangs or gun-toting isolated fanatics. She and her grandfather had seen their share of both as they'd moved north and east to Boise.

Just to be safe, Robin stayed watchful for signs of habitation, out-of-place sounds, food smells, or smoke. There was nothing.

"The houses are farther out of town, mostly farms on the far side. It'll be dark soon. A motel might be okay," Kory said, breaking the silence. "If we can get in. Ones that take key cards are tough but regular, old-school style key locks are easy to pick."

He probably could kick the other doors in, but then they might not close properly, and therefore wouldn't be secure, so weren't worth the effort.

It was too dark to see farther than across the street when they found a roadside motel. Without the sun, the temperature had already dropped and a few stars winked above in the darkening sky. It was clear tonight and would be well below freezing. She shivered as they examined the ramshackle building. It would have been outdated and in need of remodeling and some paint before the asteroid hit. Nowadays, you took what solid shelter you could get.

They trooped behind the building and chose a room accessible from that direction. Without a chimney or fireplace, they couldn't light a fire inside to heat their room, but they could hide one back here in the parking lot while they cooked. Well, boiled water, which would be all that cooking entailed most nights while on the road. There was no stockpiled firewood, but they could scrounge. There also might be something inside to burn; wadded-up pages from obsolete phone books made excellent kindling.

She worked on the lock, her hands turning bright red with her gloves off, while Kory gathered branches and sticks from under the trees growing behind the motel. When the locking mechanism clicked open, she entered, holding her breath. Two beds, standard room. Thank god it hadn't been gutted. She could use a bed for her weary body tonight. Out of habit, she flicked the light switch. Nothing. She'd heard rumors of places where random pockets of electricity still functioned. She'd just never been lucky enough to find anywhere that it was true.

The stale air and dust-covered furniture made it obvious that no one had been in this room for a long time. Maybe years. She unpacked one of her new candles from the first house and lit it, discerning additional details in its yellow glow. The dark wood paneling and the dingy room smelled musty, but not damp. No roof leaks yet. Once it had probably been clean, but a fine, bone-colored ash had settled everywhere in a thick film.

Setting down her pack by the door and placing the candle on the small round table, she stripped the quilt from the first bed into a bundle and shook it outside. She did the same for the second and for the fluffy pillows. The less ash on her skin or in the air, the better.

By the time she finished housekeeping, Kory already had the fire going with his blackened cooking pot half in the flames, the lid on. The water would boil in no time. She left the door open to air out the room while she waited. It wasn't like the temperature inside was any warmer than outside. Not yet.

"Tomorrow, we head up Highway 26," she said. "It joins the 20 and the two highways run together past Craters of the Moon." Her teeth chattered and her feet felt like two icy bricks now that she wasn't walking. She stomped them to restore circulation.

"Have you checked if the water works?" said Kory, glancing up from the flames.

She shook her head and returned inside.

In the bathroom, she tried the taps for the sink. Nothing. Then she remembered a handy tip her grandfather had shown her. Sometimes the water had been shut off. She searched under the sink, turned a valve, and hoped. She tried again. At first, there was nothing, then a humming noise in the wall and a bang, like the pipes knocking. The faucet spat and lurched, spraying water into the basin in several brief spurts. By the third longer spit, it ran freely and came out clear.

She got her pot so they could boil a second one for extra drinking water and washing. Hot water wouldn't go to waste. If nothing else, she could drink some to heat her inside. Maybe Kory would like to shave. She'd noticed him scratching the stubble covering his face a couple of times today, though he might be warmer with a beard.

Waving away billowing smoke, she set the second pot of water across the fire from the first. "Good call," she said with a shiver, moving out of the smoke. She put her gloves back on and huddled close to the small blaze.

Kory opened his pack and dug out two mugs from a side pocket. He removed a Ziploc sandwich bag filled with assorted tea bags. Her mouth watered. They might be stale, but they'd be fabulous. She'd even spotted sugar packets inside a covered plastic tray with coffee fixings.

"You want tea?" he said, looking up. At her nod, he dropped a tea bag in one cup. He poured water into each mug and let the tea set, then switched the bag to the second, which he passed to her to hold while it steeped. "We'll be warmer soon."

She collected two rock-solid sugar packets, packed the remainder, and gave one to Kory. He winked and added it to his tea.

As the heat seeped into her aching digits and the sugar and caffeine hit her system, she blinked back tears. Would she ever have an actual home again or was life on the road the only option? She'd lived hand to mouth for so long, anything else was fading into a distant memory.

Sipping tea, she returned inside to prepare the rest of their dinner. They'd crammed their backpacks full of the pouches from the stockroom at Eddie Bauer that she and her grandfather had raided. She took out two, hesitated, and added a third. She emptied the packets into bowls, making one considerably larger than the other, though they shared the extra pouch of pasta and sauce.

After the water boiled, Kory brought both pots inside and poured water into the waiting bowls. She took the smaller one and stirred. They tasted better if they were mixed and then sat for a couple of minutes to rehydrate the pasta and dried meat chunks. He brought the rest of their belongings inside and dumped snow on the embers, which sent up a hissing wall of thick steam.

When he finished, he locked the door and flipped the deadbolt. Robin checked that the curtains fully covered the windows, not wanting stray light to give them away if there were prowlers or other travelers. Outside was now inky black and they ate by candlelight. Though it was early, Robin considered going to bed. Sleeping alone would be a hell of a lot chillier than last night, but less confusing. At least she had a proper bed and would be inside her sleeping bag and under the sheets and quilt. Plus, there were pillows. She yawned, her jaw creaking.

She was all set to go to bed when Kory brought out another candle lantern, which illuminated the dingy room well with its steady flame. He also produced a deck of cards and a cribbage board, the kind that folded in half and didn't take up much space. His pack was full of treasures. No wonder he kept it close.

He raised an eyebrow and tapped the cards on the table. "You play?"

She nodded, a flutter of excitement running through her. Her Uncle Luke had taught her as a child, and she had Grandpa Clay had played hundreds of games of crib the last few years. They'd turned them into a two thousand-game tournament. Her grandfather had been ahead by about ten games at the last tally. They'd made happy memories playing cards, even in tough times.

"Low card deals?" Kory removed his gloves and shuffled the cards with a swish, then bent them into a bridge to fan them back together with another. He must have played cards often as well. He cut a three to her queen and then dealt the cards.

She'd always played quickly, and while Kory's movements appeared slow and deliberate, he didn't take long thinking about his cards either. They played without a lot of chatter, but it was pleasant to forget about the cold outside and the long journey ahead.

"It would be nice if we had music to play. Something upbeat to break the silence," said Kory. "Maybe some Foo Fighters. Dave Grohl and Taylor Hawkins knew how to rock."

That was the first crumb Kory had dropped about something he liked. "Or Taylor Swift," said Robin. "Taylor's Version of anything."

"Not sure I've ever listened to Taylor Swift. Not on purpose," said Kory, lifting his gaze from the cards. "What do you mean, 'Taylor's Version'? She sang her songs. Doesn't that make them all Taylor's Version?"

Robin shook her head as she counted her cards. "Fifteen two, fifteen four, and a double run is twelve." She counted with her back peg, and then picked up the crib hand, scoring another six points. "A few years ago, Taylor tried to buy the rights to her own songs. Her record label refused and sold them to someone else. So, she left the label, released an indie album, then rerecorded several previous albums, and she got all the money from the new Taylor Versions."

She'd love to listen to Taylor's Red right now. She had a cap in her bag that matched the one Taylor wore on the re-released cover. The most gorgeous deep cherry red color she thought of as Taylor red. In the summer, it was often the one spot of color she wore.

That night, alone on her side of the chilly room, Robin dreamed of Dillan and his leering face again. It morphed into the series of men from that long-ago group, each scruffy face imprinted on her brain as she'd fought to escape. That's often where she woke up. Even her subconscious couldn't relive everything she'd endured.

Despite the cold air, she was covered in a sheen of sweat and her breath sounded loud in the otherwise quiet room. Her throat ached again. If she went back to sleep immediately, she'd loop through the dream again. Better to calm down and concentrate on something else. Not always easy in the middle of the night.

As her heart slowed, she realized she wasn't alone. Beside her bed, Kory's tall shape loomed—a charcoal shadow in the pitch black. She sucked in her breath.

"You okay?" He whispered.

"What?" Her sleep-fogged brain wasn't working yet.

"You were screaming."

She winced. "I'm sorry." She'd woken her grandfather for months when she'd first arrived at the farm. Dillan's attack had brought everything back to the surface. That feeling of helplessness. The pain of waking up alone, having lost Shelby. Her chest constricted as it always did at the thought of her younger sister. What had happened to her?

"You're shaking," Kory said. "Your teeth are chattering."

Robin was almost glad she couldn't see Kory's face, to try to figure out what his expression meant—that had never been her strength. His tone implied a concern that she hadn't imagined.

"I'm fine. I didn't mean to wake you." She felt too awake now to go back to sleep.

"Shove over."

She didn't understand what he meant until he sat on the edge of the motel bed, his sleeping bag rustling. He must still be inside it, as though preparing for a potato sack race. She smiled at the image of him hopping across a field, competing with children in their smaller burlap sacks. She slid farther over and he swung his feet up on the bed, wrapped in his own sleeping bag, and tucked in next to her, under the quilt. Was it out of pity?

"You didn't wake me. I wasn't sleeping, anyway. It's colder than a witch's tit in here." Kory wasn't wrong. He also wasn't trying anything. He hadn't touched her in ways that would make her uncomfortable, nor had he given any sign he intended to make a move. She sighed. The bed was already warmer with their combined heat.

She wanted to protest, but he didn't act as if he were interested in anything except warmth to sleep. Nor did he seem angry that she'd disturbed him. She flipped onto her side, facing away from him, and snuggled deeper into the bed, completely inside her sleeping bag. Her body calmed and her eyelids became heavy as she once again grew drowsy.

In the morning, the blankets crackled when she moved, and her breath plumed white in the frosty air. Inside the motel room was frigid. Beside her, Kory stirred. It was warm enough in bed, but she experimented with her hand and discovered it was cold enough that her bare skin almost burned. It must be minus forty or colder inside. Another example of extreme weather in the new world.

"I don't think we should go out there today," she said, peeking out in Kory's direction. "I've seen this happen a few times—pockets of

Arctic air that last two to three days. There's no protection out there. We might freeze to death or get frostbite."

They fortified the room as best they could, using the sheets from the second bed to cover one set of windows, reserving the second for later when the outside light faded. Robin stuffed towels against the base of the door, wishing she'd blocked that draft sooner.

They opened one set of curtains for light and stayed in bed, reading most of the day. Robin had fingerless gloves for just such a purpose, while Kory wore one glove. He held the book with that hand, flipping pages with the other that was otherwise kept tucked into his armpit or sleeping bag.

To her surprise, it was a companionable day for all she tired of sitting in bed and became restless to be on the road making progress. If it stayed this frigid for long, they'd need somewhere better to stay— somewhere with a stove. She glanced at Kory, reading the missing copy of *The Hating Game*. She never would have pegged him as a reader, which just went to show that you couldn't always judge a book by its cover.

Being stuck here with him could be worse. They had water and ate cold food directly from the pouches. They kept their canteens in bed to keep the water from freezing.

To conserve supplies, they didn't light the candle the second evening until it was fully dark. After dinner, they played cards again by candlelight for a couple of hours. Robin was up eight games to four after the two days combined—not that she was keeping track.

"I thought I had you that time," Kory said, as she won a third straight game. He tossed his cards down in disgust.

She gathered them and shoved them into his worn card box, passing them back. "It's probably late enough I could sleep, even if we didn't do much today."

He nodded and spread the second quilt over where they would sleep. They took turns getting ready for bed and climbed back in when done.

Kory had been quiet and pleasant company today and her throat seemed improved. It was still uncomfortable to speak, but no longer painful. She nestled down to sleep, Kory nearby, hoping tomorrow the cold snap would break so they could continue their journey.

CHAPTER 10: KORY

On the third morning in Carey, Kory woke almost too warm, the blankets heavy and his body damp with sweat. The cold snap must have broken at last. He had to hand it to Robin, she'd called the length of time. While he'd chafed at their lack of progress for the last two days, he and Robin were a lot more comfortable around each other than before. Yesterday, she'd even teased him when she'd skunked him at crib. She was still sleeping beside him, flat on her back, both arms over her head. She must trust him to sleep so deeply next to him.

It was nice waking up beside someone. Especially her. He found himself thinking about her often and noticing little things. Like her obsession with vitamins at dinner every night. It could have been annoying, but it was just an interesting quirk, another thing that made him want to get to know her better. Not just because they were traveling together, but because she was an attractive woman and fun—two things missing from his life for a long time.

Kory had tried to clamp down on his fantasies, but with just the two of them, some of them crept back in. This surprising feeling had crept up on him. How had he gone from not wanting to get involved, not being depended on, to wanting a partner?

Was she interested in him, too? It didn't seem likely. He had a crush, and she was wary. He would wait. And see.

Robin rolled toward him, snuggling into his chest with a soft sigh. She had exactly seven freckles on the bridge of her nose. He enjoyed the feel of her and waited until her eyes popped open before he rolled away, toward the edge of the bed. They'd be back on the road today and the extra rest would be beneficial. She seldom slept well.

He flashed her a smile as he got up to use the bathroom first, then repacked his belongings while she got ready. After a quick fire to boil water for their oatmeal, they bundled up and headed out into the more moderate wintery conditions. It was still cold, but no longer in a freeze-your-ass-off way.

They walked on the frozen solid snow and occasionally broke through to the softer snow beneath. Several times Kory almost wiped out, his feet shooting out unexpectedly on the slick surface.

They paused when they reached the outskirts of town at a residential neighborhood for a quick check of the nearby houses. By mutual agreement, they worked the houses together. He took the downstairs while she went up. Although there was minor damage inside, someone had picked the houses clean of food, candles, batteries, soap, and anything useful.

Once more, Kory grew uneasy. Maybe someone lived not too far away and shopped here. He maintained a higher level of alertness as he searched. Robin bit her lip and glanced around as they hurried from one house to another. She must feel it too and probably had the same idea. Someone might be pissed they'd wandered into their territory. Especially if pickings were slim. He and Robin would need to be vigilant.

They found very little of use and gave up after the first dozen houses, with nothing much to show for their time. They had too far to go to waste more time here. All they took were a couple of sets of ski poles to keep them from slipping while they trekked.

Back on the road, the countryside became flatter and more desolate the farther they walked from Carey into what appeared to have once been quiet farm country. The road became difficult to pick out, but they followed the roadside reflective markers at the border as guides. The plains were exposed, and the wind picked up that afternoon, its bite chilling his face.

He adjusted his scarf to cover more of his skin, glancing at Robin to see how she was faring. Her nose and cheeks were rosy from the cold, but she seemed otherwise fine. Every bit as tough as he was for all she appeared fragile and birdlike. Some of that was her inner strength that he admired.

The main indications when they neared isolated farms were the stands of trees planted around them as windbreaks and for summer shade. Passing one, he took a long look, hesitated, and then kept walking because it was too early to stop for the night. Though the temperature had been warmer today, Kory didn't like the dark clouds moving in. There might be more snow coming. The farther they traveled today, the better.

The idea of the two of them not being alone remained foremost on his mind, though they'd seen no signs of people.

Cresting a gentle rise in the road, they looked down on a faded farmhouse set back from the road on the left—a dozen leafless trees clustered around it. Smoke rose from the chimney—which they would have noticed before they'd gotten so close if it hadn't been for the thick clouds overhead. A crooked mailbox sat near the road, labeled Jones.

Kory stared at the house. He wasn't inclined to hide or slink away. Besides, there was nowhere out here to hide. Most of the land was flat near the road and gently rolling further away. Pretty much a desolate, frozen wasteland. Still, he doubted someone living in such an isolated place would welcome strangers. These days, people on their own shot first and asked questions later.

"What do you think?" His breath plumed white in the cool air. "Should we go around?"

"Too late." Robin pointed to a flash at a window. "Binoculars. They've spotted us." She swallowed and adjusted her beanie with a deep sigh. "I'm not a fan of strangers."

"Let's stay on the road and keep walking. We can see what they do. They might not care if we're just passing by." He doubted it would be that easy.

They hadn't gone more than another dozen yards when the front door of the house flew open with a bang and someone came outside with a rifle. The man pointed it in their direction but didn't raise it to shoot. Kory clenched his jaw and kept moving. Two additional men joined the first on the porch. He and Robin were outnumbered.

Beside him, Robin tensed, but followed his lead and continued walking. He moved closer to her and angled himself in front of her.

"Stop right there," the first man shouted from the porch. "That's close enough."

Kory and Robin stopped. He glanced at her from the corner of his eye. She was trembling. It made him itch to protect her—she had enough horrible memories.

"We don't want any trouble and don't mean any harm." Kory raised his voice so it would carry to the older man with the gun. "Just passing through."

"You have one minute to get off my land," said the original man on the porch. "Then, I shoot."

Grabbing Robin's hand, Kory broke into a shambling run, half skating on the slick road. She followed, and he released her as soon as he could tell she was moving. The cold air hurt his lungs as he slid and ran with an awkward gait. Their heavy backpacks bumped along on their backs. If it hadn't been for the ski poles, he'd have fallen a dozen times as they crunched through the white-blue snow. He didn't dare look back to see how far they'd come. It wasn't far enough, but their time must be almost up.

He glanced around, still moving, gasping for breath. The road dipped just ahead. If they could get there, they should be out of sight of the house.

A bullet whizzed over their heads as the rifle shot cracked through the still air—maybe a warning. The next one might be more accurate, and he tried to shrink into himself to become a smaller target. Not the best time to be a big guy. He crouched, half running, half sliding as they skidded the last hundred yards, where the road curved and headed down an incline.

"I doubt we're off his land," Robin said with a gasp as they slowed to a walk. "I want to be well away from here before nightfall." She resumed walking and gliding, still keeping a brisk pace, the poles swinging at her side.

Kory agreed but saved his breath and hustled to keep up.

They continued as fast as possible for another hour as the light faded. He kept watch over his shoulder as the sun sank lower on the horizon until just faded bands of pink and purple remained in the nearly dark sky. They had a decision to make soon. Push on, hoping for another house before nightfall, or camp. They'd be easier for others to find if they shacked up in a building—buildings would be logical places to search, but outside would be colder. They'd need a fire, which would also be a beacon for searchers.

"Chance another house? Or tent in the snow?" He didn't want to decide for both of them. They were in this together.

She cocked her head and squinted at the remaining light. "We only have about half an hour before it's dark. Why don't we stay at a house if we reach one in the next twenty minutes? If not, we make for that ridge." She pointed to the right. "Then camp on the other side." She picked up the pace.

They hadn't gone much farther when they spotted a low dark patch on the left, stark against the snow. Probably trees, so, with luck, a house. This one further removed from the road than many they'd encountered. They might make it that far before nightfall.

They pushed on, arriving close enough to see buildings among the tree trunks just before it grew too dark to continue. Kory turned as a low whine and vibration reached his ears. An engine. Shit.

Grabbing Robin's hand again, he sprinted. If they reached the cover of the trees, they could at least hide. He glanced back just as they left the road. He misjudged his footing and stumbled, rolling his ankle.

"Fuck." He slowed but kept moving. The pain was manageable. The injury didn't seem too serious.

Sure enough, there was a house. It was small and unlit, probably uninhabited, but it would be the first place someone checked. The engine sound drew closer, and a headlight shone from across the snow. Each passing second brought it nearer.

"Barn," Robin gasped. "We can hide."

He turned, changing direction on his sore foot, slipping again. All his weight, the pack included, went down with a crash on the ice. A shooting pain rocketed from his right ankle up his leg. He could have sworn he'd felt something snap this time. When he got to his feet, his entire foot burned. Shit. Gritting his teeth, he forced himself to move, no matter the agony. Robin reached the barn and stopped to wait. He waved her inside.

With a deep breath, he broke into a jog and slid in behind her, bumping the wooden door closed, trying not to make more noise than necessary. It wasn't fully dark inside, with the eaves open above, but he couldn't make out anything. He suppressed a sneeze; the interior smelled like hay.

"Psst," Robin hissed from his right. "Up the ladder."

He followed her voice and met her at the bottom, where she climbed a steep wooden ladder. He followed, wincing with every step. At the top, scattered hay littered the loft floor, and he was tempted to haul up the ladder but didn't have time. It might also scrape and give away their hiding place. One side wall held musty hay—bundles stacked eight feet high. He shoved a couple of lone bales that had fallen on one end and built a bunker to hide behind.

Huddled behind their flimsy cover, he whispered, "Get down." He placed another bale on top of the first two and sat beside her, facing the outer wall and the dim light outside, which grew brighter as the engine stopped outside.

Maybe a snowmobile. Not the Wings then. A terrific idea in these parts. Regular fuel would have turned by now, but in isolated areas like this, purple gas or other fuel might still work if they knew someone with additives and a way to mix it. Even diesel would be degraded by now.

He pressed his eye to a knothole in the outer wall, searching for a glimpse of whoever was outside, trying to see what they were up against. Two men. Probably the two younger men from the house not far back. Both with rifles. They checked the house first, their boots thumping on the boards of the porch.

"No tracks or snow on the porch. They didn't go in." The speaker continued around the back of the house. "Not this way either," came the shout.

Kory held his breath, still pressed to the wall, watching below. The barn had been the better call. Smart girl.

The men searched the grounds in a cursory fashion. His hands grew damp. Would they find the places he'd stumbled? Or had they driven over it in the dark? A clear footprint would be a problem.

"I doubt they made it this far," said one. "They might have slid off the road in a dozen places we missed since it was almost dark.

"I'm just going to check the barn," said the other.

Kory glanced upward. Even the faint light from outside was all but faded, other than the snowmobile's headlight, which illuminated slow twisting flakes of snow. Falling again. He looked at Robin and could just make out where her face was. She pressed her gloved hands over her mouth and slouched against the hay bales, unmoving, wide-eyed. She hadn't moved or made a sound since they'd hidden.

They remained frozen like statues, straining to hear the searchers below.

For the first time in days, his hand strayed to the knife on his belt, popping the snap open without a sound. He wouldn't move unless he heard someone on the ladder, then he would shove it down. He wouldn't be much good in a physical fight right now. Not injured.

The outer door banged open against the outside of the wooden barn. Then nothing. He waited. A crashing sound followed by cursing broke the silence. Someone must have tripped over something below. Tools or derelict machinery?

"I can't see a goddamn thing in here," the man hollered from almost directly beneath them. Kory prayed he didn't notice the ladder.

"Aiden, the snow's picking up. We should head back. Dad and Pops said to return before nightfall and we're already late."

"Yeah. It's too dark to keep searching, anyway. Those two looked pretty harmless. As long as they really kept moving, it's fine. I wonder how they'll deal with that nut at the Visitor Center. No one gets past him."

"If he's even still there. Dad saw him a couple of months ago, but that's it." The voices faded as the men returned to their snowmobile and left.

Kory listened until the sound faded before he moved. He stood and took stock, keeping his weight on his left. His right ankle was fucked. He ignored the pain, but it hadn't diminished while he sat. Pursing his lips, he considered. He and Robin should be safe to stay in the house overnight, but they'd need to move on tomorrow—and walking on a buggered ankle wouldn't be pleasant. He could wrap it and hope that made a difference.

The miles to Idaho Falls now seemed insurmountable. Winter wasn't going away; it was early this year. Again. Idaho Falls had been the first destination he'd had in mind, simply because it was old stomping grounds, but it had been scoured clean and would only have been temporary, anyway. He had one stash of food that might still be there. Enough for a couple of weeks, anyway. Less, since there were two of them now. Now it didn't look like they'd be making it that far. Shit. South Dakota was a helluva long way on a busted foot.

Maybe there'd be another farmhouse up the road farther, out of easy range for the family who'd just left but somewhere to hole up for the winter. Tomorrow, they'd have to look for a driveway or a side road, something off the beaten path. He wouldn't get far, but they couldn't stay here. It was too close to the occupants of the other house, which included at least four men by his count. Aiden, the brother, Pops, and Dad.

Kory closed his eyes, took a breath, and got out his headlamp. "They're gone. For now. Let's check out the house."

Robin exhaled a long breath. "Just for tonight." She must have reached the same conclusions.

Somehow, he climbed down the ladder and hobbled to the house, letting Robin pick the lock. She had a soft touch and opened doors faster than he did. They stepped inside and shut the door. Like the house on the first night, it was cold, dark, and silent.

Further exploration revealed a wood stove that sat in a cozy living room, close to a matching recliner and loveseat, facing a blank TV screen. He eyed the space on the floor. It looked hard and his Thermarest wouldn't change it enough. Dragging a mattress down from upstairs would be a bitch on a bad ankle, especially for just one night. There might be one on this level. He could use a stroke of good luck.

A quick check of the downstairs revealed a bedroom after all, and the two of them lugged the mattress down the short hall and maneuvered it into the living room. Robin shoved the recliner out of the way and let the queen mattress drop with a thud.

"Were you going to mention what happened to your ankle?" She raised an eyebrow.

"Probably sprained. I slipped when we were running for the barn."

"Go sit down." She waved him toward the loveseat while she pulled the drapes firmly across the windows and inspected the cast-iron pot-bellied stove. "Not a lot of wood inside. I'll go outside and look around. Maybe there's some left behind in a shed."

Kory lit his candle lantern as she left with the other light. The chimney seemed fine—the stovepipe was still intact. Still fiddling, he ensured the flue was open before he gathered the wood chips from the bottom of the wood bin. It would be enough to start a fire, but not to burn overnight. There'd been a couple of buildings outside, but he would be surprised if there would be much firewood. The people down the road would have consolidated supplies if they were smart. Odds were, they were the ones who'd stripped the houses in Carey as well.

Turning toward the covered window, he wished he could see outside. Would they have a fire tonight or not? He hated waiting.

He couldn't believe he'd wrecked his ankle and couldn't help more. Tomorrow, walking was going to be excruciating. He sat and propped his foot up, prepared to inspect the damage, but hesitated. Once his boot came off, it might not go back on easily. He would wait until Robin returned, and they'd started the fire. She might need help, though so far she seemed competent. Besides, the men on the snowmobile were gone, and she should be safe. Still, he listened, waiting in silence.

About fifteen minutes later, though it could have been longer, Robin returned with an armload of split wood and some mismatched lengths of two-by-four. A dusting of snow covered everything, including her hair and eyelashes. Holy shit. She wasn't just cute; she was beautiful. The stray thought knocked the wind from him, leaving him as breathless as a hard fall.

CHAPTER 11: ROBIN

To Robin's surprise, she and Kory didn't discuss what the man had said about the nut farther up the road. Maybe it didn't seem worth talking about without more information, but someone who was unstable sounded dangerous. That's all they needed. Maybe Kory was preoccupied with his injury. She already knew him well enough that for him to admit his ankle hurt, it must be truly painful. He started the fire while she went back outside into the snow for a second load of firewood.

She glanced around the almost empty shed. There were a few long lengths at the back of the woodshed, but they would require a saw, so she gathered the last of the smaller pieces. They shouldn't need more than two armfuls for one night. At least they only needed to heat one room again.

She dropped off the second load and wiped the wet patches on the floor with a raggedy towel from the linen closet so they didn't slip. She wrinkled her nose. The ripped and dirty cloth smelled like mold, but she wasn't using it on herself, so the stench didn't matter. After cleaning up, she returned to the living room. Despite Kory's injured ankle, he was still on his feet, chopping potatoes to boil for dinner. He wasn't good about sitting still for long unless he had something to do—something they had in common.

She carved off a couple of chunks of icy snow from near the untrampled back stairs and tossed them in the second pot. The snow should be clean, or at least clean enough after boiling. She'd become an expert at pouring off the water from the constant ash sediment.

In the living room, Kory stood by the fire. His forehead was creased and his mouth seemed tighter than usual. If she hadn't known and seen the limp, she never would have guessed he'd injured himself. He'd done what was necessary in the barn and since. She still had an almost full bottle of Tylenol. She could share.

"Go sit down. You should stay off your foot."

To her surprise, he took her suggestion and sat on the loveseat with a long sigh. He unlaced his boot and loosened it before he slid it off gingerly. He let out a deep groan that made Robin's stomach clench in a peculiar way. Sliding off his sock, he wiggled his toes and winced. "I don't think it's broken." His foot and ankle had swollen and were turning lilac on the outside all around his ankle bone. No wonder it hurt. She wouldn't have been as stoic.

Robin met his warm brown eyes. "We aren't getting to Idaho Falls this winter. Are we? It's still over a hundred miles."

"Nope."

"We can't stay here." A tightness rose in her chest while her stomach fluttered and her cheeks burned at his intense gaze. What was wrong with her?

He nodded in acknowledgment of her words and at last looked down, poking his discolored foot.

"We need somewhere safe. With food and fuel." That was just the essentials—stuff she'd left behind in Boise. She wished they could have carried more of her garden's bounty.

"Water too, if we're lucky. Places out here might have a well, otherwise, we'll use a ton of fuel melting snow for drinking water." His calm demeanor kept her from panicking.

"That's asking a lot. We have food for about six weeks. You might be mobile by then." It was uncertain how the weather or snow conditions would be in December, but having a backup plan is better than extreme rationing and slow starvation. The second winter on the farm had been rough. She didn't think she could do that again.

"I might. It's only mid-October, but we've seen the ass end of fall." He leaned back on the threadbare loveseat, his expression one of disgust or frustration. She couldn't tell, though he was easier to read than a few days ago and his tells were subtle.

She handed him a dozen tablets. "Tylenol."

His eyebrows rose, perhaps at her generosity with the medication. Painkillers were hard to find now. Somehow, over the last few days, they'd started to feel like a team. If a sprained ankle sidelined him, she was sidelined, too. Her chance of making it through the winter out here improved if they worked together. Even injured, he would be fierce and would protect her if he needed to. She no longer doubted that. Her fingertips grazed her throat, thankful again that Kory had returned to stop Dillan.

Once again, they went to bed early, not lasting much longer after dinner and clean-up. Though bone-deep weary, Robin couldn't sleep, her brain spinning with worries. What if they didn't find somewhere to stay? Too bad she didn't have her phone to look up information about Craters of the Moon. It would have allayed some of her worries. Having facts was usually comforting, but having information at her fingertips was no longer possible. Once her phone had seemed essential, but it hadn't taken long to learn to live without.

She seldom allowed herself to miss technology anymore, but it would have been useful. She had no idea what to expect from the National Park. Robin had seen the signs on the interstate, of course, but had never been, though she'd suggested it several times when she was younger and obsessed with volcanoes. Her mother had always vetoed the trip, saying it was too far out of the way and scorching in the summer's heat. It certainly wasn't too hot now. Under the snow lay the lava fields with crumbled dark gray, dull red, and deep purple volcanic rock. She remembered that much from pictures. Were there buildings? Would there be people?

Perhaps this quiet highway gamble would still pay off. Or it could be a disaster. Time would tell. Hours after Kory lay snoring next to her on the floor mattress, she still fretted.

The next morning, when Robin woke, she didn't know if she'd dreamed. For once, she'd also slept through the night. At some point, Kory had wrapped his arm around her again. It surprised her to discover that she didn't mind. He made her feel safe. Maybe that was why she slept better when they were next to each other. She didn't like the idea of relying on someone else so much. She'd have to be careful not to become too attached.

She slipped out of bed and checked the window. Outside was white and still snowing. They should get moving. Kory would struggle to hike any distance today.

She grabbed a pan from the icy kitchen to fry the rest of the boiled potatoes from last night. One more hot meal before they headed out. Pulling out her map while breakfast cooked, Robin guessed their approximate location. She traced their route, starting at Fairfield, past the first house, the camping spot, and through Carey.

She estimated they'd walked close to twenty miles each day. Less yesterday because they'd searched houses in the morning. That meant they had about ten or fifteen more until the Visitor Center at the Park, the only roadside landmark shown in Craters of the Moon. At least that gave them a goal.

When their canteens had been refilled, the dishes cleaned, and everything stowed in their proper places, Kory double-checked the tensor bandage on his ankle and pulled on a lightweight sock, rather than a heavy winter one. While she watched, he adjusted the laces of his boot and shoved his foot inside with a grimace. He dry-swallowed two more Tylenol.

"How does it feel this morning?" she said as he stood.

"I'll survive. Let's go."

They collected their packs and their poles from beside the door, then headed out. Robin surveyed the expanse of white from the porch. She took a deep breath and forged onward. The temperature remained cold and steady but without the wind, which had died down. Thick white clumps of snow still fell. It had likely snowed all night and the new accumulation on the road was over a foot deep and thick to wade through. Luckily, her rain pants covered the tops of her boots or she would have been soaked in minutes.

Robin led, breaking a trail in the deep snow. The exercise warmed her before long, enough for her to take off her beanie and unzip the front of her jacket. She'd be cool if they stopped, but she kept trudging. When she looked back, their trail was easily apparent but filling in fast. As long as the flurry continued, in a couple of hours, it would bury all traces of them. Though the snow looked white in the air, on the ground it had a pale ivory cast—still filled with ash from the asteroid-related volcanic eruptions.

How long would it take for the climate to return to normal? Years? Maybe never. People had done a great job messing it up even before the asteroid. While she'd been growing up, climate change had been a problem and in the news daily. Still, with only a fraction of the world population still living, compared to the old days, at least it wasn't getting worse from new human pollution.

To keep her mind from her fears and to fight the boredom of walking, she cast her mind back. For a while, she and her grandfather had checked in on the Emergency Broadcast System periodically. It hadn't changed after the first year and the original evacuation orders for the West—which they'd disregarded. The president and his important people would still be in the underground command center bunker under the White House. Or that was where it was rumored to be, anyway. They were supposed to stay there another seven to ten years while everyone else fended for themselves. By the time the government emerged, there wouldn't be an America to return to. It was already gone.

The West Coast was a deserted wasteland of rubble and ash. The Southwest was on fire, some tire factory that smoldered non-stop, spewing greasy smoke into the air. From what she'd gleaned from the broadcast, the East spent its time dealing with the refugee problem.

Not to mention the lack of government, starvation, and a resurgence of disease.

The rest of the world had disappeared, dealing with their own issues. Volcanoes, earthquakes, flooding, and violent storms plagued the world with accelerated climate change and extreme weather. She'd concluded years ago that nobody was coming to the rescue. Anyone who would survive in America needed to do it on their own. Sometimes she wondered about Mexico and Canada, but assumed they also had problems.

Yanking herself out of her reverie of dark thoughts, she looked back to check on Kory. His jaw had been clenched all day as he toughed it out, dealing with his sprained ankle. He didn't speak but kept moving, making the most of the uneven trail she broke and leaning harder on his ski poles than yesterday.

Perhaps noticing her regard, he stopped. "Want a rest? I can take over for a bit."

She shook her head and continued.

Sometime later, they took a brief break.

"Lunch?" He passed her a couple of strips of jerky.

She took them with a weary smile. He wasn't much of a talker, but then, she often wasn't either. They had more to do out here than chat, as moving required a great deal of energy.

By mid-afternoon, the new snow reached above her knees; while light and powdery, there was no sign of the flurry letting up. The sky remained white and visibility limited. What if it snowed like this for days? Weeks? She was almost spent. Now that she was no longer lost in thought, a noise similar to yesterday's met her ears. Another snowmobile.

There was nowhere to hide, and she was too exhausted to try. Maybe whoever it was would miss them in the snowstorm. Perhaps the machine was off-road and not even on the buried highway. Her heart thumped harder. There was no hiding their recent trail where they'd floundered through the deep snow.

As the whining sound grew, it didn't come from behind as she expected, but from ahead.

Robin felt like slumping to the ground and resting, but she might not get up. She jammed her poles deep into the ground and held on, no longer moving her feet, instead bracing herself for whatever happened.

"Maybe it's the person the young men mentioned last night." In her exhaustion, her words came out as gasps. It would be better than the return of the Joneses.

"You mean the nut," said Kory, flashing her a quick smile.

"If he doesn't shoot us, I can handle odd. At least short-term." She wouldn't be alone with the stranger—she would stay glued to Kory.

A couple of minutes later, a snowmobile stopped on the snow-covered road ahead of them, almost too far to make out details. The rider switched off the engine and waited beside the machine, watching them with binoculars—no rifle in sight. That was something. Still, her shoulders tightened and her heart raced.

"Let's go talk." Kory rested a hand on her arm and forged into the lead. "I got this."

Taking a deep breath, Robin trudged forward in Kory's wake.

When they were about twenty yards from the watcher, the newcomer called out. "Did you folks buy a National Park pass?"

She and Kory stopped and looked at one another. He raised an eyebrow.

"There was no one at the ticketing booth," said Robin. They'd passed a roadside hut within the last hour. Or was it two? That must mean they'd entered Craters of the Moon.

"You need a valid pass," the man insisted.

"Can we buy one from you?" she said, glancing at Kory, who shrugged. She could play along.

"Back at the Center, I can sell you a day pass. But it will cost extra." The man's gloved hand drummed against his leg.

"How much?" said Kory.

"Well, that depends on how long you're staying at Craters of the Moon," said the man. His eyes slid past them to their tracks in the snow.

"We haven't decided yet," said Robin. "What is there to see in the Park this time of year?" Snow. Ice. More snow. Maybe some frozen rocks.

"The Visitor Center is open from twelve to four every day. I had to reduce the hours because I'm on my own." He glanced over his shoulder, presumably back toward the Visitor Center.

"Have you had many visitors?" said Kory.

The ranger's eyes narrowed. "Why do you want to know? What were you told?" He took a step forward, glaring. "Who do you work for?"

"A minute ago, we were paying guests," Robin whispered under her breath, her voice soft enough that only Kory would hear. The ranger's quick change in attitude made her uneasy. Odd was fine but unpredictable could be dangerous.

"He's fickle." Kory turned his face to mouth the words just to Robin. He faced the ranger once more. "We're on vacation and playing it by ear. As you can see, we've had a minor setback."

"That's right. I couldn't help but notice you were limping," said the ranger with a gesture toward Kory. "You're a big guy to be walking around on an injury like that. You might do permanent damage."

"I just twisted my ankle," said Kory, waving off the pain. Probably to make light of it. "My girlfriend and I aren't having the greatest holiday. How much farther is your Visitor Center? Is there somewhere we could rent or camp? We'd appreciate a place to stay for a few days."

The man hesitated.

"After we buy a pass for at least a week," said Kory.

The man licked his lips. "The Center's less than a mile back. I can rent you one of the deluxe rooms."

"Perfect." Robin whispered to Kory. "Can you make another mile?" She wasn't sure she could, but she would. She would rather lie down and sleep for three days. Every muscle in her body screamed for rest.

"I'll have to," he said, giving her a thoughtful look. He squared his shoulders.

"The girl can ride with me. Because of your limp, I brought the trailer and can haul you back," said the ranger, waving behind him. They'd missed the trailer in the snowmobile track and deep snow.

Another disquieting thought jumped into her head. How long had he been watching them? Perhaps not long in the storm, but how had he known to bring the trailer? Maybe he always towed it. She swallowed, her mouth going dry. There was something off here. She didn't want to ride with the ranger and shot Kory a wide-eyed, panicked look.

"I'm Kory and this is Robin." Kory took charge again as she froze up.

"I'm Everett. Officer Everett James." The ranger patted his chest. Maybe there was a badge or name tag under his coat. "Hop on. We'll head back to the Center for that pass and for orientation. You can choose a program for the week."

His friendly words didn't reach his shifty eyes. Was he up to something? Perhaps he wanted them thrown off guard. Robin didn't trust him.

"Thanks." Kory led the way to the snowmobile. After his second step, he reached back his gloved hand for Robin's.

She took it. She could trust Kory.

Up close, Everett was older than Robin had initially guessed. White stubble covered his cheeks and chin while wrinkles creased his weathered face. His pinched features gave him a distrustful air. Or was that her imagination?

Still, a ride. They'd just have to be careful on the other end. The words from last night came back to her—no one got through from the other side. What happened to travelers?

Kory sat on the trailer, which was like a wide sled, his legs on the outer edges. He patted the spot in front of him, between his legs. "We'll ride double back here." He must not be comfortable with this guy either, or he'd registered her hesitation. Either way, she moved to the trailer, rather than the snowmobile.

Everett pulled up his goggles and started the snowmobile with a push of a button.

Robin removed her pack and sat, hugging the pack in her lap while Kory held her from behind. She was dying to talk to him in private and tell him about her misgivings. Was leaving with this man a mistake? She hated being in a position where they didn't seem to have a choice.

Robin yawned, and her jaw creaked.

"Hang in there," Kory whispered in her ear, his breath warm on her cold cheek. It was difficult to hear over the roar of the machine, but she nodded and leaned back, trying to gather her strength. Her muscles felt like rubber. Plowing through the deep snow all day had been exhausting. She'd sleep like a log tonight.

The ride took only a few minutes before they pulled up outside a long, snow-covered building with a steep roof. Smoke rose from a chimney at the far end. It might be warm inside. Kory could put his injured foot up, and she could sit.

"Go ahead. You can wait in the lobby. Sorry I haven't turned the heat on in that part of the Center, just the staff quarters. I'm going to put the snowmobile away, then I'll see you inside in a few minutes." Everett waited for them to unload. "You two look like you could use a hot meal." He pointed them toward a door where he'd cleared the snow on the sidewalk. A snow shovel leaned against the outer wall.

Suddenly, Robin felt horrid for mistrusting the old guy. He might be harmless, and just lonely. If he was still out here working, he could have been alone for three years. That had to make you eccentric. Maybe he just wasn't good at talking to people anymore. Like her.

•   •   •

Ten minutes later, after they purchased a week's pass with a fake credit card number, Everett invited Robin and Kory to the back of the Center where the staff quarters were located.

"You can use this room," Everett said, waving toward a doorway that he unlocked with a key from a jingling bundle from his pocket.

Kory opened the door. Inside was a bedroom and bathroom. Hardly deluxe, but better than anything else they might have found. Out of habit, Robin flicked the light switch and, to her shock, the light turned on. Kory turned it off and on again with a grin.

"I'm surprised you have electricity out here." Kory turned to Everett.

The old man smiled, the first real one they'd seen. "We have our own electricity, water, and heat out here. I understand not everyone is so lucky. There's a pantry too. The former director was a Mormon, and she stocked this place to the rafters with supplies. Not much variety, but I can whip something up for your dinner. Meet me in the kitchen in ten." He pointed down the hall. "The kitchen and my room are down there." He strode away, leaving them to settle in.

Robin sat on the bed and flopped back onto the quilt. If it wasn't for the prospect of hot food, she wouldn't move again. "Your girlfriend is beat." She smiled and quirked an eyebrow in Kory's direction. What would he say about that?

He shrugged. "Seemed like a reasonable explanation about why we're traveling together." He dumped his pack in the corner. "We're almost done. Let's have dinner, then go to bed early. I need to get off my foot." He grimaced.

"It'll be dark soon. We might have just made it here by nightfall, but I'm glad we got a ride for the last part." She yawned as she forced herself to sit.

"Me too." He flashed her another fleeting smile.

Further investigation revealed that the bathroom had running water. Even hot. Robin almost cried. This was incredible. Maybe the old man was lonely and would want them to stay for longer than a week. Perhaps they could help him with things and win him over. Perhaps they could stay through the worst of the winter and head out in the spring when the snow receded. She took a breath, trying not to get ahead of herself. Dinner first.

After they'd cleaned up and put on fresh clothes, they followed the short hall to the kitchen. Everett stirred a steaming pot on the stove and then opened a can of fruit cocktail, which he split into two equal portions in white bowls. He rinsed the tins and tossed them into the garbage in the corner receptacle.

"Aren't you going to eat with us?" said Robin.

"I ate before I headed out on patrol," said Everett. "I try to only eat two meals a day to conserve supplies. I'm going to go watch a movie in my room. Please don't wander around or go anywhere else. I can show you around tomorrow if you like, but most rooms are locked and kept closed to conserve heat."

Something about the way he mentioned the locked doors bothered Robin. Her imagination must still be playing tricks. Since arriving, Everett had been perfectly nice and almost normal. What was real and what was an act?

"Thanks for everything," said Kory, as Everett dropped off two full bowls of steaming soup on the table. They sat where he'd set spoons and napkins. Kory glanced at Everett, who hovered nearby. He lifted his spoon. "This looks amazing. You don't have to stay while we eat. Don't worry, we'll clean up."

"See you tomorrow." Robin smiled and waved. "We really appreciate a hot meal and a place to sleep." She took a bite of soup and lifted another to her mouth.

"Night," said Everett as he left.

His room was the last room on the left, where he closed the door with a thud. From inside, a TV flicked on, blaring the loud sounds of an action movie—something Robin hadn't heard in ages. She hadn't missed TV as much as she'd expected.

She dove into her clam chowder with a hearty appetite. After three more bites, she looked up. Kory wasn't eating. "What's wrong?" She set down her spoon.

"I'm allergic to shellfish," he whispered, glancing toward Everett's room. "I didn't want to seem ungrateful, especially when he's unstable. I'll eat something from our stock."

"I'll get it," said Robin, jumping up to save him from hobbling back to their room. She returned with dehydrated beef stroganoff, filled the kettle, and continued eating while she waited for the water to boil. She lined up her dinner vitamins on the edge of the table to take after she finished her soup, and most of Kory's.

Kory ate several bites of canned fruit while he waited for his dinner to be ready.

When they finished eating, they washed the dishes and left them to dry on the rack, before heading back to their room. It looked like this place could work, at least for a few days. It seemed like Everett was open to their staying, at least for the week. Short-term was better than nothing.

A moment of uncomfortableness ensued when she and Kory climbed into bed together wearing pajamas. This was the first time they'd slept together without separate sleeping bags. Neither of them offered to sleep on the floor. Robin kept to her side of the mattress and snuggled into the downy pillow without looking at Kory. She closed her eyes and felt the thrum of her tired muscles as they relaxed. As expected, she dropped off to sleep in a matter of minutes.

●　　●　　●

The room was almost pitch black when Robin woke, her stomach twisting. She lay in bed, hoping the moment passed, and that it related to a nightmare. Instead, her stomach cramped harder and churned. She tried to remain still, so she didn't disturb Kory, but she couldn't get comfortable. A surge of heat ran through her and stabbed her gut. She pushed the quilt lower and rolled into a tight ball, willing the excruciating pain to leave. The position provided some relief, at first, but only for a few minutes. A wave of nausea ran through her. This wasn't period cramps. She was going to be sick.

Flinging the covers aside, she dashed for the bathroom, closing the door and flipping on the light. She made it just in time as she heaved the contents of her stomach into the toilet bowl with a splash.

Another volley of violent cramps followed. Breaking out in a sweat, she vomited again. She felt so gross, with barely time to catch her breath, as another spasm wracked her exhausted body. She heaved several times more until all that came up was a watery greenish fluid.

Too weak to return to bed, she flushed the toilet, rinsed her mouth, and curled up on the floor to wait for the next round, her hot cheek pressed against the cool tile. Must be food poisoning. Tonight was going to be a long night.

Chapter 12: Kory

Kory woke to the sound of retching. Robin's side of the bed was cold and empty. The clam chowder must not have agreed with her. For a split second, he was grateful that he wasn't sharing the same fate, and then his heart went out to her. This was the last thing she needed. Some canned food was spoiled after three years, especially anything with dents or misshapen cans. He should have insisted on inspecting the cans before they ate, but it would have come across as rude and ungrateful.

He should have known better than to trust a stranger to be as cautious as he was about expired food. They both should have. She'd eaten a healthy portion too since he'd given her his share.

Light outlined the bathroom door, so he waited in silence, trying to decide if he should offer to help. She may have been in there for a while. She ran the water, probably washing up. Another gagging sound followed it and more throwing up. The toilet flushed, but Robin didn't return to bed. The clock read 2:15 a.m.

Kory swung his feet to the cold floor and hobbled to the door, where he knocked. "Robin, you okay?" He kept his voice low.

She didn't answer. Maybe she hadn't heard.

He inhaled, debating. Help or not? When he was sick, he preferred to be left alone to suffer in silence. His older sister had liked someone to hold her hand and pamper her a little. On more than one occasion, he'd done that. "Robin?" He spoke louder.

From inside came a low groan. He cracked the door open and peered inside, blinking at the bright light as his eyes adjusted. Robin sat hunched on the cold tile floor, near the tub, with one hand on the edge as though steadying herself. She looked up at him with red, swollen eyes. This must have been going on for some time. What a day.

"I'm sorry I woke you." Her voice was raspy again, though most of the bruises on her throat had faded to dull yellow and pale green.

"Bad food," he said, sitting down beside her. "That's rough."

"I should be okay in a day or two," she said. "I've had food poisoning once before." She shuddered and moaned. She rested her forehead on her folded knees. "Everything is spinning."

Her stomach must be a mess. With her exhaustion, it would hit extra hard, plus she didn't have any extra meat on her. He rested his hand on the back of her neck. Holy hell. Her temperature must be well over a hundred degrees.

"I'll be right back." Kory hopped to the kitchen, keeping his wrapped ankle from taking much of his weight. He flicked on the overhead light, taking a second to marvel at how easily that instinct had returned. As he searched the cupboards, taking care not to bang anything, he located a large plastic mixing bowl. He grabbed it and a mug from the cupboard before returning to their room.

He arrived just in time for her to be sick again, so he held her hair back as she threw up. Her skin was as hot as a furnace, but she wasn't sweating. She was probably dehydrated. When she finished, he helped her to the sink, where she washed her face and rinsed her mouth. Heat radiated off her in waves as her body fought the bacteria.

He handed her the mug. "Sip. You need to be careful not to get dehydrated."

She took a couple of careful mouthfuls and passed the mug back.

"Come back to bed. You need rest." He wanted to fold her into a hug and tell her it would be okay, but he didn't think she would appreciate it right now.

She wobbled as she walked, and he wrapped his arm around her for support as they made their way to the bed. Her normal pep and independence gone, she accepted his help without a word.

"I'm putting the bowl here beside you. Just in case." He tucked her in and then cleaned up the bathroom better, keeping an ear out in case she vomited again. His own stomach didn't feel great, churning a little. He didn't think he'd be sick like her, but the fruit also may have been too far gone. He wouldn't make that mistake again, rude or not. Any sign of distended ends of cans meant he wouldn't eat what was inside, especially if it was also long past the expiry date.

Any canned food could be suspect, and any serious illness from spoiled food could be a death sentence. Winter was cruel and without medical help, you never knew what would be life-threatening.

Kory peeked into the bedroom through the slit beside the almost closed bathroom door, not wanting to let the light fall on Robin's face and disturb her rest. She looked peaceful, though she was pale as chalk with almost white lips. He was about to turn off the light and join her, when the bedroom door opened from the hall.

Everett tiptoed into their room, pale light spilling into the darkened bedroom from the hall. They must have woken up their host as well, and he was checking on them. Kory's first inclination was to feel guilty that they'd bothered the old man. Then he spotted the knife in Everett's hand as he continued into their room. What the fuck? Kory's fist clenched, and he turned on the tap as cover. His muscles tensed as he waited for his moment.

Everett glanced around. He didn't seem concerned about the light and water in the bathroom. The man must think Kory was in there. If anything, he seemed reassured that Kory was occupied. Maybe he thought they were both sick. Maybe that had been the ranger's plan.

Kory turned off the water and made a fake retching sound, still watching the room.

Everett stepped closer to the bed and raised his knife.

Kory sprang into action. Ankle forgotten, he charged out of the bathroom with a roar and caught the spindly old man's arm, wrenching the blade away.

"What the hell?" Kory's yell woke Robin, who scrambled farther away across the bed, her deep blue eyes open wide though she didn't make a sound.

The ranger fought back harder than Kory would have imagined, wrestling his arm free and bolting. Everett made it only to the hall. Kory caught him and twisted Everett's arm up tight behind his back.

"I asked what the hell you were doing in our room?" Kory hissed. "You have three seconds to explain." His body shook from fury and adrenaline. He could snap the old man like a twig for a wrong answer.

Everett's head whipped around, his eyes blazing. "You were both supposed to be incapacitated," he spat.

Making them sick had been deliberate. Kory's fury turned to ice. "What should I do with you?" It was a rhetorical question. If he left the old man free, he and Robin would spend the entire winter looking over their shoulders. There would be no peace, and they could never trust him. The old man would be like a cockroach and return until they dealt with him. He needed to be squashed.

Kory glanced over his shoulder. Robin watched from the bed, glassy-eyed. She couldn't travel tonight. He made a quick decision and shoved Everett farther down the hall as his own stomach lurched again. He didn't want to hurt anyone, but he had to do something.

"What are you going to do?" snarled Everett. "Kill me?" He peered over his shoulder and must have read Kory's intentions to do just that. The old man struggled and tried to get loose again, to no avail.

Kory had a firm grip as he propelled the man toward his bedroom, past the kitchen. "You gave us food poisoning and were going to slit our throats in our sleep." His voice emerged as a deep growl.

"They'll come looking for me," Everett said, his voice shrill as he seemed to shrink into himself. "I live alone, but I have customers. They supply me with fuel. I sell them meat."

Kory felt sick, suddenly understanding what happened to waylaid travelers who disappeared along this route. Everett must have thought that injured Kory and Robin would be easy marks. This man would kill them if Kory gave him a chance. He'd killed others, possibly children. Children like his sister, who he hadn't been able to help. Children like those at the center who he'd let down. Women like the Wings' women. Once again, guilt from spending years as a bystander washed over him.

He took a deep breath, shoved the old man against the wall, grabbed his head with both hands, and twisted. Everett's neck snapped with a sickening crunch. He slumped to the floor, his eyes vacant.

Kory stared at his shaking hands as though they weren't attached to him. He'd become a killer. "Two." The word slipped out. He'd killed two men. He hadn't wanted to be one of the Wings, but he'd earned both wings. One for each side of his leather jacket—not that he would wear it again as he'd left it behind with the bike.

"Kory," came Robin's weak voice from the bedroom.

"I'm fine," he said, loud enough for his voice to carry. He felt strangely calm. "I'll be right back." He grabbed Everett by his heels and dragged the man's limp body into his bedroom at the end of the hall. The room stank of stale body odor, dirty laundry, and something sour. Thick dust covered the surfaces of the furniture. The TV had been paused on a familiar movie—Die Hard. Kory turned off the TV with the remote. He would deal with the body in the morning.

At the last second, he snatched Everett's keys from the dresser and left, locking the door behind him.

Robin threw up every fifteen to twenty minutes for hours while Kory kept her tucked into bed and held the bowl as needed. When she was able, she sipped water. Neither of them got much sleep, but he would rather help than make her deal with it on her own. She was a wreck. Caring for someone besides himself—it was something he could get used to. He liked being needed.

Just as the sun peeked over the eastern horizon in a glorious pink sunrise, she fell into an exhausted sleep. Kory checked that he'd locked the bedroom door with the key, and dropped into bed beside her, hoping for a few hours of rest. At least they could stay in bed late without being disturbed. They should have the place to themselves. For now. What would he find in the locked rooms? Tonight, the sound of Everett's neck crunching might keep him from a peaceful sleep.

•   •   •

It was late morning when Kory woke. He hadn't been sure he would sleep, but killing the ranger had been necessary, and his actions hadn't tormented him for long. Yesterday had been exhausting, and he'd still been tired when his sleep had been interrupted. He yawned and stretched. His ankle throbbed, but he still had several Tylenol left from Robin's generous handful; he'd been rationing them. He would take one when he got up. Gingerly, he flexed his foot. Maybe he'd take two.

Today and the next few days, he would take it easy so his ankle would improve. Walking on it all day yesterday had made it worse. His eyes felt like they'd been filled with sand as he rubbed them and yawned again. His jaw creaked.

He rolled onto his side. Robin still slept, clutching the top edge of the plastic bowl. He peeked and was thankful to see the bowl was empty. Her color remained pale, but more pink than yellow was a favorable sign—as were the last few hours of uninterrupted sleep. Food poisoning typically lasted about twenty-four hours. With luck, she was past the worst.

Chances were, she wouldn't be able to keep much down today, but perhaps he could find something soft and bland to feed her, like instant pudding or plain oatmeal. More tea.

He'd have to deal with the ranger's body today, too. At least it was cold enough outside that he would find somewhere to store it. It would freeze solid and it should remain that way for months. Maybe he could temporarily leave it in an outbuilding. Burying it in the frozen ground would be difficult and would have to wait until his foot was healed.

Now that he possessed the Visitor Center keys, he should check the supplies and the other rooms to see how this place was stocked. Already his mind was spinning. This wouldn't be a horrible place to recover for a few weeks or even to spend the winter, as long as the neighbors didn't investigate too soon.

He couldn't get the disturbing meat situation off his mind. The neighbors must have been desperate to resort to cannibalism. The people down the road may not have acknowledged where the meat came from, but they must have some idea. After all, they'd noticed the lack of travelers as well. He'd done the math on his own, so they could too. In this case, two plus two made four.

Kory couldn't imagine eating human meat, but he couldn't quite find it in himself to condemn those who made the choice out of desperation. The will to survive was strong and starvation was slow and awful. Of course, he didn't hold with killing others for their meat. That was one step too far. Everett's choice was worse than the family or families down the road who were his customers.

Behind one of the locked doors, Kory found an extensive pantry. Floor-to-ceiling shelves lined with powdered food. Everett hadn't been exaggerating about being well-stocked. All the remaining canned goods were piled at one end, separated from the rest. Most had been shoved against the back wall. There, most of the ends were bloated and bulging; they were inedible. The ranger had probably eaten everything decent.

Most of the remaining stock on the shelves was gallon containers of dehydrated food. Upon closer inspection, the majority remained three-quarters full or sealed and unopened. There were also shelves of dried goods that stored well, such as flour, sugar, rice, beans, lentils, and pasta. Everett hadn't been starving, and there was enough food stored to last for years.

One end of the room held other supplies. Though he and Robin didn't need candles and matches here, with the power still on, they could restock their supply when they left. If it weren't for worrying about the neighbors, this would be an excellent place to winter. They'd have to decide how long they were comfortable staying.

Behind another door, he found a long white freezer that emitted a gentle hum. Kory opened it and slammed the lid immediately. Packages of meat wrapped in white paper almost filled the freezer. He didn't want to see what else might be stored with them. He left and relocked the door, making a mental note not to return.

As he searched the complex, Kory watched for bullets or a gun, but found nothing. Not even in Everett's room. He also located the electrical panel for the building inside an office of the main Visitor Center, noting the breakers that had been switched off. He changed nothing.

Two of the other guest rooms were stained and destroyed with soiled bedding heaped on the beds. Kory closed those doors and relocked them. Robin wouldn't want to examine the blood-stained mattresses any more than he did.

On that note, he checked on her and found the bed empty, and the shower running. That was another positive sign. She might not be better, but she was improving. Kory returned to the kitchen to wait for her. He mixed some instant vanilla pudding and cooked plain rice, things that would be easily digestible if she wanted something in her stomach. He also made mushroom soup from powder for himself. The finished product had a faint chalky texture but was otherwise satisfactory.

A dust-covered bread maker sat in the corner. He might haul it out later and see if he could make bread. He checked through the drawers and found a manual with several dough recipes. For the next couple of days, they spent most of their time recuperating. Robin's food poisoning passed by the second morning, though her energy and appetite took longer to return.

At the back of Kory's mind were the neighbors, but for now, he and Robin got to be in recovery mode while winter settled in, snowing almost every day. The banks of snow stood almost three feet deep already. They were here to stay, at least as long as the weather and Kory's injury trapped them, or it remained safe.

CHAPTER 13: ROBIN

Robin and Kory settled into the staff suite of the Craters of the Moon Visitor Center while the winter whistled outside and thick snow fell. Robin worried little about the neighbors showing up while it stormed. It had horrified her when Kory had explained his cannibalism discovery and revealed what Everett had done. But regular everyday stresses took precedence over the horror—things such as laundry and cooking. That was balanced by spending quiet time with each other. The Visitor Center had a small bookstore, and she intended to read most of the fiction while she had a chance.

Things had changed between herself and Kory. They had been different since they'd left Boise, but it was more obvious than ever here, sharing time, space, and a bed. They hadn't spoken about their status, and neither of them had acted, but there was a tension between them that was new; and while a little uncomfortable, it was also exciting. Robin bit her lip, not sure what she wanted to do about the shift. She hadn't minded being referred to as his girlfriend.

Sometimes she felt Kory's eyes on her and her skin tingled, and thoughts of having a relationship with him were intriguing. She couldn't deny her powerful attraction, even if she froze up and stammered every time it happened, often turning back to her book to avoid acting on it.

Several times that week, she'd caught him studying her with an expression like he considered her a puzzle to be solved. Maybe he wasn't sure what came next, either. Allies to friends. Then lovers? It no longer seemed an unlikely progression.

From what he shared, she gathered he was usually a loner, so perhaps he was also confused. She didn't know what he'd guessed about her past, but he hadn't made a move. Maybe he was leaving it up to her, but she felt clueless. If she chose to do anything, having a physical relationship would require a gigantic act of faith. She wasn't sure she was ready.

Robin climbed into bed that night, still wondering how to proceed. The silence stretched as Kory climbed in next to her. Tonight, he wasn't wearing a T-shirt, just pajama bottoms. Not only did he have broad shoulders and solid muscles, he had a good amount of chest hair. It seemed to make him even more masculine. His stubble had turned into a short beard, which suited him.

She wished she were brave enough to reach out and touch him. His skin looked smooth and hard at the same time. Some of her thoughts may have shown on her face because Kory turned on his side, his head propped on his hand, staring at her instead of turning off his light.

Her face flamed and butterflies romped in her stomach. She stared into his warm brown eyes. His gaze gravitated to her mouth.

"Can I kiss you?" His voice was quieter than she would have imagined. "I think about it all the time."

She nodded, her mouth suddenly dry. She hadn't kissed anyone since her boyfriend in eleventh grade, over four years ago, and she hoped she hadn't forgotten how. Kissing Kory would be different—he wasn't an awkward teenager.

Kory brushed a few strands of hair away from her face and tucked them behind her ear with a soft smile.

She swallowed, still holding his gaze. "I'm nervous."

"I won't hurt you. I don't know what happened, but I'm not like whoever hurt you. If you change your mind, I'll stop. I also won't be offended if you tell me to go slow." His eyes were like calm pools she could fall into. "If you aren't interested, tell me."

"Thank you," she whispered, sliding closer to Kory, and she closed her eyes as he caressed her cheek, leaning into his touch. She liked Kory. More than anything, she wanted to feel connected and close.

The first touch of his lips was so soft, she could almost have imagined it. As the kiss grew, she responded and warmth zinged throughout her like a low-grade current, setting her nerves on fire. The sensation raced everywhere, even her toes and fingertips.

Kory wrapped an arm around her and tugged her closer so that her body pressed against his larger, hotter one. Being this close reminded her of his solid power, but it wasn't frightening—it made her feel safe. When his lips claimed hers again, more of his desire became apparent. He was hard everywhere. She must be doing this okay, and opened her mouth as his tongue flicked against hers. They kissed for several minutes, long enough for her lips to feel tingly and swollen when they stopped to catch their breath. Kory rested his forehead against hers.

"I don't want to scare you," he said, his hand sliding beneath her shirt to rest along her ribs. "Your grandfather told me you had trouble in the past. I want to know you better."

His incredible warmth spread to her with the skin-to-skin contact.

"And if you're willing to tell me, I'd like to know what happened. Out there?" He gestured to the outside world.

This moment felt like a crossroads. Robin had kept her pain to herself for so long, in part to spare her grandfather the burden of knowing, but also, as if refusing to talk about it, would erase the attack from existence. But that wasn't realistic. Instead, the details of the assault had become a heavy weight she carried alone. Safe and wrapped in Kory's arms, for the first time, she wanted to share.

"It happened near the beginning." Her chest tightened, but she was tired of shutting down and avoiding the past. "When the news broke, Mom gave up and refused to leave Portland, so in the first days after the asteroid, I was with my sister Shelby. We hitched a ride with a family friend who dropped us off outside town, helping us get beyond the mayhem in the city. The two of us hiked into the mountains, where we found shelter in an unoccupied cabin. The second night, the volcanoes erupted, and we hunkered down to wait out the ashfall."

Kory remained quiet, perhaps thinking about where he'd been at the same time. It wouldn't be something he'd forget.

She took a breath. "About a week later, four guys on motorbikes found the cabin." She shivered, remembering the sound. "We heard them coming, but had nowhere else to go. At first, they seemed like they'd be polite enough and respected our wishes to be left alone, even if they were a little rough around the edges. They camped downstream, and we listened to them partying until late."

She shuddered and took another deep breath. "We fell asleep. I woke up when they kicked in the door and yanked us out of bed. They took turns raping us." Her breath became ragged, once more feeling the rough wooden floor beneath her and the alcoholic fumes of the drunken, unwashed men. "Shelby was only sixteen and I couldn't protect her."

Kory brushed a tear from her cheek with his thumb.

"Shelby kept begging me not to struggle. Said it would be over soon, but I couldn't stop screaming, kicking, and scratching. They took turns holding me down. They beat me to make me stop fighting. By morning, my eyes were so swollen, I could barely see and they'd cracked my ribs. They kept us tied and used us for days. At least two, maybe three, though my memory of that time is spotty. We got water, but no food. I hurt all over, was covered in bruises, and was raw below." Her voice had gone far away as she related the events. "On the last day, one man choked me while he fucked me. I couldn't breathe and I passed out."

Her voice stopped, and she took several heaving breaths, trying to regain her composure before she told him the worst part. She closed her tear-filled eyes and her voice shook. "When I woke up, they were gone. Shelby with them. I think they left me for dead."

"But you were tougher than they thought. You didn't stay there and die." Kory's voice surprised her. She'd almost forgotten he was there—he was an excellent listener. There was no judgment in his voice.

Having shared the worst, her voice became more relaxed.

"I scavenged some clothes, since they'd shredded mine, and followed the trail deeper into the mountains. I stole food where I could and remained hungry when I couldn't. It took me weeks to make my way to my grandfather's farm. I don't remember most of the journey. When I got there, I tried to convince him to chase after Shelby, but we didn't know where to start. The bikers could have taken her anywhere or left her behind somewhere else. It kills me that I'll never know what happened to her. She was my responsibility, and I failed her."

"You didn't fail her. Society did. Those men knew better. It wasn't your fault they chose violence." Kory wrapped both arms around her and tucked her into an embrace. Her head fit under his chin, holding her while she wept—three years' worth of guilt and pain in her sobs. "Your grandfather was right," he said a few minutes later. "You've got grit."

A chuckle burst from her as her tears slowed to a trickle. "He said that?" Warmth filled her. That was high praise from her tough old grandfather, who'd been a soldier in his youth.

"He did." Kory kissed her again. "Let's get some sleep. Thank you for trusting me with your story. Tomorrow, I'll tell you mine."

She flipped over and snuggled into him, allowing his solid presence and clean soap smell to surround her. She fit perfectly against him. Though she felt Kory harden at the close contact, he wouldn't hurt her or try anything. That she could trust. She wasn't ready to be intimate physically, but she enjoyed his touch and yearned to be closer at some point. Tonight, she was drained.

The next night, they climbed into bed and Robin couldn't wait to hear Kory's story. Her emotions had felt raw all day after sharing something so personal. Still, hearing about his past would balance things between them. His story might also be unpleasant. Everyone who'd survived had been through hard times.

"Can I touch you when we talk?" Robin said, looking at him. He no longer seemed like a giant. He seemed like Kory—steady, reliable, and someone she trusted. That might not seem exciting, but it was. Not that long ago, she never would have pictured lying in bed with a man, comfortable enough to tell their personal stories and be vulnerable.

"C'mere. Let me hold you. We fit better like this." He wrapped his arms around her again. "What would you like to know?" He was as toasty as an oven and she enjoyed feeling his heart beating against her back and his warm breath on her cheek. After so long without touching anyone, it was extra nice to be held. She sighed and relaxed in this newest safe space. This was the connection she'd craved.

"Why did you leave Portland?" She had a lot of questions. Suddenly, she wanted to know everything. "Actually, start at the beginning, with the important facts before leaving Portland." If she wasn't specific, he might give the short answer, and she wanted more.

"My dad left before I can remember." That was something else they had in common. "My first stepfather left when I was seven. My mom and my second stepfather died in a car accident when I was thirteen, so I spent several years bouncing around foster care. The last couple who took me were alcoholics, dependent on the payment from the state for my upkeep." He maintained his usual even, growly voice. These must be old hurts he'd learned to live with.

One of his hands wandered up to stroke the underside of her breast. The sensation distracted her, but in a way that she liked.

"January of my senior year, I turned eighteen and my foster parents cut me loose because there would be no more funds coming from the state. I couch-surfed at first but didn't have many friends I could impose on for longer than two or three days. Later, I slept nights at a church close to the high school. Your mother figured out I was on my own and brought food for me to school. As soon as I graduated, I split because I had no reason to stay."

"Where did you go?" Her heart ached for the younger Kory, who'd thought he was alone. Reading between the lines, he'd felt nobody cared or would miss him.

"I hopped trains for a year, crisscrossing the country before I returned to the West Coast. Milder winters in Seattle than in Denver or New York state. That's for sure."

"You said you lived on the streets." She cringed at her impudence but couldn't help herself. His patience for answering her questions made her ask more, even if they might be intrusive. If he didn't want to answer, he wouldn't.

He kissed the side of her throat and continued his story.

"I did. A fluid community of us lived in downtown Seattle in the parks. Most of the time I slept in a tent and worked casual pickup jobs when I could."

"Did you have girlfriends?" Curiosity made her ask. The motion of his hand stopped for a heartbeat before it resumed.

"A couple, but it was always casual, and they moved on after a few months."

"You said you did jobs for cash or drugs. What type of drugs?" He didn't drink, smoke, or do drugs now. Once, that kind of history would have scared her, but nobody was the same as they'd been in the old days. She peeked over her shoulder and caught a flash of a smile.

"I stayed away from the hard stuff. Mostly weed. It was legal in Washington." His voice seemed amused.

"When did you quit smoking?"

"After the asteroid. I spent a few months at a refugee center in Spokane. I cleaned up there and decided if I was going to live, I didn't want to spend my life altered or turn out drunk like my foster parents. My survival needs took precedence over vices."

"Is there anything else I should know about you?" Her voice dropped.

"I like you a ridiculous amount." He squeezed her in a brief hug.

She smiled and snuggled closer. "Anything else?"

"I miss music." He trailed kisses along her throat and neck. His new beard scratched just enough to add friction. She liked the sensation.

"What kind of music?" It had become more difficult to focus on her inquisition.

"Rock. Some newer, some classic. Remind me to show you my favorite CDs tomorrow. I have a small collection. Things I want to play someday if I'm lucky enough to have or build a stereo."

She swiveled so that his next kiss landed on her mouth.

She forgot everything else as they made out, losing track of time, enjoying the feeling of closeness. The feeling of intimacy grew as they touched each other, enjoying being together. Though never hesitant, his every touch seemed gentle and caring.

When Kory stopped kissing her, he said, "Goodnight, Robin." He promptly fell asleep. Robin's disappointment that they'd stopped startled her in its intensity.

•　　•　　•

Three nights later, after similar nights of conversation, making out, and going to sleep frustrated, Robin showered before bed and came out of the bathroom wearing nothing but one of Kory's T-shirts. It hung down to her thighs—as long as a short skirt. Her stomach fluttered at her daring. Kory set his book down and watched her without a word, his eyes never leaving her as she climbed onto his lap and straddled him. She tilted her head and smiled.

"Are you trying to kill me?" he said in a strangled voice. His hands cupped her bare butt cheeks. Holding her in place.

She shook her head. "Maybe if I start half-naked, we'll get farther."

He made a noise in his throat that was difficult to interpret, but he seemed surprised and, from the twitch of his mouth, amused and not upset. He didn't ask her to leave.

She wrapped her arms around his neck and kissed him. Without breaking contact, he slid away from the headboard, so she wrapped her legs around him. When he kissed her in return, goosebumps broke out all over her skin. He deepened his kisses, becoming more demanding. Because she trusted him, his every touch turned her on, making her skin tingle.

He broke off the kiss, yanked the shirt he wore over his head, and tossed it to the floor. Next, he peeled his T-shirt from her, leaving her wrapped around him on his lap, naked. When they resumed, his hands roamed everywhere, leaving a trail of heat and desire on her sensitive flesh. He cupped first one of her breasts, then the other, his thumbs teasing her nipples, which made her gasp.

Their kisses became yet more heated. She gasped when his tongue flicked inside her mouth and she flushed all over, feeling a wetness pool between her legs as she ached for his touch. For more. God, she wanted him. She couldn't believe this was her choice, but she was tired of being afraid. This was the first time she'd been with a man of her free will, and it was fabulous. She switched from kissing his mouth to nibble his neck and sucking below his ear. His sizeable hands wrapped around her and he squeezed her ass on either side. He groaned as their lust picked up steam.

"Fuck, Robin. You're so goddamn hot I should ravish you." His intense voice seemed sincere.

She smiled against his skin and whispered. "That's an excellent idea."

When he sucked on her nipple, she gasped. When he took the rest of her breast in his mouth and sucked harder, she nearly came apart in the most incredible way. Nobody had touched her like this; it was far different from inexperienced and uncomfortable teenage groping. She melted into him, on fire inside, her skin more sensitive than ever. The sensations could have been overwhelming, but instead left her further aroused.

Every touch unlocked more heat inside her core. Small gasps escaped from her throat and her breathing became uneven. Kory may have been in better control, but not much. His skin flushed and was hot to the touch while his breathing became punctuated by low moans. He moved one hand from her ass and dipped it between her legs. She was so swollen; she hadn't known her body was capable of that.

"You're so fucking wet," he panted, swirling his thick finger onto her swollen clit and she squirmed to allow him better access. She gasped again, pushing herself onto his hand. She should be embarrassed, but she wasn't now—the pleasure was too intense.

"Can I finger you?" he whispered. "I promise I'll make you feel good."

She couldn't imagine feeling better than this, but she bit her lip and nodded, too lost in desire to speak.

She slid off his lap, and he repositioned her onto the bed and lay down beside her. He slipped a finger inside her, leaving his thumb to rub outside while he thrust deeper. The pressure made her ache more, not less. He cradled her in his arms and against him while she writhed and arched her back. He added a second finger, picking up the pace. With the increased speed and pressure, she couldn't remain quiet. She threw back her head and called out his name.

"Oh, Sweetheart," he said, in a husky voice. "Come for me."

She didn't know if it was his hands, his mouth, or his words, but she lost what little control remained, shaking and grinding as white light exploded in her mind. Again, she cried out. This was new and amazing. For several heartbeats she pulsed around his fingers, riding the climax of this fabulous orgasm.

As her shuddering slowed, she was almost embarrassed to look him in the eye, but his kiss was so tender and gentle, she forgot to be self-conscious. She kissed him back, still breathless.

"Thank you," she said when at last she could speak.

"You are so very welcome," he said with a wide grin. "Anytime." He slid off the bed and stood up, his massive erection obvious through his pajamas. "Excuse me while I deal with this." He turned for the bathroom.

"Where are you going?" she said, disappointment surging through her. She wasn't ready to let him go yet.

He hesitated. "I'm going to shower and jerk off. Like I do every day or I'd be hard non-stop." He ducked his head, looking almost shy. "You can watch or help. If you want."

She tugged her shirt back on, embarrassed, and averted her gaze. Her cheeks flamed.

"Hey," he said, coming back to perch on the edge of the bed. He took her hand. "I don't think you understand. I want you." He glanced down at his tented pants. "Badly. Every day, I know you better and fantasize about you more. The smell of your citrus shampoo surrounds me every night, and I can't wait for bed. I want to inhale the hint of vanilla that your skin smells like all the time and lick you like an ice cream cone." He ran his fingers through his tousled dark hair.

"But," she said, her eyes on the floor. Was his avoidance because she was damaged?

He tipped her chin up. "But we don't have birth control. If we have sex, we're risking you getting pregnant." He let those words sink in.

She turned pale, then her cheeks burned anew. She hadn't thought that far ahead.

"If we decide to stay together, we'll deal with whatever happens. If this is nothing more than convenience or hormones, that isn't fair. I'm falling for you but we're early days. I always swore I would be a proper dad if I got a chance, not some absentee father. If I have kids, I want to be there. Not just for you and for them, but for me, too. Does that make sense?"

His foresight put her to shame. She'd only thought about feeling pleasure.

"Don't get me wrong," he said, his gaze still holding hers. "I'm thrilled I no longer terrify you and that you're considering having sex. I'm tempted. But we have time." He grinned. "We have months to practice and decide. We can make each other feel terrific in dozens of other ways. Let's start with the shower."

He took her chilly hand in his, pressed a kiss to her forehead, and they headed for the shower together.

CHAPTER 14: KORY

Not knowing the exact date rarely bothered Kory, as it seldom mattered, but Robin had talked about Christmas. Several times in the last few days. It had been some time in mid-October when they'd reached Craters of the Moon and they'd been here just over eight weeks. What mattered was his ankle had healed, giving him only a twinge at odd moments. If he had to walk miles on it, he would be okay. The time had flown by faster than he would have credited for being stuck in one place.

Most of that was because, during this time, he'd fallen head over heels in love with Robin. His days of watching and trying to convince himself he didn't care about the suffering of others felt like a different lifetime. Protecting Robin and getting her to her uncle and aunt was all that mattered. He'd also never considered how it would be to have someone to protect and trust as a matter of course. That was a life he'd thought beyond him, but now that's what he was lucky enough to have found. It seemed too good to be true that not only was he in love, but he also suspected that she returned his feelings.

His feelings had nothing to do with their history or her mother, and everything to do with how she accepted him without making him feel less for having a complicated past. She saw his best qualities, and either hadn't discovered his flaws or didn't see them that way. What did history matter? He and Robin clicked and spent pleasant times together.

Just thinking of her brought a grin to Kory's face. For the first time in years, he was content. More than that—happy. She was the reason, and he wanted to do something special to show her. It should be Christmas in a few days, and he'd love to surprise her with a present.

Christmas wasn't his favorite holiday, but she'd mentioned it more than once. He hadn't celebrated it since his parents had died when he was thirteen. Money had been tight, so they had been pretty low-key. He'd discovered Santa was a lie at six or seven when his mom had said they were too broke for a Santa gift. Christmas had sucked since then, as they'd never had excess to spend on gifts.

Still, Christmas was important to Robin. She'd talked about special family celebrations involving lavish food, presents, and time with her loved ones at her grandfather's farm. He'd already decided to give her the copy of *The Hating Game* he'd grabbed in Boise for her birthday, which was in early January, just days before his own. She'd read it before, but he'd seen her eyeing it when he was reading it. And she would love receiving the book she said was her favorite.

He also wanted to get her something new. His shopping options were limited, but he wanted to try. He grabbed Everett's keys and steeled himself for what he might also find as he searched some of the blocked-off rooms, as well as the sheds outside. He might discover something interesting he'd missed before.

In one, he found several pairs of snowshoes—not huge, old-fashioned, clunky ones, but sleek modern ones. When they left Craters of the Moon, they could add the snowshoes to their gear. A present for both of them, but not what he had in mind for Christmas.

On his search, Kory ventured into the room with the freezer that he'd avoided. In the back corner, he discovered heaps of camping and trekking gear, clothing, and several backpacks—probably from the missing travelers. It felt strange to go through their belongings, knowing they'd been killed here. But they were gone. It wasn't much different than searching houses and taking useful items.

He was about to leave when a handwritten schedule posted on the wall caught his attention. The title at the top read, "Collection Dates." January first was circled in red and it listed three family names below: Jones, Foisy, and Cooper. Taking a deep breath before examining the contents, Kory opened the freezer. Each of the packages was labeled with capital letters that matched the same three names.

He clenched his jaw. January must be less than two weeks away. He didn't want to leave here that soon, not in the thick of the winter storms, where they seldom went more than three days without flurries and serious wind. On the road, they would be in trouble. He and Robin would be insane to leave somewhere with food, water, shelter, and heat—not without a pressing reason. They would have to decide if the people showing up according to this schedule constituted a serious threat.

If the neighbors needed the meat and expected it, should he and Robin make it available? He'd prefer not to be involved with cannibalism—the idea was repugnant. But the travelers were already dead, and he hadn't been a part of that atrocity. Supplying the expected meat might buy more time before he and Robin had to leave. There was no good choice.

They'd talked about their plans for the spring, agreeing it would be best to wait until March or April to hike out into this desolate country. If the snow melted earlier, they would be prepared to depart before then. They hoped to arrive in South Dakota before next summer. His thoughts circled back to the current problem.

If they had more fuel for the snowmobile, they wouldn't have to hike out and could load the backpacks in the trailer and start with additional food supplies. They'd saved her rations for traveling, eating the bulky potatoes and supplies from the pantry.

He would talk to Robin about staying or going, as it would also be her decision.

Kory found her in the Visitor's Center office, her back to him, as she examined the electrical panel. She flipped one with a sharp clicking sound.

"There you are."

Robin jumped, as though caught doing something she shouldn't, a guilty look flashing across her expressive face. What was she up to?

"I just wanted to see if we could get power in here, too." She glanced at the panel.

"Any particular reason?" He winked. She was cute when at a loss for words.

Her eyes flicked back to the panel with the breakers. She shrugged. She was a terrible liar. Either that or he knew her too well. He also knew her well enough that whatever she was doing wasn't deceptive or hurtful.

Which one had she changed? Perhaps she was planning a surprise too, as she kept an accurate tally of the days. She must know it was almost Christmas.

He let the topic drop. "I was thinking of putting together dinner. You interested?"

She smiled and nodded. "I'll be inside in a few minutes."

Kory headed into the kitchen to make hot drinks and dinner, and she joined him minutes later.

Later that night, when Robin was showering, Kory crept back into the chilly Visitor Center gift shop. Other than travel mugs and books, they'd left the souvenir shop alone, but now he was looking for something specific. Robin had given him an idea. Just because she might not use something now, a gift might send a message and be saved for later. He scanned the darkened racks, illuminated by his headlamp.

His heart sank at the boring array of T-shirts and hoodies. Maybe something from the jewelry counter? Or from behind the counter on the far racks. Her ears weren't pierced, and he didn't know what else she might like until he spotted a stack of CDs tucked in the corner.

Music. Someone on staff must have left them behind, as they weren't new and covered in plastic.

He'd love to share the gift of music with her. Give her something to add to their someday collection. He flipped through the options and grinned. Three Taylor Swift CDs. *Reputation*, *Midnights*, and *Lover*. Not his favorite artist, but one of hers. He slipped them into his jacket pocket. Later, he would read the lyrics and decide which seemed the most appropriate. He would save the others to give her another time—for her birthday or just-because gifts. He left the store with a smile. At last, he'd found something special.

Kory returned to their room, where it was warmer and bright, and slipped the CDs into his pack. Since their arrival, he'd stopped sleeping with his backpack. He trusted Robin, which had been a revelation. Now his pack sat at the far side of the room, containing his most precious belongings, while he used a dresser drawer for his clothes. More civilized and settled than he'd been in years.

He did an extra fifty push-ups while he waited for Robin to emerge, undress, and slip under the covers.

"I didn't see much of you today," she said as she came out of the bathroom in a cloud of floral steam, toweling her hair dry. "What were you looking for today that kept you so busy?"

He wasn't going to lie, nor give away his surprise.

"I wanted to see what else was here that we might have missed. I found some snowshoes we can use. They'll be helpful when we leave unless we wait for the full thaw." He took a moment to think of how to broach the other subject. "Of concern, I found a schedule on the wall with a series of collection dates. Three families are due here January first for their supply of meat."

"The packages that might be human meat from the freezer room." She spoke slowly, and her nose wrinkled with distaste.

Kory nodded. "What do you think we should do? They're likely to be upset to find Everett gone."

"If we don't give it to them, they might force their way inside to get it. They're probably depending on it." A crease appeared on her brow.

He'd considered that. There were just the two of them, and they'd be outnumbered. Perhaps by a lot. Each name could represent several larger groups or families. Robin had given him a handgun from her pack and six rounds of ammo that her grandfather had left behind. She wasn't familiar with how to shoot it. That might not be enough to protect themselves. Tomorrow, he would show her how to shoot in case of an emergency.

"I think we'd be foolish to leave in the dead of winter, except as a last resort," he said.

Robin sat cross-legged on the bed beside him, tracing the quilt's pattern with her index finger. "Maybe we should give it to them. We don't want it. When is the following collection date?" She looked up.

"March 15th." By then, it would be almost spring. There would probably still be snow, but the end would be approaching. That was close to when they'd need to be underway, anyway.

"What if they ask about Everett?" She winced when she said the ranger's name.

"We tell part of the truth. He didn't make it and we're living here now."

"They might think we're taking over his business and have expectations for the future."

"Let them. It might buy us the rest of the season." Kory had spent the day considering their options. He was in favor of staying, as long as she was willing to take that risk.

"Could you do that? Give them human meat and accept their fuel in exchange so we can stay here longer?" She bit her lip.

"I could. I don't love it, but it would keep us safe for longer. I doubt we'll get travelers through in winter. Our arrival in October was unusual enough for Everett. We'll have to deal with the neighbors just this once."

She didn't answer right away.

"If you would rather leave, I'll go." He picked up her hand. "Winter or not. My ankle is healed."

Robin turned and flopped back onto the bed, her head landing on her pillow as she stared at the ceiling. She remained silent, thinking. "Is it baffling to want to leave? We have shelter here. We even have electricity and running water." She sat up halfway. "In some ways, this would be an exceptional place to live."

His eyebrows shot up. "Long term? What about South Dakota? What about your uncle?"

"It's still over six hundred miles away." Her eyes looked sad.

"We can make the hike." He waved off her concerns. "We don't want to live here. We'd depend on the goodwill of neighbors who are willing to eat each other. Our food will eventually run out and we won't take over for Everett long term and kill people."

"You're right. Uncle Luke and xTerra just seem so far." She slumped back down.

"Do you know today's exact date?"

"Today is December 22nd, 2028." She hadn't needed to look at her tally; she'd known.

They had ten days. If they were going, it should be soon. He held his breath.

"I think you're right. We should stay until early March and leave before the next collection."

"We supply this one delivery, then?" He wanted to be clear. This shouldn't only be on his conscience.

Robin nodded and sat up. "I don't want to leave yet, and everything you've said is true. Spring is a better time to travel and this would be a lonely place to live forever. Plus, with the volcanic rock out there, it's probably four hundred degrees in summer—with no shade."

Kory wouldn't be lonely without others. He had Robin and couldn't imagine better company, but this was a temporary refuge. Not a home. He hadn't had one of those in a long time, not since his mom and stepfather had died in the car accident. They hadn't been much as parents, but their loss had taken him from everything he'd known. He'd been without a home for half his life. Someday, he'd like to live somewhere permanent, but this wasn't the place—a few shabby rooms of an abandoned National Park Visitor Center. No thanks.

He and Robin talked for a while longer and agreed that on January first, Robin would stay out of sight and he'd handle the guests. His size, her gun, and the meat would be ready. He hoped everything went as planned. Counting on other people to be predictable was a gamble.

•   •   •

After dinner on Christmas Eve, Kory and Robin planned to exchange presents, and they'd wrapped them in magazine pages. Their festivities on Christmas Day would include cooking a "lavish" meal together. Robin had also assembled the ingredients to bake cookies as a Christmas treat. She said she and Shelby had made this recipe so many times they'd memorized it, though with the substitutions she had to make, they would be "Robin's Version." He got the impression that baking them made her feel connected to her sister. She never talked about Shelby, but at this time of year, Robin must miss her sister the most.

Celebrating on separate days would spread out the holiday, giving them more to differentiate their pent-up, monotonous winter days.

Robin bounced on her toes. "Open this one first." She held out a wrapped box not much longer than her hand and about as high.

Kory peeled off the tape, unfolded the glossy paper, and opened the metal box inside. She'd given him a watch. Not a cheap one either. It looked well made and once it would have been expensive.

"It still works?" He hadn't worn a watch in years and this was nicer than anything he'd ever owned, but the battery appeared to be dead.

"Put it on." She gestured, wanting him to try it immediately.

He slid it onto his wrist, fastened the metal strap, and checked the face. The second hand moved. He held it up to his ear. It ticked. Nice trick. He raised an eyebrow.

She smiled. "It doesn't use a battery and runs when you wear it. It's self-winding and is powered by kinetic energy."

He kissed her, impressed by her ingenuity. "Great idea. We can't exactly look at our phones to know the time anymore." Not that time mattered much anymore, but it was the first Christmas gift he'd received in a dozen years.

"That isn't your only present," she said, standing up before he gave her his present. There was more? "We have to go next door for the other part. I couldn't wrap it." She took his hand and tugged him toward the door, grabbing their jackets on the way. He tucked her present into his coat pocket.

She'd been in the Visitor Center again today, preparing for his surprise. He hadn't figured out her plan, though he hadn't tried for long; he hadn't wanted to ruin her fun.

Once inside, she flipped a breaker. It was warmer inside than usual and the lights turned on, so whatever the surprise was, it probably required electricity.

Robin led him to a couch and pointed. "Sit here." The couch used to be on the other side of the lobby.

Kory sat, leaning back, his arms outspread, resting across the back. "Like this?"

She grinned. "That'll do."

She trotted over to the information desk and fiddled with something under the counter. A crackled of static alerted him, then the unmistakable, melodic sounds of Pink Floyd's *Dark Side of the Moon* filled the room. He almost didn't breathe. He wanted to hear every note. She'd positioned the couch halfway between a pair of overhead speakers.

Wordlessly, he patted the couch beside him. She sat next to him, tucking her feet beside her. He adjusted, bringing her closer, and closed his eyes, letting the music wash over him. A lump formed in his throat as he soaked up the music.

Kory didn't speak for forty-three minutes, not until the last sound faded.

"You liked it." Her eyes shone.

"I loved it. Do you take requests? What else did you find?"

Robin chuckled. "It's my only CD. It belonged to my Grandpa. I brought it because he said it was the most perfect album ever made. Also, Craters of the Moon seemed the perfect place to play an album about the moon."

Kory laughed. "It's true. He also had exceptional taste. I haven't heard it in years. It's even better than I remembered." The lump in his throat remained. Feeling suddenly shy, Kory took the chosen gift CD from his pocket and handed it to her, his hands damp. He hoped it was appreciated as much as her gift of music, which blew him away.

She picked at the tape, unwrapped her gift, and hugged it to her chest, beaming from ear to ear. "Taylor Swift. We have to play this right now. How did you know this is one of my favorites?"

"I took a chance. I couldn't tell if it was a 'Taylor's Version.' Not usually my thing, but I remember you talking about her. I bet you were a Swiftie." He winked.

Her cheeks turned pink. "Maybe."

He took the CD, walked over to the information counter, and scanned behind the desk. He'd missed the small CD player, tucked into the shadows of the overhang. Taking a deep breath, he removed Dark Side from the tray and inserted it into the case before putting on the CD he'd chosen to the selected track, track three. After reading all the lyrics, he'd chosen this album and this song.

Kory cleared his throat. "Will you dance with me?"

Robin jumped up and trotted across the room as he hit *Play*.

The first line said something about Christmas lights, but he concentrated on Robin and her reaction, not the music. He tugged her into his arms, his hands on her waist like a high-school dance. Not that he'd ever gone to one. She reached up to clasp her hands around his neck, her slim body pressed against him as the slow music drifted around them. The song was about falling in love, a song called "Lover."

He shuffled his feet to the music, enjoying the feel of dancing with Robin. She rested her head on his chest as they swayed to the mellow music. He could feel her mouthing the words along with the music. When the song finished, he looked down into Robin's shining eyes. He cleared his throat again, but she spoke before he could.

"I love you." Her words resonated in the empty room and his breath caught. "And I want to be with you. Not just here, but after." Her deep blue eyes were serious and full of emotion.

Robin wanted to stay with him. His heart lurched as she continued.

"I don't care if we stay or go to South Dakota, or find somewhere between here and xTerra. You're everything I want."

"We can listen to more of this tomorrow," he said, releasing her with a smile. She remained on the dance floor while he turned off the music. Taking her hand, he tugged her toward the door to the staff quarters. Fuck safety. He wanted her.

"Where are we going?" She followed his lead.

"Our room. I'm going to make love to you unless you object." Kory raised his eyebrows. She shook her head with a breathtaking smile. "If you aren't naked in two minutes, I'll be disappointed." He ached and couldn't wait to be balls deep, and his mind went no farther than that fantasy that was about to become reality.

She laughed and flicked off the extra breaker on the way past the panel, plunging them into near darkness, the moonlight turning the snow a glowing blue outside.

"I loved your surprise," he said as they reached the door to their room. He kicked off his shoes and swept her into his arms again. Though he was hard and would love to have her flat on the bed already, he knew better. He'd played this moment out in his mind dozens of times. Despite their practice, he needed to go slow and worship every inch of her.

Her lips were warm and her hands eager as they undressed. He wanted to savor every moment, but he was shaking from anticipation after having blue balls for months. He flicked her bra open and when she let it drop to the floor, he held her upright as she wriggled out of her pants—leaving her clad in lacy pink underwear he hadn't seen before. She'd kept a few surprises under wraps.

"Sit on the edge of the bed." It would reduce his height advantage.

Robin did as he suggested, and he knelt in front of her, sliding between her legs. He kissed her, her lips warm and pliant. He cupped her small but firm breasts, warming them with his heat. Despite her petite size, he didn't feel clumsy or huge, like an oaf, around her. Their bodies fit each other as well as the rest. His hands were the perfect size for her breasts, for her ass, her hip, for cradling her head.

She moaned when he caressed the sensitive undersides of her breasts. The urge to bury himself in her remained, but he took his time.

Kory kissed and touched her everywhere, caressing her familiar body and soft skin, leaving her pretty underwear in place. His cock strained against his boxers, but he left them on. For now. He lost himself in her mouth and her touch. Eventually, they switched places and Robin took him in her mouth. They'd done this many times in the last two months and she knew what he liked, keeping him rock solid. Tonight, he stopped her twice before he came.

Moving further onto the bed, he lay beside her, kissing her until he thought he must be drunk on lust. He slipped his fingers beneath the edge of her drenched underwear. He couldn't wait much longer. Sliding them down, he slipped first one finger into her, then two almost right away, stretching her. She was so damn wet, and the eager little noises she made as she rocked her hips made him almost forget his last vestiges of control. Still, he played until she came. Watching her orgasm took the last of his patience.

He shifted his weight, keeping most of it on his elbows and knees, he checked with her one more time. "Are you sure?" He gazed into her deep blue eyes.

"Absolutely." No hesitation.

She took his breath away.

It might be best if he made her come again first; she would be more relaxed, but he wanted this almost more than he could bear. He guided his tip into her wet pussy and stopped to let her body adjust as she stretched to accommodate his size. She was so fucking tight. He clenched his jaw and slid in deeper, loving every inch he gained. She gasped and so did he. He kissed her and slid in further. He tried to go slow. This was new, and he was substantial. Still, she was made for him and took all of him.

Kory reveled in the sensation, deep within her before he moved, sliding part way out, then in. Her eyes closed as she relaxed into the sensation. Their months of playful experimentation had chased away any fear of sex. God damn. He could come now.

"I won't last long," he gasped. He gathered his strength and slid all the way out and all the way in three times, slow, careful. The motion left him on the edge.

"You won't hurt me. I'm not fragile." Her eyes were closed, but she knew what he needed. Her words shot straight into him, filling him.

"I love you." He'd never said those words before. Not to anyone. To have her love and her trust, touched him inside like nothing else. Her eyes opened, and he held her face and jaw with one hand and kissed her deeply, enough to leave them both breathless.

Only then did he thrust the way he'd wanted all along. Hard. Robin's eyes flew open again. Not hurt, but startled. She nodded, and he did it again. He was in so deep, and his control was ragged. Then, he changed his mind. The next time he slid out, he leaned in and kissed her again, teasing her lips and mouth, drawing out their pleasure. He'd been patient this long, and it had only made things better. He went slowly, lasting longer on the brink than he'd thought possible. When at last the pace quickened, she cried out and rode him, her hips tilted to meet each thrust.

Bliss came hard and fast, his climax shuddering through him, rocking him to the core. To his surprise, Robin pulsed around him and came seconds later, convulsing with him, his orgasm triggering her own. He'd had sex before, but not like this. When he pulled out, he held her while they basked in the relaxed state of after. Worth waiting for, and then some.

"Fuck, Robin," he said, cupping her jaw. "I'm so in love with you. You know that. Right?" He needed her to know this was the truth.

She nodded. "That's why this is so incredible."

He kissed her again, enjoying the softness of her full lips. "Merry Christmas."

As Kory drifted off to sleep, tangled together with Robin, he made a mental note to ask her about her cycle. They might risk getting pregnant, but perhaps they could minimize their chances. Still, he'd never noticed her having a period. She may be too thin or malnourished for it to be consistent. They might be playing with fire, but he didn't want to walk their relationship back.

Tonight had been perfect—his first perfect Christmas.

•   •   •

January first dawned clear and cold. Kory had shoveled the sidewalk in front of the Visitor Center yesterday. When he'd examined the packages of meat, each was marked with a letter and a number: J, C, and F with a 2 or a 3 beside them. This morning, deciding that the numbers meant the second and third deliveries, he packed three boxes of meat into the frigid lobby—one for each family. The boxes would be close enough to the door he could get them quickly if someone arrived, but without heat, the meat wouldn't defrost.

He kept his ears cocked, listening for snowmobiles. He didn't have to wait long. When the first whining sound of an engine reached his ears, it was only ten a.m. He wore the gun holstered in plain view on his belt and his knife in its sheath, since he didn't want guests to think he would be an easy mark. A balance. His goal was to appear tough, but not an immediate threat.

Two snowmobiles arrived together, both dragging sleds. They stopped thirty yards from the shoveled area and cut their engines.

Kory took a breath and stepped outside the Center. Best he took the initiative instead of waiting for them to pound on the door. Their goggle-covered faces turned to him as they stepped forward.

"Where's Everett?" said one man, turning from his snowmobile to look in both directions, as if the ranger might still appear. He shoved his goggles onto his head, as did the other man.

"He isn't here anymore," said Kory. "He didn't make it."

The second man twitched toward his rifle, held in a scabbard alongside his snowmobile. "What happened to him?"

Kory's hand dropped to his holster, and he hardened his voice. "I wouldn't do that." The man retracted his arm. "Let's keep things civil. Everett is gone, and the calendar says that y'all would arrive for a collection. Identify yourselves."

"You're making the drop?" said the first man.

"That's the intention," Kory said. "Assuming you're the proper people."

"I'm Glenn Foisy, that's Cooper. I'm guessing you also expect either Alan, Kent, or Aidan Jones."

Kory nodded. "Where's the payment?"

"Coop, unhook the gas can," said Foisy. "Show us the meat."

"Wait here." Kory went inside, took another deep breath, and grabbed the box on the left with meat labeled C2. Hefting it, he carried it outside and set it on the frozen ground halfway between the Visitor Center and the men with snowmobiles.

"There's another box." He backed away, watching them until he reached the walkway. There he turned, went inside, and returned with the second box. In the distance, a third snowmobile approached from the south. Shit.

He would have preferred the pickups to be staggered. What if they banded together to take him down, thinking he was alone? Or cheated him of the fuel. He hurried with the second box. While he'd been inside, the men had switched the jerry can for the first box of meat. Cooper strapped it to his sled. "See you in March," he said, starting his snowmobile. He left, nodding to the new arrival on the way past.

Foisy loaded the second box as the third man turned off his machine.

"You're not Everett," said the third man, his eyes narrowed.

"Nope. I'm Kory. Everett is gone. I've taken over here."

The third man flicked a glance at the departing Cooper and Foisy, who waved. "I see they got what they came for."

"Wait here," said Kory. "I've got a third box inside. What have you brought?"

Unlike the other snowmobiles, Mr. Jones had brought a wooden crate strapped to his trailing sled.

"Same as usual. Canned fruit and a few things from last summer's garden." His words seemed normal, but his expression was unfriendly. Downright surly. His eyes flicked toward the Visitor Center. Was he already rethinking the deal?

The third box was the largest. Kory nodded and went inside to retrieve the heavy box. His mouth watered at the idea of fresh food. He returned outside.

The third man said, "I remember you. You and someone else came through just after the first snow. My boys chased you that night but lost you. Looks like we drove you here and Everett tried something. Didn't he?"

Kory's heart stopped. "He tried to kill my girlfriend. He didn't survive the attempt."

"What did you do with the body?" said Mr. Jones, his eyes remaining flat.

"He isn't in the packages, if that's what you're asking," said Kory. They'd propped Everett's body up in a corner of an outbuilding. Frozen solid.

"So, you aren't stupid," said the man in the snow. "Should we expect you to be here in the spring? This is a lucrative place to set up. Or it could be." His eyes weighed Kory, scanning him from head to toe, lingering on the gun.

"We'll see," said Kory. "The March 15th drop is ready." He got the impression that the other man might like the operation for himself, though it could be paranoia or his imagination at work. Oh, shit. Kory could kick himself for sharing that tidbit. Still, he schooled his face to remain impassive. He and Robin would have to be on guard.

There were at least four men in the Jones family, the men they'd encountered their second last afternoon on the road. If the families worked together, he and Robin would be in trouble. They should hike a perimeter on non-blizzard days to be sure they remained on their own. Plus, they could use the exercise and practice on the snowshoes.

Kory lugged the third box to the flat place in the snow where he'd deposited the others and hefted the other man's box in trade. Jars clinked together inside. "We'll see you in March." Kory's back twitched when he carried the crate toward the Center without looking back. They would leave early. Jones made him uneasy.

Minutes later, the third snowmobile left, following the track made by the others as they departed Craters of the Moon. If there was a problem, the Joneses would spearhead it. Kory hoped they'd wait until spring, when he and Robin would be long gone.

Chapter 15: Robin

Robin glanced out the kitchen window on the last day of February. The icicles on the eaves dripped steadily, hanging down almost far enough to obscure her view. While she watched, a section broke and crashed to the ground, clearing her line of sight. All afternoon chunks had been falling outside. Spring might not be far away. Hard to believe she and Kory had been here almost all winter—over four months. They'd woken this morning to a warm chinook wind and the thaw.

A thick chain of clouds remained in the east, while the west was clear.

The cold would probably hit again soon—winter probably wouldn't be over this early into the new year, but it might be time to pack. They wanted to be ready to leave without notice if the weather changed for more than a couple of days. One of the few things to count on in this post-asteroid world was extreme and unpredictable weather.

Robin broke from her reverie at the sound of Kory stomping his boots at the end of the hall before joining her in the warm kitchen, his cheeks red from being outside in the fresh air.

"I relocated Everett," he said, scrubbing at his hands with soap under the intense pressure of the sink's running water. "I hauled his body toward the hills and buried him close to a clump of trees. Digging was almost impossible because the ground is like iron, thaw or not, so

I stopped. He's got a shallow grave. The ground is still frozen for at least two feet down, so scavenging coyotes or something might find him."

"At least the Joneses can't eat him." A wave of nausea rose and dissipated in seconds. All day, she'd imagined the faint smell of decomposition from when she'd helped load Everett's body for transport. At least the corpse was finally gone.

"It was practically balmy out there most of today, but the temperature was dropping like a stone as I put the snowmobile away. Back to cold tomorrow." He kissed her and nuzzled his cold nose on her neck. She squeaked but didn't move. "You smell good." He looked down with a mischievous smile.

"Anything else interesting out there?" She handed him a mug of hot chocolate and threw in a handful of shriveled marshmallows.

He winked as he stirred the marshmallows, fished them out with a spoon, and scooped them into his mouth. "A fresh set of tracks. Somebody's come as far as the last knoll behind us, at least twice since the last dump of snow four days ago. Looks like they stayed a while because they flattened the snow. Our visitor left on foot, back to their snowmobile. Farther away, the snowmobile tracks turn southwest. Probably Jones and company, monitoring us." His words were at odds with his playful tone.

"Maybe they want to make sure they can get their supplies in a few weeks." Robin felt sick again, her stomach churning.

"Maybe they're wondering if they need to wait." His eyes met hers over the rim of his mug. Their twinkle had faded.

"There haven't been any more tracks close by." Her brow furrowed.

Three days ago, they'd found a black glove with red stripes dropped in the snow—near the snowmobile shed. Last week someone had come as far as the front sidewalk and tried the exterior doors of the Visitor Center. The intruders had also poked around near the locked sheds. She hadn't been outside alone since, and until today, neither had Kory.

"If we're taking the snowmobile, we should leave at first light. I doubt they're camping out there to watch us. They go home for the night."

"Is there still enough snow for us to travel that way?" She looked back out the window and at the piles of fallen ice.

"We're going to get another heap of snow tomorrow, I think." He took a long swig of his drink.

"I was thinking I'd pack tonight. Just in case." She didn't like the idea that they were being watched. The creeps.

"Can't hurt." Kory wasn't one for false reassurance. He was worried—with good reason.

•   •   •

Hours later, Robin awoke with a start, her heart racing—the bed beside her empty. Kory was up and dressed, sliding on his boots. She threw back the covers to get ready, too.

"What's going on?" Her voice trembled. "Are we leaving?"

"Voices outside. Under the window." Kory whispered. "I'm going outside. I'll slip out the back. Can you let me out? Then I don't need keys. Safer that way." He strapped on the gun in its holster and tugged his jacket down over his knife. A fluttery feeling appeared in her gut. She hoped he wouldn't have to use either of his weapons. Still, better he wore them with the threat posed by the Joneses.

Would she be in a kill-or-be-killed situation again? Hopefully not. She hadn't done well last time. At least, she was stronger now with all the pushups Kory had overseen.

She threw on pants and a sweater, and jammed her bare feet into her shoes. They crept down the hall in single file. At the back door, she put her hand on his solid arm. "Please be careful."

"I just want a look around. If I can listen to their plans or see who it is, I will."

Her chest tightened. What he was doing was dangerous.

He kissed her. "I'll say your name to get in. They know mine, but not yours."

Robin nodded. He cracked the door open and slipped into the freezing night. She relocked the door with a faint click and carried a chair over from the kitchen. Sitting in the dim hall, with only pale moonlight shining in from the kitchen window, she didn't turn on a light, concerned that she would alert anyone outside that they might be awake. She didn't dare leave, afraid she'd miss Kory's return. Sitting there, she strained to hear anything from outside that might let her know he was all right.

After a while, she shivered and dashed back to their room for socks and her jacket. The night stretched toward dawn as time crawled. She yawned and her head nodded, drifting toward her chest. With a jerk, she got up and paced to stay awake, not going farther than the kitchen, always listening for Kory's voice. If she had a clock nearby, she would have been watching it for too long. Her wait seemed interminable; it must have been hours. Standing off to the side, she peeked out the kitchen window at the sky. He'd been gone long enough that it was changing color. Sunrise was closer each time she checked.

First, a faded jean color replaced the blackness of the sky, then a stripe of dull yellow became brilliant swaths of orange layers filling the eastern sky. With a clear sky, it must be well below zero this morning. Soon it would be daylight and Kory still hadn't returned. It was hard to stay put inside while he was out there. She put on the kettle, keeping away from the frost-coated kitchen window before returning to her post. He'd be cold when he returned.

What was taking so long? Had they caught him? Robin took a deep breath. She had no proof that anything had happened. He was smart. Perhaps he couldn't get back to the door without being seen and had hidden.

The tight feeling in her chest remained.

It was full daylight and two cups of tea later when at last Kory's voice came from outside the back door.

"Robin. It's me." He must have waited to be confident he was alone.

Her hands shook as she unlocked the deadbolt and threw open the door. Despite her efforts to remain calm and patient, she'd imagined horrible things that might have happened at the hands of the neighbors. He stepped through and she launched into his arms as soon as he locked the door. His face was rosy from the cold, but he seemed otherwise unharmed.

"You're okay." She searched his face for signs of distress.

"Tired and cold, but safe." His teeth chattered as he spoke.

"You must be freezing." She returned to the kitchen while he peeled off his coat and boots. She poured him tea and whipped up pancakes for breakfast while he related what had happened since he'd gone outside.

"I circled around and stayed hidden by the corner of the building, listening to the men. There were six of them." When she handed him his steaming drink, he wrapped his red hands around the mug before drinking. He sighed.

"They didn't see or hear you?" Robin spooned batter into the hot frying pan.

"No, but I didn't dare leave in case they did." No wonder he was cold. Standing still so long in the sub-zero night.

"Jones has got the others set on taking this place before the fifteenth. He and his oldest son have been taking turns watching us." He didn't seem surprised—that had been their guess.

"Are they coming back today?" She looked up from the frying pan.

Kory shook his head. "In three days. Jones is leading. He mentioned setting up his old man here to replace Everett. They agreed the ranger had been so successful because he was old and unassuming. He gave people a false sense of security, thinking he was just a harmless old man." He shrugged. "Like we did."

"I say we go to sleep early. Leave at daybreak." She flipped her pancakes, the sweet smell filling the room.

"Agreed. Twenty-four hours from now." Kory got up and grabbed cutlery, setting it on the table while she finished cooking.

Robin's chest tightened. She didn't want to leave so soon, but it was necessary. They couldn't risk being outnumbered and overrun. Bile rose in her throat. She wouldn't be their dinner. Neither she nor Kory talked as they ate the pancakes, washed up, and took stock of their supplies. She would miss hot water and electricity the most, but she'd proven she could live without.

The day flew as they prepared, packing as much food as they could from the pantry in addition to the travel rations they'd saved from Boise. They'd eaten all the potatoes, so they replaced their bulk with lighter containers and bags of pasta. They should have enough food for their trip. She also packed a jar of sugar as a luxury item. To have a little for a treat seemed like wealth.

Her other items of value remained in her pack—almost forgotten. She showed Kory. Sewn into a hidden pocket that looked like a seam, she'd stashed several gold rings with diamonds from the mall in Boise. She would need to rip out the stitches to get at them, but they'd be there if she needed them. Maybe once they reached South Dakota, they could use them to purchase supplies or membership in the community. Her grandfather had called it her insurance policy.

Robin and Kory woke before dawn in the coldest stretch of early morning and prepared by dim candlelight, in case the Visitor Center was already being watched. Her stomach rebelled at being up so early, but she muscled down some oatmeal; she would need the energy. After they'd eaten, she filled a thermos with hot tea, then collected their full canteens. Feeling as ready as they could, they dressed in their warmest clothes, grabbed their packs, and headed out the back door.

Kory locked it. "No sense making it obvious that we've left or make it easy for them to get inside." He kept his voice low as they stole into the crunchy snow.

Every step made her wince, and her stomach remained unsettled. Maybe breakfast had been a bad idea.

A blanket of cloud cover in the still dark sky hid the stars and the light of the crescent moon was pale but lit the snow. The snowmobile shed had boot prints around it from yesterday, but there didn't appear to be fresh ones. Hair raised on the back of her neck. There were new scratches near the lock where someone had tried to break in.

"They'll probably bring a crowbar next time," said Kory, as he unlocked the door. They stepped inside and strapped their packs to the trailer. He'd topped up the tank last night with the gas from the January payment. He'd also packed a small tool kit and the snowshoes besides their personal gear. There was nothing else to do. They were ready.

The snowmobile engine stuttered as it started, but caught on the third try.

Kory drove the sled outside. Robin relocked the door and hopped aboard, resting her gloved hands on Kory's sides, reminding her of their motorcycle ride last fall. That felt like a million years ago, when they'd been strangers. They took off, headed for the road, which ran almost due east, toward Idaho Falls.

They took a risk leaving via the snow-covered highway, but it was the most direct route, and following it would keep them from getting lost. They'd discussed traveling cross-country but decided against it in unfamiliar territory with unknown hazards.

Robin glanced over her shoulder and swallowed. They left a trail that would be easy to follow. They just had to travel farther today than it would be worth chasing them. That might be ten miles. It might be twenty or fifty. There was no way to know when the others would give up. Maybe the neighbors would be happy to take the Visitor Center without force. She didn't think that would be the case because she and Kory would also be wanted for their meat. She gagged and shoved the thought away. All that mattered was they were away.

They rode for about forty-five minutes before the snowmobile coughed and sputtered to a stop. Ahead, the sun rose in bands of orange and pink, while the surrounding silence seemed ominous.

"What's wrong? We shouldn't be out of gas yet." She shoved her gloved hands into her armpits while she jumped up and down to restore circulation to her cold feet.

"My guess is that the gas they gave us is shit and degraded faster than it should have. This thing is done. Let's strap on the snowshoes and get the hell out of here. We can't waste all morning trying to figure it out. When they show up to watch the Visitor Center, they'll see our trail. We might have a few hours' head start." He squinted up at the sky. "Snow is coming. That'll help. We probably rode half the distance we need. Let's go."

Chapter 16: Kory

Kory had downplayed the danger to Robin yesterday. He didn't need to amp up her fear. The men outside had watched them for weeks and knew more about their routine than made him comfortable. The group he'd listened to had also been determined to get both of them for their meat, considering them straightforward marks if ambushed. These men were hungry and had families to feed, which lent them stealth and cunning, even if this was the first time they would do their own killing. No way in hell would Kory make it easy.

He and Robin left the snowmobile behind as the snow fell. Small flakes carried on a brisk wind. It was the coldest it had been in days, but he worked up a healthy sweat as they traveled. The snowshoes kept them from breaking through the deep snow at every step, and he was thankful they'd practiced and could move at a fast clip. Still, it was at least another forty-five miles to Idaho Falls. They wouldn't make it today. It would be two long, grueling days on foot. He looked around. The weather reminded him of their first night on the road. In the four months since, he and Robin had become a solid team.

They would have to camp out overnight. He'd hoped to get twice as far by snowmobile, but there was no sense in being upset. It's just how it was. With luck, the Joneses would give up before discovering he and Robin were on foot after about seventy miles. No sign of them so far, but he doubted that luck would last.

Kory planned for the week ahead, as much to keep his mind occupied as for a genuine need. He and Robin would come into town from the west. There were several neighborhoods in that direction that might stretch far enough up the smaller highway to provide shelter. Not tonight, but tomorrow. With the temperature so far below freezing, that was a concern, even in town, because he wouldn't dare have a fire. They needed to stay hidden.

There was no point in dwelling on what they couldn't have. There probably wouldn't be much firewood after the Wings had wintered there last year, plus there was the security factor. He hadn't assessed who else might be around Idaho Falls, so it was best to lie low. Robin agreed.

Kory continued to run through his adjusted plan as they hiked, their breath loud in the barren landscape. Tonight, they needed somewhere they could heat water for food on their burner, and he would set up his tarp tent to make somewhere warm enough to sleep. It would be cozier than the last time they'd slept in his makeshift shelter on their second night on the road.

He glanced at Robin. She was light on her snowshoes and seldom broke through the top crust, maintaining a quick pace. He gave her a smile of reassurance.

His thoughts continued to whirl as they traveled. The falling snow limited their visibility. Still, it proved a screen for their pursuers. Either way, it left him on edge. Since they'd left the snowmobile so early, he wished for the snow to fall faster to cover their tracks. That was an advantage they needed. He cracked his knuckles. With gloves on, it was unsatisfying.

He scowled. At least three of the men behind them owned rifles. If it was the Jones brothers, they could each have one. Among the Jones, Foisy, and Cooper families, they had several hunters. He and Robin had only the handgun. In a pinch, he'd have time for a couple of shots, but they'd have to be at close range.

Kory glanced back. He'd seen no one on their trail, but once he caught the whining sound of an engine in the distance. Hopefully, it was still far behind, a trick of the wind, or their pursuers were crisscrossing paths out there, hoping to find them. At some point, the pursuit would require too much fuel and no longer be worth the trip. He hoped they'd passed that point already—or would soon. Still, he wouldn't rest until he and Robin were in town, with shelter and hidden. It would be a long couple of days and a longer night.

They ate lunch on the move. The land around remained desolate and windswept, with few hills or landmarks discernable in the snowy expanse. He was glad they'd stuck to the road. It would be easy to become turned around in the sameness of the winter landscape.

They kept going, following the tops of the roadside markers that resumed after they'd left Craters of the Moon. Several times, he grew fatigued and considered taking a break, but the temperature continued to drop and nipped at his exposed skin. Robin readjusted her scarf to cover most of her face, and he followed her example. The only way to keep warm was to keep moving.

It was nearing sundown when another whining sound reached him. This one accompanied a hint of vibration in the ground beneath his feet. He checked on Robin. Her deep blue eyes looked enormous as she met his gaze.

She nodded. "I hear it too. It's probably them."

They put on a burst of speed. He glanced over his shoulder. He couldn't see far enough back to gauge the distance or how much time they had before they were caught. With the sound growing louder but remaining invisible, their pursuers might be running without lights. With thick snow falling, the snowmobile would be almost upon them before he would see it.

"Over there." Robin pointed to the right.

Off the road, straight across what was probably a field, was a pale-yellow square of light—maybe two hundred yards away. It shone steady, a beacon through the whiteness of the flurry.

A light meant people, which was a risk, but strangers were better than the probability that the snowmobile was carrying the cannibals on their trail. They would have to chance the unknown.

"I'll try not to look threatening," he said, scrambling down the bank, trying not to wipe out as they left the road. He made a beeline for the light and Robin followed, stumbling in her exhaustion.

The snow was deep enough that they didn't need to go through the barbed wire fence; Kory lifted Robin, pack, snowshoes, and all over the top two strands above the snow. He stepped over and they continued. The snow here was deeper, softer, perhaps drifting down from the road, but they kept moving, even if sometimes they broke through and floundered.

The rumble of the snowmobile grew closer. Kory's heart rate increased.

The light ahead came from a house window. Though tempted to hide outside and wait for the snowmobiler to leave, that might not be the best option. He was still trying to decide how to proceed when they reached a picket fence sticking out of the snow. A shoveled path beyond led to the front porch of a two-story southern style home and to the weathered barn behind the house.

The fence surrounded both buildings and a woodshed—one half-filled with chunks of split wood. The air smelled of smoke and roasting meat. Kory's stomach gurgled. He hadn't eaten real meat since he'd left the Wings, just jerky and unidentifiable dehydrated chunks of chewy protein, which did nothing to satisfy his cravings. These people had better not be cannibals, too.

The metal latch clinked as soon as Kory touched it, and a dog barked inside the house. His muscles tensed. No way to be stealthy now. He stared back at the road. Silhouetted against the snow, the outline of two men standing beside a snowmobile. Too damn close. They were probably watching through binoculars or a rifle scope.

Kory's muscles twitched. He couldn't make out faces at this distance, but he'd bet at least one man was a Jones. He tugged Robin aside, out of sight of the road. The corner of the house blocked them from the men and the snowmobile. The engine sound remained.

"Go on," he said to Robin, holding open the gate. She pushed through and he squeezed her shoulder before letting go. They took another couple of awkward steps on the cleared walkway, their snowshoes clacking on the flat stones beneath less than an inch of snow. Someone must have cleared it in the last half hour.

The front door opened, and light spilled out from inside. A burly old man with white hair, dressed in a navy sweater, overalls, and work boots stepped out onto the porch carrying a rifle. He closed the door behind him. From inside, the dog barked again.

"We haven't had company in quite some time. Seems a helluva bad day to travel." His voice was friendly, but his expression remained wary.

The man pointed his gun at Kory's chest.

Kory froze.

"We spent the winter at the Visitor Center out at Craters of the Moon," said Robin. "It must have seemed too cozy because the neighbors wanted it and ran us off."

He was grateful to let her take the lead this time.

"Looks like they want you back," said the man, nodding toward the snowmobile still stopped on the road. "Y'all take something they want?"

From the man's tone, he didn't seem in cahoots with their pursuers.

"There's a reason you don't get travelers from the west," said Kory, deciding to tell the truth, hoping this man wasn't in league with the others. "The previous tenant at the Visitor Center sold human meat to the neighbors. He's been killing travelers for two or three years. We didn't want to fall into their hands."

"Cannibals?" the man said with a grimace. "Folks would have to be pretty desperate to resort to that. Don't worry about us. We raise pigs, so we've got enough to eat." He cocked his head. "If you'd headed for the barn first, where I keep my animals, we might be having a different conversation. You'd be talking to the business end of my rifle." He stared at them when they didn't respond, probably debating what to do. The rifle swung to the right.

Kory let out the breath he'd been holding. He believed the man's words that he wasn't working with the Joneses.

"I'm Robin. This is my boyfriend, Kory. We're originally from Portland. I spent the first couple of years after the asteroid at my grandfather's ranch. If you want to put us to work, we can do chores. We're just looking for shelter overnight."

"We'll move on in the morning," added Kory, glancing toward the road, which was still blocked from sight.

"It feels like another of those freeze snaps coming on," said the rancher. "You won't make it outside for a couple of days. You'll freeze solid as rocks."

They waited for another heartbeat. Robin was shivering.

The man nodded as he seemed to reach a decision. "I'm Jeb Croft. Come in. Take a load off. My Martha made a pork roast and vegetables. We can share." He half-turned toward the door and stopped before they moved toward the house. "You take anything, touch her, or the dog, I'll shoot you dead." His matter-of-fact tone was more menacing than any loud threat. He meant every word.

"We're grateful for the food and shelter. We'll be on our best behavior." Kory unclipped his boots from the snowshoes and Robin did the same. He stepped backward and took a last glance at the road. He exhaled. The men were leaving. The snowmobile turned around, flicked on its headlight, and headed back the way it had come, the sound soon fading into the storm.

The man's warning was meant to be taken seriously, and Kory hoped they'd left the cannibals behind. Still, if anything inside gave him bad vibes, freezing cold or not, he and Robin would take their chances outside.

Inside was warm enough that Kory's cold face almost burned as it tingled in the heat.

"Leave your gear here," said Jeb, pointing to a long mat in the hallway. "I won't touch anything."

Kory leaned their snowshoes against the wall. He took his pack off and looped the straps through his arms. He'd prefer to keep it in his sight.

"Is it just you and your wife here?" said Robin as she checked out the photos on the wall. Framed pictures of two boys at various ages and stages hung in the hall, including two graduation photos with caps and gowns and at least one wedding photo.

Jeb turned. "Our boys are grown and live back East. We got a packet of letters from them last spring, delivered by a traveler. As far as we know, they're alive and well."

"That must be a relief," said Robin. Someone at xTerra might know a way to send a letter back to Portland, even if it wasn't the old postal service.

When they got there, Kory would remind her to try. She worried about her mom.

Jeb nodded. "Martha," he called into the kitchen. "We've got guests for a night or two. Come meet them."

Martha came to the doorway between the hall and the kitchen, pushing aside a heavy blanket dividing the two sections of the house. It would make an excellent heat barrier. She had snow white hair in a bob, a round face, and a pleasant smile that further eased Kory's tense shoulders. She seemed genuine and exuded a feeling of warmth.

"I'm Martha. It's so nice to have someone new to talk to. Jeb and I have been rattling around here on our own for some time." Her eyes sparkled with mirth as she shot an affectionate look at her husband.

"I'm Robin and this is Kory." Robin rested her hand on his arm and spoke with a soft voice and a partial smile.

Kory let her do the talking, since she seemed comfortable enough. She said she wasn't great with strangers but must be getting good vibes from the old couple. He used the toe of the opposite feet to scrape off his boots and placed them on the mat. He hung their jackets on a hook and shed his other winter gear while Robin did the same.

"If you don't mind, I'd like to keep our packs," said Kory, picking it up once more.

"As long as you put your knife and gun away, that works," said Jeb with a nod.

Kory unfastened both weapons from his belt and slipped them into the top of his backpack. He'd been wearing weapons long enough that going without in an unknown space with strangers, he felt naked.

"Can I get you two hot drinks?" said Martha. "You look like you're freezing."

"Thank you. That would be much appreciated." Kory rested his hand on Robin's lower back. He wanted it clear that they were together. He met Jeb's eyes and the older man winked.

"Martha, your pork roast brought them in from the road. Sounds like they've had a long day of traveling. I thought they could stay in Mark's old room overnight. If we get one of those deep freezes tonight, they might stay a couple of days."

"We won't be a bother," said Robin. "Please let me know if I can help with dinner or anything else."

"Maybe tomorrow, dear," said Martha. "You go with Jeb, pull out the table, and he can add a couple of plates. I'll get your room set up with bedding." She grabbed a lamp and headed up the stairs. "Hot drinks first and dinner will be in a few minutes."

Kory grabbed his pack, and Robin's, and they followed Jeb into the kitchen. Kory set their stuff on the floor where he could watch it. The air here was considerably warmer than in the hall, and the delicious scent of the food was stronger. His mouth watered in anticipation. The dog didn't make a sound but followed his movement with its intelligent eyes. Kory ignored the animal, trusting Jeb enough to stop anything unexpected from the dog.

The Crofts' kitchen window was the one they'd seen from the road. An ordinary range must have been replaced with an old-fashioned wood stove with a cast-iron top, a warming oven, and chrome legs. The stove with a kettle on top stood at one end of the toasty kitchen. Several kerosene lamps lit the room, making it almost as bright as electricity from the overhead lights. Jeb pulled a rectangular table out from the wall and Kory moved the chairs. Jeb retrieved two extra plates from the cupboard and collected a handful of cutlery, which he passed to Robin to set.

Martha returned and bustled around the kitchen, waving everyone to the seats at the table. "You all sit. I just need to finish up." She made two hot teas, which she delivered to the table. Across the kitchen, she opened the oven and removed the roasting pan. Kory couldn't take his eyes off it as the meat's aroma wafted through the room, richer than ever as she made gravy.

Kory almost couldn't wait for dinner. The smell alone had brought his hunger to the forefront. Potatoes and carrots had roasted in the pan with a hefty haunch of crispy pork. He closed his eyes and inhaled the scent. He took Robin's hand and squeezed it as they sat.

Jeb sharpened a carving knife and sliced even pieces of meat, setting them on a blue and white platter while Martha dumped the vegetables into a matching bowl and poured her gravy into a gravy boat.

Taking a pot from the stovetop, she drained the water with a lid into the sink and dumped bright green beans into another bowl. They must have been able to grow a garden last summer too. He was dying to eat the succulent food.

Kory tried not to inhale his food, but he ate steadily, savoring every bite of the delicious dinner. Robin's lips twitched, probably amused by his obvious enjoyment. Martha chattered about her boys, Mark and Richard, and the grandchildren back East, filling the table with laughter and conversation.

He and Robin contributed little while Jeb told stories about his neighbors and why they'd stayed instead of evacuating. Thoughts of extreme weather and the danger of their pursuers faded in its urgency, with terrific food and pleasant company.

Hands down, it was his best meal since the asteroid. Hell, the best meal he could remember eating.

When he finished everything he'd taken, he leaned back. Martha spooned another portion of everything onto his plate with a smile. "I like a man who appreciates my cooking." She shot Jeb a look.

"Don't look at me. I've enjoyed your cooking for forty years." Jeb pretended to be annoyed, but his mouth twitched.

Robin ate more slowly than Kory had, but also finished everything she'd dished up. She covered her mouth as she yawned, then rearranged the cutlery on her plate, laying it down to show that she was done. She looked up to find all eyes watching her.

"Pardon me. I'm so tired. We woke up early and snowshoeing all day was quite the workout." Dark shadows ringed her eyes.

Kory wished he'd noticed sooner that she was so tired. He'd assumed she could keep up, and she had.

When the meal was finished, Robin jumped to her feet to help clean up, but Kory took her plate from her hands. She looked up in surprise and he kissed her temple. "You're exhausted. You sit. I'll help."

Under Martha's guidance, Kory cleared the table and stacked the dishes on the counter. She ran cold water into the sink, adding soap and scalding hot water from the canner on the stovetop so Kory could wash the dishes. He set them in a rack to dry as he finished and wiped down the counter.

At the table, Jeb watched with what looked like an approving smile. "I'll put those away in the morning. I know where everything goes."

Kory and Martha rejoined them at the table.

"Where are you folks headed?" Jeb asked.

Kory looked at Robin and raised his eyebrow.

"Have you heard of Vita xTerra?" Robin's voice sounded tired without her usual enthusiasm.

"That's the bunker city in South Dakota, right?" said Jeb. "I've heard rumors. They supposedly have guards, walls, and electricity. It's supposed to be amazing."

She nodded. "It's real. My uncle and his family stopped at my grandfather's farm right after the asteroid hit. They own a bunker and were on their way to South Dakota. My grandfather sent them ahead because he was waiting for me to arrive. We had trouble with the military evacuation and gangs. We couldn't ever catch up."

"What happened to your grandfather?" Jeb's eyes looked sympathetic.

"He got lung cancer this spring and passed away in the fall, just before the snow hit. Kory and I left Boise, but the storms socked us in at Craters of the Moon. We're headed for South Dakota again, and this time we're going to make it." Her voice held a ring of determination.

Kory smiled. There was his Robin.

"You stopped there for most of the winter," said Jeb. "But you don't look like you're starving. The Visitor Center must have been okay."

"The staff quarters had power, water, and tins of dehydrated food," Robin said. "Nothing like dinner tonight." She turned to Martha. "I haven't had food like that in years. Everything was amazing. Thank you again."

Martha waved off Robin's thanks, but the older lady's smile said she was pleased with the compliment.

"Seems like a plum place like that would be occupied already." Jeb's eyes narrowed as he looked between them.

"It was," said Kory. "A man claiming to be a ranger invited us in, purposely gave us spoiled food, and tried to kill us in our sleep. He didn't survive."

Jeb cut in, his eyes flicking to Martha. Perhaps he didn't want to scare his wife with talk of cannibals on their doorstep. "Sounds like a good place to live, which is why the neighbors eventually chased you out." He hesitated. "We'll keep an eye out for them here. They must have a way to get gas since they were traveling by snowmobile. How many men have you seen?"

Jeb wanted to know what kind of threat was out there. "There's at least six men and three snowmobiles among three families. My guess is they have twice that number of people. They live between Carey and the Visitor Center." The closest must be at least seventy miles away.

Far enough on foot, not far enough if they had vehicles. The Crofts would need to be careful.

"I appreciate the warning," said Jeb. "We've got a few neighbors out this way, too. I'll have a conversation with them and alert them when the weather improves."

Kory nodded. The cannibals might have their own trouble in the spring. He looked at Robin, who'd been quieter than usual tonight. Her eyes drifted closed. As he watched, her head nodded lower, and she jerked upright, forcing her eyes wide open. She was falling asleep at the table.

"That was the best meal I've had in years, ma'am," Kory said to Martha. "We don't mean to be rude, but my girl is just about asleep already. If it isn't too much trouble, can we get settled for the night?"

"Robin looks wiped. That must have been some trek today," said Martha. "We aren't offended at all." Her calm manner and pleasant smiles made Kory believe she told the truth.

"Since it's going to be a cold one, might I borrow you tomorrow to do barn chores with me? Speed up the process," said Jeb. "Not early."

"Of course," said Kory. Robin had fallen asleep again. "Sweetheart," he said, resting a hand on her shoulder.

"Hmmm?" Her eyes fluttered open.

"Time for bed."

She stumbled to her feet and he collected their packs.

Jeb grabbed one lamp and lit a candle, passing it to Kory. "I'll show you to your room."

The temperature in the rest of the house seemed cool after the warmth of the kitchen, but it wasn't cold like outside. With his hands full, Kory couldn't help Robin on the stairs, but now that she was awake, she seemed fine—though they'd probably both have sore muscles tomorrow.

Jeb opened the first door upstairs on the right. "Bathroom. The toilet flushes and you can run water, but just cold. Looks like Martha already laid out some towels for you. We sleep downstairs behind the kitchen and have our own facilities. Sleep as late as you like. The stock will be fine on their own until late morning."

"Thank you." Jeb and Martha had done a lot for a couple of strangers, and Kory was grateful for their generosity.

Jeb opened the door on the left. "This room's over the kitchen and should be the warmest."

Inside was a queen-sized bed. Clean sheets, two thick blankets, and a quilt were folded at the end of the bed. The blinds were down, covering the window. The cinder block chimney rose in the corner, giving off heat.

"You two settled?" said Jeb from the doorway to the hall.

Kory nodded.

"This is fantastic," said Robin. "Thank you. For everything." To Kory's surprise, she stepped forward and kissed the old man on the cheek.

Jeb smiled. "One more thing," he said, turning to leave. "My dog sleeps in the kitchen. Wait until you hear me up and about in the morning. You wouldn't want to startle him."

The German Shepherd dog had sat alert on his bed in the kitchen throughout dinner. His eyes had stayed on Kory and Robin. He'd seemed obedient but hadn't been friendly. The dog had every right to be protective and territorial these days.

"Got it." Kory nodded. No nighttime wandering.

He and Robin made the bed and got ready for sleep, using cold tap water to brush their teeth and wash up. He locked the bedroom door before undressing and strung up his wire. Probably unnecessary, but it was the first night in a new place. When he slid between the cool sheets, he blew out the candle and hugged Robin's naked body to his, having learned from experience that body heat was the best way to stay warm. She relaxed in his arms and fell asleep almost immediately.

Jeb and Martha seemed solid, pleasant, and trustworthy, but Kory planned to sleep with one ear open. He'd been fooled before. He soon followed Robin into slumber.

CHAPTER 17: ROBIN

After a mid-morning breakfast on the fifth day with the Crofts, Kory and Jeb stomped into their boots, and once bundled up, headed out to the barn. The cold snap had lasted longer than usual, but if the pattern was the same as the first few days, the men would be gone for a couple of hours. Not only were there pigs to feed, but a flock of chickens, at least two cats, and half a dozen long-haired goats to tend.

Robin cleared the plates and ran cold water into the sink to counteract the boiling water on the stove so she wouldn't burn her hands washing dishes.

"If you were staying longer," said Martha, interrupting Robin's thoughts about the ratio of hot water to cold, "I'd teach you to spin and weave. I've been saving the goat hair and have an enormous bag. I've been working on it all winter. An extra set of hands would be appreciated."

"That sounds like a handy skill," said Robin as she poured scalding hot water into the sink, leaning back to avoid the steam. Setting the pot back on the stove, she tested the water, added a squirt of soap, and swished the water to create suds.

"Maybe we should start with crocheting today," said Martha. "So you can make the baby a few things. I've got lots of leftover yarn upstairs I can share. Plus patterns and a hook or two to spare."

Robin's cheeks burned and two tears escaped, trickling down her flaming cheeks as she focused on the dishes in the water instead of looking at Martha. Martha had figured out her secret. It wasn't even a secret yet, just a suspicion.

"What gave me away?" Robin's voice shook. If it was becoming obvious already, she needed to tell Kory sooner rather than later. A lump formed in her throat. She would have talked to him already, but she hadn't been certain. To have someone guess made it real.

"I've been pregnant myself." Martha took a clean dish from Robin's hand to dry. "Your expression when I dished up the eggs this morning was the key. It was all you could do not to run and throw up. Right?" Her voice was gentle.

Robin nodded. It had been close. The smell had been nauseating. She'd stuck to bacon and oven-toasted bread with homemade strawberry jam. Even now, the idea of eggs made her stomach churn.

"Are you afraid Kory will get over-protective once he knows?" Martha smiled. "He seems the type, since he worships the ground you walk on."

Robin nodded, her cheeks still flaming. She didn't trust her voice not to break, or more tears to erupt. She took a breath. "We'd considered the possibility of pregnancy. We aren't dumb, but a baby would have been more convenient once we were closer to xTerra."

"Babies don't care about convenience. You will just need to travel this spring and early summer, before walking becomes too uncomfortable." Martha took another plate to dry and added it to the stack in the cupboard.

Robin scrubbed the pan used to cook the scrambled eggs, her stomach once more roiling at the odor. She got it under control and scoured away the remains.

"How far along do you think you are? Martha asked gently.

"Two months." Even if she'd gotten pregnant at Christmas, it couldn't be much longer. Robin shot a glance at Martha as she reached for the dripping pan.

"That fits. During the first trimester, I was so tired. There were times I pulled my car over and did jumping jacks beside the road, so I didn't fall asleep at the wheel. I went off eggs and cheese, and always wanted cookies."

Cookies. Robin sighed.

Martha laughed. "We should bake cookies this morning and surprise our men. I have a little sugar left."

"Thank you," said Robin. "For more than just the cookies." Her secret felt less frightening now that she'd shared. She needed to tell Kory. She wasn't scared to tell him, but she worried everything would change and she wasn't sure she was ready to face the consequences. Plus, it gave a more urgent deadline for their travels. Traveling heavily pregnant or with an infant would be infinitely more difficult. Plus, the idea of delivering without a hospital or doctor was terrifying. They needed to get to xTerra. If anywhere had a doctor, they would.

She and Martha baked chocolate chip walnut cookies with supplies stored in the cool pantry, supplemented by the sugar Robin had brought from the Visitor Center. They sprinkled in the last of the chocolate chips.

"Thank you for using your supplies of goodies for me. I've been craving sweets for weeks." Robin said. The cookies were baking in the oven, and she couldn't wait until they were done.

"The chocolate needed to be used," said Martha with a smile, her eyes crinkling, "and it's my fault for mentioning cookies." She hesitated. "If things don't work out on the road or xTerra turns out to be too far, you two should come back. Jeb can use help with the farm and I'd love the company." She took a deep breath. "It would give me a chance to be a grandma again." Her eyes sparkled with unshed tears.

The offer touched Robin. Martha must miss her actual family.

"If my family weren't out there, we'd think about staying. It's tempting, anyway." She would mention it to Kory, but she wanted to continue. Walls and bunkers at xTerra sounded like the safest place left in this lawless world.

"The creeps that ran you off from Craters of the Moon are still close and I got the sense that your Kory is running from something." Her eyebrows lifted.

The Wings. He still worried Jake or his guys might find them and make him pay for killing Dillan. Idaho Falls wasn't far from Boise once the roads cleared. Kory was convinced it would be one of the first places they would check. Their stay would be brief.

Robin nodded, but didn't speak.

They switched to talk of recipes and baking while the scent of melted chocolate and sugar filled the kitchen. It was all Robin could do to limit herself to two fresh-from-the-oven soft cookies. They melted in her mouth and tasted like heaven.

When the men returned, it was to over two dozen cookies spread out on cooling racks, piping hot tea, and ham sandwiches on thick slices of homemade bread. Robin had also picked up the basics of crocheting and was working on a sample piece. She grinned at Kory's expression.

"New hobby?" He kissed her and swiped a cooling cookie from the rack beside her on the table.

"Martha thought I should learn," she said, glancing at the pale green yarn. It didn't look like anything, but she'd figured out the proper tension and how to do all three stitches Martha had demonstrated. Martha was going to find her a couple of patterns from the attic. "How's the temperature this afternoon?"

"Warmer. The snow started melting this afternoon. Another of those rapid swings with a warm breeze. We should pack, so we're ready to leave tomorrow." He pointed to the window where the icicles dripped. "If we wait much longer, the ground will be bare."

She couldn't help the surge of disappointment. Kory looked around the kitchen, perhaps also realizing they were alone. Martha might be running interference, so Robin and Kory could talk.

"Jeb asked if we wanted to stay." Kory pulled out a chair and sat beside her.

Robin liked how direct he was, though she couldn't read the look in Kory's dark eyes. Did he want to stay?

"Martha talked to me, too." She bit her lip. "If you want to stay, we should discuss it."

Kory picked up her hand, his thumb circling on its back. "It's too close to Boise and the Joneses for my preference. Plus, if the Wings catch me, I'm a dead man. Jake will see me killing his nephew as a serious betrayal. He won't let it go."

"That puts Jeb and Martha in danger, doesn't it?" That was something neither of them could live with.

"So, we leave." He squeezed her hand. "It might be difficult for them anyway, but I don't want it to be our fault."

She nodded, the tight feeling in her chest lessening. "I promised my grandfather I'd go to South Dakota. It's the safest place left. If it wasn't for that, I'd at least think about staying. They're good people."

"If we can't get to xTerra or they won't let us in, we could come back." Kory's eyes probed hers. "Even if it won't be close."

"We can get there." She wanted to tell him the other reason, about becoming parents, but the dog barked in the hall, signaling Jeb's return. That might be a discussion best left for when they were back on the road. She didn't want to rush.

The next morning, after a breakfast of pancakes spread with more of the delicious strawberry jam, Robin and Kory prepared to leave. They'd stayed with the Crofts less than a week, and it already felt like it could have been home, but it just wasn't theirs, no matter the temptation.

Martha tucked a small packet into Robin's hands when she went upstairs to grab her backpack. "I know you can't take much, but I hope this helps."

Robin peeked inside. The package contained several hand-copied patterns, white and yellow yarn, an extra crochet hook, two newborn sleepers, and two receiving blankets. The care package contained a start. Her eyes misted over. They'd only been here a few days. It would be harder to leave later. It was best they were leaving before they got more attached. She hugged Martha.

"If there's ever a way to repay you," Robin started, her voice choking in her throat.

Martha held Robin at arm's length by her shoulders and shook her head. "Don't worry about that. If you need to come back. You do that. We'll take you in, no questions asked. You, Kory, the baby, any time. You're always welcome."

They went downstairs together, and Robin hugged Jeb, too. Then she stomped on her boots, adjusted her pack, and picked up her snowshoes. She looked at Kory. "Let's go."

•   •   •

Robin had exhausted herself again, hiking through the melting snow from the Crofts to Idaho Falls. She couldn't wait to fall into bed. The plan was to spend the night outside town in a place where Kory had stayed before he'd met the Wings, then carry on tomorrow. She clenched her jaw and kept moving. Warmer temperatures after the deep freeze had melted the snow, leaving it wet and heavy. Even with snowshoes, she'd broken through often. Without them, it would have taken twice as long to slog this distance.

Sundown approached, and hopefully, it was time to stop soon. Buildings had become more frequent, and they'd passed two exits into Idaho Falls. They were headed to a house Kory had stayed before. Or that was the plan.

She was sick of snow and her legs were like rubber. She'd been counting steps all afternoon but kept losing track as she stumbled more often. To distract herself, her mind drifted to thoughts of xTerra. Her cousin Jess must be almost five years old. The little girl wouldn't even remember Robin—she'd been a baby at the time of the asteroid. Luke and Ella may have had other children since then, too. Robin's child might have cousins to grow up with. She clenched her jaw, even more determined to join them.

"How much farther are we going tonight?" She tried to keep the weariness from her voice.

"We're almost there." Kory answered. "The house is out of the way and as safe as I could make it. We can cook inside but shouldn't stay more than overnight. Especially with the snow melting, I want a head start on Jake and the Wings. Now that we're on the move, I don't want to stop more than necessary."

She agreed. The sooner they made headway toward South Dakota, the better.

Kory avoided the major streets after they exited the highway and trudged into a neighborhood. It was as quiet here as everywhere else. The dominant sound was that of dripping water. No smoke plumes filled the sky and no scents of cooking food wafted through the air. If anyone lived here, they were discreet. Kory stopped twice to examine tracks in the snow. At the periphery of Robin's vision, a tabby cat scooted around the edge of the building and disappeared.

"Nothing newer than several days old is my guess. But it's getting harder to tell as the snow melts. We probably have less than a week before most of the snow is gone."

Which meant the Wings could travel any day. Boise was less than three hundred miles away via the interstate or four to five hours by motorcycle. That wasn't far if the trip was connected for another reason, such as supplies or to meet up with the gas supplier.

Robin and Kory continued until it was dark before stopping in front of a brick house that looked like most of the others on the block—very middle-class. That was old-fashioned thinking. There was no such thing anymore.

"This is it." Kory led her to the back of the house, where he removed a loose brick and extracted a key hidden inside the wall. He held it up where it glinted in the light of the rising moon.

"Did you leave it here?" she said, keeping her voice hushed.

He nodded. "About two years ago. We could get in without it. I just wondered if it was still there. I ran out of food and left. I wandered the city, looking for overlooked supplies. A week later, Jake found me trying to boost some of their groceries—stuff they'd cached. Instead of shooting me, he took me in and introduced me to the guys."

"Jake sounds like a decent guy," said Robin.

"Not always," said Kory, staring into space. "But, yeah. Most of the time. I'm not kidding myself, though. If he finds me, it'll be bad. My leaving could make it seem as like he wasn't in control. There was a faction within the Wings that would love to challenge him for leadership. My killing Dillan without reprisal could give them a reason."

"Will he know to look here?" She glanced at the house.

"I never brought him here, so I don't think so." Kory frowned.

Maybe he wasn't as certain as he sounded.

The back door stuck at first and Kory shoved like a linebacker to bash it open, forcing his way in. Stale air rushed out. A faint aroma of mildew followed, but the floor seemed dry and the ceiling intact, at first glance.

They removed their snowshoes and propped them inside a closet by the door with several dusty pairs of rubber boots and faded holey sneakers. They stepped inside, where it was pitch black. The windows must be covered. Kory found his candle lantern and lit it before he shut the door so they weren't plunged into total darkness.

He held the light aloft as they ambled through the living room and kitchen. She spun, peering at the dim rooms. It smelled like rodents. If they were going to stay, she would have lured a cat inside to deal with them. There was no sign anyone had been here in some time. No dishes, food containers, or sleeping bags. Most of the furniture was gone, leaving just a kitchen table and three faded vinyl-covered chairs with metal legs.

"I don't think anyone's stayed here since I left," he said. "It looks just like when I locked up."

"Where did you sleep?" Robin wanted off her feet and to set down her heavy pack. She'd look around later, but a quick nap before dinner sounded fantastic.

"I slept on the living room floor, but if rats haven't overrun the master bedroom, that's our best bet."

She looked at him in inquiry. Maybe she should flop on the floor. She was too tired to wander or search, even if the house had a standard layout.

"Down the hall. We can cook in the kitchen with the burner by a cracked window. There's a hardware store nearby where we can stop in the morning to grab another fuel canister or two."

"No fire tonight though," she said. There was an empty fireplace, but if they were hiding, they shouldn't have a fire. Nor did they have wood to burn. At least it wasn't too cold.

"I'll keep you warm tonight," said Kory with a grin. "Let's check out the bedroom." He turned down the hall, and she followed.

Inside, a king-size bed dominated the space. The bedding had been stripped, leaving just the bare mattress. "No idea about sheets," he said from where he stood in the doorway. "Might be some in the closet, but it'll be nice to stretch out."

"We can zip the sleeping bags together." She smiled. He hadn't complained about any of the beds they'd slept in, but they'd all been cramped for his gigantic frame.

"Why didn't you sleep here before?" She couldn't imagine choosing the floor over this bed. It looked so comfortable.

"It seemed too nice. I was afraid I'd relax, sleep too deeply, and get found. The only thing I used this room for was to hide things. I built a compartment into the crawlspace under the floorboards by the wall."

She nodded. Knowing him, everything he said made sense. "You should have. This is a you-sized bed." She unclipped her pack and dropped it beside the bed. Sitting on the edge of the mattress, she bounced and then flopped backward onto the surface. Her muscles felt heavy, and she stifled a yawn. "Yep. This is good." She sat up. "Be careful. It's a trap." If she lay down for more than a minute, she might miss dinner.

Kory watched her with a smile. He did that more often than he used to. Since their time at Craters of the Moon, he seemed softer. As if his rough edges were being polished. Probably not to strangers, but at least with her.

After a quick dinner and wash, they climbed into bed.

Robin should have been exhausted, but her mind wouldn't rest. She'd been playing the same conversation in her head all day. It was time to share her news with Kory.

"I have something to tell you." She rolled to face him. Though it was dark, she made out his general shape, though not his expression.

"You can tell me anything," he said with a yawn. "Do you regret leaving Jeb and Martha's?"

She took a deep breath, reached out, and placed her hand on his firm chest. Touching him gave her courage. "No." She would need to be direct like he was. "I think I'm pregnant. About two months along. Martha thinks that's why I've been so tired lately."

Kory's silence felt like forever. "I wondered." His voice was soft. He tugged her closer and his warmth filled the slim space between them. He kissed her slowly while their bodies rearranged and tangled together. One of his capable hands stroked the underside of her breast. She gasped as his hand curled around it.

"Your boobs are fuller," he said. "Just a bit. Maybe more sensitive, too."

"You aren't upset?" It became difficult to maintain her level of concern when his hands were so distracting.

"Sweetheart. We knew what we were doing. I was there with you and we knew the risk. It was worth it." He stroked her hip and cupped her butt, pressing her against him. He was like iron. Currents raced through her at the evidence of his desire.

"I'm going to be a dad." His voice was barely more than a whisper.

"I think so. Does that change our plans?" She touched his bristly jaw, her fingertips tingling. Her eyes had adjusted enough for her to see his tender expression.

"Not much," he said. "First thing in the morning, I'll see about those fuel canisters and see if I can pick up a pregnancy test. It'll be expired, but it might set your mind at ease to know for sure." His cock tapped against her and he grinned, his mouth on hers. "I can't hurt the baby. Right?"

"Right." She loved that this was his reaction.

He slipped a hand between them, stroking her belly. "Your stomach is still flat, though." He slid his hand lower. "Do you have enough energy to make love?" He whispered his words against her lips. She moaned when his tongue flicked hers, teasing hers to respond.

"I'll take that as a yes." His touches and kisses were slow and deliberate as always, but after all this time together, he knew what turned her on. When his hand dipped between her legs, she gasped at the slick movement of his fingers. She was so wet and ready.

They kissed for long enough that time ceased to matter on their cozy island of bed and flesh.

He whispered, "Do you trust me?"

"Always." He'd never hurt her.

"Flip onto your belly. I need to go deep. Feel all of you. Let you feel all of me."

His words make her stomach flutter. Deep meant she would feel it everywhere. She ached for him to send her into ecstasy. She rolled.

He moved above her in the dark, his weight settling onto her as he spread her legs with his bulk. Instead of being stifling, his mass was comforting. All of him, which was considerable, would protect her. He guided himself to her where she was wet, without a hand, like a missile locked on target. Though he was careful to take most of his weight on his elbows, she was pinned in place.

He slid farther, stretching her until she cried out as he moved over her, sliding in and out, gliding deeper with every thrust. She'd never felt more complete, more part of something. They were together; they were one.

Every nerve ending she possessed caught fire, burning from within as she pulsed around him, sliding into an orgasm between one breath and the next while he maintained a slow, even rhythm like a metronome. The consistent pace shouldn't have been sexy, but it was.

He remained in control while she lost all sense of herself, spiraling away and exploding into white light and heat.

Only after she shuddered and returned to herself did Kory pick up the pace. She met him thrust for thrust until he came.

"Shit Robin. Fuck me." He collapsed, still mindful not to crush her. He rolled off and pulled her into his arms. She rested her head on his chest where his heart hammered rapid fire beneath her. They lay in the dark, enjoying the blissful silence as their bodies thrummed. It would be easy to fall asleep like this, still entwined.

"I love you," Kory whispered. He hadn't told her with words very often and they made this moment more special. Though she couldn't see his face, his expression would be both tender and intense. She'd seen it before.

Her eyes filled with happy tears. "I love you too." She moved forward to claim his lips, wanting him to know that he, too, was cherished.

"I don't know how this works anymore," he said, "But I want us to stay together. To have you next to me always. That together we're home. Wherever we end up."

"Of course." She snuggled closer. He was so warm and solid.

"I'm not saying this well," he muttered. Rolling on top of her and resting his forehead against hers, he said, "Robin. Will you be my wife?"

"You're asking me to marry you?" She held her breath, waiting for his answer. How would that work? Obviously not a wedding.

"I am. This is my commitment to us."

"I will." Wishing she could see his face, she held his jaw and kissed him again.

CHAPTER 18: KORY

Kory extracted himself from the bed, being careful not to wake Robin. He would let her sleep for the hour it would take him to gather the supplies and return. Gazing at her form in the bed, he was tempted to wake her and make love again, but there would be a lifetime of chances and they should hit the road soon.

He had a spring in his step as he slipped outside into the March morning. It was just bright enough to see without a light as he jogged down the block, avoiding a few slushy patches of remaining melting ice. He'd wanted to do this early so they could still leave just after daybreak.

A grin tugged at his mouth. He was going to be a father. Robin's news made his heart almost burst with joy. He would have a child to protect and raise, and a family to depend on him. That should probably scare him, but caring for Robin had awoken a need inside him. She made him better—she made him somebody that took action. He'd be there for her and for their child and keep them safe.

Collecting supplies was easy. The back room at a local hardware store still had several boxes of fuel canisters. Natural gas hadn't deteriorated yet. They were still viable, but he couldn't carry more than two or three. Robin might have room for another. The more they had, the better off they would be, as traveling in the mountains would be cold and water would take longer to boil. He grabbed one with each hand and packed them into his bag before selecting a third and heading for the drugstore several blocks away.

This might be trickier. The Walgreens looked deserted, but stores with high-demand items were more often visited by others, and perhaps some folks who he wished to avoid. Several sets of tracks led in and out of the broken doors. Idaho Falls appeared to have more residents than Boise.

Kory glanced in all directions before leaving the cover of the neighboring box store to cross the adjoining parking lots. There were lots of bare patches. Most of the snow and ice had melted, and dark clouds menaced overhead—probably too warm to be more snow. He ducked inside the building, crunching shards of glass and dried leaves underfoot in the sheltered entryway.

Light streamed in the broken front as he headed deeper into the store. Bare shelves were common now, as was scattered inventory. He grabbed another tube of toothpaste and some floss as he passed an almost empty shelf once dedicated to oral hygiene.

When he reached the correct aisle, he stopped and exhaled. There were several varieties of pregnancy tests available. No condoms, though. They'd gone ages ago. He couldn't see a difference between varieties, other than packaging. Tucking two different ones into his daypack, he started back.

Kory circled the block and zigzagged his way back toward the house, watching behind him. He didn't want to be followed and lead anyone to Robin. He checked over his shoulder several times. The streets were deserted.

He turned a corner and a furtive movement caught his eye as someone ahead ducked around a corner. Kory followed, watching as a slim figure with long greasy hair and grubby jeans slunk along the building and continued into the nearest alley. Some loner, probably, much like he used to be. He waited several minutes to be sure he was alone once more before continuing.

At the house, Kory stepped on bare concrete to walk an unseen path to the door as drizzle fell. It would be wet today and miserable conditions for hiking. Inside, the sweet smell of oatmeal greeted him and his stomach gurgled. He'd left before breakfast. In the kitchen, he swung Robin around with a kiss. Though she hadn't been up long, she'd been busy; everything other than breakfast and their dishes had been packed. She must have dealt with the bedroom too, as their full backpacks leaned against the wall, once more proving she made a terrific partner.

"Thanks for letting me sleep," she said. "Did you find the canisters?"

He nodded and tossed the pregnancy tests on the counter. "And these."

"How long do they take?" Robin dished up their breakfast and sprinkled each bowl with a few chunks of dried apple from another resealable package. She always worried about their health and eating proper nutrients, taking care of him too. She would be a fantastic mom.

"Three minutes. Why don't you pick one? Pee on it. Then we'll eat. That way, we can have something to do while we wait for the results."

She nodded. "Good. So we aren't just sitting." She grabbed a box and disappeared into the bathroom, returning a couple of minutes later. She set the white plastic stick on the counter.

"Three minutes." She took a deep breath. "Let's eat."

He gobbled his breakfast in no time, even after scraping his bowl with a spoon for every crumb. He wanted to check the stick, but she should be the one, even though he was excited and fluttery about the prospect of confirming he would soon be a father.

Interrupting his thoughts, Robin said, "Let's look together." She took his hand, lacing her fingers through his.

The pink line confirmed what they'd known. He picked her up and kissed her, a deep, thorough one that she must know meant he was speechless with love.

"We should clean up and go," he said as he returned her to her feet. "Idaho Falls is busier than I'd like."

They wiped and packed the dishes, and Kory scanned the room, giving it a last check. He froze and cocked his head. An out-of-place sound reached his ears. The distinctive rumble of motorcycles. He listened for a few seconds and his heart started racing. They were coming closer. Had they been discovered? Robin's eyes widened. Striding over to the boarded-up kitchen window that faced the street, he peered through the cracks.

"Fuck." The curse wasn't much more than a breath. He could just make them out, but a few faces he would recognize anywhere. The lanky teen he'd spotted this morning rode on the bike with Jake. Zeke and Gus also carried passengers. Six men. Too many to fight.

Kory stepped back. He and Robin wouldn't have time to slip away, even escaping out the back. The Wings were too close and there was nowhere else close he and Robin would be safe.

"Jake's here. Back in the bedroom," he hissed. "The hole for my emergency stash will be crowded, but it's the best I've got." He would worry about how they'd found this house later.

They snatched their packs and sprinted for the bedroom. On the far side of the bed, he tore up three loose floorboards and tossed the packs into the darkness below. His cubbyhole was three feet deep, five feet long, and three feet wide. Tight, but possible for two adults and stuffed backpacks. Scurrying little feet scritched on the wood as the bikes stopped directly out front. The damn mice would have to share or leave. He and Robin only had a minute.

Robin jumped in and sat, scooting away from the opening. He followed and crouched as he rearranged the planks above. It was still bright enough to see with streams of light filtering in through the narrow slits in the flooring. He sat, keeping his eyes riveted on the room above while he and Robin huddled below, shoulder to shoulder.

He'd no sooner slotted the last board back into place when the thump of several sets of feet pounded on the front stairs. Someone rattled the doorknob. Locked. They shook the door in its frame. He passed his knife to Robin, who clutched it so hard her knuckles turned white, and he slid his gun free, turning off the safety. He didn't want to shoot anyone, but he would if it came to it.

Jake's voice was clear from the front stairs. "Break the door down. We don't have all day."

There was a muffled crash. Then another as the door splintered open after a second kick. Footsteps sounded in the house as the men spread out to search.

Kory held his breath. Beside him, Robin sat motionless and wide-eyed. He covered her icy hand with his. This hiding spot was the reason he'd risked somewhere familiar, though he'd always hidden food and travel gear. Not people. A scene from an old Star Wars movie popped into his head. Han Solo, Luke Skywalker, and Chewie had hidden from Stormtroopers in compartments under the flooring of the Millennium Falcon. Han had said something about never expecting to smuggle himself. That's how Kory felt about hiding here. He hoped it worked.

"He's not here, Boss," said Zeke's deep voice. "The kid just said he saw someone big; it might not have been Kory. Besides, the guy was probably on his way out of town."

"Maybe." Jake's voice carried in the almost empty house. "The guy in town might not have been him. Kory might not be alone."

"Nobody lives here. There's no sign of a fire or garbage. So much for your hunch," said Gus's more nasal voice. "Why are you so certain he won't be alone? All winter you've been certain he shacked up with the mystery woman from the mall, but we haven't seen anything to prove they left together."

"It's just too convenient that Gus spotted her in the mall, but we never found her. We ripped Boise apart searching, even found that bolthole in the parkade. Somebody lived there and left town in a hurry. Dillan had an appetite for pain. He and Kory probably fought over the chick and Dillan lost. Kory's still with her." Jake's tone remained confident.

Kory couldn't tell if his former leader was angry or impressed. Maybe both.

"What makes you so certain he'd come back here, Boss?" said Zeke. "We've used a lot of fuel on your hunch. He could have gone anywhere."

"This," said Jake. The footsteps converged in the kitchen as the conversation paused. What had he found? "She's pregnant. He wouldn't leave her like that."

Kory felt like smacking his forehead. They'd left the pregnancy test on the counter in their hurry. Of all the stupid moves. Robin covered her face with her free hand.

"That could be from anyone. Anytime." Gus wasn't the sharpest knife in the drawer, but he made a point that Kory hoped Jake would consider.

"It's recent. There's no dust on it. We're catching up. The snow will be gone in a few days and we can get everyone up here to search the whole damn town. We'll flush them out." Jake's voice filled with menace. "I want to have a long chat with Kory. He'll either complete our initiation and take Dillan's place or we shoot him. Either way, Trent's men will back down once they see I've handled the Kory situation."

There wouldn't be much talking if Jake had his way. The man carried a grudge.

"He won't choose a piece of ass over the Wings," said Zeke.

Kory ground down on his molars and glanced at Robin. She was so much more than that. She understood him like no one else. He never would have believed he'd use such a cheesy phrase, but she was his soulmate.

"He already did," said Jake. "Let's go. I've got two more prospective hiding places he might have used. Places we'd seen him before I caught him stealing. One had a couple dozen tins of stashed food. He can't run forever."

Kory hadn't known someone had noticed or followed him before Jake had found him, but he shouldn't be surprised. Jake had acted as though he'd trusted him, but the wily leader had been careful. Coming here had been risky, but Kory had been complacent about their head start because of the early winter.

Once Jake was gone, Kory and Robin would have to check their route out of town. They'd head for high ground next, into the Grand Tetons, where the snow would last longer. They should lose Jake again going somewhere the bikes would hesitate to follow. There would come a point when Jake would give up, but the evidence he'd just found would keep him searching longer. Damn.

The men clomped their way out, leaving the broken front door ajar.

Kory and Robin remained hidden for several minutes after the roaring sound faded in the distance. At last, they emerged to find the house deserted and the pregnancy test gone. Jake would probably be back tomorrow or the next day and keep checking. Kory checked the window. It was full daylight. They'd be exposed to every eye in town if they left.

"I don't think we should go right now. We should stay inside and leave before first light tomorrow. We can't have anyone seeing us leave town before we head into the wilds. They might report to Jake."

•　　　•　　　•

Kory carried both sets of snowshoes strapped to his backpack as they slunk through town, staying away from the worst of the snow patches and mud in the predawn silence as they snuck out of Idaho Falls. With the bare ground and damp patches of earth, it smelled like spring. Despite his worry, they didn't see anyone as they hit the highway. They shouldn't need the snowshoes until higher elevations, assuming there would still be snow. Robin's map listed the elevation in Idaho Falls as 4700 feet. The first day back on the road would be one of their easiest.

He hoped to reach Teton Village, Wyoming after three or four days. It was at the base of the former Jackson Hole Mountain Ski

Resort, where the elevation was 8100 feet. Maybe the fourth day was more realistic.

Those would be strenuous days with steep sections of road. Still, they should be through the mountains and into the homestretch in three weeks. With five hundred fifty miles to go, they needed to average twenty miles a day. Tough, but not impossible. Best to travel as far as possible now, before the pregnancy affected Robin more.

Both food and fuel should stretch for almost a month. There would be lots of water around, so they could purify some each day. With a little luck, they would be in South Dakota in early to mid-April. By then, they should have left behind the Wings and trouble.

Kory and Robin trekked along Highway 26. Cracks spidered through the worn asphalt and crumbled sections near the edges were broken off. Scattered potholes littered the surface, some filled with water and loose pebbles where the freeze-thaw action had destroyed the pavement. What would the surface look like in ten years? Twenty? It wouldn't be long before the road became little more than an overgrown path.

Some places might get repairs near towns that were still inhabited, maybe Salt Lake City, but not here. Few vehicles, other than motorcycles, used the roads. Transportation was mostly on foot. Twice last year, the Wings had spotted trains running, but they'd never gotten close to one that stopped.

Without tourism in modern times, any remaining inhabitants of Teton Village would be isolated and need to be self-sufficient, through farming or scavenging. Most people wouldn't have remained somewhere so remote. The West had become more like the Wild West of the past, without modern transportation, communication, and technology. It would probably slide even farther before it improved.

Painted signs that looked new were interspersed along the fence line on both sides of the road, reading Property of GreenCorps. The company owned a lot of land—their logo was everywhere. Did they own the land or simply claim what had been left empty? It was difficult to know. Kory cracked his knuckles, thinking about the spare population of the West. Perhaps one day people would return.

The destination goal for the first day was Swan Valley, where they'd leave the 26 and head into the mountains. After the turnoff, he took advantage of a viewpoint to scan back the way they'd come. No sign of movement below on the other highway.

Swan Valley was quiet, the wind whistling through the valley. Patches of green fields showed through the taller, golden grass that was flattened, but no longer covered in snow. The land here was flat, with low rolling hills in the distance that looked blue on either side. After a long uneventful day, they found an uninhabited motel where they fell into their beds and slept after about fourteen hours of walking. No sign of pursuit.

On the second day, they headed onto Highway 31, the mountains looming closer. The road grew steeper, a constant upward slope that made Kory's calves burn and both of them gasp for air. The air grew colder as they gained elevation. Though they'd worked out at the Visitor Center, their cardio was lacking. Still, it was pleasant to be somewhere new. This country looked like what he'd always imagined as ranch land, mountain slopes that should be littered with horses and cattle. Now both were scarce and the ranch houses looked deserted. The GreenCorps signs tapered off after lunch.

By midday, he and Robin were back to traveling on the snow and using the roadside markers to keep them on the road. Their pace slowed with the grade and the deep snow. Without snow-clearing equipment and snowbanks, he didn't know how far above the ground they were. He was exhausted as they laboriously snowshoed into Victor, a ghost town in the Grand Teton Mountains. It was the last stop before they left Idaho and crossed into Wyoming. Passing the 'Leaving Idaho' sign tomorrow would feel like progress.

Deer and rabbit tracks criss-crossed the town and once a quick motion of a coyote or fox slid out of sight. Without people around, many of the wild animals had moved back into former urban areas as they expanded their habitat. The town had been built in a beautiful setting. Jagged mountains rose above them as they searched for somewhere easy to stay. He didn't have the energy to keep looking. They settled for the ground floor room of a fancy hotel—the kind Kory never would have been able to afford in the old days. It meant another king-size bed and a solid night's sleep before they tackled the pass through the summit.

On day three, the views became glorious the higher they climbed, the rugged mountains jutting sharply above the winding mountain highway where they turned onto the Old Jackson Highway toward Teton Village, their next destination.

The air was thinner here and his lungs labored for a full breath. Robin looked half asleep on her feet as they trudged into town at sunset on their third day. The wind picked up, and the deserted gondolas and ski lifts above the town rose and fell on their cables, swaying in the wind with a vibrating whine. The structures would last longer than the roads, but were no longer of any use. The dangling cars reminded Kory of spaceships or escape pods. He smiled to himself. Maybe he'd read too much science fiction.

For three days, they hadn't heard the Wings or any other vehicle noise, but this town was somewhere that could have people—best to be on guard. Sure enough, moments later, he spied thick smoke rising at the far side of the cluster of condos and townhouses—mostly fancy cedar and wood construction. They weren't the only ones in town.

He'd never been to a resort town like this when they'd been operational and busy. No rustic cabins or dusty farmhouses here. Once this town had been expensive, filled with travelers from across the world. It wasn't somewhere he'd stayed, even when hopping trains and crossing the country. What would it have been like to have had money to fly somewhere like this for a ski vacation? He would never know.

Kory glanced at Robin and she smiled. Who needed fancy vacations? He had what he wanted, a simple life and pleasant companionship with someone he trusted. Now they just needed a safe place to live.

They broke into a log cabin, one of the smaller ones that would be easier to heat and near their trail out of town. Dropping their belongings inside, they scrounged firewood from nearby sources, finding a couple of armfuls. They didn't risk a fire until after dark when the smoke wouldn't be seen.

They had only two hours of warmth before they retreated to bed on a slightly chewed mattress riddled with tiny holes. He gave the top several solid thumps that sent mice scurrying. He and Robin exchanged a glance. Somewhere else wouldn't be much better, unless they moved to one of the fancy condos that might be sealed better but be more dangerous because it would be closer to the other occupants of the village. Best to tough it out for tonight.

Kory woke once to a scratchy tickling feeling on his arm and bolted upright. A mouse had run across him. As he sat up, three or four more scattered across the top of the bed. He yanked the sleeping bag higher to cover everything, including their heads, and tried to return to sleep. Constant rustling from the floor and from deep within the mattress kept him tossing and turning, unable to settle.

At first light, he jumped from the bed, scaring some of the creatures back into hiding. He made breakfast, discovering mice had spoiled several bags of food. Anything opened by mice, he didn't dare eat. He counted what was left. They should still have enough, but it would be tight. They couldn't afford any more delays.

CHAPTER 19: ROBIN

Robin stifled a sigh as she walked, placing one foot in front of the other. It felt as if they'd been on this highway for weeks, not four days. There was a certain sameness to the mountainous landscape—rocks, trees, and yet more snow. Beautiful, but frigid. She was sick of winter and longed for warmth and the green of spring. Her fingers and toes ached from the cold—a background pain that persisted throughout the day. The temperature must have dropped again, even though it was March 13th.

It would be their first night without a roof and four walls, but it couldn't be worse than having creatures scampering around on them all night. She shuddered, remembering the most recent cabin. She wasn't scared of a mouse or two, but that volume of mice had been gross. Neither of them had slept well.

Despite the similarity in the landscape, today's hike was the steepest yet, with a series of three peaks to traverse on the mountain pass. With lofty peaks looming on either side, they'd probably be in the shade, even at midday.

The snow-capped Rocky Mountains reminded her of the coastal mountain range near home, though on a grander scale. Actually, the familiar mountains of home must look different now than the way they had during her childhood. The recent series of volcanic eruptions triggered by the asteroid would have changed the whole coastal skyline. A lot had changed in the last four years—even the mountains, that were supposed to be permanent.

If even the earth underwent drastic change, would everything continue to feel temporary?

Robin and Kory plodded up the mountain highway for hours, making steady progress. Sometime well after lunch, they came around a corner to discover that the road ended at an enormous swath of thick dirty snow. The solid wedge rose several yards above their heads and continued over the side of the mountain like a frozen waterfall. Trees and rocks stuck haphazardly out of its mass. Robin's heart plummeted. Sometime over the winter, an avalanche had engulfed the pass, and taken out half the forest, as well as the highway.

Could they go around? On one side was the mountain slope, on the other, a steep cliff that dropped several hundred yards. Her spirits sank as she stared, her feet turning numb as they stood there, stuck. How far would they have to go to find the road again? There wasn't another route or highway through the mountains.

There didn't seem to be an alternative. She scanned the slope above again. The collapsed section extended up the mountain as far as was visible. It was difficult to be upbeat when exhaustion had settled in every bone.

"Do you think it's safe to cross?" It had better be. Going back wasn't an option.

Kory strode closer to the face of the avalanche and pounded the grayish ice. His fist made little impact, but at least this edge seemed solid. "It seems stable now. We should be able to go over it if we're careful. I don't see an alternative. Hopefully, it isn't too wide. We'll know better once we're on top."

He chopped several hand and footholds with his hatchet, strapped his snowshoes to the back of his pack, and went up the face of the blockage. Dangerous or not, they were going across.

She took a deep breath and gathered her will. She could do this. Using Kory's hacked path, Robin climbed with no problem.

When she reached the top, the surface had a sheen the treads on her boots couldn't penetrate. It wasn't easy to hold still. Up here, walking might have to be done in controlled slides. Kory took out a length of rope and tied it around their waists, joining them together. She felt safer on the slippery surface once anchored together. They kept their snowshoes packed, hoping their boots would have enough grip.

From up here, lower mountain peaks and valleys lay before them in one section, back the way they'd come, as did a turquoise glacial stream, cascading over the edge, gurgling through thick icicles.

He smiled. "The rope is just a precaution. I'll use my ski pole to test the ground before we move forward. Then you step where I step." He raised an eyebrow to check her understanding before they proceeded. "One more thing. We shouldn't talk much up here. We could set off another avalanche if the mountain above is unstable because of the melt. There's still a lot of snow up there." He kept his voice low.

While the avalanche field seemed solid under her feet, another entire mountain of snow could come crashing down and swallow them. Great. Her lungs constricted when she tried to take a deep breath. She exhaled and nodded.

They started across, taking slow, even steps that crunched on the ice. In smoother sections, they boot-skated. With each shuffle forward, Kory stabbed the translucent snowpack. As instructed, Robin followed his path, placing her feet where he had, trying not to look too far ahead. One step at a time. The silence pressed downward and sweat trickled down her back, pooling beneath her backpack. Now that she shouldn't talk, Robin wanted to speak to lessen the tension, but refrained, finding she held her breath most of the time.

They were three-quarters of the way across, with only a hundred yards to go before the wedge of avalanche debris sloped downward, when Kory's pole jab created a two-foot-wide hole in the snow—an air pocket in the rotten ice.

"Stay back." Kory shifted and pivoted uphill for his next thrust. Again, the top crust crumbled, leaving a hole. Moving back and left, he repeated this several times as they inched uphill, but couldn't find anywhere that led closer to the far edge. This final section, where it was more exposed to sunshine, had melted and become unsafe.

Robin's shirt became drenched with sweat and her shoulders ached from constant tension. The bright sliver of late afternoon sun seemed to mock them as it slid further behind the mountain peaks in the west. It wouldn't be long before they lost the sunlight. Glancing over her shoulder, her weight shifted to the right and the ground beneath her feet disappeared, becoming powder.

She yelped and scrambled for solid footing, but the rotten ice and softened snow crumbled further. It felt as if time had slowed. With every movement, she slipped deeper into the chasm beneath her feet. Soon, her head was lower than the surface and she was still dropping.

Her chest constricted, and she flailed, trying to grab something, anything. With a desperate lunge, she caught a branch embedded in the icy wall of the hole and halted her slide. With her heart lodged in her throat, she took a shuddering breath and gripped with both hands—praying she could hold on. More snow slipped away beneath her feet, leaving them dangling in mid-air. There must be tunnels riddling the inside of the avalanche field.

She stared upward, blinking unwanted tears from her eyes.

Kory appeared at the top, lying on the surface to peer down. His bearded face and brown eyes had never been so beautiful. She wasn't alone.

"Good job grabbing the tree," said Kory.

How could he be so calm when her insides were churning?

His face disappeared, and the rope around her waist pulled. In her panic, she'd forgotten they were tied together and hadn't noticed their connecting rope—now taut.

"I've got you." Kory's voice came from just beyond sight and was as much of a lifeline as the rope. She lurched upward, the rope angling into the more solid mass on the left as he hauled her toward the surface.

Robin didn't release the branch until she was too far above to hold on. Her heart pounded against her ribs until she reached the lip and Kory pulled her to safety.

Her legs felt rubbery, and her hands shook as she scrambled to her feet. Her pants were covered in snow and her legs and hands were cold.

"You okay?" Kory wiped some of the snow from her clothes, perhaps checking that she wasn't injured.

At her nod, he wrapped his arms around her and squeezed. He whispered, "I'm thankful we used the rope. We'll clean up your cheek once we're off this thing and you can put some of your ointment on it."

She peeled off her glove and touched her numb cheeks. The ice had scuffed one side and her hand came away sticky with blood. Thank goodness she'd gotten nothing more than a scrape. It could have been so much worse.

Kory seemed calm, but his body shook as she pressed against him. In an instant, she'd almost been gone. He must have been as frightened as she had been.

Unable to speak, she lived in his hug, letting her trembling body return to normal. After a few more breaths, she spoke, her voice shaking despite her efforts for control. "We should get going. I'll be fine, even if I was scared for a minute." More like terrified. But she'd be better when they were off this chunk of ice and back on solid ground.

He tightened his hug for another beat. "I don't know what I'd have done if I'd lost you." His low, growly tones gave her confidence.

Robin's voice became stronger. "I'm really okay. It'll be dark soon. We need to go." She wasn't okay yet, but she would be.

Kory gave her a look that said she hadn't fooled him, kissed her hard, and released her.

She took another deep breath. Backing up, they found thicker crust again and eased across a gravelly patch almost to the edge. They were so close. The far side remained steep and wooded, and it appeared impossible to hike through the trees. Splintered and shattered trunks stuck at angles out of mass and offshoots of dirty snow and ice continued into the forest. Where was the road?

Kory leaned forward, craning his neck for a better look, and knocked a couple of chunks from the near edge.

Robin stepped back and tread with care as they inched across the slope, searching for a way down. She watched for a break in the trees or some sign of the highway, somewhere flat or changed by humans, such as signs or blasted stone. She glanced at the sky as the shadows lengthened, stretching toward them with expanding dark tendrils. The steep mountains blocked most of the light, though it was only afternoon. A chill ran down her spine—or maybe it was almost evening. She'd lost track of time during the crossing. She looked where the top of the mountain glowed pink with alpenglow, reflecting the light of the sunset on the western side. Definitely later.

She and Kory needed to get down and find a safer place to camp. They hadn't expected to make it to Moran tonight, but this setback meant they'd only come about twelve miles today. Which meant they would have to make that up if they wanted to stick to their timeline.

They hadn't spoken for most of the tension-filled, sweaty crossing, other than the rescue, but Robin broke the silence when she spotted a broken chunk of a bright green highway sign sticking out of the grayish-white expanse.

"The avalanche field tapers off that way," she said, speaking low. "That flat patch might be the road."

Kory adjusted their direction, aiming toward the solid piece of green.

It took another half hour and the last of the daylight before they were safely off the avalanche path. She eyed the slope above. The danger zone was still too close for comfort. They shouldn't linger.

She shot several nervous glances at the mountain and breathed a sigh of relief when at last the ski poles didn't seem necessary. They were back on the couple of feet of regular snow they were used to traversing.

Kory unpacked his headlamp and flicked on the light, illuminating a flat expanse of snow toward the road where it wound around the corner. "You sure you're good? It would be preferable to get a few more miles in." He glanced uneasily up the slope and clipped his snowshoes back onto his boots, and passed hers over.

"Sure. We have another steep pass tomorrow, then a long downhill to Moran." At last, her voice sounded normal.

The road angled downward with a steep grade and slippery sections as they trekked. That, combined with the low light and icy surface, kept Robin on edge until they'd wound down several sets of sharp curves into a wooded area—one without precarious snow-covered slopes. They tromped further until the road swooped in the opposite direction from the mountain, and they found a protective outcropping of bare stone.

"Let's camp here. I'm spent," said Kory. "There's a lot of downhill tomorrow so we can make up the mileage then."

With no argument, Robin unfastened her pack, let it drop, and leaned it against the stone face—relieved to have its weight off her back. "Let's camp right on the road. I'm done."

Kory laughed. "Let's at least set up in the trees so I can use branches to keep up the tarp."

Settling in, they ate a quick dinner and retreated to the tent for the night.

The next day's journey was uneventful and brought them to Moran, leaving them two hundred and fifty miles to Casper, Wyoming, the last decent-sized town before the homestretch to xTerra. Robin calculated that they had come one-half of the total distance from Boise to South Dakota. Not bad, considering their initial delay caused by winter. Her nausea had stayed manageable, and they were making good time. If only the rest of the trip continued to be as straightforward.

•　　•　　•

Robin and Kory trudged into Casper at nightfall on day seventeen since leaving Idaho Falls. This was the three-quarter mark of their journey. With so many possibilities to search, the Wings should be left behind once and for all. Robin couldn't wait to be done walking for the day. Her date tally showed that today was March 26th. If everything went according to plan, they had another eight days of hiking. They had ten days' worth of food remaining.

She yawned. They'd finally caught up to spring again, and had taken off their snowshoes, hopefully for good, the day before yesterday as they left the mountains behind.

"Want to spend an extra day or two in Casper? We can rest our weary bones?"

"Sure." She'd rather keep going—they were in a rhythm now, and the sooner they reached the bunkers in South Dakota, the better— but they'd earned a day off.

They broke into a fancy house near the edge of town—a massive stone and brick edifice with a fenced backyard, a woodshed, and a chimney for a fireplace. She couldn't wait to sleep inside for the first time in five days. Perhaps there would even be a king-size bed. She wanted to wash better and rinse out their clothes. They were both ripe from traveling. She'd already worn everything she owned several times.

The house was perfect inside, and with the spring weather, they would be warm enough at night to sleep in a bedroom, not by the fireplace on the floor. Her jaw creaked with another yawn. Though she was still tired at night, the exhaustion seemed less today. Either the pregnancy was getting easier, or her muscles had become accustomed to walking. Maybe both.

"A place like this might have books you can trade for." Kory winked. "You can look around and check for supplies while I boil water for dinner."

"I'll pick a room too," Robin said, starting on the main floor. That was more than a fair trade. He kept doing things like that when they stopped, giving her the simple jobs.

The master bedroom looked the most comfortable with the spacious bed she'd been hoping for. She closed the dusty blinds and laid out their sleeping bags, zipping them together before she continued to poke around.

On the second floor, an entire room was lined floor to ceiling with built-in bookcases filled with books. Most were history books, but one shelf had paperback fantasy novels and she chose a couple that she hadn't read. Her pack had gotten lighter as they'd eaten most of their supplies.

She wandered into the bathroom and set her candle lantern on the counter. She hadn't looked in a mirror for weeks. Her hair had grown enough that the sides curled and the back was long enough for a short ponytail. She gathered it behind her and let it fall. Maybe she'd continue to let it grow when she got to xTerra. She missed having long hair.

Robin turned sideways and lifted her shirt, rotating back and forth. No change yet. So far, her stomach still looked flat, though Kory maintained her breasts had grown. It wasn't obvious to her, but he might be right. She smiled in the mirror as Kory appeared behind her as though summoned by her thoughts. He stooped, wrapping his arms around her from behind, and nuzzled her neck, his beard soft now that it had grown in.

"You're beautiful," he said. "You ready for dinner?"

"Mm-hmm," she said, turning into his arms and kissing him. "Maybe tomorrow I can do laundry. Then back on the road the next day. It won't be long until we get to South Dakota."

"What's left? A hundred and sixty miles. Eight days. We can do that. Piece of cake."

"I remember when it was eight hundred. I can't believe we're almost there."

With their evening decided, they went downstairs for dinner and an early night.

CHAPTER 20: KORY

Kory woke the morning they planned to hit the road with a sore tooth. It wasn't like he could make a dentist appointment, so he'd just have to deal. He poked at the sorest part with his tongue, unable to leave it alone—the usual place. His wisdom teeth sometimes flared up, inflaming his gums. This had happened before and would pass, but it hurt like a son of a bitch. He tried not to take his irritation out on Robin, though his mouth burned like fire ants were swarming and biting. Twice he was short with her without meaning to be. He apologized and shut up to bear the pain.

The hiking wasn't difficult, with a gradual downhill, and they made great mileage that day and the next. They weren't far from Douglas as it approached nightfall and the shadows had lengthened on day twenty since leaving Idaho Falls. It had been raining for hours and the wind picked up, but they should be able to find shelter soon. He'd ask for Tylenol when they stopped. They'd walked over fifty miles the last two days, and it was time to quit for overnight.

Kory glanced at Robin. She'd worn a ball cap to keep the streaming water from her face and she wore full rain gear, but she was still drenched. Her lips had turned a pasty white and her teeth chattered, but not one complaint. His girl was tough and deserved a rest— somewhere warm and dry.

The Grand Teton Mountains, Yellowstone, and Thunder Basin Grasslands had all been parks, so permanent residents were few and had always been scattered. The outskirts of town differed from many they'd passed through, with buildings spaced farther apart than most places. Maybe it was because this area was so remote. Even in the old days, there hadn't been many people who lived in this region.

Several stores, such as the hardware, pharmacy, and grocery stores, had been boarded up and still looked like they'd been left untouched, which was a surprise. He squinted at the red letters painted on the damp wood, trying to make out what they said. Property of the Slains Brothers? The same words had been scrawled on several businesses, and those buildings had been padlocked and secured.

Twice his peripheral vision caught the slight motions of curtains twitching while they crossed a residential area on the way to the bridges leading out of town. Coming into the clear, he got an extended look at the river. The near bridge was out and so was the second downriver. They'd need to take the other, the only bridge across the North Platte River that led east toward South Dakota.

They bunked down in a motel for the night. Robin guessed something was wrong and handed him two Tylenol with a pointed glance. No fooling her.

"Wisdom teeth," he explained. "The pain started this morning."

She got out the creased map and laid it on the small round table.

Tomorrow they'd cross the river, then they'd be camping their way across the plains for five or six days. Vita xTerra had started to feel reachable, and it was difficult not to get excited about their journey's end. What, and who, would they find on the other end? He hadn't thought about their reception until now. What if Robin's family hadn't made it to the walled city? Would he and Robin still be welcome? He could also be called out for Robin being pregnant when they arrived.

The pain from Kory's tooth kept him awake half the night while he listened to the wind whistle. It could be rough crossing the flat plains in this kind of weather. It was going to be a long week.

In the morning, his jaw still aching, he accepted more Tylenol and they hit the road. Picking their way through town in a light drizzle, they discovered that someone had blockaded the remaining bridge. Spying movement, they stopped a few streets away behind the corner of a brick building to confer. Kory squinted at the group of men manning it mid-span, counting.

"Six men." He peered around the corner and counted again. Same result.

"There's no way around it unless we go two days out of our way. Should we find out what they want?" Robin bit her lip. She clearly didn't want to interact with strangers anymore than he did. They'd done well avoiding people for weeks.

"We need to go that way. Their roadblock doesn't look temporary. There are probably men stationed there every day. Good chance they have the other way blocked, too." Kory ground down on his molars and winced, having momentarily forgotten his sore tooth, which now flared hot with pain.

"Maybe they just want some kind of payment. Like a toll." Robin tilted her head, thinking.

"I doubt we have anything they want." He wasn't about to give up food or fuel. They had enough for their journey, but not excess.

"I have the jewelry in the lining of my pack."

"Can you dig out something small, so you don't have to search in front of them?" If they saw more gold, the problem could escalate.

She nodded, slipped out her pocketknife, and slit a couple of stitches from the concealed inside pocket in her pack. With a little effort, she worked a gold and diamond ring out of the slot. She slid it onto her ring finger. "It might make a better show to take it off if I have to give it to them."

It wasn't the worst idea.

Still, he hated approaching a fortified position while he and Robin would be exposed and at a disadvantage. He took a deep breath. "You ready? Walk with your hands out to the sides to show you aren't a threat. I'll do the same."

She slid her gloves back on and adjusted her pack. "I have a bad feeling about this."

"Me too. But I don't see an alternative."

"Should we go the long way around?" Robin looked at him, though it had already been discussed and discarded.

"There's no guarantee the bridge on the Interstate is intact, plus we'd spend days working our way back here on the other side." His tone was more impatient than usual.

She shot him a look but said nothing.

"Sorry, my teeth make me irritable. I shouldn't take it out on you."

She nodded before she peeked out at the men on the bridge again. "I still don't like this. Let's get it over with."

He looked her over, trying to see what the men would. With longer hair than last fall, she looked like the attractive young woman she was. Even tucking her hair into her cap wasn't enough to be a disguise. Getting through the blockade wouldn't be easy. "I'll do the talking. I know you dread that part."

She nodded. "Hostile strangers. No problem. You got this."

They stepped out from behind the building and strolled up the wet street, their hands in clear view, and headed toward the bridge.

Kory expected a flurry of activity when the men spotted them, but the group remained at their posts—two forward and four at the barricade. His skin prickled with unease. He and Robin must have been seen yesterday. These men may have been informed of their presence in town, which meant that they were expected. Two of the men watched through binoculars.

He walked until the front men's faces were clear and they were close enough that he could monitor their hands. Their rifles were slung across their chests but held low and ready.

"I'm Kory and this is Robin." He projected his voice, unsure who to address. The men looked roughly the same, with no clear leader. Camouflage rain jackets, tan pants, boots, and faded caps.

A man of average height with long hair in the back, probably in his forties, stepped forward. "You're on Slains property." His gravelly voice carried a warning.

Kory turned to face the spokesperson, angling his body in front of Robin. "We're just passing through. Headed east. We're hoping to use the bridge, seeing as the others are broken."

"*Our* bridge," said the same man, "Not *the* bridge."

Shit. "You're the Slains brothers?" Kory's hand indicated the group.

"I'm Rodney and I'm married to a Slains, so I'm senior here." In other words, there were likely a lot more folk nearby.

The other men's eyes drilled into Robin and Kory. No one cracked a smile. The guards meant business.

"You were waiting for us," said Kory. Best to lay some cards on the table so this didn't take all day.

"That's right. One of our citizens reported seeing you two while on a patrol last night in town." Rodney moved to stand in line with the foremost men, now three abreast. "He wasn't exaggerating. You're a tough-looking customer. We could use someone like you."

"We don't want any trouble," said Kory. An outright refusal of their offer would be an insult and therefore a problem. He'd met people like this before, including with the Wings. This time, he didn't have Jake and the guys to back him up.

"You found trouble just the same," said Rodney in his raspy voice. "We could use someone like you. You have a choice. Be smart. Join us. Both of you." He didn't have to say what would happen if they chose no, but the other men shifted their weight, their hands adjusting their rifles. This could get ugly.

Kory lifted his hands a little higher. "Let's keep this friendly. My wife and I just want to cross the river. We'll keep going and you'll never have to see us again." Beside him, Robin stiffened.

"Wrong answer," said Rodney, his eyes narrowing. "Play nice, or we shoot you and take your woman. She looks smart enough to recognize a good thing."

Kory's right hand drifted down to touch Robin's arm. She was shaking. "Can we discuss your offer?" This was her most extreme reaction yet to strangers.

Rodney shrugged. "You have five minutes to decide. Stay in sight."

There was no way Kory and Robin were getting off this bridge without agreeing. Fuck. He led Robin back twenty yards so they could speak on their own, turning so the men couldn't see their mouths or hear their whispers.

"I think they might leave you alone since you're with me and they seem to want someone with muscle. We'll ditch them later, but we're going to have to accept. I don't see an alternative."

Her eyes filled with tears, though she blinked them back. "These people are terrible."

"They haven't shot us yet because they want something, but we don't know enough to say what they're like. Good or bad. It's not usually that straightforward." He looked more closely. She wasn't just upset, she was unraveling and alarm bells went off in his head. This wasn't like her.

"What's going on? Are you okay?" He didn't know how to get them out of this situation without violence.

"The one on the far right was one of them." Robin's blue eyes darkened and narrowed. "From the cabin in the mountains."

Them. The sick fucks that had raped her and her sister and left her for dead. That put a different spin on things, even if it didn't solve their immediate problem.

Her voice shook. "I don't think he recognizes me. It was almost four years ago. But I want nothing to do with these people." She shouldn't have to confront her rapist on top of everything else.

Three. Kory tallied the man's death in his head. He glanced at the man, who he would call Three, memorizing his features, clenching his fist at his side. If he got an opportunity, he would make the creep with the pinched face and hard mouth his third kill. To work with these people, he'd have to be patient.

"Two minutes," called Rodney in his grating voice.

"No matter what, I want to keep you safe. Do you trust me?" Kory looked down into her gorgeous eyes, now shiny with unshed tears while she struggled to control her fear. She was terrified. He took both of her gloved hands in his and squeezed. "If we say no, they'll shoot me."

She nodded, her chin quivering, but she kept it together. God, she was tough. If something happened to him, she would be stuck with these assholes and have more to lose than he did. He continued to hold her hand, and they walked back to Rodney.

"What do you need me for?" Kory kept his voice free of inflection.

"We've got this county locked down, but we're expanding and have a few alliances about to come into play. We need to deal with a few isolated holdouts all at once before they can band together. You're joining our militia to smash stuff and beat sense into some farmers."

"How long do we need to stay for this job?" Maybe this could be a one-time thing.

"That isn't for me to decide," said Rodney. "John Slains will make the call, but I'd say at least a year."

Kory's heart sank. No way in hell they would stay that long.

"You'll love being on our side," Rodney continued. "I bet you'll never want to leave. We live like princes out here and nobody messes with the Slains."

"Damn straight," said the man on the left.

"You tell'em, Rod," said the one on the right.

"We're in." Kory kept his voice calm but firm. Robin's grip tightened.

"You're making the right decision," said Rodney. "Hand your gun over, then let's go. You'll get it back when you've earned the right." He turned to one of the other men. "Put them in the jeep."

Kory dropped his pistol in Rodney's outstretched hand. He wasn't surprised and was pleased they hadn't also asked for his knife. He wouldn't be without a weapon meeting the leader.

The man on the left motioned with his gun for Kory to lead as they crossed the rest of the bridge on foot. Rodney, the man with the gun, and Three followed.

At the mud-splattered jeep, Rodney said, "I drive. She sits up front with me."

Robin didn't look at anyone as she climbed into the passenger seat, while Kory took the seat behind her and rested his hand on her shoulder. For all she might not like to be touched with Three so near, she would do better with a little contact as comfort.

Rodney jumped behind the wheel and the two henchmen slid in beside Kory in the back. Three aimed a handgun at Robin's back. Kory ground down on his sore tooth, the pain keeping him alert and from doing something stupid.

"We're ready," said Three with a smirk at Kory. Whatever expression he read on Kory's face wiped his smile away. He rested the gun in his lap and faced the other direction.

The jeep drove north for half an hour, away from Robin and Kory's intended route. They passed an off-white three-story hotel and a boarded-up blue and white diner called "Penny's" in what seemed to be the middle of nowhere. Why anyone would have visited this godforsaken back-of-nowhere place was beyond comprehension. They turned right down a bumpy gravel road and parked outside a barricade made of squashed and rusted cars. A patchwork metal fence extended around the property. A house sat back from the fence on the far side of the compound.

Rodney parked the jeep beside two others. In an open shed nearby, three filthy dirt bikes stood in a row. The door to a small office was locked with a padlock. Behind the shed, in a field, several pickups had been jacked up and had their tires removed. The Slains had a few kinds of transportation and must know someone who mixed gas and sold it to them. Maybe the alliances Rodney had mentioned.

Rodney banged on the rusty sheet metal gate fixed into the barricade. "It's me. I've got them. Let us in." At the first sound, a dog barked from inside.

So, they were expected here as well. The Slains might even have radio communication with an operation like this. Something he and Robin would have to learn.

With a screeching sound of metal grinding against metal, a section of the wall opened. A partially overgrown driveway, now a path, lay on the other side.

"John's expecting you," said another of the Slains men, dressed in the usual garb—camo hunting jacket and tan pants. Did they wear the same thing for convenience, or was it a uniform? Kory preferred his jeans. They might not have anything in his size.

"Wife or girlfriend?" said the guard as they passed. His gaze raked Robin from head to toe. "She's got a nice ass."

Robin stiffened, but kept her mouth shut. Best for her not to react to statements like that.

The Slains would expect Kory to be tough. He shot the guard a pointed look and barred his teeth in what they might consider an evil grin. "You can admire her fine ass, but if you touch my wife, you'll answer to me."

The man blanched, perhaps taking in Kory's bulk for the first time. The guard swallowed and closed the gate, motioning the dog to move. "Outta the way Rex."

The others continued on foot toward the main farmhouse, two hundred yards away. The weather-beaten house had been here awhile and could use another coat of white paint. They'd built several newer cabins on each side in a half-circle, reminding Kory of one of those cabin resorts. He counted at least a dozen. Several men stood near two larger ones in clusters. By his count, there were at least fifteen additional men on site. Probably more.

Rodney led as they clomped onto the porch and he entered the house through the front door without knocking. He held it open as Robin and Kory passed.

Three and the other man stopped outside, taking up positions on either side of the door. "We'll make sure you aren't disturbed."

Kory took Robin's hand again. He didn't care if that might make them look weak. It was best everyone understood his cooperation depended on her safety—that she mattered.

John Slains stood as they entered the kitchen. He wasn't a tall man, nor was he short. His gray-streaked brown hair had been cropped close on the sides, but he wasn't much older than Rod. Perhaps forty-five. His skin was weathered as if he'd worked outside for years. Maybe he'd been a farmer. Now it seemed he was a leader, perhaps some kind of new world lord.

John held out his hand to shake Kory's and, with just the smallest hesitation, Kory took it and gave it a firm shake. No power games or crushing grip. Just an acknowledgment of the two men meeting.

"Welcome. Rod, you wait outside too. I'll fill you in after." John must feel confident in his superiority here at his headquarters with his men stationed outside and at the gate.

There was no argument from their escort as he turned and headed back outside, leaving Robin and Kory alone with the leader.

"I understand you're John Slains. I'm Kory Walker and this is Robin. My wife."

"That's the thing," said John, shooting Robin a speculative look. He addressed his remarks to Kory. "There are wives and there are other women. We have a pretty strict definition here. Wives have privileges within the compound and are off limits for anyone except their husbands. They keep to themselves and work with the other wives."

"Meaning?" said Kory, not liking the direction of this initial conversation.

"Other women are communal whores. I don't condone what goes on, but men will be men. We've got forty-four men and eight women under my protection. Not including you. You see what I mean."

"Fixing your ratio isn't our job." No one else had better touch his Robin.

"No. But," John smiled an easy-going smile that didn't reach his cool eyes. "Wives are breeders. Pregnant. Slains men tend to be the fathers. We're invested in the future."

Kory wanted to tell John Slains to fuck himself and leave, but instead grinned back, pain once more flaring from his sore tooth. "Easy. She's three months along and the baby's mine. No Slains required."

John's smile dropped away to be replaced by a harder expression. "Be that as it may, she's going to stay here in my house while my men borrow you for a few months."

Fuck. Robin would be a hostage and he'd be away without being able to ensure her safety. He'd expected it on some level, but it still came as a gut punch. Being separated would make escape that much more difficult.

"Are there other wives she'll be able to stay with?" Kory maintained eye contact with the other man. Could he have his blade on the leader before anyone heard a ruckus and charged in? Probably not. He readied himself to charge if this went further sideways, even if getting out of here would be difficult.

"She doesn't look pregnant," said John Slains. "You'll need my say-so to get her wife status." His hard eyes raked Robin from head to toe.

What the fuck did he want? Kory stared at him, letting the other man reach his own conclusions. Kory wouldn't help them with shit, not without an iron-clad guarantee of her safety. Robin was his family and his home. Without her pregnancy and their dwindling rations, they'd have slipped away in town. They'd never gone near the fucking bridge, but getting her to South Dakota was his mission. Unharmed.

They stood in silence while John took Kory's measure.

At last, John Slains' eye twitched. "Maybe you'd like to meet the other wives. There are four of them. She can stay with Rod's wife, Amanda, while you're out on raids and patrols. She's my sister. That safe enough for you?" His mouth twisted with disdain.

Kory shrugged. "Let's meet them."

John raised his voice and rotated his head. "Ladies, I expect you're back there listening. Get in here. I'd like you to meet the newcomers."

The far door swung open and four women poured through the opening, two at the back, casting nervous glances at John. The other two glared at each other and jostled to be at the front. Those two reminded Robin of children squabbling for attention.

John indicated the taller of the pair. "This is my sister, Amanda."

"Robin!" The youngest of the women shoved past Amanda and flung herself at Robin.

Beside Kory, Robin let out a small gasp and stiffened.

"I thought you were dead," gasped Shelby, clutching Robin in a tight hug. "I can't believe you're here."

"And Shelby. My wife." For the first time, John seemed surprised as he stared at the young women.

Robin shot Kory a look of disbelief and carefully wrapped an arm around her younger sister. She looked stunned.

"So, do we beat the holy hell out of you and lock your wife up with the whores? Or will you leave her with us for a couple weeks at a time? Time to decide." John wanted an immediate answer.

Kory nodded at the women. "Guess that makes me your other brother-in-law."

John pursed his mouth and turned his gaze on the sisters. "I guess so."

CHAPTER 21: ROBIN

Shelby lived with the Slains and was married to the leader. Robin's mind had trouble grasping the idea. That seemed like a tremendous step up from the scumbag she'd left with. Clearly, she'd arrived with the creep Robin had identified on the bridge since he was also with the Slains. She wanted—no, needed—an explanation, but that would have to wait until everything was settled and she could have a private conversation with her sister.

Despite remaining calm on the outside, Robin still seethed about the leader's words. There was no way in hell she would be a communal woman. She'd stab anyone who came near her. She inhaled, the fresh air from the open window helping to calm her.

Kory had said for her to trust him, and she was doing her best. It wouldn't be easy to get along without him in such a hostile environment when they were separated. He wouldn't be here to help if some low-life tried to take advantage in his absence. Including John Slains. Inside, she was quaking about Kory's departure. She'd been reluctant to depend on someone else, but they were better as a team. Shelby had adjusted to life in this place, but Robin could already tell she wouldn't.

"You two will have your own cabin when you're on-site," John said to Kory.

"What about while he's gone?" Robin asked.

John's steely eyes flicked to her. "Shelby, can you explain the rules to your sister?"

Shelby's head dipped. "Yes, John." She turned to Robin. "I can't believe you're really here. Let's go have a chat and catch up."

Kory stepped forward. "It's nice to meet you, Shelby, but I'm not comfortable letting Robin out of my sight until I see where she's staying."

John Slains tapped his cowboy boot on the hard floor, some of his impatience seeping through. His jaw flared before he spoke. His patience must be nearing its end. "I will not tolerate your overprotective bullshit." He turned to Robin and hissed as he spoke. "Listen, Missy. I don't like being spoken to by uppity women who aren't used to how things work. You only have status if your husband does. We're the ones who provide and protect. Without us, you're nothing but sinners. I won't send your husband off without letting you two say your goodbyes. Go with Shelby. Now."

Robin clenched her jaw and shot a terrified look at Kory, keeping another batch of tears pricking her eyes at bay.

He nodded, so she let Shelby lead her from the room.

"Who the hell does he think he is?" Robin said once they were several rooms over in the living room. She kept her voice pitched low so it wouldn't carry back to the others. John Slains seemed ordinary on the surface, but he was strangely cold. She was certain there was a terrifying edge below.

Shelby checked behind them before she spoke. "Someone you'd better listen to. John's decent when he isn't drunk or angry. He keeps the creeps and assholes here in line. They're all scared of him and think he's got a direct line to God." Shelby looked proud as she hugged Robin again before sitting on the brown leather couch. She patted the cushion next to hers. "Sit. Let's chat. Tell me everything."

Robin took a deep breath and took in Shelby's appearance, noticing the differences for the first time. Shelby had grown up in their time apart. Her skin had cleared up, her figure rounded, and even without makeup, she was striking. She must not get outside much as her skin was milky white, a sure sign of wealth or status in this world. One thing was the same. Even without her glasses, Shelby's greenish-blue eyes were still hard to read.

Maybe she was interested in Robin's story and being genuine. If their positions had been reversed, Robin would want to know everything. Still, a nagging voice in the back of her head told her not to fully trust her sister. Shelby might have been assimilated by the enemy.

Robin summarized her life since waking up alone after the assault; how she had made her way to Grandpa Clay's farm, and about their time in Boise. She swallowed hard at the lump in her throat as she explained that he'd passed away last fall. She glossed over the Wings coming to town and what had led to their flight, but said that Grandpa had asked Kory to look out for her. "I hadn't trusted anyone in a long time, but I trust him."

"Is it true that you're pregnant?" Shelby's eyes flicked to the side as she spoke.

Something was up. Was she supposed to pump Robin for information and tell John what she learned? "Of course," said Robin. "I'd never make that up."

"That's so exciting," said Shelby. "Our children can grow up together."

"Kory and I planned to keep heading east," said Robin. She didn't feel like sharing Vita xTerra as their destination. A vague east sounded safer.

Shelby pouted. "You wouldn't leave me again?"

What the hell? The taste of bile filled Robin's mouth at the memory of that morning. Shelby was the one who'd done the leaving. Still, best not to argue. It would be counterproductive. She was here to get along and put her sister at ease. Maybe Shelby stayed against her will, too.

Robin double-checked that they were alone, before she leaned in and whispered, "When we leave, you could come with us." Seeing a sliver of shrewdness gleam in Shelby's eyes, Robin regretted her words.

"Did Uncle Luke make it to xTerra?" Shelby picked at the edge of one of her inflamed nails, which were bitten to the quick. Then she shook her head before Robin had decided if she should answer the question. "I can't."

Robin took her sister's hand. "If your husband is mean to you, just leave." It was a long shot, but she couldn't live with herself if she didn't bring it up once.

Shelby snatched her hand away. "I think you've got the wrong idea. I've married up. John Slains is the top dog, the kingpin, so that puts me on top too." Her eyes narrowed. "Even if his sister sometimes forgets. Besides, I can't leave, because I'd never leave my son."

"You have a son?" said Robin. That changed things. Her first instinct had been correct. She couldn't trust her sister to help them escape. Now for damage control. She wouldn't mention leaving again.

"John Junior will be three in June," said Shelby. "I arrived with Travis about two months after the asteroid. He woke me up in the middle of the night a couple of weeks after we thought you died, and we ditched the other two. He didn't give me a choice. We headed east and were passing through north of here near Wright. We ran into a patrol with one of John's younger brothers and their right-hand man. Rodney offered him a job, which Travis jumped at."

"That doesn't explain how you ended up married to a man more than twice your age," said Robin. "And the leader, to boot." Maybe she would be the one gathering important information—two could play that game. Robin wanted to learn more about John Slains and this place—anything that might help them escape.

Shelby shrugged. "John isn't old. He's experienced and a tough leader. He's a man of God and well-respected."

"So?"

"Well, Travis didn't care one way or another if I was his girlfriend or just some whore. John invited me into his bed and said if I got pregnant in the first six months, I could be his wife. Keep him warm at night and raise his heirs." Her eyes lingered on Robin's hand, where she still wore the diamond ring, and Shelby's mouth flattened at the corners.

She must be jealous. For all John called her a wife. Maybe they weren't married.

Robin took a chance with her next question. "How does your husband know the kid is his?"

Shelby didn't seem offended. "He got his sister to babysit me for two months to make sure nobody else came near me while he put out word I belonged to him. When the time was up, I got pregnant almost immediately, so we got married. He was a preacher before the asteroid and he performed a ceremony. Now, I have John Junior. My John dotes on him and I'm pregnant again too, so he's pleased with me." Her hand dropped to her abdomen. Now that she was sitting, her small but defined bump was more obvious.

"I'm glad you're doing well and making the best of the situation." Robin had forgotten that Shelby seldom listened to anyone except herself and that she'd always needed to be in charge. With Shelby, popularity mattered. Perhaps being married to the leader was the closest her sister could get to status in this world. Robin changed the topic. "What rules are you supposed to explain?"

"Women don't talk to men here unless they're answering direct questions. Except for your husband, of course. Which, by the way, your Kory is one handsome hunk of a giant. Way out of your league and not what a brainiac like you would have chosen in the old days. Lucky you." She laughed, "I would have asked John if he wanted a second wife, but it looks like you've got a protective husband already."

No way would Robin have agreed to be a sister-wife to Shelby. Her skin crawled. A control freak like the Slains leader wasn't what she had in mind for a partner. "So, I can only talk to you and Amanda, and the two other Slains wives that were with you?" Robin asked. That was ridiculous. On the other hand, she didn't want to speak with the strange men. Especially Travis. The sight of that rapist made her stomach churn.

Shelby nodded. "Honestly, the other two wives don't have a brain between them. Hannah and Jenn were married to John's brothers before the asteroid. His youngest brother got killed on patrol early on and John doesn't want his nephews in charge one day, which is why it was so important for him to have his own son." Her eyes shone with pride.

Apparently, John Slains was starting his own empire.

"What does he need Kory for?" Robin asked her sister.

"None of our business," Shelby said. "No talking to the men. Do what I say. Do what Amanda says, and most of all, do whatever John says. That's all you need to remember. Got it?" She chewed on the sore-looking side of her thumb.

"Yes." There was no point in more discussion. Robin would just get angrier if they kept talking about what wasn't allowed.

"Good. I'll take you out to your cabin and wait for your hunk to join you. The next patrol leaves in the morning and he'll be with them. He should bring you back to the main house when he goes. I'll look after you."

"If we get our own cabin, why can't I stay there?" Robin wasn't interested in staying in the main house near John Slains. No matter that he was married to Shelby, she didn't trust him. She'd prefer the privacy of her own cabin, with the door locked, while Kory was away.

"A. Because John said so. B. Because if you stay out there and the other guys figure it out, you're fair game." Shelby smiled. "You're better off inside."

"This place sucks," said Robin. "How can you stand it?" She'd meant to keep her mouth shut, but the words slipped out.

"It's no worse than anywhere else out there and better than a lot of places." Shelby tossed her long ash blonde hair over her shoulder. "You'll get used to it." She stood up. "Let's go. The only empty cabin is number six, so that's your new place."

Shelby led Robin out the back door and across the muddy backyard to a cabin—off-center on the right. It looked the same as the other numbered cabins, except with a black number six painted on the door.

Inside was nicer than Robin had expected. On one side sat a wood stove, two recliners, and a small round table with matching chairs. A peek into the separate bedroom showed a proper bed covered by pristine, new-looking bedding. The walls seemed solid and at least it was clean.

"Not bad, right?" said Shelby, indicating the interior. "It was my idea to outfit the bunkhouses and cabins from the hotel about two miles back. Everyone has decent furniture and bedding. No kitchen needed as we deliver the meals from the main house." She sat on the bed.

"What will I do when Kory isn't here? When I'm staying in the farmhouse?" Robin had a feeling that she would be cooking and doing laundry for a host of men. It could be worse.

"The usual, I guess," said Shelby with a shrug. "Cooking, cleaning, laundry."

Her words confirmed Robin's fears. She was a servant.

"Oh," Shelby continued. "You're such a book nerd, I'll suggest we put you to work teaching. The kids have been running wild. They need someone to teach them how to read and do basic math."

"What about you?" said Robin, her eyes narrowing. Her sister had never liked chores.

"I mostly supervise," said Shelby, tossing her long hair.

Robin nodded. She itched to make a run for it. She and Kory were so close to xTerra that stopping now was frustrating. It must be only a few hours up the highway by jeep. Still, they were going to be stuck here for a while because everyone would keep a close eye on the newcomers for some time. They wouldn't be permitted outside the gate together, and certainly not near a vehicle. They'd have to manufacture an opportunity.

CHAPTER 22: ROBIN

Robin and Kory woke to pounding on the cabin door, and her stomach plummeted. Kory would leave on patrol for ten days at a time, which made her insides churn. She yawned. They'd been up most of the night, making love and planning. She could do this.

"Patrol leaves in twenty minutes, Lover Boy." Rodney's distinctive voice carried through the door.

"I'm up," called Kory. Before rolling out of bed, he grabbed Robin for another extended kiss. "It's just a delay. We aren't staying." His quiet words helped lessen her pounding heart and soothe her shattered nerves. Kory swung his feet to the floor and got dressed. "I'm leaving my CDs with you. Is that okay?"

Robin nodded. He was asking her to believe that he would return unscathed. "Can you leave your blue T-shirt too? So, I can sleep in it?" She wanted something that would make him feel close.

He smiled and tossed it to her with a wink.

She caught it, forcing herself to return his smile. Lifting the shirt to her nose, she inhaled. It smelled like Kory, which was just what she needed.

"I need to get ready too," Robin groaned. She stretched before getting up. She didn't want to room with Amanda or stay in the main house. The other woman had shown no interest either, and, if she read them right, Shelby and Amanda battled to be in control of the women and to have John's ear. Robin didn't want to be caught in the middle, but she might have no choice.

She dressed and grabbed her pack, tucking the extra items from Kory inside. He'd come a long way from the days when he'd guarded his treasures, even from her. She straightened the bed while Kory stuffed his feet into his boots. He would take his pack with him. They wouldn't leave anything in the cabin for others to snoop through. They owned little, but what they had was important.

Kory pulled her into his arms for a long last kiss and hug before he took her hand and they headed to the main house. A bottomless pit developed in her stomach as they walked toward the house. Shelby and Amanda stood on the front porch while the men who were leaving milled around on muddy patches of ground with scattered clumps of flattened brown grass that was the front lawn.

Kory joined the men while Robin climbed the stairs to the porch. There were several whistles from the waiting crowd. She stiffened, but pretended not to notice. Shelby caught her eye and tossed her head toward the door. As Robin reached her sister, John spoke to the gathered men from the top of the stairs.

"Men, you're headed out today to relieve those on the north watch near Wright. A group will carry on mid-week to Gillette to deal with the rogue farmers and spread the word of our expansion. Rodney's in charge of both groups. We'll see you back in ten days. You'll have a week of duty at headquarters and three days off before you rotate back to the north. The new guy is Kory. His wife is Shelby's sister."

There were a few disappointed looks, but most of the men looked ready for business.

"Fall in," said Rodney, addressing the assembled men. "You five are with me. Johnson will drive the second group."

"C'mon," said Shelby, tapping her foot on the porch and tugging on Robin's arm. "You don't need to watch them leave. We've got work to do. Today will be easy, compared to tomorrow, when the other group arrives from the north. They'll have laundry and will double who we need to feed. Then we have three slow days until the southern patrol rotates."

That meant about twenty-five men would be here at a time with another twenty or so out, split between two locations. Escape would be risky.

Robin gave Kory a half-smile and a wave and turned to follow Shelby. Best to listen.

Inside, Shelby brought Robin to a mountain of laundry baskets, overflowing with clean sheets, towels, and clothing. "Start folding. Bedding and towels go on this side. Clothes on the other. When the kids get up, I'll introduce you. Breakfast is in an hour." Turning on her heel, she departed.

Robin folded everything, stacking the mound of white sheets together. Clothing was labeled with Sharpie on the tags with initials. Though she didn't know who they belonged to, she grouped items by the letters on their labels.

Shelby arrived to take her to breakfast in the dining room where they ate with John and two men who, based on their similar coloring, must be his younger brothers and their wives. Robin sat and tuned out John, who appeared to be in lecture mode to his brothers. She choked down toast and bacon, but the sight of the runny scrambled eggs made her feel sick and she left them on her plate. The egg smell was almost more than she could tolerate.

"You should eat up," said Amanda. "We don't waste food here." She sniffed as though she smelled something foul.

"Since I've been pregnant, eggs don't sit well," said Robin. "If someone else would like my share, please take them."

One of John's younger brothers grabbed the plate with his long reach. "Don't have to tell me twice." He smiled, showing a mouth full of yellowed teeth.

Robin opened her mouth, but before she spoke, a sharp kick hit her shin. Must be Shelby reminding her not to talk to the men. Cheeks burning, Robin kept her eyes down and her hands folded in her lap while she waited for the others to finish. While they ate, four boys and two girls arrived and were served breakfast at the counter. Their ages ranged between about twelve, down to the youngest, who looked no more than three. John scooped the youngest boy onto his lap and tickled him.

John Slains smiled, transforming his face for just a moment as he dropped his guard.

"Daddy. Stop," said the squirming boy.

That must be John Junior. Her nephew.

"Kids," said John, his face becoming serious. "This is Robin. She's in charge of teaching you this spring and summer. She's going to make sure you can all read and learn some math." Shelby must have suggested it to him.

"John, I wanted to teach her to make bread," said Amanda. "It would be nice to reduce my workload." She shot a poisonous glare at Shelby. "Afternoons then, I suppose."

Shelby smiled back, a sweet and innocent smirk. Robin bet Shelby would fill her afternoons too, making Robin a pawn in the power struggle between the women.

"When can we play?" whined the tallest, and probably the oldest, boy. His dark shaggy hair needed a cut.

"Lessons until lunch," said John. "Five days a week, starting now. Then Shelby wants her sister for dinner prep."

Amanda threw her hands in the air. "I'm supposed to be in charge of the kitchen. It would be nice if I were consulted." Her look challenged her brother, who stared until she dropped her eyes. Family or not, nobody could stand up to John Slains.

"Amanda. Remember your place." He returned his focus to the children while his sister's face paled and she turned away.

"Uncle John, school all morning isn't fair," said the second oldest boy, who was perhaps eight or nine. "When will we play? We just finished building the fort." He looked at the older boy, who nodded.

"No argument. The Slains family is going to be the best-educated family around, which means you need a teacher. We'll watch for an educated man to take over, but for now, Robin is it. Take her to the schoolhouse when you've finished breakfast." John stared at each of the older boys until they dropped their gaze. "Listen and learn."

"Yes, Uncle John," said the oldest. His dark, sullen eyes flashed to Robin, giving her a speculative look that immediately put her on edge. How could someone as young as he seemed, be so unsettling?

The kids didn't want lessons, and teaching children who wouldn't be respectful to her because she was a woman was going to be difficult. Plus, how was she supposed to teach an almost three-year-old? Maybe counting, his alphabet, and letter sounds? He wasn't old enough for kindergarten—she would be a glorified babysitter.

After Robin helped clear the breakfast dishes, the flock of children escorted her to the largest separate building out front. Inside was cold, and she spent several minutes lighting candles. A thick film of dust coated everything. When was the last time anyone had given the kids lessons? Had there been nobody in the four years since the asteroid?

The schoolhouse was sparse inside—a table, half a dozen chairs, and smaller tables as desks. Her chest tightened. She didn't know how to teach. Under the windows, she found a shelf with picture books, another with chapter books, and a third with assorted textbooks that may have been scooped from the local school. There were sharpened pencils, a box of assorted pencil crayons, and stacks of notebooks with lined paper, but not much else for supplies. For games, they had some dice and several decks of cards. That would help with Math.

Robin had never been much of a babysitter, preferring to avoid those jobs. Mom had been the teacher and Shelby had been the one to take jobs minding children for money. This was unfamiliar territory.

"Let's get acquainted with each other?" said Robin, taking a deep breath. "Come sit at a desk and you can tell me your names and how old you are. If you can read, tell me that too."

"I'm Bobby," said the oldest boy. "I'm almost thirteen. I finished grade three at the actual school and am the best reader." He glared at the others as though daring them to argue. The oldest girl flinched under his gaze and turned her eyes to the floor, almost in tears.

"I'm Sam," said the next boy. "I'm nine. At the old school, I went to kindergarten, so I can read too. Everyone else is too stupid."

"Maybe they'll learn now that I'm here," said Robin, trying not to be annoyed with the boys' attitude.

"I'm Daisy," said the oldest girl in a quiet voice. "I'm nine too." Her sad eyes remained riveted on the floorboards. Robin's heart went out to her.

"I'm Ava," said the second. "I'm five." She kept chewing on her grubby fingernails.

"I'm Little Rod," said a boy who was missing one of his front teeth. "I'm five too." He lifted his hand and showed his fingers outstretched. "Five. I hate school 'cause Bobby said it's dumb. Plus, he said we don't have to listen to you." For all his negative words, the boy was friendly and spoke with a lilt of good humor.

Bobby, huh? "I recall your Uncle John having a different opinion. You're going to have to obey me when I'm the teacher." Robin channeled her mom's teaching manner and turned to her nephew. "You must be John Junior." He had thick brown curls with golden highlights that reminded her of her own hair and eyes like his father.

"He's not even three," said Little Rod. "He's the baby."

"Am not. I'm big," screamed Junior as he jumped off his chair. He threw himself at his cousin and punched him in the midsection.

Little Rod crumpled to the floor, moaning, tears trickling down his flushed face.

"Junior," said Robin, putting authority into her voice. "You can't hit each other. Especially not at school." She didn't know if that was a rule they'd heard before. "You need to apologize."

Junior stared at her with his father's cool, grayish-blue eyes and his face lost all expression. Damn. He wouldn't apologize. What should she do? Her mouth turned to sand as she wracked her brain for a new plan. The kid had just won the power struggle, and he wasn't even three. She glanced across the room as Sam rose to his feet.

He strode across the classroom and smacked Daisy. The snap of his palm on the little girl's cheek hovered in the air. "We can hit the girls. They aren't allowed to talk back." He glanced over his shoulder as if daring Robin to do something.

Daisy held her cheek and a lone tear trickled down her scarlet face, but she didn't protest.

"The rule applies to everyone," said Robin. "John Junior and Sam, you'll have to stay back for fifteen minutes when the others leave for lunch." There needed to be consequences, so they would follow her rules. She needed to gain control and stop the violence so everyone would feel safe. She wasn't trying to make long-term plans, but she couldn't help but want to do a decent job. Maybe she could win them over, at least temporarily. Changing their beliefs long-term might be unrealistic.

Bobby's reading was halting and Sam's was no better as they struggled through a Grade 2 level reader. Robin watched Daisy following the words with her finger, her lips moving without sound. She'd bet the girl could read well, even if she pretended she couldn't. Daisy also would have finished kindergarten before the asteroid.

Robin ran through the alphabet with everyone, and they discussed how the letters sounded. The big boys glared at being included, but followed along. She labeled notebooks and passed them out so the children could practice writing letters, both uppercase and lowercase. Everyone could use a review.

After about an hour, Amanda dropped off a snack tray of sliced apples and individual small containers of peanut butter for dipping. Including one for Robin. She called a break for recess and took a few deep breaths. Other than the initial problem with behavior, so far, so good.

Afterward, she read aloud from a faded copy of *Harry Potter and the Philosopher's Stone*. It was too challenging for any of the kids to have read it on their own, but it might be a story that they'd all enjoy. She gave the older three some addition problems to work on while she sat with Rod, Ava, and Junior to practice counting. They found a jar of buttons that she divided into piles for them to use.

Though none of the children had seemed keen to be in school, everyone had cooperated with the lessons—perhaps remembering John's words. Maybe this wouldn't be a bad way to spend the mornings until she and Kory could leave.

At noon, Shelby returned. "Lunch."

"Sam and John Junior need to stay back for a few minutes," said Robin. "They were disrespectful." Sam stopped near the threshold, hesitating.

Bobby sidled out the door with a smirk for his younger cousins. Daisy stayed behind, straightening the books on the shelf while the others raced for the door.

"Sam can stay," said Shelby, tossing her long hair. "Junior doesn't get punished."

Sam stopped and flopped into the nearest chair. "Aunt Shelby. I'm hungry."

His whine grated on Robin's nerves. "He and Junior both hit someone. They can't hit their classmates."

Shelby gave Robin a look and extended her hand to Junior. "C'mon." They walked out the door, ignoring Robin's quiet seething.

Her cheeks flamed as she went to speak to Sam. She crouched beside his desk. "Do you know why you're here?"

"Ya. Cause my bitch mom didn't collect me like Aunt Shelby did Junior." He swung his legs back and forth, kicking at the floor with his scuffed shoes.

Robin ground down on her teeth. "I'll talk to Junior's mom later. Nobody hits anyone at school."

Sam looked up, his eyes filled with hate. "I don't have to listen to you. You're a woman and a sinner." He jumped off the chair and ran out the door.

Robin gritted her teeth. This was Shelby's fault. If she hadn't taken Junior, Robin could have reasoned with the boys together. She looked around the classroom. Daisy remained by the books.

Robin checked that nobody else had come in.

"You can read too, can't you?" she said, sitting down next to Daisy on the floor.

Daisy looked up. "I'm not supposed to do anything better than the boys." Her brown eyes were earnest and her lip trembled.

"Looks to me like you might want to keep it hidden, but there's no reason you can't read better and do math, too. When I went to school, the girls could do everything the boys could."

"I remember my kindergarten teacher," said Daisy with a lilt in her dreamy voice. "She wore fuzzy sweaters that smelled like flowers and she said I was smart."

"I'll help you," said Robin, her heart aching for the little girl who had to live here. "Why don't you eat lunch and we can meet here for a while after? I'm sure my sister will assign me chores, but I need to plan something for tomorrow. If she lets me, you can come back for an extra reading lesson. Would you like that?"

The little girl nodded, pink staining her cheeks. "I can keep a secret." She smiled and skipped out of the classroom.

Robin's instinct was to make the little girl's life better, at least for now. She'd feel guilty leaving Daisy behind when she left, but it wasn't enough to make her want to stay.

When Robin returned to the house, she ate a ham sandwich and followed Shelby into the back room for a private conversation. As soon as they were alone, Shelby whirled around and smacked Robin across the face. The blow snapped her head around, her cheek smarting. Her hand itched to return the favor, but she restrained the urge. This would escalate, and she was alone and not the wife of the leader. She inhaled. She had to be smart and not react.

"Never tell Junior what he can and can't do," said Shelby, pointing a finger with its chipped nail in Robin's face. "He's the next leader, and you'd do well to remember that."

Robin's hand rested on her burning cheek, still feeling the impact. "What the fuck?" she whispered.

"It was for your own good," said Shelby. "You're not in charge here. I'm your superior." Her gaze shifted once more to Robin's ring. "That's from your husband?"

Robin nodded and shoved her hand in her pocket. Shelby didn't have a ring and seemed jealous that Robin did. She swallowed, biting back the retort she had ready. She would play the game, for now. "May I please take an hour this afternoon to plan tomorrow's lessons? I will teach better if I prepare."

Shelby nodded as though pleased. "Since you asked first, it's fine with me. Amanda's bread-making lesson will have to wait." She smirked and held up her finger. "One hour. I'll retrieve you at the end. You're on dinner prep this afternoon."

Robin nodded. Her sister was the enemy. Robin hadn't wanted to admit how low her sister had sunk. Her heart broke to think that her little sister was so callous and mean. This nasty side of Shelby severed the last of Robin's loyalty. Some of the harshness reminded her of their mother.

The rest of the day passed in a blur. She gave Daisy the secret reading lesson, planned which letter sounds to cover tomorrow, and wrote a few pages of practice sentences in the notebooks. Too bad she couldn't print them on a computer or copy machine. Hand copying was tedious. Then, Robin made three sheets of math problems for the older kids and made three rough Snakes and Ladders boards to teach them a game the next day. It would be beneficial for all the kids to practice counting.

After an hour, Shelby took her back to the house, where Robin chopped vegetables and made soup with Jenn and Hannah, the two quiet wives. Neither of them spoke or were friendly, but they worked hard. They were also nervous, jumping at every loud noise in the kitchen.

At dinner time, Robin stayed behind to wash the dishes. Shelby and Amanda ate with the Slains family. Robin gobbled a few bites alone in the kitchen when the dishes were almost finished, grateful for the time alone. With the mark still burning on her cheek, she couldn't face her sister right now.

At the end of the night, Robin collapsed into bed—a lumpy mattress that smelled faintly of urine—on the floor in Amanda's room. Wearing Kory's T-shirt, Robin closed her eyes and imagined he was there and what she'd tell him about her day. She took several deep breaths, trying to relax. He had to be okay. They could get out of this together.

She slipped into an exhausted sleep, only to be awakened when it was still dark to help cook breakfast before teaching school for the morning. She got the extra hour for prep and read with Daisy. Robin helped with vats of laundry in the early afternoon before heading to dinner prep later. Feeding the Slains family and the men stationed here would keep her busy.

On the third day, she slipped up to her room to crochet for an hour in the afternoon before once more helping with dinner and clean up. That was the only time she was alone. Cooking for thirty was hard work. Plus, twice every two weeks, when the patrols returned, they'd have the men's laundry to add to the daily chores. Shelby kept her occupied, so Robin hadn't been able to help Amanda yet or learn her method of baking bread. That could turn into a problem.

Robin kept her head down and worked, counting the days until Kory returned. She saved her frustration and tears for bedtime after Amanda had gone to sleep. Without him, Robin reverted to her loner self, not speaking to anyone except in the schoolroom. There, she focused her attention on the students that wanted to learn, particularly Daisy and, to her surprise, Little Rod. He sucked up knowledge like a sponge and had an instinctive sense for numbers that was far beyond his years.

Her teaching time became the only part of her day that brought her joy. Helping Daisy especially was the highlight. The rest of the time, Robin spent in fear, waiting for Shelby or Amanda to take offense and smack her—they often hit Hannah and Jenn. So far, she'd avoided John Slains entirely, except at breakfast. Sometimes she felt him watching while she ate, but she kept her head down, avoiding eye contact.

Robin couldn't wait until Kory returned so she could get out from under her sister's thumb for a short while. Maybe she'd get a full night's sleep. She didn't know how much more hostility and silent treatment she could take. Nights she lay awake, obsessing over things she wished she could say and do.

Maybe when the men returned, she and Kory could escape.

Chapter 23: Kory

Bunking with the men at the patrol camp wasn't much different from when Kory had stayed with the Wings. He'd survived living with them and he'd make it through this, too. Half of the group was sent to cut firewood, gather supplies, and do whatever needed doing, while the others remained at a barricade on the main road. Every few hours, they switched on and off active duty.

Kory kept to himself and followed orders. Several times, the hair on the back of his neck rose as he felt Rod's eyes on him, evaluating.

The first change to this routine came on day five.

"Everybody up," said Rod, striding into the canvas wall tent where all but the night watch slept. Their smaller tent was right beside the road. "Greg and Jim, you've got the blockade today. The rest of us are going on a raid. There are a handful of farms up north that need a reminder that they pay tribute or we'll make them wish they had."

The men ate a quick breakfast and hit the road, piling into the jeeps.

The first place they stopped was a rancher-style home several miles past Gillette.

"Take anything you want," said Rod to the group in his jeep. "We've been here once before, but stayed outside. We're going to step it up. This time, smash anything they won't need for cooking, canning, baking, or other food production. Scare the holy hell out of them. If the husband talks back, this time we're taking his wife."

The other men nodded and grinned. Kory felt ill.

The couple who owned the farm rushed outside when the Slains arrived, pleading to be spared.

"Face down. On the ground. Don't move," Rodney called.

The homeowners threw themselves onto the hard-packed muddy surface.

The jeep doors opened and Rod strolled over to stand above the couple. "Stay down."

They didn't move. The Slains had visited before and they seemed to understand the need to be cautious.

The men from the jeeps rushed past them, sprinting for the house. Kory included. While hesitant at first, Kory dumped a desk and kicked the chair over. As he continued, he knocked picture frames to the floor and smashed photos off the wall, getting into the spirit of destruction. He got swept up in the feeling of power, the rush of control. The Slains men whooped and hollered as they bashed, making holes in the walls and rifling through drawers, flinging clothes onto the floor.

Kory stopped, taking in the wanton destruction. They'd ruined everything of personal value in this house. He sobered. He didn't want to be like these ruffians. To calm himself and slow his pounding heart and heavy breathing, he ducked into the kitchen, away from the group, hoping to catch his breath.

Inside was cozy but there wasn't a lot of food in the pantry. Half a bag of grainy flour, a cup of rice, and a small, almost empty bag of dried beans. These people weren't holding out on the Slains—they had nothing to spare. The taste of bile filled Kory's mouth.

He returned outside to report to Rod. "They have nothing."

"Check again. They probably hid the best stuff behind walls or under floorboards. They expected us," said Rodney with a wave.

Kory returned to the house, tapping on walls and thumping on the floors, listening for hidden compartments. All around him, guys carried clothes, tools, and household items that they'd plundered, crunching through broken glass from the smashed pictures. Kory had done that to the house. His stomach clenched—he hated himself for taking part in the destruction.

He was about to give up on finding anything when a thump on the back wall of a closet boomed with a hollow sound. He checked the panels and ripped off the loose pieces. Holy shit. A cache of seven rifles and more than a dozen boxes of ammo lay within a hidden compartment. He glanced around. He was alone, so he removed two of the rifles, leaving the nicest ones inside, and grabbed three matching boxes of shells. They could keep the rest.

He fixed the compartment, adjusted the hanging jackets, and headed outside with his ill-gotten booty.

"Nice work, new guy," said one of the men.

"Good work," Rod said, slapping him on the back. "That's what I'm talking about."

He kicked the husband, who curled up on the ground. "I hope you learned your lesson."

Rodney took the guns and ammo and stashed them in his jeep. "Okay everyone, we got what we came for." He turned away from the couple on the ground who hadn't moved. "Message received." He blew a whistle from his pocket, the sound piercing.

The remaining Slains men roared out of the house like a pack of wild dogs.

The farmer on the ground watched Kory, his eyes never leaving him. He must have noticed Kory had only turned over some of the weapons. He nodded once when he caught Kory's eye and the others were busy climbing into the jeeps.

Back on the road, Rod drove for fifteen minutes before arriving at their second stop. This clean, prosperous-looking house had well-tended flower beds, with the first tender shoots of daffodils and tulips rising from the black earth.

Kory didn't want to ruin somewhere so well taken care of, nor did he want to get caught slacking. He wasn't sure what to do, but he had a fine line to walk. He stepped out of the jeep.

The farmyard smelled of manure—they must have animals.

The men started their search and seizure with the outbuildings.

Sure enough, the barn was filled with pigs, chickens, and three cows. Rod directed several swine to be put into the trailer behind one jeep. His men didn't take everything, perhaps what the Slains felt they were due. They'd been here before, but like the other house, the search hadn't progressed inside the last time.

The homeowners stood in the doorway of the house while the Slains were busy outside. They were an older couple who reminded Kory of Jeb and Martha Croft. The familiarity was another punch to his gut. Rod let them return inside the house while the men searched. He might not consider them a risk because of their age.

Rod called Kory over from where he'd been hovering near the porch. "Find something like you did at the last one. Maybe you have a talent for finding hidden shit."

The old couple sat at their kitchen table, holding hands, while the Slains ripped their pantry apart, stole jewelry, and cheered over a gallon jar of coins from one of the bedrooms. Kory grimaced at the sound and shrugged at the farmers. He took a deep breath and got to work.

Kory thumped on walls and floors once more, going from room to room.

After checking the kitchen, the farmer followed him. "Why are you here? We haven't done any harm. John Slains instructed us to supply pigs at harvest and we did. We deliver eggs every second week to the collection point. We were told we'd be left alone if we complied."

"Rod thinks you're holding out on them." He couldn't look not-Jeb in the eye, a sense of shame washing over him. Continuing to search, Kory located two empty wall compartments. No guns. No weapons. He descended into the basement, the farmer still trailing. Nothing.

Kory turned to leave the gloomy cellar when someone sneezed. He whirled and looked at the old man, whose eyes widened and the creases on his face deepened. The old man fake sneezed a second too late. Kory wasn't buying his act.

The sneeze hadn't been him.

Kory's eyes narrowed as he scanned the room again, checking for inconsistencies. This room was shorter than the length of the house upstairs. The far wall might be false, concealing a hidden room. He thumped on the wall in question. It seemed solid, but he continued, tapping every few inches, listening for the sound to change.

Near the corner, he moved a clothes drying rack and found a seam in the wall. His tap sounded hollower. He pushed near the crack several times, working his way across the wall. A handleless door popped open from a second line in the corner, revealing a narrow room. Inside, two teenage girls sat on the floor, hugging their knees. Their tear-filled eyes glanced up at him. The girls looked to be about fifteen or sixteen years old. His chest tightened, and he clenched his fists. What to do? There was no fucking way he could turn them in. He knew their inevitable fate. He wouldn't have that on his conscience.

"We couldn't work the lock, Grandpa. It's stuck," said the older one. Her voice quavered, and she looked past Kory to the farmer.

Ignoring the girls, Kory jammed the door closed and replaced the drying rack, adjusting the hanging shirts. His mouth was as parched as drywall dust as he prayed no one from upstairs would interrupt. He grabbed the older man who'd remained silent and hauled him back upstairs by the bony elbow. He propelled him into an empty bedroom where clothes and books had been strewn across the hardwood floor. "I won't say a thing about your guests, but I need something to keep Rod happy. He won't believe I found nothing."

"Why would you help these monsters?" The old man nudged the door shut with his dusty work boot.

"They've taken my pregnant wife hostage," Kory said, surprised into being honest.

The old man nodded and reached underneath the scratched wooden dresser. He removed a bundle that had been fastened underneath, out of sight. "Give him this." From somewhere else in the house came the sound of breaking glass. The man winced and turned toward the noise.

Kory took the cloth bag and unwrapped two handguns. He looked up, his eyebrow lifting.

"They were my father's," said the farmer, pitching his voice low. "Or I'd have turned them in sooner. We've been compliant, hoped not to attract attention."

Kory stood right next to the older man and whispered. "You shouldn't stay here. Take the girls to xTerra, the walled city near Edgemont, and see if they'll take you in. It isn't safe for them here. No matter how careful you are. If I found them, someone else could, too."

"We don't want to leave our farm." The man's jaw set in a determined line. "My granddaughters will be more careful."

"Women have no rights with the Slains," said Kory. "For all John Slains preaches about keeping order and following God's plan, his men will rape them. Hurt them. If you love them, get them out of here. I won't say anything, but next time it will be someone else and you might not be so lucky."

He spun on his heel and headed outside, holding the guns aloft like prizes when he reached the porch.

"Holy shit, kid," said Rod. "You're better than a drug dog but for weapons. We can always use guns." He slapped Kory on the back and blew the whistle, signaling for the others to return. The sound of smashing dishes stopped.

Kory breathed an inward sigh that this hadn't been a test. If someone had seen him, he would have failed. He needed to fit in better. He couldn't keep taking risks. Not just his safety, but Robin and the baby's depended on it.

Once more, the rest of the men poured outside with armfuls of loot.

"I trust you've learned your lesson," said Rod to the farmer. "We're doubling the number of pigs we'll need this fall. Better hope you have plenty of piglets." He turned to Kory. "You ride up front with me. We have one more place this afternoon and two tomorrow. Then, we wait at the collection point for eggs and other regular tribute. Won't be long until we rotate back to headquarters and you can see your girl. You've earned it."

Kory nodded. He'd been counting the days. His anxiety over hers and the baby's well-being remained high. No matter how pleased Rod seemed, John Slains hadn't been pleased to grant Robin status or be part of the family. Would Rod have orders to make sure he didn't survive the summer, leaving Robin on her own? The question dogged his every moment, keeping him from sleeping. He bit down on his aching teeth whenever he needed a reminder to resist becoming one of the Slains. The pain kept his mind sharp.

Rod's voice continued. "At the next few places, we're making first contact. Our policy is less grabbing, more intimidation."

Kory shrugged. "I'll do what you want." He prayed there wouldn't be killing.

Rod nodded. "You're smarter than you look. Your job specifically is to scare the fucking shit out of these people. Yell, scream, go apeshit—look like some sort of Viking berserker for all I care. Make them believe you'll rip them limb from limb if they don't join us."

That was the last thing Kory wanted, but he'd play the role. It would keep Robin and their unborn baby safe if he acted like he was on board. No half-measures.

For the rest of the ride, he pictured living in xTerra with Robin, planning how to ditch these brutes. He had to keep the long-term goal at the back of his mind while he did what he needed. For now, he just needed to stay alive and get back to Robin.

CHAPTER 24: ROBIN

Sundown approached on the tenth day since Kory's departure, when the roar of jeeps outside the wall made Robin's head jerk up from where she'd been peeling a basket of dusty potatoes. Her heart raced. Kory should be with this group. Dinner prep was almost complete, but either Amanda or Shelby would put her back to work if she stopped. Best not to draw any attention. She bit her lip, longing to sprint to the gate to greet Kory. She had a moment of misgiving. What would he say about her black eye? He'd be livid.

Her eye was courtesy of another smack from Shelby. Junior's behavior had remained difficult, and Shelby wouldn't listen to reason. When they'd faced off a second time, Shelby had demanded Robin's ring as the price for not involving John. Robin had passed it over without a word, her face stinging. The confrontation had been deliberate. Shelby's smirk of satisfaction when she slid the ring on her own finger had been confirmation.

"You owe me this much for abandoning me in the mountains," said Shelby, holding her hand up to let the diamond sparkle in the sunlight.

Her words slashed Robin's heart. Shelby had left Robin for dead. With the accusation hanging in the air, Robin bit down on a retort. Shelby was a lost cause. As much as it hurt Robin, she'd leave Shelby without another thought. Her sister had become a Slains. She'd chosen her life, and she would have to live with the decision.

Tonight, Robin would get out from under Amanda's and Shelby's watchful eyes with Kory back. At least for a while. Some party was scheduled for tonight to celebrate the raids, which had been wildly successful, or so Robin had gleaned from the snatches of conversation she'd overheard. It was going to be huge too since she, Hannah, and Jenn had been prepping all day.

Robin went back to peeling potatoes until her quick peek at the window showed the returning men inside the gate. Her heart raced as she watched Kory stride past the corner of the house, probably on the way to their cabin. Screw this. She wanted to see Kory. She set down her peeler and headed for the back door, only to find Shelby blocking her exit.

Her sister shook her head. "He can find you if he's interested, but you can't ditch work to find out." She pointed at the kitchen and followed.

Robin had cut only one potato into chunks when Kory roared, "Robin. I missed you. Get out here."

She shot her sister a triumphant look, dropped the kitchen knife with a clatter, and ran.

Kory stood in the open doorway by the front door. He grinned as she sprinted toward him and flung his arms wide. She jumped into them. He lifted her off her feet as he squeezed, holding tight. His familiar pine scent filled her lungs when she inhaled. She didn't want to let him go and her arms shook. She kept herself from bursting into tears of relief. They weren't alone. Part of her had wondered if he'd ever return. She'd been terrified he'd be injured or killed.

He whispered in her hair. "I'm about to be a jackass. Don't take me seriously."

He pulled back, taking in the sight of her black eye, and his expression darkened. "Come help me unpack." He threw her over his shoulder and headed for their cabin, passing almost a dozen men milling around nearby. Jars of moonshine were already being passed around. It might get rough here tonight. Dozens more were being unpacked from a crate near the gate.

Several of the men jeered as Kory marched past, carrying Robin.

Robin's face flamed. "Put me down. Stop being a Neanderthal."

He laughed and smacked her ass. Not hard, just a tap for the watchers.

She squirmed, but couldn't get down.

"Hey, Goliath, take a jar. We'll see you later." Rodney handed Kory a jar filled with clear liquid as they passed.

"Thanks," said Kory, taking it with his free hand. "A drink is second on my list." He patted Robin's butt as he continued to their cabin.

He was laying it on a little thick, and Robin didn't appreciate being part of his show, but he must have a reason. Cheers followed in their wake.

Inside the cabin, he let her down and stroked her cheek with his thumb—below her blackened eye. "You're okay? And the baby is too?"

At her nod, some of the tension left his shoulders. "Who hit you?" he growled.

"My sister," she said, staring at the floor. "I'm thankful I know what happened and that she's alive now, but I can't save her. She belongs here." Kory had better still be planning to leave. This place was a nightmare.

"Hey," he said, tilting up her chin. "Are you okay? For real?" His touch sent shivers coursing through her body. Flames licked at her core. How long until naked fun time?

"Shelby acts like she's the queen and I'm a servant. She accused me of abandoning her and took that stupid ring as payment. She thought it was my wedding ring." Robin took a breath, letting thoughts of her sister go. "I survived. I missed you and I hate it here." She hadn't meant to spill everything in the first second. "How are you?"

He perched on the edge of the bed and patted his knee. She sat, basking in happiness, enjoying that he was back. He tilted in for an extended kiss that left them both wanting more. When he released her, she took a deep breath, feeling most of the tightness in her neck and shoulders dissipate for the first time since his departure.

Kory's mouth remained flat and his face devoid of expression. Something was wrong, and she wouldn't let him keep it to himself. Part of being together meant they shared.

"What happened out there?" She stroked his whiskered jaw, looking him in the eye. She wanted the truth.

He opened his mouth to speak, and nothing came out. Then, his face crumpled, and he sobbed onto her shoulder, pulling her close. Hot tears soaked her shirt. She'd never imagined Kory being upset this way. He hadn't even reacted this way to killing Dillan or Everett. Had they made him hurt innocent people?

She hugged him back, making soothing sounds, hoping she was doing the right thing.

When at last he could speak, he pitched his voice to be quiet while she sat on his lap, enjoying their closeness. He must know too that even if they were alone, they'd have to be careful. She wouldn't put it past Shelby to send someone to listen to their private conversations. John, too, for that matter.

Kory filled Robin in about the first two raids where he'd tried not to get caught up in the mayhem and destruction and how he'd worried that he hadn't done enough to be convincing. The next ones, the men had been given the green light to intimidate, smash, and destroy. More than that, ordered to wreak havoc. So he had.

"I freaked myself out," he said, his voice breaking. "I was a brute. A monster. I terrified those people."

"You were supposed to," she said. "That was your plan. Rodney would have known if you weren't doing your part. You said you would try to fit in and take away their suspicion."

"Mission accomplished," he said, bitterness dripping from his voice. "I'm Rod's favorite. His new number one."

"I'm missing something. You're upset about being too convincing?" She leaned back to better see his face.

His eyes looked haunted. "I scared the holy hell out of innocent people and made them join the Slains kingdom. What I didn't expect was that I enjoyed it." His voice dropped. "I felt like a beast. If we stay here, I'm scared, that's what I'll become forever." His voice cracked at the end.

She took his face between her hands and stared him in the eye. He needed to see how serious she was. "You are kind, thoughtful, and caring, and I love you." She kissed him. "We'll get out of here." She infused more confidence into her words than she felt. She didn't know how or when, but they would. Soon. He wasn't the only one who couldn't take much more. Every interaction with her sister chipped off another piece of her soul.

"We go tonight. I'm not going on another patrol or more raids. I'm done." His hands shook, and she took them and squeezed.

"What's the plan? You seem certain, so you must have one."

He nodded. "The party. Guys will be drunk, even the ones on active duty. They're drinking already. The moonshine is flowing, and soon they'll be drunk. Travis makes it. He bragged the entire way back about its potency. Said it can strip rust from nails and have you hammered with less than a jar." Kory's face hardened again. "John only lets them drink every couple of months and tonight's the night. Never on patrol, only here at headquarters where they are secure."

Robin's voice shook. "They're going to expect you to drink with them, especially if you're the hero of the hour." What if he miscalculated and got too drunk to leave? She could see the mess now. A bunch of drunken, sex-starved men would be terrifying. She needed to hold herself together; she couldn't afford to panic or freeze.

"I don't drink and I'm not starting tonight. I'll go out in a while, after I've had some proper time with you." He smiled, allaying some of her worries. He'd be okay. "I'll reek of booze and slosh some around; to them, I'll already be drunk. I've seen enough alcoholics to be convincing."

Not just with the Wings, but growing up, he'd seen plenty.

"I slipped a jar to the guard on the gate tonight. He'll be in no shape to stop us." Kory stood up and yanked his shirt off over his head and sniffed it. He grimaced and tossed it onto a chair. "I can't believe you let me hold you when I stink."

"Can you get us a jeep?" She remained stuck on the plan for leaving, even if the sight of shirtless Kory and his solid muscles were distracting. "If not, they'll catch us in no time."

He nodded. "I know where they store the keys. You've got a light touch with locks. Have your wire and shear ready. You can open the shed, no problem, while I stand guard. I'll drive. We're less than three hours from xTerra with wheels. We're halfway between the northern and southern routes. Once on the road, we'll head north. We only left two men stationed near Wright tonight. That's it until the reinforcements leave at dawn. If we go south, we hit a full patrol of ten or twelve." His eyes met Robin's. He clearly didn't like those odds.

Now that he'd filled her in about the plan, she had more pressing needs.

"There's wash water over there," said Robin, pointing to a water pitcher and basin on the dresser. Shelby had sent her out to ready several cabins, including her own. She'd also taken time out to wash after lunch. Sex would be a great distraction.

Kory smiled. "What have they had you doing most days?" He poured water and grabbed the bar of soap.

While he cleaned up, she told him about the school lessons, the power struggle between Shelby and Amanda, and Junior being a spoiled brat. She fiddled with the laces of her hiking shoes. Looking up, she found him staring at her cleavage. He looked like he was starving and she was a full-course meal. It turned her insides to jelly.

"Before we do anything else, I'm taking you to bed. I've been thinking about you for days." His voice became a growl. "I need you."

"I thought about you, too." She placed one of her icy hands on the muscles of his solid chest, and he grinned. The air in the room heated as they switched to a more private topic; she shed her clothes, letting them drop piece by piece to the floor while Kory's hands caressed her skin, sending tingles everywhere.

They took each other's hand, lacing their fingers together. Kory led her to the bed.

• • •

Robin and Kory remained in their cabin for another hour and a half, soaking up each other's presence. A knock at the door interrupted their interlude.

"I'm sorry to bother you." Came a quiet voice. "Dinner." Someone must have brought a tray with their food.

"I'll get it." Kory pulled on his jeans and opened the door.

Robin dressed as well.

The mousy blond outside was Hannah. She kept her eyes on the ground and cast a quick glance toward the front of the house, where the party had grown to a moderate roar of loud voices. "Rod's looking for you. Amanda said to pass the food along."

"I'll be out when we've eaten." Kory slurred his words as he took the tray.

Hannah's eyes widened, and she flicked a look at Robin before heading for the back door of the main house, avoiding the raucous men in the front yard. Wife or not, she'd do best to stay inside. Robin almost wished she could enjoy that safety herself.

She dished up their dinner of venison stew and freshly baked bread at the table.

Kory slid into a chair and shoveled in his first few bites of stew. "After we eat, we'll mingle and I'll be social. I'll stagger around and be an ass for maybe an hour or two, then I'll almost pass out. Then you'll have to get me back here to put me to bed. When it's dark and quiet, we're outta here."

Robin couldn't eat much dinner, but forced a few bites down. She'd need fuel and energy for tonight.

After dinner, Kory said, "Are you ready?" At her nod, he swished his mouth with moonshine and spat it into the empty wood stove. He sloshed more onto his shirt and swished some in his mouth again. He spat it out. "How's that?" He leaned close.

Alcoholic fumes rose in waves. She tried not to inhale too deep and turned her face away.

"Ya. You stink now." She swallowed. "The other wives aren't outside. I think they're hiding in the house." She wanted to preserve the plan, but she didn't want to be sent away or left here to wait, hoping he stayed sober and the plan worked.

He took her hand and squeezed. "It fits if I don't let you out of my sight. Our little show will fit with what they know of me. Overprotective brute that I am. Rod and John won't think anything of you being tucked under my arm. I'm just sorry we have to go out there. I'd rather stay here and skip the party, but they'll suspect less if I seem happy."

She bit her lip. She didn't want to go outside, but she trusted Kory to keep her safe.

"Let's get it over with." The stench of hard alcohol carried negative associations, and she would force herself to deal, even with Travis out there. Plus, as one of the few sober people outside, she'd have an advantage.

Kory wrapped his arms around her waist and kissed her temple. "I won't let them hurt you."

Robin took a deep breath. "Okay." She tucked her chilled hands into her pockets.

The party was in full swing when they joined the crowd. Three women wearing tight clothes passed around mason jars. She didn't recognize any of them.

As Robin watched, several men groped them on the way by or whispered in their ears. That could have been her fate. Her heart went out to these women. Tonight would be difficult and busy. Another woman emerged from Cabin One a few minutes later, fixing her hair and adjusting her skirt. As Robin had expected, the wives must be inside, as there was no sign of Hannah, Jenn, Amanda, or Shelby.

John Slains stood on the porch with Rod, passing a half-full jar back and forth.

She watched, noting that John kept his sips small. If he was drunk, it wasn't obvious.

The men in the yard talked over each other and it was all she could do not to cover her ears at the cacophony. How could anyone enjoy themselves amidst this racket? Several men staggered from group to group, almost spilling their drinks as they moved between conversations that seemed mostly bravado and stories about being shit-faced or violent.

Several sets of eyes bored into Robin as she and Kory moved deeper into the noisy throng. Travis sidled up, scanning her from head to toe with a leer. Kory's arm tightened, though his expression remained neutral.

"Hey, Goliath. You're sharing, after all?" Travis turned to Robin. "I didn't recognize you at first, Sweetheart. You still like it rough?" He was staring at her breasts when Kory's fist smashed into his face.

Travis hit the ground, landing on his back with an audible whoosh of air. His eyes rolled back, and he stayed down. A roar went up from the nearby bystanders, who seemed to think the scene was part of the evening's entertainment.

Kory swayed on his feet but stayed upright. "My wife is off-limits." He slurred and turned his back on the fallen Travis. "Where can I get another drink?"

With her peripheral vision, Robin noticed John and Rod watching the interaction.

One of the younger Slains brothers brought Kory a fresh jar. He ignored the fallen Travis and stepped around him. "Cheers." He clinked his container against Kory's.

"Thanks, man." Kory touched his jar to a couple more held in his direction before lifting it to his mouth.

She and Kory moved on, circulating through the crowd. She swiped her sweaty hands several times on her jeans, and when he stumbled, she tucked herself under his shoulder to support him. Her throat tightened. He was convincing. What if the other men thought he was too drunk to protect her or to fight?

John and Rod remained on the porch above the others, still talking. How long would they stay and be watchful? Neither seemed tipsy, let alone drunk. The escape hinged on most of the Slains men being out of commission or dead asleep. Robin took pains not to be obvious when watching them.

Rodney's gravel voice became louder and his hand gestures grew bigger as he and John started another jar. Robin tried not to show her relief that they might only have John to worry about. All the other women took turns disappearing, but Robin stayed glued to Kory's side. Though several speculative looks came her way, nobody touched her. Several men glanced at Kory, perhaps noting his size or remembering what had happened with Travis. They gave her a wide berth as they moved through the crowd. The men who'd been on patrol with Kory seemed friendly, while the others who'd been stationed here were more reserved.

The minutes crawled by and as the sun went down, the temperature dropped and the crowd thinned. Two of the guys had passed out on the ground and John disappeared inside. Though it wasn't full dark, Kory lurched and grabbed onto the handrail of the porch stairs to stay upright. Time for another show.

"Are you okay? It might be time for us to go back to the cabin." She didn't have to pretend concern.

"I'm fine, woman," he growled. "Don't tell me I've had enough to drink." Several sets of eyes turned in their direction at his loud voice.

"I just thought maybe you'd like us to spend some more time on our own," she said. "I've missed you." She pouted for their watchers.

Kory stumbled and half-fell, spilling the rest of his drink. He touched one knee to the ground and stayed down.

Robin struggled and couldn't lift him to his feet.

"I'll help," said Rodney, trotting down the stairs. He wasn't too steady on his feet, either. Good to know.

He grabbed Kory on one side and Robin took the other, and they half carried, half supported the sagging Kory to Cabin Six. He didn't help, other than moving his feet, letting Rodney and Robin struggle. Kory protested the whole way, making a convincing drunk.

"Leave me be. I can do it."

Robin opened the door and Rodney helped drag Kory to the bedroom, where he collapsed onto the bed and lay unmoving, his eyes closed.

"Make sure you lock the door tonight," said Rodney to Robin. "Everyone conscious knows Kory is going to sleep hard tonight. He had a fair bit of Travis' special sauce."

"I wish he'd stayed awake." Robin backed away from Rodney, not wanting to be too friendly even while they spoke. He seemed nicer than most, but what if he got the wrong impression?

"You two have ten days to get reacquainted before we rotate back on patrol," said Rodney. "Don't be too hard on him about tonight. Everyone needs to blow off steam from time to time." He stopped, one hand on the doorknob. "Speaking of steam, now I've got to convince my wife to unlock the bedroom door." He winked.

"Thanks again for your help." Robin bit her lip and glanced back at the bed where Kory was splayed out, his arms straight out from his sides. It didn't look like he'd be moving anytime soon.

"Let him sleep it off. In the morning, you can stay in bed too. John said you're excused from teaching tomorrow. Thought you might like to know, Kory was a real asset out there, and I made sure John knows too. You two will fit in great. See you tomorrow." He nodded on his way out.

When Rodney left, she locked the cabin door, and she watched through a slit in the curtains as he wove his way back to the house.

She double-checked the covering on the windows, lit a candle in the main room, and set it on the table. They would have to wait before venturing out.

Kory emerged from the bedroom. "Thank you for being a good sport. That couldn't have been easy. You ready to leave as soon as it's quiet?"

She nodded and set out the crib board. "I never unpacked. Cards while we wait?"

Chapter 25: Kory

After two hours of waiting, the noise of the party fell quiet. They turned out the lights and Kory wandered outside. He urinated in the bushes near the cabin, using that excuse to scope out the situation. Two different men had passed out on the hard mud near the buildings, but most had retired inside the bunkhouse and cabins—even the stragglers were gone. The yard was deserted and the lights in the main house were dark, with everyone settled for the night.

Kory peeked around the corner again. No sign of John, Rod, or the other Slains brothers. He would deal with the gate guard, if necessary, but the jar of moonshine should have done the trick. Kory checked his watch.

Midnight. Time to go.

He slipped back into the cabin. "It's clear."

Robin grabbed her pack, and he did the same before they slid out the door. The night was almost black, with the light of a half-moon and a blanket of stars scattered across the inky sky. His eyes adjusted while they navigated their way to the fence. His heart drummed against his ribs as he unlatched the gate. He winced at the slight squeak of the hinges as he swung it wide enough for them to slide through. Once outside, he closed it with a faint click.

The inattentive guard sat passed out beside the jeeps, leaning on the nearest, facing the house—an empty jar overturned in his lap.

Three of the five jeeps the Slains owned had been parked near the shed where they kept the keys. There were half a dozen pickups lined up in the back field that no longer ran. Kory had asked a few quiet questions while he'd been on patrol. The jeeps were the only currently operational vehicles besides the dirt bikes. They'd been gassed up and made ready to leave at dawn. Hungover or not, ten fresh men were being sent north to Wright to patrol the north highway and the new Gillette region.

Robin produced her lock pick and shearing wrench from her back pocket and set to work while Kory kept watch. She strained to listen to the night noises, watching the drunken guard for signs of movement. Every scratch or whisper of sound made his heart lurch.

A coyote yipped in the distance, and another answered.

The noise of the engine would be a problem in the deafening silence. They'd need to deal with the motorbikes as well, just in case. He used his pliers to remove the valve from their tires, the faint hissing loud in the night. Slashing them would be faster, but noisier. He would do the spare jeeps next.

"Got it," whispered Robin, standing up.

The other tires could wait. Kory slipped past her and into the shed. The keys lived on a rack right inside the door. He groped across the pegs, feeling for them, and slid a set from the third peg. Squinting at the key chain—number three. He turned, then grabbed all the other keys and shoved them into his pocket. Anything to slow the others down. The minutes wasted retrieving spare keys or hot-wiring a vehicle would be vital.

He checked the first key matched the ignition on the jeep spray-painted with a three, the one farthest from the sleeping guard. They worked.

Instead of starting the ignition, he popped the jeep into neutral.

He slung their backpacks into the back seat. "You steer, while I push."

"We need to knock the others out of commission or they'll catch us." Robin slipped her multi-tool from her pocket and pulled the valves from both back tires on the other vehicles. The steady hiss of air didn't bother the inert guard.

"Front too?" She looked at him, the whites of her eyes gleaming in the dark night.

He nodded. While she dealt with the one vehicle, he moved onto the one the guard was propped against. He cringed as the man shifted at the sound of the nearest tire's air being released, but the guard didn't wake. The house remained dark, so it seemed they might get away without a hitch. Then, from inside the yard near the gate, a dog barked. Shit. Then, it moved closer, alerted by the continuing hiss of air. Kory's heart slammed into his ribs. At the sustained barking, the passed-out gate guard stirred. Fuck.

"What's going on?" the man said, blinking. He stood groggily, turning toward the commotion. "What's up, Rex?" He walked toward the house and gate. He must not suspect anyone outside.

Kory nodded to Robin and motioned for her to stay crouched on the ground, hidden behind the jeeps in the shadows. He took a deep breath, steeling himself for what came next.

It was a pity Travis hadn't been on guard. Kory hadn't had an opportunity to get revenge for what the man had done to Robin. The punch earlier would have to suffice.

Kory tread with care on the soft ground, sneaking up behind the man and slit his throat. Not Travis, but the third man he'd had to kill. He and Robin couldn't get caught out here beyond the gate. Kory eased the body to the ground. Inside the compound, the dog continued to bark.

They had to go. Now.

Robin slid behind the wheel and turned the jeep as Kory pushed from the front, then the rear, to direct the vehicle onto the long gravel driveway. Despite the level ground, sweat dripped from his face as he labored to keep the jeep rolling.

The silence pressed downward, magnifying every noise. Every time his boot scraped the ground, or the wheels crunched on the small stones, he winced, praying the sound remained undetected. Soon, the gate disappeared into the night and with it, the slain guard. Another couple of hundred yards from the shed, dripping with sweat, Kory had pushed as far as was reasonable. The dog had fallen silent.

He took a long swig of water. "Time to drive."

Robin hopped into the passenger seat and he took the wheel. With a deep exhale, he turned the key. The engine roared to life. He slammed the jeep into gear and drove onto the highway, heading north. He checked the rearview mirror. Behind them, lights flicked on upstairs in the main house. First in one room, then another. Shit. At least two of the Slains were awake. He'd bet one was John.

He and Robin still might get caught. Kory flicked on the headlights and drove as fast as he could on the cracked and pitted highway. Speed now mattered more than stealth. At least there wouldn't be traffic. Going this way, he'd seen the empty road and knew when they would reach the barrier outside Wright.

He and Robin flew through Wright and turned east. He slowed the jeep, turned off the lights, and they crept up to the barricade across the highway where he'd been posted. The two remaining men stationed here were supposed to be awake, but those coming to relieve them in the morning often found them sleeping. Another tidbit of information he'd picked up in advance.

Sure enough, nobody met them on the road. Without wasting time or energy, Kory jumped from the vehicle, and dragged one end of the heavy sawhorse out of the way, swinging it aside to create a path for the jeep. He hurried back and pressed the accelerator, counting on surprise to get them through the gate before anyone clued in to what they'd done.

They rolled through the opening, but a light appeared in the wall tent as someone lit a lantern. The remaining men would investigate. A shadowy figure emerged. Greg or Derek? Fuck.

"Stop. Get back here," said Greg, running toward the road. "Stop or I'll shoot."

The road here was straight, and there was nowhere to go but forward. Kory tromped on the gas, slamming the pedal to the floor. The jeep shot ahead.

Greg fired several times in quick succession, the sound rocketing through the night. One hit the jeep with a glancing blow and a metallic rip.

Kory hunched inward to reduce the smaller target for the shooters, but he was too big to hide. He'd have to trust his luck with the poor light.

Seconds after the next shot, a searing pain tore through his left side, leaving his left hand and shoulder on fire. He removed that hand from the wheel and kept driving, pressing his elbow against his side. He gritted his teeth at the fiery sensation. His right hand shook and sweat dripped down his face. His left side burned and then became numb. He kept driving, unable to determine the extent of his injury—he was still alive, so that was something.

Soon they were clear of the men at the blockade who had stopped shooting once they'd disappeared into the night. The limited patrol of two had been left without wheels overnight and couldn't follow.

Kory flicked the headlights back on and increased their speed, each bump jarring his injured side. Still, he pushed. They needed to get far away from here, and he didn't know how much longer he could stay upright. Every second might count.

"You okay?" Though the pain was agonizing, he kept the sound from his voice. They needed to stay calm. Robin must not realize he'd been shot.

Wide-eyed, she nodded from where she'd crouched in a ball on the jeep floor. "They're a long way back now." As long as he could continue and they didn't get cut off, he and Robin might get away.

Robin returned to her seat, checking behind them several times as she fastened her seatbelt.

The countryside remained dark, as did the highway in both directions.

If the Slains had phones or even radios, this escape wouldn't work. But he'd learned that the Slains had no form of quick communication, relying on messengers, short distances to drive, and the number of men within their territory.

Kory pictured the map Robin had studied in the cabin. It should be another hour to Newcastle, where they'd turn south and then another half hour or forty minutes to the turnoff to xTerra. Depending on road conditions, they could be there in another two hours. If only they could get through xTerra's gate and behind the walls before the Slains arrived. His goal seemed tantalizingly close, but with the burning in his side, he couldn't drive much longer. It was getting difficult to keep pressure on his wound.

It was all he could do to keep the jeep on the road, and his vision blurred. He blinked hard several times, and he grew cold. He might have lost a fair amount of blood.

He glanced down at his ribs, feeling fiery pain shoot everywhere at the slight movement. He carefully peeled his elbow away from his side. Hot blood trickled down his side where his shirt had stuck to him. XTerra had better have a surgeon; he needed an operation to remove the bullet. Plus, there was a serious risk of infection. He would need antibiotics. Getting to xTerra was more important than ever.

Soon after he turned the jeep onto 85 South, he had to face facts. He couldn't drive.

He slowed, halting in the middle of the pitted road, leaving the engine running.

Robin turned to him in confusion. "What's going on?"

He tried to speak, but the pain had become too great and blood loss was making him slow. It took a few seconds to get words out. "They shot me. You need to drive the rest of the way. Forty minutes to the turnoff. Another thirty or forty to xTerra." His voice was weak and shaky.

"You were shot. You're just telling me now?" Her words had a frantic quality. "Can I help?"

"I need the doctors at xTerra. You just need to drive. You can do it." He stumbled out and climbed into the back, shoving the packs to the floor. He slumped onto the back seat, wedging himself in, leaving the door open. Should he get her to try to stop the bleeding? No, they didn't have enough of a head start.

Robin jumped out and ran to the driver's side, slammed his door, and climbed in. "I haven't driven since the farm. Thank god it's an automatic."

He recognized the nervous flutter in her voice as she spoke out loud to herself. He'd like to reassure her, but the words wouldn't come.

She fastened her seatbelt and took a deep breath. The jeep rolled forward, slowly at first, but picked up speed.

He fought to stay awake, so he ran through the escape so far. The Slains needed to change four flats. Eight if they wanted more men for the chase. They would need to start a vehicle. That meant they would need at least an extra ten minutes. His head swam, and he struggled for coherent thought. The southern route appeared marginally shorter on the map—they'd probably go that way and pick up extra men from that patrol—sober ones. If they arrived at the xTerra turnoff first, it might be a problem. Kory was in no shape to fight as his strength leached away and his mind grew foggy.

"Why didn't you tell me?" Robin glanced in the rear-view mirror once she was up to full speed, meeting his eyes. She looked terrified, but was holding it together.

"Just wanted to drive as far as possible. I want to keep you safe." His words slurred as it became more difficult to concentrate on anything except the burning sensation from the hole in his side. His breathing became ragged, and he wasn't sure he made sense anymore. He was getting delirious. "You're a great driver because you're so beautiful."

He tossed his pistol onto the front seat beside her. Her startled eyes met his in the mirror again. "In case they catch up at the turn. They might take the other loop." She would understand.

He blinked hard. Fog filled his brain, but he had one more thing he needed to do. He grabbed the first aid kit jammed in the pouch on the back of the driver's seat and opened it with a shaking hand. Unwrapping the biggest gauze pad, he held it against his side, and wound the tape around his abdomen and ribs to hold it in place—adding pressure to the seeping wound. He used his teeth to rip the tape.

It hurt like hell to move, but he had to slow the bleeding or it wouldn't matter how far xTerra was. His tape job would have to do. He grit his teeth and slumped back again. Every bump jarred his injury, but Robin needed to drive fast, and she was. He hated being helpless.

Kory fought to stay conscious, but the lights of the jeep dimmed. He couldn't keep his eyes open. With everything dark and muted, it took too much effort to stay awake. The sound of the wheels running on the old asphalt faded, and he drifted away.

CHAPTER 26: ROBIN

Robin clutched the wheel with her sweaty hands. Her fingers ached from gripping the stiff wheel and her stomach churned. Kory had fallen silent in the back seat at least twenty minutes ago.

"Kory?" He still didn't answer when she tried for the umpteenth time. Her veins chilled. What if he'd bled to death?

She pressed the accelerator harder and increased her speed to over eighty miles an hour—as fast as she dared. The engine didn't appreciate how hard she was pushing, shaking with a horrid high-pitched whining noise. She wanted to clap her hands over her ears to shut it out, but she resisted the urge as she fought the chattering steering and the uneven pavement. She couldn't go any faster on unfamiliar roads in the dark—not without risking an accident.

Beside the road, a sign flashed by—*Watch for Deer and Antelope*. It was the second one along this stretch. If anything wandered onto the road, at her speed, it would be too late to slow down. She would hit them. Robin strained her eyes, peering into the darkness, drops of sweat racing down her back and pooling near the waistband of her pants. She shifted forward to avoid sticking to the seat.

A crash would be all she needed. She focused, scanning both sides of the road ahead for orange eyes reflecting back at her. She flew past a pair of animals in an adjacent field. Another one moved roadside, but stayed out of her way.

She prayed for no further problems—enough had gone wrong. This drive was already urgent. A red light near the speedometer caught her eye. The fuel light was on. A bullet may have hit the gas tank too. They were almost out of fuel. There had to be enough. She choked back a sob.

Her shoulders were so tight it hurt to move, and her arms ached. The night air rushed past the open window and she grew chilled, but the bracing air kept her alert. She didn't have a watch and the back seat remained quiet. Her chest ached and breathing was difficult. If she'd realized Kory had been shot, maybe they could have stopped to bind his wound. Maybe he wouldn't be bleeding to death. Any serious injury could be fatal in this world, let alone a gunshot wound. A meltdown seemed imminent, but somehow, she kept it at bay. The turnoff must be close.

She still didn't dare slow up to check his condition. Even now, they could be intercepted. Maybe she would be shot, too. Tears filled her eyes, and she blinked them back. She needed to hold herself together. What would she do without Kory? He'd become integral to her world.

Robin didn't want to die. She wanted to see her Uncle Luke and live at xTerra with Kory. She wanted a chance to hold her baby. The silence in the back seat became more ominous with every minute. It might already be too late for a happy ending.

The road sign for Edgemont, the closest town to xTerra, flashed by on her right. Shit.

She'd missed the turnoff. She slammed on the brakes, reversed, and lurched onto a narrower bumpy road.

She hadn't driven long when she passed a *Welcome to South Dakota* sign. So close now. They were almost to xTerra. She sped up as the road improved and she flew through an abandoned town, dark and boarded up. Edgemont. Vita xTerra was south. At the edge of town, she made a hard right, following the signs.

Just outside town, her headlights revealed another roadblock that prevented her from continuing. A massive concrete and rock wall stretched across the road and into the darkness in both directions. There was no way around.

She braked hard, spraying loose gravel from the pock-marked asphalt as she screeched to a halt. She slammed the steering wheel with her palm. Twice. What now? Her chest constricted again, causing stabbing pains along her ribs. She couldn't afford a delay.

She exhaled, took a couple of deep breaths, and studied where she'd come to a stop. She inched forward and the engine coughed, then sputtered and died.

Her headlights showed a heavy wrought-iron gate across the road—a permanent fixture with a smaller building tucked into the trees behind the massive wall. Maybe a gatehouse? Was there anyone here? Perhaps she could talk her way through the gate. On the other side, a second wall and gate blocked her view beyond.

She hopped out to inspect the barrier and the near gate. The fuel gauge hovered below empty. She glanced back the way she'd come. What if the jeep wouldn't restart? The road remained quiet, but the Slains could be here any second. John Slains wouldn't let them go without a fight.

She took two steps forward, and a floodlight blinded her. She threw her hands in the air, blinking against the sudden intense light, and turned her face away.

"Identify yourself," called a loud male voice from near the gate.

"I'm Robin. You don't know me. I'm trying to get to Vita xTerra. My husband has been shot and we need help."

"How did you hear about xTerra?" The voice came from behind the light, and it was impossible to discern anything about the speaker.

"I think my uncle lives there." Her voice shook, and she blinked back tears, her eyes burning with the effort.

"Who's your uncle?" demanded the same loud voice.

"Luke Wilson. Do you know him?" In a closed community such as xTerra, there was a chance.

"Is your grandfather with you?" said a different voice from further left.

Her knees trembled, and she grabbed the jeep's hood to steady herself. "You know my uncle Luke." She could have sobbed in relief, but it still wasn't time. Getting Kory medical attention was her priority. She took another deep breath. "My grandpa died last October. Lung cancer. He made me promise to find Uncle Luke and Aunt Ella."

"She's for real. Her story checks out," said the same man. "Open the gate."

The blinding light flicked off, and a regular lantern lit the area in front of the barricade. In the distance, the whine of an engine came from the direction of the highway behind her. The Slains must be close. The sound became louder, perhaps several vehicles, and a series of faint lights appeared. Three jeeps were almost here. The Slains must have opted to send a single jeep as soon as possible and met up with those from the south. Damn. This could get ugly.

"Please help. The Slains are coming." Her voice took on a strident quality and her knees trembled.

"You're in one of their jeeps," said a third voice. "Maybe this is a trap."

She clenched her fist. No time for a discussion. "We stole it and I'm almost out of gas. They shot Kory near Wright. I'm not sure he's still alive. Please hurry."

"Open the gate," said the man in charge. "We're out of time. Grab your stuff. Leave the jeep. We'll get your husband."

Someone unlocked the clanking gate with a key, swinging one side open.

Three shadowy figures jogged from behind the solid barrier while another held the lantern aloft. Robin grabbed both backpacks and hauled them from the jeep. In this dim light, it was impossible to see if Kory was still breathing. His eyes were closed, and he was as white as paper—his expression was blank. He'd wrapped several rounds of medical tape and a thick gauze pad around his side. Soaked in blood, his bandaged side appeared almost black.

She stepped away from the jeep.

The men dragged Kory from the back seat and lugged him toward the gate. If they struggled to carry someone his size, it didn't show. They half-ran, and she followed, both packs looped around her shaking arms. The adrenaline that had gotten her this far was wearing off.

"He's a moose," said one man as a fourth held the gate open.

The fourth man relocked the gate after those on foot passed through and dashed ahead to fling open the second gate. On the other side sat a truck facing the road to Vita xTerra.

Robin felt a surge of hope.

"Lay him in the back," said one of the three men carrying Kory.

They hefted Kory into the bed of a dark pickup, sliding him along the cold metal with a scraping sound that set her teeth on edge. Two of the men returned to the barricade and locked the second gate as Robin jumped in beside Kory. Crouching beside him, she rested her hand on his chest and felt his heart beating. Slow but still there.

He was still alive. A shuddering breath escaped her. He still had a chance.

The last man slammed the tailgate and looked at her with strange, mismatched eyes. One light, one dark. "I'm Ryan. Luke's my friend. I'll get your husband to the doctor as fast as I can."

She nodded and took her first full breath since learning Kory had been shot.

Ryan jumped into the cab and started the truck with a roar. A blast of exhaust filled her nostrils. He took off fast, gunning the truck straight down the road, her body lurching with the sudden motion. Her last view of the barricade was with the floodlight turned on once more. The three men at the gate pointed rifles at the oncoming jeeps.

The Slains' jeeps screeched to a halt behind the one she'd abandoned, its doors left open like wings, as the pickup sped away. The faint sound of shouting came to her ears, but nobody followed. She listened for gunshots, but there were none.

The truck turned a corner, and she lost sight of the gates, the glow of the floodlight the only sign of their existence. She repositioned, resting Kory's head in her lap so it wouldn't bounce against the hard metal, and wrapped his icy fingers in her own—squeezing tight, hoping he could live until they reached xTerra.

Inside the cab, Ryan spoke into a walkie-talkie. "This is Ryan coming in hot with a gunshot victim and his wife. Have medical on standby and find a surgeon. The guy's still alive. Get Captain Wilson and Ella to intake. The wife says she's Luke's niece." There was a pause, then a garbled response. "Family has always been welcome. It was my call. If the mayor doesn't like my decision, she can yell at me later. See you in twenty minutes."

Robin leaned against the cold metal of the truck and took another breath. Leaning forward, she pressed her hands against Kory's side to add pressure. There was no reaction. They were almost to xTerra and Luke. She closed her eyes and prayed it wasn't too late.

Chapter 27: Robin

Though her eyes only closed for what seemed like a minute, Robin started awake; the truck was slowing. A glow ahead made it easier to discern detail in the flat landscape, but right now, nothing mattered. She focused her eyes on Kory. Her hands were dark with blood, but she hadn't let go.

The truck didn't stop. As they approached, a massive gate beside a wooden tower opened in a wall that was several yards high. They drove through. The solid metal gate closed behind her and the pickup stopped in a pool of yellow light lit from overhead. Ryan jumped out of the front.

"Is he still alive?" He stood next to her, his arms braced on the back of the truck. There was sympathy in his unusual eyes.

Her voice shook, and she bit her lip. "I think so."

"Robin," called a man's voice from farther away. Footsteps pounded the ground as people sprinted toward the parked truck, the squeak of wheels accompanying them.

Her whole body trembled. Uncle Luke's voice penetrated her haze of fear, but she couldn't answer. She'd come all this way to find her uncle, but she couldn't tear her gaze from Kory.

Ryan spoke. "She's in the back of the truck with him."

Two figures opened the tailgate and climbed aboard. "We're doctors," said one. "We got the call that your husband's been shot.

What's his name?" The woman's voice was calming. "Do you know his blood type?"

Robin shook her head. "Kory. His name is Kory." She should know his blood type, but she didn't. She clenched her jaw, still trying not to succumb to tears. Not while she needed to provide answers. The tightness in her chest increased.

"How did this happen?" said the other doctor. He didn't wait for her response. "It was those damn Slains again, wasn't it? Something is going to have to be done about them before long." He shot a look toward the walls, back the way they'd entered.

Robin didn't take her eyes off Kory while they slid him the length of the truck and, with Luke and Ryan's help, transferred him to a gurney. The doctors took off at a run, wheeling him inside. Robin couldn't move as Kory disappeared into the low building. Her muscles seemed frozen, but she shifted her attention to Luke and she choked back a sob.

"Please let him live." Her desperate plea slipped out.

The truck bounced as Luke and Ryan climbed into the back.

Ryan gathered their fallen backpacks. "I'll take these inside for you. The doctors have him and they're rushing him into surgery. I'll leave you two." He headed into the building, following where the doctors had taken Kory.

"Ella's inside too, waiting. Our friend Elizabeth came to sit with the sleeping kids." Luke crouched beside Robin, resting a hand on her shoulder. "You're here and you're safe. Are you hurt too?"

She shook her head. Her relief at making it to the only family she had left was palpable. A tear slipped down her cheek.

"Is any of that your blood?" His voice remained soft.

She looked down. "I. No. It's all Kory's." She lunged and hugged her uncle. His arms wrapped around her, holding her up. She couldn't hold back her tears any longer. Uncle Luke was so much like his dad. She'd forgotten how much he resembled Grandpa Clay. The few tears that had squeezed out earlier were nothing as the dam now burst. She fell apart, sobbing—terrified that she'd lose Kory. He'd been so pale and, near the end, his breathing had been so shallow.

Luke said nothing. He held on and let her cry.

When at last she got herself under control, he released her with a final squeeze, something Grandpa Clay had always done. "Let's talk inside. It's standard procedure for Medical to check anyone new." His voice changed as she struggled to her feet where the light struck her face. "Who hit you?"

She dreaded explaining about Shelby, so she hedged. "It's a long story, but it wasn't Kory."

Luke nodded. "While your husband's in surgery, we'll have time to catch up."

She hoped they were equipped for an operation like this. They might not be set up for gunshot wounds. She forced herself to focus on Luke's words. Kory could be in surgery for hours.

"We stopped at Dad's the day after the asteroid strike and stayed three days. He wouldn't leave because he was waiting for you. Did you make it to his farm?" Luke steadied her as she jumped from the truck and they headed toward the building, leaving the pickup in its pool of light.

She let out a shuddering breath, her hands falling to her abdomen as if to reassure their baby. They had electricity here. And doctors. Even a surgeon. Maybe Kory would be okay.

"Grandpa Clay and I were together for over three years." She looked at her uncle and swallowed. Explaining what had happened was still hard, but the pain had become manageable. "He died of lung cancer last October." She glanced at Luke as they walked. It wouldn't be easy for him to hear that his father had died.

His eye twitched and a flash of pain crossed Luke's face. "I'm glad he wasn't alone all this time, and that you had each other." He hadn't asked about Shelby yet. What could Robin say about leaving her behind? She wished that wasn't how it had turned out.

"Kory and I trekked from near Boise to get here. We holed up for the winter in the Visitor Center at Craters of the Moon, and hit the road in March, just before spring arrived. The Slains picked us up twelve days ago in Douglas. We didn't know before that, but Shelby's with them."

Robin hesitated before continuing after another deep breath. "Shelby and I got separated early on and we didn't know if the other was alive." Robin shot her uncle a sideways glance. How would he react to her next piece of news? "She's Mrs. John Slains now. Mother of his heir. She's the one who hit me." Her voice still sounded shaky.

Did her abbreviated explanation make sense? Her mind was already elsewhere, with Kory, but Luke nodded and held open a glass door. To her relief, he didn't ask anymore about Shelby. "We've heard a lot about John Slains." His voice had hardened.

"Aerin? Your mom?" he said as they entered the long building marked *Office and Intake*. "I had a letter last year from Kimmy. She's safe in New York and works with the refugees. She's doing well."

"That's good," said Robin. She'd hoped her Aunt Kimmy was safe back east. She took another breath before launching into what had happened the day of the asteroid. "Mom wouldn't leave Portland. I haven't heard anything." Robin swallowed, feeling new tears welling up. She'd assumed her mother had died, but she would never have proof or closure.

The pain of losing her mom was distant, but tonight she was raw. With Kory's injury, anything could set her off again. She tamped the feeling down. She wished to avoid crying any further in front of her uncle. This was the first time he would see her as an adult and she didn't want to act weak or like a child. She was embarrassed enough already about the tears.

They strode across a carpeted lobby with a waiting area and tall potted plants—it seemed so civilized and normal, other than the silence. It smelled clean—like lemons and sunshine. At this time of night, the cozy office behind the counter appeared closed with the lights off. Luke leaned over the desk and grabbed a clipboard and pen.

"I'll fill in your intake forms with you once we're in Medical."

"Do you think we'll be able to stay in xTerra?" She hadn't let herself think beyond their arrival, but some of Ryan's words were returning. Something about the mayor being unhappy. They'd worked so hard to get here, pinning all their hope on making this their home.

"Despite the Slains, we're filling up, but there are still several dozen empty bunkers," Luke said. "You two made it this far. You are welcome." There was no mention of the mayor or anyone who might disagree.

She hoped he was right.

Her uncle led her down a short flight of stairs and through a hallway, past a cafe with half a dozen tables that was closed for the night. He sent her into a washroom to clean up.

She avoided looking in the mirror, scrubbed the blood from her hands, and headed back out. At the end, they came to a set of swinging doors labeled, "*Medical.*"

Inside was a waiting room with a dozen chairs and a desk with a nurse in pale blue scrubs sitting behind it. She smiled at Luke as they entered.

A petite blond in jeans jumped to her feet from one of the chairs. It took a second for Robin to register that it was her Aunt Ella, Luke's wife. "They took him into surgery straight away. Come, sit." She patted the chair next to hers.

Luke and Robin took seats beside her. Once settled, Luke asked several questions from his forms. At last, some questions Robin knew the answers to.

"Your husband's full name and age?"

"Kory Walker. He was twenty-six on January seventh." She kept her voice steady.

"Occupation."

She hesitated. It wasn't her place to talk about Kory being homeless before the asteroid strike. It might not matter, but it could affect their admittance to xTerra.

Luke looked up and raised an eyebrow. "Before the asteroid, at least."

"He's worked a lot of jobs," she said. "Security. A bar. No college or training, but he can do most anything he's shown these days. He says he can drive anything. Plus, he's built like a house."

"Medical history? Drugs? Alcohol?"

She remembered the ruse for the Slains, which now seemed a distant part of their past. Kory's clothes still reeked of moonshine. "He doesn't drink, smoke, or do drugs. Earlier tonight, we tricked the Slains into thinking he was hammered. That's how we escaped. I don't know much about his medical history or his blood type."

"To the best of your knowledge, has he killed anyone?" Luke's calm gaze met hers.

She nodded. "Three times. Out of necessity, or we wouldn't be here."

Luke said nothing as he wrote on the paper. She wished she could see what he'd scrawled.

Her uncle looked up. "I put us down as your references."

She was grateful she didn't have to deal with the forms.

"Blood type unknown." Luke looked at her. "They always have a stock on hand, but we'll donate blood to replenish the supply."

Like a lightning bolt, a thought streaked through Robin's mind. "I'm O negative. A universal donor," she blurted. "He can have mine." She wrung her hands, wishing she'd remembered sooner.

"You're also pregnant and exhausted," said Luke, his voice gentle and his eyes softened. "So, unless it's an emergency, and they don't have enough, I suggest you wait and donate blood later."

Her jaw dropped. "How did you know?" Her pregnancy shouldn't be obvious yet. Besides, he hadn't seen her in four years to witness the subtle changes.

He winked. "In my old life, I was a private investigator and now I'm head of security. I pay attention."

"He always sees things like that," said Ella with a soft smile.

"Thank you for waiting with me," Robin said. "Probably not something the head of security and his wife usually do in the middle of the night." She bit her lower lip.

Ella squeezed her hand. "You're family. We're just grateful you arrived safely."

"I've wondered about you girls, my sisters, and my dad hundreds of times." Luke cleared his throat. "Even when the news isn't all good, knowing what happened to everyone is better."

"Don't you have to get up with Jess soon? It's almost morning." Robin said, noticing a clock on the wall. It read three a.m. No wonder her eyes burned. She'd been awake since five a.m. the day before when she'd started cooking breakfast for the Slains men.

"And her little brother Bryan as well," said Ella with a weary smile. "My friend Elizabeth came over to stay with them for the rest of tonight. She'll let me sleep in tomorrow." Her gaze flicked to the clock. "Well, later." She shrugged.

"You should sleep too," said Luke. "Surgery could take a while. Hours, maybe. Plus, I'd imagine your Kory will sleep afterward in recovery."

If he died, they might know sooner.

There was no way she could sleep. "I'm not sure I can. My mind is too busy. But you should." Robin chewed on her lip, looking down the hall past the nurse. She needed to know about Kory.

Both Luke and Ella shook their heads. "Not until they've attended to you as well. It's standard to do a health check on every new arrival. With a life-threatening injury, Kory has priority, but someone will come for you soon."

Luke set the clipboard with the forms on the counter with a nod to the nurse.

After another two hours, a doctor returned from the back. Her scrubs had patches of blood on them, but her hands were clean.

Ella took Robin's hand, and she held her breath, bracing for the news.

"The operation was successful," said the doctor with a weak smile. "The bullet is out, and it didn't do extensive damage. Our best guess is that the seat of the vehicle slowed the bullet or it would have been fatal. We're cautiously optimistic, but we'll have to see what happens overnight. He lost a lot of blood."

Robin stared at the ceiling, blinking back tears of relief as an enormous weight lifted. She took a few breaths and returned her attention to the doctor.

The doctor picked up the clipboard with the forms, scanning them. "Let's give you a quick check as well. Then we can all get some rest."

Robin followed her to a curtained area down the hall and sat on the edge of the bed to be examined.

The first questions were about Robin's overall health, the next about her faded bruises and her black eye, the last about her pregnancy. Other than the bruises and exhaustion, the doctor pronounced Robin in excellent health.

"Would you like to have a sonogram of the baby?" said the doctor with another, more genuine smile. "We can schedule one in a few days."

Kory would love to be included. She would wait until he could be part of it.

Robin nodded. "That would be terrific. Thank you." She hadn't considered that level of technology would be available in xTerra.

When she returned to the waiting area, Ella stood and stretched. "I'm going to head home for a few hours sleep." She kissed Luke and hugged Robin before saying, "We're thrilled you've joined us in xTerra."

Luke stayed, but soon nodded off in his chair, his head resting against the wall behind, his feet braced before him on the floor. It must be uncomfortable.

Robin couldn't sleep but closed her eyes, hoping to at least doze. Every time she tried to relax, visions of Kory dying played through her mind.

•   •   •

Sometime later, with sunlight streaming into the waiting room of the medical center, Robin awoke with a start, her heart racing. Luke was gone, his jacket left on the chair beside her. It took several seconds for her brain to catch up and remember where she was and why she was in a hospital. Like the old hospitals, the faint undertone of bleach and blood lay underneath everything. She blinked and yawned.

A different nurse was stationed behind the desk. This one was older, with thin gray streaks in her long brown ponytail.

"You're awake," the woman said with a friendly smile. "Your uncle left strict instructions that we let you sleep as long as possible. It must have been a long night. He's gone to grab breakfast for both of you."

"Is there any news about my husband?" Robin's voice quavered.

The nurse maintained her cheery expression. "He's alive and stable, but he hasn't woken up yet. We've moved him from recovery to a private room. I can take you there so you can sit with him for a few hours. Luke will bring your food soon."

Robin got to her feet and followed the nurse, their shoes squeaking on the polished floor. Everything here seemed too clean and bright. Electric lights and polished surfaces weren't what she was used to anymore. Hopefully, they'd get to stay, and she'd have time to adjust.

She stopped and peeked into Kory's room before entering. His face was still like chalk, except for two faint pink blotches on his cheeks. Even unconscious, he took up a lot of space. His feet stretched to the end of the hospital bed and they'd propped him up with two fluffy white pillows. With his eyes closed, he could have just been sleeping.

"Oh good, he has color again," said the nurse, walking over to the bed. "That's a positive sign. I'll leave you two alone, but if he wakes up, just press this button." She picked up a call button on a cord and set it on the blankets beside Robin.

The nurse left at Robin's nod. She pulled a chair closer and sat, taking Kory's hand. It was cooler than she was used to—usually, he was hot as a furnace. He didn't move or show any sign that he noticed her presence.

To keep herself calm, she talked to his still form, explaining what had happened since he'd stopped driving. She told him about leaving the angry Slains behind and arriving at xTerra where she'd reunited with Luke and Ella. Her eyes burned. They'd been through so much to get here. "You'll like them. They're good people and we could use a few friends."

A noise of a throat clearing behind her made her head jerk up. She wiped her eyes in case tears had escaped, making herself presentable before turning to face someone at the door.

Luke's sleeves were rolled up, a Band-Aid on the inside of one elbow. He must have already given blood.

She took the small plate with a bagel he held out and put it on the bed.

"Tea okay?"

Better than okay. Tea sounded amazing.

At her nod, he handed her a steaming travel mug. She sipped, allowing the caffeine to bolster her tired self. He'd sweetened it to perfection.

Luke sat in the other chair. "I'm not staying long, but I assume you want to be here when Kory wakes up."

She nodded. There was nowhere else she'd rather be.

"I made arrangements to have another bed brought in here. Make sure you get some rest, too." Luke sipped his own hot drink. "I'm going to head home for a few hours of sleep before I'm on call for the Watch tonight. Seems there was a disturbance at the outer gate last night and we're on alert." He winked. "Someone will be by later to check on you, if not me or Ella, our friends."

"Like Ryan?" she said, nodding.

"Or his wife, Kat. Possibly Christopher or his wife, Elizabeth. We had experience with the Slains on their way to xTerra, Ryan and Kat were attacked and had to hike on foot until they met us. The Slains attacked our entire group the last night on the road. In the mayhem, Ella shot the youngest brother and a couple more of their men were killed. They've been the bane of our existence ever since."

"So you understand."

He gave her a hug. "Our hunting parties need to be watchful and on guard, as do any groups scavenging outside the walls. Five people have gone missing. Something will have to be done soon." He stood. "Not your problem. Just a reminder that we understand some of what you've been through."

Luke left, his footsteps receding down the hall. He would be up and working in a few hours. She was grateful that she didn't have to leave Kory's side.

Robin sat for a while, drinking tea and yawning until her jaw creaked and her eyelids grew heavy. Once she fell asleep, her head resting on Kory's bed beside his motionless hand. When she woke, she had a serious crick in her neck. As promised, they'd wheeled a second bed in behind her, the covers turned down. She yawned. She'd been so tired, she hadn't noticed a thing. A tray with a sandwich sat on the bedside table beside a tall glass of ice water, condensation beading on the outside.

She ate the sandwich, not noticing the taste, washing it down with cold water. She didn't know the time, but her body felt like lead and her bleary eyes seemed filled with grit. Despite her nap, she was still exhausted. Resting her hand on Kory's forehead, she assessed him. No fever. That should be a favorable sign, right? His lips seemed pinker than before, though he remained pale. She hated to see him wounded and hooked up to machines, but he was alive and being cared for. There was nothing more she could do except wait and hope.

With nothing else to occupy her mind or hands, it was difficult to keep from spiraling into what would happen if he didn't wake. The future looked bleak and lonely without him. Best not to think.

She yawned again, took off her shoes, and climbed into the other bed, facing Kory. She closed her eyes and calmed her body at last, running through an inventory of their belongings and what she had to trade or sell as seed money so they weren't destitute. The jewelry stash was more important than ever if it allowed them to be more than beggars. She took a deep breath. It would be okay, and Kory would wake up soon. Eventually, her muscles loosened as they relaxed and she drifted, trying to focus on the positives, but it was a challenge.

What if he didn't wake up? Stifling tears, she squeezed her eyes tighter, still facing Kory so he'd be the first thing she saw when she awoke. Robin was here in xTerra, where she'd dreamed of coming for so long. If only it were as wonderful as in her imagination, even if their arrival had been lacking.

CHAPTER 28: KORY

Kory dreamed aliens had abducted him, their brilliant lights shining in his face—making it impossible to see. They must have strapped him down because he couldn't move. He tried again, but remained trapped in place. He struggled harder, panicking. He had to get back. As he became more aware, he recognized his dream made little sense. He wasn't in a science fiction novel. He didn't know where he was, though the last thing he remembered was being on his way to xTerra with Robin.

Events from the previous evening and their escape from the Slains came back to him in fragmented flashes. The stray bullet and his gunshot wound. Robin's terror and her steadfast driving. She must have made it somewhere safe.

His side ached, and he was alive.

He fluttered his frozen eyelids. They were heavy and didn't want to open. He tried again. This time, they cracked apart. The overhead electric lights made him squint, eyes watering as they adjusted. It looked like a hospital room; he was hooked up to an IV, and his hand ached where the needle was attached. He shifted, wincing, his side sore where he'd been shot.

His brain was foggy. He took a breath, finding it difficult to concentrate. Focusing his effort, he turned his head. Robin slept on a bed beside his, her cheeks rosy and her hair disheveled, wisps and chunks no longer in a neat ponytail. She looked pale, with dark circles like bruises under her eyes. Had she been injured too? There was no outward sign of anything wrong—her sleep was peaceful and she didn't have an IV or bandages. His heart calmed. She seemed to be okay.

This must be xTerra.

His free hand drifted down to his bandaged side. Someone must have operated to remove the bullet and repair the damage. He was lucky to be alive. As he'd lost consciousness in the back seat of the jeep, he hadn't been sure he'd wake up.

Kory glanced toward the window. The sun was setting with muted colors in the western sky, glinting over a surrounding wall. He must have slept the day away. Yawning, he closed his eyes again. He didn't want to disturb Robin just yet, nor did he have the energy to move. It was enough to know they were safe. Later, there would be time to find out what had happened.

The next time Kory came to, Robin was sitting in the chair beside his bed, squeezing his hand. When he opened his eyes, she jumped to her feet and kissed him.

"Oh, thank goodness. You're awake." She grabbed a cord and pushed a red button. "How do you feel?"

"Like someone shot me." He may as well joke.

Rapid footsteps approached from down the hall.

"You're okay?" he asked Robin, remembering her sleeping in the second bed.

She nodded, but before she could say anything else, a doctor showed up in the doorway.

"I'm Dr. Lee. I'll be right back. I need to let the boss know you're awake."

"How long was I asleep?" The words felt strange with his thick tongue.

"We've been in xTerra for two days," said Robin, biting her lip. "We slept for most of yesterday."

"Is it everything you imagined?" He squeezed her hand.

"I haven't seen anything except the hospital."

"Is your family here?" said Kory. That was the reason they'd come all this way.

She nodded. "The Slains were in hot pursuit and I just made it to xTerra lands before they caught up. One of Uncle Luke's friends was at the outer gate and drove us here. Uncle Luke is head of security."

Dr. Lee returned. "I let Luke know you're awake too." Her smile crinkled her eyes as she took Kory's vitals. His tongue still felt odd and the inside of his mouth felt raw. Maybe from morphine or whatever painkillers they'd given him. Apprehension filled him. No matter how hard they'd worked to get here, it was still unknown, and he was in no shape to join the guard. Of course, they wouldn't expect that right away. His brain was still slow.

"No more painkillers, please. I don't like feeling foggy." He met the doctor's eyes. Best to be clear-headed. In his Seattle days, he'd had hazy thoughts when on drugs. He might need his wits about him.

"Now that you're awake, we'll let you manage your pain level on your own," she agreed. "Everything looks as well as can be expected. You just need time to heal."

"How soon can I get out of here?" said Kory, indicating the hospital. He'd recover better somewhere more comfortable and private. If this place was anything like old hospitals, people would barge in at all hours, making it impossible to sleep. He'd never be able to relax.

The doctor's smile disappeared and her mouth flattened. That didn't bode well. Was it because they couldn't pay or didn't have insurance? Those were old problems he hadn't considered.

"I was obligated to call the Mayor when you woke up. She wants to meet you both. She delayed your entry interview until you were awake and could both speak."

Interview? Kory glanced at Robin and she shook her head. This must be news to her, too.

"We might not get to stay?" She fought valiantly not to cry.

He recognized the signs—the clenched jaw and shiny eyes. The slight tremble in her voice. She must be disappointed that their acceptance wasn't automatic, though he wasn't surprised. A place like this might have let anyone in at the beginning, but four years later, they wanted a resume. He didn't blame them. He'd always counted on being seen as muscle. Someone to man the gate or the wall, to repel invaders. Being injured was a minor setback, but it wouldn't be for long. He was young and strong, and would be fit again in no time.

He reached for Robin's hand. "We're here now. If your family can help us stay, they will."

The doctor peered down the hall and closed the door to his room. She lowered her voice despite the privacy. "The Mayor is looking for a reason to keep you from joining the community. She fears you'll join the modern faction, with Robin's family and their friends. She doesn't like that newcomers now make up most of xTerra's population. Since the recent election, that group controls the majority of the Council positions and most of the Watch. She worries she'll lose power next time. Her principal support comes from the long-term residents who were here before the asteroid and her popularity has dwindled."

Her words made sense. Kory appreciated the doctor giving them the lay of the land. At least he knew what they were up against.

"If you have something valuable to give her or pay for supplies, that would go a long way. You'd be assets, not refugees." Peering toward the hall, Dr. Lee grabbed Kory's chart and made a couple of notes.

There was a sharp knock on the door and, without waiting for an answer, someone pushed it open.

An older woman stepped inside. Her pale hair, with as much gray as blond, was cut in a bob that framed her round face. It should have made her look sweet and unassuming, like everyone's favorite grandmother, but it got his hackles up. Unlike most people he'd met the last four years, she didn't look like she'd gone without food for any stretch of time. What did she know about how life was now?

Living in xTerra might have left her soft, but her eyes and mouth had sharp creases around them, despite wearing a somewhat pleasant expression. She wore a flannel shirt and jeans with dirty knees, as if she'd been called while gardening. She must have thought meeting them was important enough to drop everything when informed that he was awake.

Even with smudges of dirt, she wore an air of authority. This must be the Mayor.

"I'm Dolores Montgomery, the Mayor of Vita xTerra. You must be Robin and Kory, our newest guests." She stepped closer and shook their hands.

All the while, Kory felt her pale eyes assessing them. Her emphasis on the last word told him a lot about her view of their arrival.

Dr. Lee made herself busy, recording something else on Kory's chart before hanging it on the rail at the bottom of the bed. "I'll come back later to change your dressing," she said, excusing herself from the room.

"We're hoping to be more than guests," said Kory. No point in skirting the issue. "Robin's family is here, and we've traveled eight hundred miles to be reunited. If you don't have a bunker for us, I'm sure they'd let us live with them." He hadn't met them and wasn't sure that was the case, but it was best to start from a position of strength.

The Mayor's mouth turned down. "You need more than just family connections for citizenship in xTerra. Neither of you are skilled tradespeople, agriculturalists, doctors, or trained in professions that we need."

"Unless I'm off base, you've got a problem on your doorstep," said Kory. "Maybe more than one."

"Excuse me," said the Mayor. "You arrived two days ago and have been awake for ten minutes. I'd be shocked if you understand the situation. Not everyone who arrives penniless on our doorstep gets to benefit from our walls and our community. You have to earn your place. Right now, I don't appreciate your tone."

He wasn't a child and didn't care if she appreciated his words. Still, he kept his voice even. "The Slains, your nearest neighbors, intercepted us, and we spent two weeks with them," said Kory. "We've seen their outposts, their headquarters, and we've spoken with John Slains. There might be something useful in what we've learned." He met the Mayor's look with a direct gaze, no longer feeling sluggish from medication. His anger must have burned through the fog. She was just another bully, and he was used to dealing with those.

She blinked first. "If what you say is true, that might be worthwhile." Her mouth twisted as though admitting their knowledge might be valuable pained her.

"That sounds like vital information," said a lanky man with Robin's same bright blue eyes from the doorway.

Kory bet he was Luke Wilson.

"As Captain of the Watch and head of security, I'd be extremely interested in what you learned on the way. The Slains pose a serious threat." He strode across the room. "Mayor," he said with a nod. He shook Kory's hand and shot Robin a smile that seemed to reassure her as some of the tension left her shoulders.

"Nice to meet you," said Kory. "You must be Luke."

Luke said, "The doctor says you can get out of here tomorrow, provided you take it easy. We still have several empty bunkers, including a few in Section One, not too far from us. Your status should be settled by this evening." He turned to the mayor and raised an eyebrow. "Citizenship shouldn't be an issue, will it, Dolores?"

The Mayor pursed her mouth. "See to their accommodations and their paperwork, Captain Wilson. I'll expect a full report on the Slains and their activities by the end of the week." She stalked past them and left without saying goodbye.

She would never be an ally. Maybe they could keep her from becoming an active enemy by being polite.

Luke shook his head after she left. "It'll be good to have you up and around soon and installed in your own place. I'll have Rose at intake choose a bunker to prepare. Any special requests?"

Robin picked up Kory's hand, and he squeezed. Her small hand felt cold in his. Perhaps still nerves.

Before he could say that anywhere would be fine, she spoke. "If there's somewhere with music or a stereo, that would be fantastic." He wouldn't have thought to ask for himself, but that would be the icing on the cake. A safe place to live and music.

Kory's throat tightened. She was wonderful.

Luke smiled and turned to go. "I'll get Rose on that right away."

"Thank you," said Kory. He wanted to make sure Luke understood his value. "I wasn't making it up. Anything you want to know about the Slains, I'll tell you. I kept my eyes open."

"I'm counting on it," said Luke as he left.

•   •   •

The next morning, Robin pushed Kory's wheelchair down the hallway of the Medical Center, up a ramp, and through reception. They continued outside, to where a man was waiting beside a golf cart, their packs piled into the back.

"This is Ryan. He drove us here the other night," said Robin. "Ryan, this is Kory."

Ryan stepped forward. "Luke's on shift at the main gate, so he asked me to help you two get settled in your new place."

"Thanks for being decisive and driving fast," said Kory, shaking the other man's hand. He stood gingerly, feeling a twinge from his side. More discomfort than pain. As long as he took things slow, he shouldn't re-injure it. Robin had filled him in about the night they'd arrived, since he remembered nothing after bandaging himself in the back seat and passing out.

"Not a problem. I'd have helped anyone fleeing the Slains, but we might not have driven inside without your family connections. Luke's family, so you are too. Welcome to xTerra."

"Thanks." Kory had a feeling he would like Luke and his friends. So far, they seemed direct and no-nonsense.

"I'll help you aboard and drive you to your new digs. You're in 135, near us in 105. Luke and Ella are in 113, and Christopher and Elizabeth are nearby in Section 2."

Ryan helped Kory into the front seat. He'd been taped and bandaged enough that he didn't bend well. Robin climbed into the back seat beside their grubby backpacks. Kory glanced in her direction. They sure as hell weren't arriving with much.

Ryan must have guessed some of his thoughts. "Your arrival was a lot like mine and Kat's. Injured, exhausted, nothing to our name except what we carried in our packs."

They headed out in the Polaris down one of the smooth gravel roads. The city inside the walled compound didn't look like much—a few metal and concrete buildings near the gate, like the one with the office and Medical. Other than that, the land rolled in waves. They turned onto a long road where he had a better view of rows filled with cylindrical bunkers—one after another, identical except for the black painted numbers on cement walls at one end.

The community's outer wall curved behind them and disappeared into the horizon, the far ends lost from sight. This place was immense, truly an underground city behind the guarding walls. The road they traveled continued past bunkers with numbers beginning with a one.

Ryan stopped outside 135. Their new home.

The word seemed strange. Home was a word that hadn't applied to anywhere Kory had stayed in years, but he would give this one a chance. He was ready to live somewhere longer, to settle down and stay. Somewhere he could raise a family and be part of a community.

Before helping Kory out, Ryan said, "Whatever's in the bunker will be yours too, so you aren't starting out with nothing. A couple of years back, xTerra went through the empty bunkers and claimed some valuables and a selection of books for the library. They centralized clothing and shoes from the bunkers which had been owned by people who didn't make the journey. The Council decided that furnishing, art, bedding, etc., and a year's supply of dehydrated food would remain in the bunkers for new occupants. You'll receive coupons for clothing, shoes, and coats for no charge. It's a cushion until you get on your feet and find your place. It'll be okay."

Kory nodded his head. He didn't like to owe anyone, but he'd take what they offered. They could use a break. "What are the strings?"

Ryan gave a short laugh. "I'm hoping to influence you to join the Watch when you've healed. We can use you. Luke suggested I do the recruiting." He shot Robin a look. "You can join too, but there are lots of other jobs. What were your plans before the asteroid?"

"They had accepted me for pre-law at Yale." For once, she didn't feel bitter that her life hadn't worked out the way she'd expected. "But I might like being a teacher like my mother."

Ryan laughed again. "I was a lawyer once upon a time. I don't miss it. There are lots of useful jobs. You may also find you want one close to home for a while. Babies are exhausting. Maybe you can help Kat teach at the school."

Kory winced, curtailing his glance at Robin as she jumped out of the Polaris. It seemed others already knew their joyous news. At least they'd have help in a place like this. So much better than living alone for the rest of their lives. Still, if he and Robin didn't like xTerra, they could always take their chances and head East or back to the Crofts where they'd be welcome. He hoped for her sake they didn't have to, but he felt better having options.

Ryan helped him climb out of the electric golf cart, grabbed the backpacks, and tossed them to Robin. Ryan handed him a sheet of paper. At the top was a door code. He slid a metal panel from a keypad and said, "You guys should do the honors. It's your house."

Robin grinned and stepped up. "Let's check it out."

Ryan left. As he turned around to drive back the way they'd come, he said, "Dinner at Luke and Ella's the day after tomorrow. Bunker 113. We wrote our phone numbers on your paper and the one for Medical and for supplies. Anything you need, let us know."

Kory glanced down. He'd never met Ryan's wife Kat or Luke's wife Ella. There was also a Christopher and Elizabeth listed. They'd stumbled into a bunker family. He wasn't sure how well he'd belong, but he'd try.

The thick metal door swung open easily when they keyed in the sequence on the number pad. Inside, motion sensor lights flicked on as they entered. He held his breath, noting the change in the air inside.

The first room was the laundry, with a washer and dryer on one side and an open door to pantry storage on the other. Floor-to-ceiling, shelves were filled with gallon-sized tins of everything imaginable to eat. At least they'd dine well. Robin closed the outer door and spun a wheel to lock it behind them.

"It's a lot nicer than the underground room where I lived with Grandpa Clay." Her voice had a faint echo.

They'd come so far since they'd met, and not just the distance they'd traveled. He wasn't the solitary man he'd been six months ago. A man who'd trusted no one, helpless to make a difference in the world. Robin had changed his life, and he was grateful. He took her hand as they explored the bunker together.

The next section was a spotless kitchen, complete with stainless steel fridge, stove, and dishwasher. Modern appliances he hadn't expected to use again. The scent of lemon cleaner filled the air. Someone must have given it a quick wipe. His legs shook with his next few steps. He shouldn't stay on his feet for long. Even this short walk was making him weak and his side ache. The previous occupants had furnished the next long room with a dining room table on one side, which was separated from the kitchen by an island with four bar stools.

On the far side was a wall-mounted flat screen, a bookcase filled with DVDs, a spacious sectional couch, and two comfy-looking chairs. It wasn't like anywhere he'd ever lived, more like something from a TV show.

"I need to get off my feet." Kory aimed for the couch while Robin continued to explore. He'd taken three careful steps when he stopped in his tracks. Two waist-height tower speakers sat in the shadows. He scanned the room, searching, and spotted several smaller speakers tucked away in other places and a substantial subwoofer. Surround sound or a stereo system? He could play his CDs. He turned, examining the room. His heart thumped in anticipation as he shuffled toward the cabinet instead of the couch.

Opening the doors, he found a pre-amp, amp, receiver, and a kick-ass stereo with both a turntable and a CD player. A few CDs sat on a lower shelf where there would be room to add their music. He pushed the power button and turned it on. One of the nicest systems he'd ever been around. He turned around to show Robin, but she'd disappeared. He fumbled with his pack where she'd dropped it beside the couch. Kory was going to play *2112* here, on this system—his favorite album of all time.

From down the hall, Robin called in excitement. "You won't believe this place. Come here. You'll love it."

The music could wait a few more minutes. He followed her voice down the short hallway to the first room on the left. He shuffled inside, his jaw dropping. Inside was a massive collection of music on vinyl, hundreds of CDs, and a wall of books. Robin had already pulled out a short stack of paperbacks and was reading the back of another.

Luke couldn't have chosen a better bunker for them if he'd tried. Kory was speechless. He could have stayed here all day, but his body wasn't up for much more as he swayed in place, though his mind was racing at the possibilities.

Robin joined him, sliding under his arm to prop him up.

"Luke did an exceptional job, didn't he? We're going to have a blast going through this." She smiled, taking his breath away once more.

A quick peek in the other rooms, before heading to the couch, showed three bedrooms and two bathrooms. He'd never had this much living space. Not with his parents, and certainly not on his own.

Kory had left his CD on the couch. He sat and handed it to her while he leaned back with a sigh.

"You want me to play this one?"

At his nod, she went to the open cabinet, opened the tray for the CD player, and settled the disc inside.

As the music played, Robin snuggled into him, avoiding the bandaged side. His throat closed up as he relaxed. He'd never thought he'd hear this music again. Letting the sound of the music fill him, he listened, not knowing how to express how much it meant to have music again. At a loss for words, he kissed Robin, his hand cradling her jaw.

Somehow, they'd made it to xTerra, and they had a chance to make their life together. This was the first home he'd had for more than half his life. Plus, he had someone to share this life with. A place with Robin and their soon-to-be family.

Kory smiled, tears collecting in his eyes. He looked down into her shining eyes that mirrored the happiness of his own.

They were home.

Epilogue: Robin

The sun shone golden on the September afternoon when Robin, Kory, and their new daughter headed home from their overnight stay at the maternity ward. Kory drove the Polaris carefully, going slower than Robin had ever seen him drive. While amusing, she wouldn't have done any better. Little Aerin seemed so tiny and fragile. She'd do anything to protect her daughter.

Vita xTerra was the haven she and Kory had hoped for, but it wasn't perfect. Before she had time to consider the widening gap between the three factions and the struggles ahead, she wanted to enjoy this moment and today.

As they neared their bunker, a gathering outside the door came into focus. The noise of laughing children filled the air. Ten-year-old Jayden, Christopher and Elizabeth's son, raced toward them, outdistancing the younger kids who followed in an unruly and stumbling pack.

"Can I hold the baby first, Aunt Robin?" he said, stopping several yards in front of the slow-moving golf cart. "Mom showed me how. I'll be super careful."

Robin smiled. "When we've parked, you can be the first to hold Aerin."

Jayden was the vanguard of the welcoming committee and what looked like a homecoming barbeque. Smoke filled the air as

Christopher grilled venison burgers. She inhaled. Kory was always up for extra food and she could probably eat several after not eating yesterday. She was starving.

She glanced at her husband, who still concentrated on the road, a slight furrow to his brow. A feeling of warmth suffused her. How had she gotten so lucky?

She tugged his sunglasses onto his eyes and leaned over to give him a kiss on the cheek.

He grinned and draped his arm around her, at last taking one hand from the wheel.

They pulled onto the crunchy gravel outside their house and parked their transportation in the metal shed near the entrance. Kory came around and helped her down while Jayden hovered nearby, unable to stand still.

"Looks like your mom, Aunt Ella, and Aunt Kat have set out chairs. Let's go sit down. Then you can hold the baby." Robin held the warm bundle against her, glancing down at her daughter's eyes, which showed the promise of remaining blue. She hoped so. They were the color of her grandfather's eyes.

Jayden skipped around her while the other children caught up again. Her cousins, Jess and toddling Bryan, were the last to arrive, following Jayden's sister Allie, and Kat and Ryan's three-year-old son, Nick.

Robin settled Jayden in a chair and passed Aerin to him, checking that he was supporting her head. She sat beside him and watched the children playing in the sunshine and their smiling faces. Vita xTerra was the only world they knew and their lives, while difficult, wouldn't have the same hardships their parents had endured to get here. They wouldn't have the old world to compare their lives to or find this one lacking because of all the things that no longer existed. She hoped this was a place where they could be happy.

It was up to her and the other adults to make a decent world for them to live in.

This was their home, and for now, it was safe.

Acknowledgments

The last few years have made me grateful for the online writing communities that I have become part of. Writing could be a solitary and isolating endeavor, but thanks to these people and groups, it isn't. I wanted to take a few minutes to acknowledge some people who have made a significant contribution to my writing and my well-being.

The first group is the Creative Academy for Writers based in Vancouver, BC. Through this group, I found beta readers, my critique partner, my editor, my mentor, several readers, friendship, and a sense of belonging. As someone who struggles to connect, this is important. I especially wanted to thank the group of Creative Academy writers who recently attended the 2023 Surrey International Writer's Conference, including Bonnie, Kirsten, Stacy, Leslie, Lisa, Marie, Jenny, Phil, and Sarah. They helped make my conference wonderful. I also want to thank my early reader, Michele Amitrani, whom I also met through TCA.

I want to thank Black Rose Writing, including the publishing team and the authors who support each other. For my first book, *The Edge of Life: Love and Survival During the Apocalypse*, I asked many writers for blurb reviews. Most turned me down. That happens, people are busy with their own lives and projects. The Black Rose authors were different.

These are the Acknowledgments for my fifth Black Rose title in less than two years. Since that first contract, I have reviewed sixteen books by local authors and thirty-two more Black Rose titles. The other Black Rose authors do the same, read and enjoy each other's work. I am also grateful for a select group of Black Rose authors I can now ask for a review, even when it isn't a straight-across trade. This group includes Cam Torrens, Dave Buzan, Diane Hawley Nagatomo, Gary Gerlacher, and Karen K. Brees. I also want to thank the Black Rose Authors Book Club and Karen E. Osborne for her interview, which will air next week.

In May 2023, I organized a book signing and launch for *The Wish* near my hometown in the Okanagan. My mom hosted a backyard party, and we invited many of my long-ago teachers, childhood friends, and her former colleagues. I want to thank everyone who came and bought books, as well as my mom, for having us. It was wonderful to see them again, and their generous support blew me away.

I continue to be grateful for the two people I work with most, starting with my critique partner, editor, and friend, Tracy Thillmann. I've thanked her many times, but with her poised to do a seventh edit for me, she is an integral part of this process. I wanted to acknowledge her valuable contribution to every book I've written. She is a fantastic writing partner and her attention to detail is unparalleled.

I also want to thank Ben Brockway, who is consistently my first reader. When the draft of my story isn't ready for others yet, I count on him to put his finger on what is missing or wrong. Whether it is tension falling off a cliff, passive writing, or something missing within a character arc, he tells me and I work on it. I'm still grateful he got the agent we wanted and at his suggestion, I submitted to Black Rose Writing. Five published books later, it has turned out to be the best pivot and redirection.

I also want to say a special thank you to David King who designs the covers of my books for Black Rose Writing. They're stunning, each one more amazing than the last. I'm thankful for such beautiful and professional work.

As always, I also want to thank my family, especially my husband, Rob. Rob always cheers me on and encourages me to write, and do anything else I want. I'm lucky to be married to such a kind, generous man. He didn't read my writing until I had published books. Now he's my number one fan.

Thanks also to my mom, my daughters, my sister, my aunts, my cousins, many of my friends, and my colleagues who buy and read my books. Thank you all.

SNEAK PEEK OF

TRAIN HOPPERS – ONE

SWITCHING TRACKS

OUT OF THE TRASH

CHAPTER 1: ELSA

SoCal-2195

Garbage heaps are treasure troves if you have the eye to recognize true value. Elsa's great-grandmother had been telling her that since she was knee-high to a cockroach. They scavenged to survive. That's why Elsa had worked with painstaking care to fashion the new tunnel into the mountain of compacted refuse, where she'd reached the correct depth to hit late-twentieth and early twenty-first-century trash. This was where the paydirt was located, but scavenging was never a sure thing.

She braced and supported her excavation so she wouldn't be trapped in an avalanche of filth. Her heart rate quickened in anticipation. What would she find today?

While Elsa worked the tunnel, her great-grandmother, Granny Lee, guarded the entrance of their licensed recovery sector within the largest landfill in SoCal—referred to as the Heap. Interlopers and thieves often interfered with the sites, so Granny carried a loaded shotgun—which she wasn't shy about using. They'd worked this shaft for days and the current tunnel should be worth excavating for another week, though it was always a gamble and Elsa had been disappointed before.

Old newspapers that had been buried and never exposed to the elements were interesting and still legible at times, but GreenCorps only paid plastic tokens for pots and pans, solid plastic, and metal objects. Some metals rusted, their coating worn away, or pitted and corroded, but stainless steel was like solid gold. Not that she'd ever found much precious metal, except what could be recovered in minute quantities from extinct electronics.

Hard to believe that her finds had been considered junk a couple of centuries ago. People today couldn't be so wasteful. After almost two hundred years in this landfill, most things still intact had value as scavenger currency. Her most valuable find had been a jar of assorted coin from before 2008. That had fed them for over a year. A set of chipped cookware might yield a week's food and water for herself and Granny.

Elsa advanced her cross-brace, moved her battered lantern forward, and dug with a trowel to separate one layer of garbage from another. She stacked treasures, old clothes and shoes, and items that might have value at resale to GreenCorps. Some were worth keeping for personal use.

She reached an area with rocks and dirt—backfill—that separated it from the level below. Filling her bucket, she hauled it part-way up the tunnel before attaching it to the pulley and rope system with a tug. Granny yanked it outside, then returned the empty bucket. Elsa rotated her neck and hips, easing cramped muscles.

Elsa refilled the bucket and sent it to the surface, keeping wads of filthy plastic bags and plastic sheeting on the side to clean and separate later on the surface. They would twist and weave the flexible strips of old bags into clothing, bedding, and useful day-to-day items, even some footwear.

Returning to the face of the excavation site, Elsa's heart pounded as she uncovered a rounded chunk of smooth black plastic with a metal ring at the end. It looked like a pot handle. Heap gold.

She reined in her excitement, slowing her extraction to avoid collapsing the tunnel, and removed her bulky work gloves. Wadded-up clumps of mushy paper, broken bits of plastic, disposable diaper balloons, and chunks of rotten wood surrounded what she was trying to extract. Scattered throughout this layer were the white chunks of

Styrofoam packing that Granny said resembled popcorn. It had its uses too, but she didn't need to collect it today as she had a sufficient stash at home.

She freed the stainless pot with a gleam of satisfaction. The twenty-first century had the richest garbage, and she studied it with a keen eye. The pot had a shallow dent and a couple of spots of rust that she poked. She smiled. They weren't deep and should buff out. A little more effort rewarded her with the lid as well. The pot and its lid were nicer than anything they used at home, though they seldom cooked beyond boiling water and oatmeal. At the market, this alone should earn days' worth of food and water tokens.

Underground, it was easy to lose track of time, but her tired muscles informed her it was quitting time. She looked anew at the gaping hole. She'd try for one more item.

She groped inside, her arm encased in warm guck to the shoulder, and she fumbled for easy-to-grab, solid items. Often, she'd find treasure in patches. Today, her hand closed on a cylindrical tube—too thick around to be a pot handle.

The wall made a sucking sound as it released, and she moved it into the light of her lantern. What was it? The tube was made of metal. Her fingers tingled when she ran them over the smooth surface, the way they did when she found something spectacular.

Her back twinged, grounding her in reality. She needed to get out and stand straight. She'd take the tube home to clean and examine.

Elsa carried both the bucket and her finds up the tunnel, her back spasming as she crouched to half crawl through the low tunnel near the entrance. It was tight, even for someone of her petite stature. The constricted section made it more difficult for thieves to snoop during the night. Even if it reduced her escape options and was prone to collapse, it also made the upper portion of the passage easier to barricade. Casual, lazy robbers would be kept from poaching the exposed trash.

She set down the bucket with the rest of the day's haul about ten feet in from Granny's position and left the lantern beside the entrance for tomorrow. Though inside the Heap, there was light from outside now. Elsa consolidated her finds at day's end, shoving the metal tube into her satchel instead of the bucket. You couldn't be too careful with items of value.

She wiped the sweat from her dirty face on her sleeve and took a swig of her rationed water from her canteen. It was hot at the surface, even in March, and even hotter in the tunnel. The garbage generated its own heat with chemical reactions. It steamed all day, all year. One reason she wore gloves was to protect herself from chemical and steam burns within the trash.

The warm rot seeped into her pores, so Elsa never felt clean. Sludge ground into all exposed cracks and crevices in her skin and under her nails. No scrub brush removed it all. She wished she earned enough to pay for a daily shower or a bath. She compromised by scrubbing with sand and rinsing with previously used gray water. SoCal didn't have water for luxuries unless you were wealthy. Perhaps one day, it would be different.

She donned the standard-issue GreenCorps Uvee goggles that hung around her neck, shuffled closer to the surface, and squinted at the sky, trying to gauge the time. The sun was invisible through the perpetual dust and smog, and the light was dimming. It must be later than she'd thought. Time to go. She hoped she hadn't left leaving too late. Granny seldom questioned Elsa on the job site, but she must be getting concerned.

Working wasn't as fast as when they'd been a three-person operation. Her older sister, Avery, had quit when she'd married a GreenCorps man. Her new family had coins, not just plastic tokens, and ate without sifting through junk.

It was a fine line to walk, staying late enough for a full day's scavenge, but not so late they had to return home after dark with the day's haul. They didn't have passes to be out after curfew. At night, they risked losing their finds to roving patrols of GreenCorps recruits. The local youths who joined were bullies, eager to change sides and work for the oppressor for coin instead of plastic tokens. SoCal was a political prison disguised as a work camp, and Elsa had been born here. Talk about bad luck.

Elsa collected her loot. Besides the pot and tube, she'd found a muffin tin, two bent spoons, and a matching fork. She also bundled her soft plastic, her back aching from hours in a stooped position.

She stepped out of the tunnel and stretched, wincing at the muscles that screamed in protest. Unhooking the pail from the system of ropes and pulleys; she was freed for the day. She dropped the bulk of her treasures in the bucket, making them easier to carry and harder for others to see.

"Hey, Granny. I'm ready to go home."

Granny Lee smiled, showing the two teeth missing in the front while her wispy snow-white hair stuck out from under her sun hat and goggles. Like Elsa, her pants and poncho were handmade, woven from strips of found plastic to protect her skin from the harsh Uvee rays. Her long-sleeved shirt was fabric, scavenged from the Heap. The garment was protective and durable, even though it might feel hot.

The corner of Elsa's mouth twitched. The words used to describe their clothing also applied to Granny—especially durable. Despite her advanced age, she did a full day's work. Her great-grandmother was at least a hundred years old, and Elsa worried what she'd do when Granny became too frail to guard their site. She endeavored not to consider a future without Granny, lest darkness swallow her. Better to focus on the now. Besides, she didn't want to borrow trouble. Perhaps someday she would find a partner or hire help. Most of the women her age and older already belonged to a team. It wouldn't be easy.

Twenty minutes later, they trudged onto the packed earth and crumbled asphalt street where their home was located.

"Long day Elsa," called her friend from the doorway of the neighboring shack.

Janna worked at the beach, sifting out plastic nurdles and rounded bits of glass to sell to GreenCorps for a pittance. GreenCorps reclaimed the beaches, not for environmental reasons, but to reap incredible profits. Each storm and wind brought additional drifts of never-ending junk to shore.

"Maybe we can catch up in a few days. I'm job hunting. Working the closer beaches isn't profitable anymore. I heard they're going to try fish farming. Buy fish stocks from somewhere up north. I'd like to try that."

"Catching up sounds good." It would be nice to speak with someone her own age, though Janna was dreaming if she thought she might get one of the coveted fish farming jobs. They would hire GreenCorps favorites. Elsa nodded to Janna's father sitting on his rickety steps made of broken cinder blocks, where he was gluing the bottom of his shoe together.

"There might be perks, like the odd fish to eat," he said with a return nod.

He grinned, showing his broken and gray front teeth, leftover from his previous job working trainyard security. With people trying to leave SoCal in tough times, it was a rough job. He'd never said why he quit; between steady wages and bribes, it was one of the most profitable ways to make a living. Now his family scraped along as best they could, just like the others. The only better jobs were GreenCorps recruits and suits who traveled for the Corporation.

Elsa sighed. Her stairs needed to be repaired—the loose bricks rolled when stepped on. Their home might resemble a one-story shack more than a house, but it kept a roof over their heads, most of the time. Granny had lived here since she was first widowed and sent here to work. GreenCorps forces had killed her rebel husband and daughter during a skirmish. She didn't talk about those days. Granny had raised her granddaughter, and now her great-granddaughters, here.

The house might be a hundred years old, or at least it looked like it. The glass was long gone from the windows. Most had been boarded up from the inside, but Granny had covered two with translucent sheets of plexiglass to let in sunlight. Not that anyone stayed home during the day, except on the mandatory rest day. Elsa always looked forward to

Sunday, even if Granny said it was just a day to placate the masses and keep them complacent.

This Sunday, Elsa would work on the house. She and Granny waged a constant battle with the roof to keep the elements out. It'd been fixed so many times that the patches had patches. When it rained, which was rare, they used every bucket and dish in the house to collect water. It was too polluted to drink, but they used it for washing. The walls, too, needed attention, to keep out the hot wind, ever-present dust, and vermin.

Scavenging paid for processed food and potable water but seldom stretched beyond necessities, such as clothing and shoes. Elsa glanced down at her scuffed black boots, where her toes stuck out, and scowled—she'd need footwear soon. They fashioned sandals and clothes from plastic, but boots came from the Heap or were purchased—an over-priced luxury from the outside world beyond SoCal, brought in and paid for at GreenCorps prices.

Granny unlocked the door, then relocked it upon entering—this wasn't a neighborhood where anyone left doors open. Whatever wasn't hidden or attached could be stolen from the flimsy homes. They would visit the trading post at the market on the way to work in the morning. All the stores belonged to GreenCorps, but she and Granny frequented one with pleasant staff, though she'd been taught to trust no one. Tonight, they'd sort and wipe clean the metal and plastic items so they'd get the best price.

The house remained dark inside until Elsa turned on the solar-powered lantern. SoCal might not have much rain, but it had ample sun, even through the ever-present smoke and smog. The hard-packed dirt floor was cool compared to outside. Heat radiated from the stone, brick, and cement repurposed to build this section of housing.

When they finished their work, Granny opened the safe, and they threw the day's collection inside. Elsa kept the metal tube separate to clean it and take a better look. It was a mystery. She would put it in the safe later when Granny slept. Elsa was reluctant to show her great-grandmother, who would encourage her to sell it. The only valuables in the house consisted of a spare set of clothing, their bedding, and the battered pot for boiling water. And the shotgun, but that was never far from Granny, who slept with it in arm's reach. It came from her rebel days and was irreplaceable.

Elsa sat on the raised platform that made up her bed at the far end of the main room. The thin mattress was made of woven plastic sheets and filled with Styrofoam packing. The blankets were repurposed from old pieces of fabric. Granny always said living this way would make them tough—make them survivors. Elsa munched on her dinner ration and finished the day's water in her canteen while Granny did the same. They shared a secret smile; they'd lived another day.

An hour later, Granny's soft snores filled the room. While the woven curtain they'd hung between the two rooms provided privacy, it didn't block sound.

Outside the house, whispered voices and the odd laugh carried on the evening breeze. The young men and women who wandered the street at night were seldom loud, but Elsa sensed their presence as they wandered the dark, searching for opportunities and those unfortunate enough to be caught out late. Some of their neighbors were involved with the illicit behavior, but she'd never been tempted to join. She couldn't afford to get in trouble or risk the blighted GreenCorps patrols. She and Granny depended on each other to survive.

She didn't know how the gangs made enough to live on, but the ranks of jobless seemed to grow instead of diminishing. Some had been sentenced here by GreenCorps, others hopped inbound trains, or migrated from other SoCal slums.

Why would anyone choose to be here? What was the world like beyond SoCal? She'd been nowhere else.

Though Elsa wearied of living in the trash with no other options, she wouldn't leave Granny, and the only life she knew. They made enough to get by, but never seemed to get ahead—probably part of the GreenCorps plan. For those sentenced to live in SoCal, they couldn't leave. For those born here, there wasn't a law against leaving, but it was discouraged.

Elsa's eyes grew bleary, though she hadn't read more than a chapter of her current black-market book. She would finish soon and trade it for another. She also planned to get ammunition. Then the boots. Busy thoughts spun in her mind, making it impossible to unwind enough to sleep. Jumping up, she grabbed the metal tube and a rag with which to wipe it clean. She found it easier to clear her mind with something in her hands.

After polishing, the cylinder shone. Made from a lighter silver metal than she was used to finding, it was shiny and, surprisingly, free of scratches. When she shook it, a faint tapping, metallic sound clinked inside with no clear way to open it. On one end, a leaf symbol had been engraved beside the words *'Dept. of Agr.'*

She traced her fingertips over the emblem and its dirt-encrusted grooves. Currents of excitement coursed through her; her hand once more tingling. She'd ask Vic at the market if he knew anything about her mystery item, but she was reluctant to sell. The feeling in her gut told her of its significance. She'd had feelings about things before, but never this strong.

Chapter 2: Walker

Walker closed his travel log and tucked his journal and stubby pencil into his backpack. He crouched between the slowing train cars near the end of the train, preparing to hop off. It wasn't long before they would arrive at the next station. Hayden lounged beneath the overhang of the covered hopper, his laces undone. His brother's pinched features looked more animated than usual and his dark eyes shone. Walker wasn't sure why they'd come here now, but Hayden had pushed for the location. Something Hayden had learned in Reno had made him want to travel to SoCal's Long Beach.

Hayden jumped to his feet, his green coat flapping, but he wouldn't meet Walker's eyes. Was Hayden's agenda different than stated?

Long Beach was a train terminus, and they hadn't hopped here before, though in the last eight years they'd traveled most places the trains ran. This was somewhere they'd avoided.

The dry air tasted smoky and left a sharp taste in Walker's mouth, like breathing greasy smoke. Shit air quality and the smog-filled skies blocked the view of what was supposed to be mountains and ocean. Everything was gray and dismal. Coming into town, the infamous Heap's pungent rotting smell added to the stench. He wasn't even off the train and he wanted to leave.

The past few hours had been dark. There'd been no lights near the train tracks, no villages, no farmhouses, nothing. Nothing out this way seemed enticing. He hoped they would poke around and he could convince Hayden to hop back on the next train.

What had gotten into Hayden? What made him want to come to this forsaken shithole? He'd heard Long Beach, hell, most of SoCal, was a garbage heap, but he hadn't been prepared for the reality. The people who lived here couldn't be healthy. Most were rebels, sent here to scavenge in the GreenCorps work camps, or the rebel's families.

The Corporation thought that if people worked hard to survive, they'd stay out of trouble. SoCal wasn't as unhealthy as Texas—whose burning oil fields were responsible for the smoke overhead—but SoCal was only a step up from the lowest rung of humanity that he'd witnessed.

Walker sighed. They'd made good coin mining near Denver over the winter, so they could have gone anywhere. On the journey here, they'd stopped a couple of times, and each time he'd slipped away from Hayden for a quick detour. Walker had converted his wages to silver coins, then hidden his stash. Hayden might be like his brother, but that didn't mean he could be trusted with coin, which had gone missing on several occasions when nobody else was around. Walker wouldn't give Hayden another chance to steal, especially from him.

At least Hayden had been clean all winter.

It wasn't far from dawn, but Walker didn't know if the haze was smoke or cloud. Either way—a blessing in disguise. The lack of visibility meant they should have time to race out of the trainyard without being seen. He cracked his knuckles and stretched, warming up muscles that had seized up during the ten-hour train ride. Butterflies churned in his stomach. He hated getting off the train somewhere new. Security was sometimes lax in small places like this, but sometimes it was tight. You couldn't predict what you'd get.

He stood by the metal ladder at the rear of the covered train car, his backpack tightened and his boot laces secure. Taking a deep breath, he grimaced. How long would it take to get used to the taste of rotting garbage and smoke? Maybe this would be a brief stay.

The roar of the train kept them from talking as it slowed, so he glanced to make sure Hayden was ready. Hayden braced against the jolting train cars as they braked, waiting for the train to come to a complete halt. When the squealing and clanking stopped, they were off, quick as a flash, running for the makeshift fence that separated the trainyard from the other buildings in town. They didn't have to talk; they'd dashed like this hundreds of times over the years. Best way to deal with the security bulls was not to get caught.

In the pale morning sprint, Walker's first impression of Long Beach was that the buildings were covered in the GreenCorps logo, big letters painted two feet high. This was a corporation town. All food and all water were brought in by GreenCorps, making the people dependent on the corporation. He'd been to others besides his hometown in Santa Fe. They'd have to trade or buy tokens for their stay so they wouldn't waste coin. It was the conversion that ate your savings.

His feet crunched in the gravel until they left the station yard, ducking down a side street into town. Hayden followed. Both young men listened for footsteps or shouts behind them, but there was nothing. They dropped to a slower pace.

"See. Easy as pie," said Hayden, his walk becoming a swagger.

Hayden sounded cocky now, but running to and from the trains still made Walker twitchy.

He grabbed Hayden's arm, forcing him to stop. What was going on? "You going to tell me what made you want to come all the way out here?" Walker clenched his jaw, due an explanation, though he might not get one.

"It's an adventure, somewhere new," said Hayden, shrugging. "Plus, I heard it's warm here almost year-round."

His brother's eyes slid to the side like they did when he was dishonest. Walker had seen it before. But, if he called Hayden on it, he'd just lie.

"Let's find somewhere to sleep for a few hours. I didn't get a lot of rest on the train. I swear they're louder every time we ride." Hayden yawned.

"How about here?" Walker wasn't particular. The alley looked fine for now. It was clean enough. For a town built on and surrounded by garbage, he'd expected more debris in the alley, but it was relatively empty. A few lidded plastic garbage cans stood behind the buildings, but the ground wasn't littered with refuse. They could do worse.

They hunkered down by the fence in a dead-end behind a bar, their backpacks propped behind them. They just needed a couple of hours rest to get them through until they had more light to search for a proper place.

Though Walker had fallen asleep in more uncomfortable positions, this morning, he was unable to settle. Hayden dropped off almost as soon as they stopped moving. His head slumped to the side, a line of drool forming from the corner of his mouth. Walker grinned to himself, though he still couldn't relax. He grabbed his travel log and wrote an entry for their current stop. He used his creased, much-folded paper with sunrise/sunset charts to start the entry. With as much traveling as they did, it was nice to have something consistent.

* * *

March 20th, 2195, Sacramento to Long Beach: ten hours
Sunrise 6:55 a.m. Sunset: 7:50 p.m. Spring Equinox tomorrow.

Travel Notes:
Sacramento: Security medium, trainyard outside town quiet. Used usual campsite.

Long Beach: Security light before dawn. No pursuit, no sign of security forces as we left. Ran to an alley two blocks behind the station. Camp in dead-end behind bar.

Investigate fences and bushes on the far side of the trainyard before departure. Hidden campsite?

Two tracks: One northbound, one south. Terminus of southern track.

Sunrise a glowing ball behind thick smoke. Hurts my eyes. Will need Uvee goggles if we stay more than a couple of days.

Hopped a covered freight car, rode at the back. Standard.

Corporation town. Will need tokens.

Junkyards and scrap yards surround the station. Small business area nearby. Will investigate in the morning. Everything stinks like rotting garbage and smoke.

Walker had nothing else of import to note, so he stowed his book and tried once more to rest. He dozed for a short time, but woke as his head nodded to his chest and he startled himself awake. His eyelids felt full of grit, scratching and irritating his tired eyes.

He gave up on sleep. He hated corporation towns. Maybe that was the source of his tension. Hayden had slumped over by the fence, his head now on his pack. He looked peaceful. No point in waiting for him to wake up. It might be ten minutes or it might be five hours.

Walker stood, heaved his backpack on, and fastened the straps. Without a proper stash or hideaway, he was stuck carrying everything with him for now. He tightened his scruffy hiking shoes and headed out of the alley, away from the train station and into town. Hayden could either find him if he woke soon or they'd meet back here later. They'd been together a long time and knew each other's habits.

Walker wandered the dusty town, noting that the pale light of dawn had turned to daylight. There were about a dozen businesses, all with the GreenCorps logo painted on the window. The shops faced a market square in the center, quiet this early in the morning. He was used to the sound of birds—spring was a time for songbirds—and he found the silence eerie.

There wasn't much to Long Beach, besides the Heap dominating the skyline, obscuring his view of the ocean. Bars and brothels stretched for several blocks behind the shops up to the slope of the hill. Not unexpected, as those with coin worked near the railroad station and could afford the offered wares. A road wound back and forth across the face of the hill, to where half a dozen grand houses overlooked the town. He strolled in that direction, hoping to get high enough for a view of the area.

He walked for about half an hour before deciding visibility was too poor. He'd gotten higher than a lot of the smoke, but he couldn't see through it. In the distance, he caught the faint outline of the shoreline. Garbage littered the entire beach. So much for the clean up efforts GreenCorps advertised. He headed back into town to see if Hayden was awake. He was almost back to the alley when he noticed two women striding across the square.

They were covered almost head to toe in gray clothes that seemed like they were made from woven scraps of fabric and plastic. Ponchos draped across their shoulders and hung down past their waist. They'd cinched loose pants on with tight belts and wore tall boots that looked like they were falling apart at the seams and had been duct-taped until the boots were more tape than boot.

Their strange attire wasn't what drew his eye. It was the two women who dressed the same, walked the same, and had almost the same features. One was old, with wisps of snow-white hair peeking out from under her knit cap. The other was smooth-cheeked and dark-haired. She looked like a "before" version of the old lady. Both women were thin, not quite to the point of emaciation, but their features were angular and sharp. They had an aura of strength or toughness about them. He wouldn't want to get in their way.

The old woman walked as fast as the younger—who couldn't be more than nineteen or twenty. Her cheeks still held a hint of youth. The women didn't pay any attention to him as they marched past, but not only did they have to be related, they matched intensity. They passed his position in the doorway of one of the GreenCorps shops and he noticed their eyes. Perfect clear topaz eyes that sent a jolt to his stomach. He'd only gotten a glimpse, but the old lady, in particular, reminded him of a hawk. They entered a shop at the corner on the distant side of the square. Two fierce hawks.

About the Author

Award-winning author Lena Gibson is a storyteller as an elementary school teacher and keeper of the family lore. She holds a First-Class Honors degree in Archaeology, with minors in History, Biology, Geography, and Environmental Education from Simon Fraser University.

A voracious reader from childhood onward, Lena seeks wonderful books in which to escape. Because of her passion for different genres, she combines elements of many in her writing. As an adult newly recognized with autism, she often creates characters that reflect this experience.

When Lena isn't writing, she reads, practices karate, and drinks a ton of tea. She resides in New Westminster, Canada with her family and their fuzzy overlord, Ash, the fluffiest of gray cats.

https://lenagibsonauthor.wpcomstaging.com/

Note from Lena Gibson

Word-of-mouth is crucial for any author to succeed. If you enjoyed *Aftermath: Into the Unknown*, please leave a review online—anywhere you are able. Even if it's just a sentence or two. It would make all the difference and would be very much appreciated.

Thanks!
Lena Gibson

We hope you enjoyed reading this title from:

www.blackrosewriting.com

Subscribe to our mailing list – *The Rosevine* – and receive **FREE** books, daily
deals, and stay current with news about upcoming
releases and our hottest authors.
Scan the QR code below to sign up.

Already a subscriber? Please accept a sincere thank you for being a fan of
Black Rose Writing authors.

View other Black Rose Writing titles at
www.blackrosewriting.com/books and use promo code
PRINT to receive a **20% discount** when purchasing.

www.ingramcontent.com/pod-product-compliance
Lightning Source LLC
Chambersburg PA
CBHW030757210726
48290CB00002B/308